Lions of the Grail

by
Tim Hodkinson

For Trudy, Emily, Clara and Alice

lionsOfTheGrail@groups.facebook.com
lions.of.grail@googlemail.com

Copyright © 2011
Tim Hodkinson

Chapter 1

The dungeon stank of damp and death. The single window was so high up no prisoner could see out of it.

He had been a prisoner so long now he had lost track of time. Some days he spent huddling in the pool of sunbeams that streamed in through the iron-barred window; desperate to soak up every ounce of the precious, life-sustaining warmth. That must have been summer time. Other times he crouched by the wall, struggling to avoid the freezing sleet that spat through the window into the filthy straw that clogged the floor. That must have been winter.

How many times this cycle of the seasons had revolved he could no longer recall. All he knew for sure was that one by one, his companions had died or been taken away. None ever returned. Soon they would come for him.

The air in the dungeon was foul. Putrid straw lay in rank clumps amid festering puddles of mire on the floor. The bare stone walls glistened with green slime. At the start of his incarceration he had shared this prison with fourteen of his brethren. They were crammed in, condemned and shut away from prying eyes. They were heretics, criminals, abominations before God.

One by one the others had gone, and now he was the only one left.

He had watched some die, choking away their last moments as-weakened by cold, damp and the starvation diet-they finally succumbed to the suffocating grasp of disease. Edward Harley was the first to go, dying within two weeks of being locked in the dungeon. He had suffered much. In the fighting before their capture an arrow had impaled his foot. When they removed the arrow, Harley, like a true knight, had not flinched. A low grunt was the only indication that he had felt any pain.

All there was to clean the wound was the filthy water that ran in a channel down one side of the dungeon, providing both drinking water and latrines for the prisoners.

Within days Harley's foot had swollen to twice its normal size. It began to give off a foul stench that could be smelt even in the fetid air of the dungeon. He fell into a fever and spent his nights bathed in sweat, raving and screaming at imaginary demons that tore at his face like bats. Young and strong, the virtues that had made him a good knight had simply prolonged Harley's agonies until finally, after a week of torment, infection achieved what their captors could not in open combat. His corpse lay rotting on the dungeon floor for three days before it was removed.

A few months later, Thomas Berard had begun coughing uncontrollably. Resolutely devout, the black-haired knight from Aquitaine had continued to choke his way through his prayers every day as the disease progressed and his lungs filled with ever more bloody fluid. He had finally gurgled his last breath after a paroxysm of coughing that had begun halfway through saying his Pater Noster.

Robert Mountford, most Senior of the captured knights, seemed to simply waste away. As the seasons revolved he had got thinner and thinner, his grey hair turned to snow white and his teeth crumbled to chalky stumps that rotted in the gums. One night, as they slept in the stygian darkness, Mountford had heaved a loud groan, followed by a deep sigh and they all knew he was dead.

As the seasons became years, death in the form a pestilence claimed Brian le Jay and Guy de Foresta also.

The rest were taken away from the dungeon never to return. Geoffry de Chamberlayne was taken first. One morning the guards had arrived, the cell door was unlocked, Chamberlayne's name was called and he was lead away.

Where he went to they were not told. The accusations they were locked up for were grave, so it was safe to assume that his fate involved torture, a false confession then either the agonies of a fiery death at the stake or else the shameful, perpetual living-death of a renounced heretic.

As time passed, the same happened to all the remaining prisoners, one at a time. No one ever returned.

Now he was the only one left, and the guard had said that his time was coming soon.

Over the years his clothes had degenerated to mere dirty rags that hung around his wasted frame. The Rule of his Order had barred him from shaving so even before he was thrown into the prison his beard was already full and bushy. Now it was long, unkempt and filthy as well. His hair hung down nearly to his waist; a wild, shaggy brown mass of tangles from beneath which burned two red-rimmed eyes.

It was these eyes that most un-nerved his jailers. Even after years in the murky twilight of the prison cell they still sparkled a strange green. Their constant livid glare spoke of a man who burned inside, tormented by deep rage, tortured by the fires of hatred.

Hatred was his last remaining friend. It kept him alive when the others died: a constant, smouldering fire that vowed he would never succumb, not to them, not to anyone. His hatred had distilled into anger, an emotion that impelled him to walk constantly, pacing up and down the little cell like a wild beast in a cage. Rage boiled within him and the only outlet was to pull himself up on the bars of the door, lifting his whole body weight off the ground, so that while the others wasted away, he remained hard and lean.

He despised the men who had thrown him in jail, he detested the enemies who had conspired to bring down his Order, he loathed the hypocrites who lied and hid behind religion to justify bloody murder and most of all he hated God. The Lord who had betrayed him, lead him away from home to chase dreams that did not exist, then left him to rot in this cold, wet, malodorous dungeon.

As he sat in silence, huddled beside the wall, the sound of the key in the lock startled him. He heard bolts being drawn back and the heavy iron-bound wooden door swung open. Two soldiers clad in chainmail stood in the doorway, their drawn swords holding the casual promise of violence.

One of them wore an unpleasant smile that revealed several broken teeth.

"Sir Richard le Savage," he commanded. "Come with us. Your time has come."

Chapter 2

He had expected it for years, but the final arrival of his summons sent a quiver of trepidation through Savage's guts.

What lay ahead?

He knew too well the devices that could be employed whenever a heretic was "put to the Question". He and his companions had all heard the horror stories of what their brethren in France suffered to extort their confessions.

Some had had teeth pulled out with pliers, then iron nails poked into the bloody sockets. The feet of many were dipped in oil then suspended over charcoal braziers, inciting agony as the flesh fried and the bones blackened and dropped off into the coals. Finger and toe nails were ripped out by the root. Worst of all was the Rack: the wooden frame the Brethren were strapped to and slowly stretched. The anguish became steadily more excruciating as they listened to the popping and cracking of the sinews in their arms and legs until the joints dislocated. A spell on the rack was enough to coerce even the strongest of men to admit to planning the murder of the Mother of God herself.

The two soldiers half-dragged half-carried Savage roughly up a spiral staircase out of the dank underground cellar where the castle dungeon was. His nose twitched at a strange, sweet smell as they reached the top of the staircase. Savage suddenly realised that the aroma was the scent of fresh air, the first he had breathed for years.

As they dragged him out through a doorway into the rain and across a cobbled courtyard he flinched and tried to shade his eyes from the brightness of the daylight. After years spent of semi-darkness the sunlight provoked smarting and tears.

"Aw look: he's crying." The soldier with the broken teeth said, his sarcastic tone betraying how much sympathy he really had for the prisoner.

"He'll have something to cry about soon enough." The other soldier grunted.

They dragged Savage across the cobblestones towards a large stone castle keep. Like a dreamer waking from a long sleep, memories came flooding back from when he had arrived there, years before. Now Savage was too weak to resist the pull of the guards. Then it had taken four of them to drag him, punching and kicking like a horse, down the narrow stairway to the dungeon.

He had no idea where the castle was: they had been brought here at night in covered wagons. It was at least a day's journey from the Priory of the Order where they had been arrested, but in what direction he did not know. The castle courtyard had been deserted apart from the detachment of soldiers who had made the arrests.

Now the courtyard was full of horses and wagons. There seemed to be sergeants, men-at-arms and soldiers everywhere. Grooms and other menial servants were busy running to and fro, carrying water, preparing horses for stabling and unpacking wagons. It was obvious that a large contingent of folk had just arrived at the Castle and from the grandeur of the clothes of some of the ladies stepping out of the covered wagons and the banners of knights that were being unfurled on the battlements, these were very important people indeed. Most of them did not give a second glance at the ragged, hairy figure being trailed towards the keep. Such prisoners were common in a place like this and it was better not to pay too much attention to them in case you saw something you should not.

A cool, blessed rain splashed Savage's face, awakening memories of his last day of freedom. It was raining back then too…

Chapter 3

The Templar Commander was worried that day. He had been so since the arrival of the mysterious travellers the night before.

Just after midnight two riders had appeared at the gates of the Order's Preceptory at Garway in the shire of Hereford. Garway was one of the smaller estates held by the Order of Poor Fellow-Soldiers of Christ and of the Temple of Solomon: better known as the Knights Templar. This awkward combination of small monastery, farmstead and military barracks nestled in the remote, wild regions that comprised the border between England and Wales.

The sergeant-at-arms on watch at the gate that night was under orders not to let anyone in, especially after dark.

These were dangerous times. The Order was under assault from all sides. Terrible news came from France about the torture and executions of Templar brethren there. All over Europe the property of the Order was being seized and its members arrested. Most unbelievable of all, the Holy Father, Pope Clement, had issued a decree disbanding the Order on grounds of heresy.

Grand Master Jacque De Molay, head of the Order of Templars, insisted that these were just times of tribulation sent by God to test their faith. If they remained true to their faith, then sooner or later the truth would conquer all. They would be acquitted of all the monstrous crimes that they were being accused of and the Pope would break free of the evil influence the King of France held over him. He would reverse his decrees and the Order could get back to its true purpose: recovering Jerusalem from the Saracens.

Richard Savage was not so sure. Across the world, the tide had turned against the Order. Now even here in England-where so far they had been left untouched-there were ominous signs. Agents of the Holy Inquisition had landed in the country and were demanding of the King permission to put the Templars to "the question".

The sergeant on the gate doggedly refused to allow the riders entry until finally one asked:

"Is there no help here for a Son of the Widow?"

The gates were opened immediately. This innocuous query was actually a secret code that told a member of the Order that a brother member was in trouble and needed assistance. All brethren must respond without question.

The two riders asked to see the Commander. They were shown to his quarters and had remained there ever since.

The Preceptory was abuzz with speculation about who these men were. Savage had managed to determine that the riders were fugitives Templars from France and it seemed that they carried something important with them. Exactly what it was, no one knew.

Savage was a young knight of the lowest rank in the Order, so the Commander did not inform him about what was going on. The Order had a strict hierarchy. Knights only ever knew what their superiors decided that they needed to know.

After several years' service in the Order, Savage was finding this increasingly frustrating. Throughout the world, the Templars possessed the reputation not just as a formidable fighting force, but also as guardians of secret knowledge. He had joined to learn mystical secrets, to discover occult truths that lay behind holy mysteries, not just to fight the Muslims. Instead, he had spent most of his time so far working on the running of the Order's wealthy estates.

He had spent a year under the baking sun in Cyprus overseeing olive groves and since being transferred to England all his time had been spent on the wheat farm and mill at Garway. He was little more than a heavily armed farmer, though in his eyes that was better than the lot of many of his brethren, who spent most of their time sitting on their backsides counting the Order's money.

To Savage, the Order had grown fat, wealthy and lazy. Amidst secrets and rituals, obscured by its unbelievable wealth, its original purpose had been forgotten. Meanwhile, their world was crumbling around them. Perhaps the tribulation was a good thing. Perhaps it was the sort of purge the Order needed.

The arrival of the visitors caused quite a stir. At first light, riders were sent out to all surrounding Preceptories of the Order. The message they bore was-of course-a secret. Finally, just before midday, Savage and the other two lowest-ranking knights at the Garway Preceptory were ordered to come to the Commander's Quarters.

The three knights, dressed in their white mantles, emblazoned with the red equal-armed cross that was the symbol of the Order, stood before their Commander, Guilleme de Vere. De Vere, a vastly experienced knight with years of campaigning in the East behind him, now finishing off his service in sleepy semi-retirement running a farmstead back in his home country, was usually the most imperturbable of Masters. That morning however, he was agitated.

Beside De Vere stood another Knight Templar. A man with black hair and a goatee beard. His eyes looked out from beneath hooded lids and the smile on his lips reminded Savage of a beast called a crocodile he had once seen lurking in a river while on a raid into Egypt from Cyprus. Commander De Vere was soon to retire, and the London Temple Headquarters had sent this knight, Hugo de Montmorency, to be his replacement. Montmorency had been in Garway for a week now and from what they had seen of him, none of the Knights were particularly keen on the day he would take over Command.

"I have a task for you young men." De Vere announced. The grizzled old warrior regarded each of them with a steady gaze, his iron grey beard contrasted sharply with the white of his cloak. "Last night two of our brethren arrived here, fleeing from the unjust persecution of our Order in France. They have brought with them a fantastic item: a treasure so fabulous I believed it to be only a legend. By God's grace they managed to save this from the treasury of the Head-Quarters of our Order in Paris before it could fall into the greedy hands of King Philip of France."

"What is it Sire?" Savage queried. "A Holy Relic? A piece of the true Cross?"

De Vere smiled. "Ah, Savage: the impetuous curiosity of Youth. What our brothers carry is so important that we cannot risk it falling into the wrong hands. For that reason its exact nature must be kept secret at all costs."

Savage sighed. "Then why tell us about it at all?"

"Because I want to impress on you all just how important it is, so that you will do what I ask of you with utmost diligence." De Vere tutted. "This morning I sent messengers out to the Commanders of our Order in this shire, requesting that they come here without delay. I have also ordered Sir Hugo here to ride to Dinmore Manor and speak to the Master of the Order of St John, requesting that he should come as well."

There were a few sharp intakes of breath. The knights shuffled their feet. One coughed.

"Some of you may be uncomfortable with the Master of the Knights Hospitaller coming here," De Vere continued, "but I can assure you that what we have in our possession is so important that it transcends the petty rivalries between our Orders. Indeed, it holds the potential to unite all Christians behind it, to save our Order from its persecutions and lead us to regain the Holy Places in Outremer."

"All the more reason not to tell the Hospitallers. They cannot be trusted!" Savage said. "It was through their treachery and cowardice that we lost Acre to the Saracens."

De Vere narrowed his eyes. He straightened his bowed shoulders and drew up to his full height of over six feet tall. For the first time the young knights caught a glimpse of their Master as the fearsome, battle-hardened warrior he was in his younger days.

"Richard Savage, your impudence knows no bounds." The Commander thundered. "You were not at the fall of Acre. I was. You have not seen the carnage, the slaughter that these eyes have seen. You have not witnessed the horrors that are let loose when men wage war against each other in the name of God. For that reason I can forgive your foolish naivety."

Montmorency gave a little cough. "Commander De Vere, Surely you intend to punish this man?" He asked. "The Rule of our Order is very clear on the matter of insubordination. All Templars swear instant obedience to our superiors. You are the Master of the Order here and this man is clearly questioning your orders."

De Vere shot a sour glance at Montmorency, then looked back at Savage. "Montmorency is right. The Rule of the Order is very strict on this matter and stipulates what your punishment must be. For the rest of today you must carry out the task I am about to set you, but after that you will be in disgrace. From now on, until told otherwise, you will work with the grooms dunging out the stables. At night you will sleep in the barn, not with your brother knights in the dormitory. You will eat your dinner off the floor of the Refectory."

Savage's face flushed a deep red. He stared at the floor.

De Vere sighed and wiped his forehead as his anger subsided. "When I judge that you have learned some humility I will rescind this punishment and you can rejoin your brethren again. Perhaps you will learn to appreciate your privileges more."

Savage bit his lip. Fury boiled within him.

Montmorency smiled and looked satisfied.

"Now," the Commander addressed them all once more, "once the other Commanders have arrived we will be holding a special council meeting in the chapel. I have instructed the sergeants to guard the perimeter of the Preceptory. No one is to be let in or out once the council begins. You knights are in charge of the defence. At all costs, you much protect the chapel and let no one enter. You will stand guard in full battle readiness. Do you understand?"

They all nodded.

"Good. You are dismissed."

The three knights left the Commander's quarters and re-emerged into the courtyard. They exchanged nervous glances.

"You shouldn't have goaded the Commander like that, Savage," Geoffry de Chamberlayne commented. "It's obvious he's nervous. That temper of yours will get you killed one day."

Savage just grunted. "That bastard Montmorency had to stick his nose in though. I don't like him."

His brethren avoided his eyes, uncomfortable with the fact that Savage was criticizing the man who would soon be their new Commander.

"This place will be hard to defend." Edward Harley, another of the knights, commented. "It's a farm. It's not a fort. There's no perimeter wall, just that picket fence."

Savage nodded. "If this treasure is so precious our Masters should have taken it to one of the Order's castles instead of this place. But let's not question their orders, eh? Far be it from me to point out their stupidity." He spat on the ground.

Geoffry glanced nervously around. "I'm sure there is a perfectly good reason why they did not take it to a castle."

Richard Savage tutted. "Just you keep your head down and make sure you do what you're told, de Chamberlayne. You don't want to be helping me with mucking out the horses now do you?"

They all fell into a sullen silence.

"What do you think the treasure is?" Savage wondered aloud. He would not admit it, but he ached to know what the riders had brought. Perhaps this, finally, was an actual manifestation of the sort of secrets and mysteries the Order had a reputation of guarding. It was the lure of these mysteries that had first driven him to forsake so much at home and join. "Has anyone heard anything about it? Anything at all?"

They all shrugged.

"It must be very special." Harley said.

The rest of the day passed in a flurry of activity. The knights and the few sergeants and men-at-arms of the Preceptory did their best to secure the boundary and set up various lookout points where watch could be kept on the surrounding countryside. Savage was mostly too busy for his resentment to smoulder but every now and again indignity at his punishment provoked a surge of anger he found very hard to quell.

Throughout the afternoon Commanders of the Order from all over the Shire arrived on horseback. Each was ushered through to the chapel until finally, as evening started to fall, the three young knights were again summoned before their Commander, this time before the double wooden doors of the round chapel.

The knights were armed for combat. Their bodies cased in chainmail, shields slung by the straps over their shoulders and their swords sheathed at their sides. De Vere on the other hand was dressed in the full ceremonial robes of a Commander of the Order: a long white mantle, belted at the waist with the equal-armed cross emblazoned on his chest in crimson. He also wore a long, pure white cloak and a flowing white headdress. It was obvious this was an important meeting.

"We are about to begin." The Commander announced. "I am sorry that the Master of the Hospitallers seems not to have been able to come. That news will not disappoint all of you."

He aimed a reproachful glance at Savage who met his gaze with more insolence than the Commander liked.

"However, we can wait no longer." De Vere continued. "You men must stand guard at the doors of the chapel. No one is to be let in until I open these doors again. No one. On pain of death."

De Vere swept back into the chapel, drawing the doors closed behind him. The knights heard the rattling of iron as the bolts were drawn and the doors locked.

The three armoured knights remained standing outside as the first few heavy spots of rain began falling from the darkening sky.

Geoffry sighed and looked up at the clouds. Within seconds a steady downpour had begun.

"I've had enough of this nonsense." Savage growled and began to head off in the direction of the knight's quarters.

"Where are you going?" demanded Harley.

"I don't know yet." Savage responded without turning around.

"You can't leave. You're under a direct order." Geoffry exclaimed. "You're in enough trouble as it is."

Savage stopped and turned around. "You may be happy to stand in the rain, kept in the dark about what is going on while those old fools wallow in their own self-importance, but I'm not. I'm going to pack my belongings and then I'm leaving."

The other knights exchanged worried glances. "You can't desert. It is the ultimate disgrace. We won't let you." Harley shouted after him.

Savage's hand dropped to rest on the hilt of his sword. "Are you going to try and stop me?" he growled.

The other two knights all remained still. They trained regularly with Savage and were well aware of his ability in combat. None of them relished much the idea of fighting him.

Savage spat into the mud. "I didn't think so," he muttered and then turned his back on them to recommence his journey to the knights' quarters.

He had barely got half way there when he stopped. The desire to know the truth about what the riders had brought from France, to know what was in the chapel, itched within him like an unhealed sore. Could he really walk away from the possibility of actually finding proof that there was something greater than this miserable existence? After all, he had forsaken so much back home in Ireland to seek out the truth behind these mysteries.

The memory of the laughing face of a beautiful young woman suddenly came to his mind. Savage felt a strange pang in his chest, an uncomfortable mixture of sadness and guilt. Could he really go back now? Admit he was wrong? Would she ever forgive him?

He closed his eyes tight shut to dispel the vision.

When he opened them again, Savage saw a sergeant running towards him. The man's face was ashen grey.

"Syr le Savage," The sergeant said. "Come quickly. There is trouble."

Chapter 4

Savage shook his head. He was about to say that it was no longer his concern but he stopped himself. The sergeant was a veteran warrior, not the type who was easily vexed and the man was clearly worried.

"What is it?"

"Horsemen. Soldiers. Lots of them and they're coming this way."

"Where?" Savage demanded.

The sergeant led the way to the barn where a ladder was placed against the wall. The knight and the sergeant scrambled up the ladder and balanced themselves unsteadily on the ridge that ran along the centre of the barn roof.

The sergeant did not need to point. Emerging from the woods to the North was a large band of men. Some were mounted, most were on foot. Some carried swords, others pikes and most had shields. There were bowmen among them.

Savage took a quick look round and swore.

"God's bones! There's more of them."

To the South, across the ploughed fields more soldiers were approaching. To the East, along the road that came to the Priory from the nearby village of Garway, another convoy of riders was approaching. At the head of them rode a man in green clothes with distinctive long, blond hair.

There were soldiers approaching from three sides, while to the West any escape was cut off by the wide, fast-flowing waters of the Monnow River.

"We're surrounded: like rats in a trap." Savage breathed.

"That looks like Henry Pimlot, the County Sheriff." The sergeant said, pointing at the blond-haired rider.

"It looks like they're finally coming to arrest us." Savage said. "We have to tell the Commander."

"Well will you look at that?" The sergeant suddenly exclaimed. Savage looked to see what he was pointing at. Beside the Sheriff rode a man entirely dressed in black. Emblazoned clearly on the shoulder of his ebony cloak was an equal armed cross, the mirror of Savage's Templar insignia but white instead of crimson: the insignia of the Order of St John of Jerusalem. Beside him rode a man in the robes of the Temple: Hugo de Montmorency.

"That's Montmorency and the Master of the Hospitallers." Savage growled. "The treacherous bastard."

They both scrambled down off the barn roof and ran to the chapel as fast as they could.

"There are soldiers coming. The Sheriff is with them and the Master of the Hospitallers." Savage informed his fellow knights who were surprised to see him back so soon.

"What do they want?" De Chamberlayne said.

"They're fully armed. There's about a hundred of them, including cavalry and archers. It's safe to assume this is not a social visit." Savage said. "We've got to let the Commander know."

Savage's mailed fist hammered loud and insistent on the chapel door. After a few moments came the sound of the door being unlocked and Commander De Vere's face appeared, puce with rage.

"What is the meaning of this?" He roared.

"Sire: the Sheriff has got us surrounded. It looks like the King of England has finally given in to the Pope's demands for us to be arrested." Savage said.

De Vere's face fell in shock. "Savage. Assemble the sergeants-at-arms here. The rest of you, wait here." He ordered. The chapel door closed again.

Savage ran to get the sergeants and before long the combined total fighting force of the Priory-four knights and ten sergeants-was gathered before the chapel door.

After a few moments' anxious wait, the chapel door opened again. To the surprise of those outside De Vere and the other six Commanders emerged, each one carrying his unsheathed sword. The sight of these old men prepared for a fight sent a little shiver down the spines of the assembled warriors.

De Vere turned to Savage. "What is the situation?"

"I'd say there are about a hundred soldiers approaching from three sides." Savage replied. "Fifty from the North, about thirty from the South and a column of cavalry from the village: the Sheriff is riding with them. The river has us hemmed in to the West."

"Archers?"

"Yes. A few crossbowmen as well."

"We're desperately outnumbered, then." De Vere said.

"There's one more thing, Sire." Savage added.

De Vere raised an eyebrow.

"The Master of the Knights Hospitaller is with the Sheriff. Hugo Montmorency rides with them too."

For a second De Vere looked stunned, then he looked down and gave a bitter laugh. "Well, Savage it looks like you were right after all. I've been an idealistic old fool to think that all men would be as tired of bloodshed as I am."

Savage looked down, unsure what to say.

"Well so be it." The Commander said. "Brethren, we are facing our toughest challenge. The Rules of our Order forbid us to surrender. So we shall meet our foes at the gate."

De Vere began marching resolutely towards the large wooden gate that blocked the entrance to the courtyard. A loud banging could be heard coming from the other side.

Savage hurried to keep up with his Commander. "Sire, this is suicide," he muttered to De Vere in a confidential voice. "We're hopelessly outnumbered. It's not true that our Rule does not permit surrender. Does this have something to do with our French brethren? I see they have not left the chapel to join us."

De Vere smiled as he walked. "Perceptive and nosey to the end, Savage." He replied in a confidential tone. "As I have wronged you I shall let you into a secret: In the chapel, beneath the altar, is the entrance to a secret passageway that leads underground out of the Preceptory. It was built years ago with this very situation in mind. I will not tell you where it leads. Our French brethren are making their escape that way. We must buy time for them and allow them to get away. What they carry is so precious that we cannot allow it to be captured."

"What can be so precious as to be worth the lives of so many men?" Savage argued.

"I cannot not tell you, Savage. If you knew then you must follow us." The Commander smiled again, his eyes had a strange, glazed appearance. "I give thanks to God that that shit bag Sir Hugo Montmorency has not been here long enough for us to have revealed the secret of the passageway. The Commanders, however, all know about it. We cannot allow ourselves to be captured. Our persecutors have instruments of persuasion in their torture chambers that can break the resolve of the strongest men, and we are all old. Savage, you must promise me this: When all the Commanders are dead, you will surrender. Save the lives of the Sergeants and you young knights. Once we have created time for the French brothers to escape there is no need for everyone to die."

"No Sire," Savage objected. "We must all fight and die fighting if necessary."

De Vere smiled. "Savage. I'm an old man. I have lived my life and I've seen enough of death and killing. We Commanders have no choice now, but do not throw away your life needlessly."

Savage could not reply. His throat felt strangely choked and his eyes stung.

At that moment there was a crash as the Preceptory gate was smashed open. Through the splintered remnants of the gates, several armed horsemen burst through into the courtyard. As they quickly arranged themselves in a defensive line they were followed by the Sheriff and the Master of the Hospitallers, both with swords drawn. Behind them foot soldiers and archers began pouring in.

"Commander Guilleme De Vere." The Sheriff shouted. "We have come with a warrant for the arrest of you and every Templar here. You are all charged with the crime of Heresy and must answer before a court. Surrender."

De Vere raised his sword. "Never." He yelled. "Beauseant!"

At the sound of the battle-cry of the Order of the Temple, the other brethren ripped their swords from their sheaths and echoed "Beauseant" at the top of their voices.

The sound of this famous war cry made the Sheriff's men hesitate for a second. De Vere charged towards them and the rest of the knights and sergeants followed, screaming and brandishing their weapons.

The lead horseman recovered his wits and spurred his horse forward, intending to cut De Vere down. With surprising dexterity the old man spun around, avoiding the sword blade that chopped down towards him. The Commander thrust his sword upwards, back over his head and the blade sunk into the riders back as he rode passed. With a scream he collapsed backwards off the saddle, landing with a heavy thump on the courtyard ground.

Savage felt like cheering the Commander's skill and wondered what a fearsome warrior he must have been in his younger days.

He did not have long to contemplate this though. Another horseman was galloping towards him. The rider swung his sword down. Savage hoisted his shield to protect himself. The heavy impact made him stagger sideways. Savage swiped in vain at the horseman like his Commander had done but he had already galloped on towards the other knights, looking for another target.

The other old Commanders surged forward, swiping at their mounted attackers with similar expertise as that displayed by de Vere. Soon the first charge was over and the Sheriff's men had retreated to the gate again. Five of their horses now had empty saddles, their riders lay in pools of blood on the courtyard.

The Order had taken no casualties.

"Forward again," De Vere roared. "Drive them back out the gates."

The knights surged forward across the courtyard towards the Sheriff's men.

"Shoot them." The Master of the Hospitallers shouted. "They're fanatics. Shoot them down like dogs."

The ranks of Sheriff's men at the broken gates divided and their archers came forward. In an instant they loosed a volley of arrows that tore up the courtyard into the charging knights. The sergeants and the armed knights fell to a crouch behind their shields. Savage heard the thump of an arrow colliding with his shield and saw another glance off the iron helmet of one of the sergeants beside him.

The Commanders stood no chance. Their grand ceremonial robes gave no protection and the deadly missiles plunged into their bodies. As Savage watched, Guilleme De Vere stumbled and collapsed forward, one arrow transfixing him through the chest and another through his thigh. All five of the other Commanders also fell, each one riddled with arrows. Harley had gone down too, an arrow having glanced off his shield into his foot.

Rage boiled in Savage's chest and for a few moments in his eyes the scene before his eyes took on a strange, red hue. He clenched his eyes tightly and took a couple of deep breaths.

At all costs he had to remember his training and stay calm while in combat.

"Take them now." The Sheriff yelled. The horsemen surged forward again, this time in a more concerted charge. Sheriff Pimlot aimed himself at Savage.

Savage dodged sideways, then spun back round. He swung his sword in a chop that caught the horse across the flanks and connected squarely with the Sheriff's knee joint. With ease the blade separated the bottom half of the Sheriff's leg from the rest of his body. The horse whinnied in pain. Pimlott shrieked and instantly lost his balance. He toppled out of the saddle, landing with a sickening crunch on the ground.

Melee ensued. Sergeants and knights on foot tried to defend against the horsemen who wheeled around them, slashing and cutting. Several of the sergeants went down. Bright crimson blood splashed across the cobblestones of the courtyard. Behind the riders the foot soldiers of the Sheriff came surging forward in an overwhelming tide.

They quickly overpowered the defenders by sheer weight of numbers. Savage desperately slashed at the first two men that came at him. His blade missed the first one but connected with the side of the head of the second. The man's iron helmet saved him but the force of the blow sent him staggering sideways into the path of a charging horse. The weight of the beast thumped him to the ground and a nauseating crack issued from his chest as the horse planted one its back hooves on him.

Savage heard the crash of splintering wood behind him. He turned to see Hugo Montmorency had smashed down the chapel door and was going inside. Savage began sprinting towards the chapel himself but as he did so a horseman riding past swiped at him with his sword. The blow landed on the crown of Savage's head. His helmet absorbed most of the damage but the impact stunned him and he fell forwards, the weight of his shield dragging him over.

The moment he hit the ground three soldiers pounced on him and began raining punches, kicks and blows from the butts of their swords on him. His arms were pinned and the remnants of his damaged helmet ripped off.

"Surrender. Give yourselves up," Savage shouted to his brethren. "It was Commander De Vere's last order."

Looking up, he glimpsed Montmorency emerging from the chapel, a look of rage and frustration on his face. With some satisfaction Savage surmised that his French brethren had made good their escape.

Twisting his head he caught sight of a cudgel raised above his head. It fell and the Sheriff's soldiers battered him into unconsciousness.

When he awoke, he found himself with the fourteen other survivors of the fight, bound and locked in a covered carriage that bounced its way through the darkness of the night. Finally it arrived at the castle with its dungeon that was to be their prison for years to come.

As these memories replayed themselves in Savage's mind his guards dragged him into the Castle Keep. They went up another flight of spiral stairs and across a hallway until they finally came to a large set of double doors. Two more men-at-arms blocked their way with swords drawn.

"The last prisoner from the dungeon, as requested: Syr Richard le Savage," the guard with the broken teeth announced. The men-at-arms nodded and opened the doors.

Through the doors came a welcome breath of warm air. Savage was dragged into the room and just had time to note the sumptuous tapestries on the walls and the roaring open fire that blazed in the grate before he was dumped unceremoniously on the floor.

"So," said a cultured voice in Norman French, "this is the Irish Knight Templar."

Chapter 5

Savage looked around him. Compared to the dungeon, the room was a riot of colour that overwhelmed his senses. Embroidered woollen tapestries shrouded the walls. A fire blazed in a huge iron dog grate at the end of the room. The floor was carpeted with deep, clean rush matting and furs.

A long table ran along the far wall. A tall man was lounged in a brightly painted chair behind it. He was in his mid-thirties, his face ended in a long, pointed goatee beard and his chestnut brown hair was combed straight and hung to his shoulders where it was curled in. At the brow, his hairline had receded, leaving a high-domed forehead that lay between a middle parting. Even though he was seated, it was obvious that he was a big man: very tall and powerfully built. His clothes looked expensive and a large black bear fur was wrapped around his shoulders.

The man regarded Savage with a curious gaze and a slightly sardonic smile played across his lips.

"Am I to be tortured?" Savage demanded.

The man snorted and his smile widened. "My dear Syr Richard, this is England. The use of torture is against the Law here."

Savage tried to struggle to his feet but one of the guards forced him back down again.

"Kneel before the King, heretic!" The guard shouted.

Savage looked at the man at the table again, a confused look on his face. What did he mean by 'King'?

The man in the bearskin stood up to his full height, which was well over six feet and gestured to the guards to leave. "Out!" He commanded. "Syr Richard was a member of the Order of Knights Templar. They did not recognise any earthly Kings and their only Overlord was the Pope." He gave a little chuckle. "Which is rather ironic, given what happened to them. Tell my Lords Lancaster and Mortimer to join us."

With expressions on their faces that betrayed that they were as confused as Savage, the guards left the room. Savage struggled to his feet again.

"He called you King…" He croaked.

The man at the table poured himself a goblet of ruby red wine. "I am Edward Plantagenet, King of England, France and Lord of Ireland." He announced.

Savage did not know what to say. He had expected beatings, torture and being hauled before a bishop at a Church Court. Instead he was standing in front of the King of England. What was going on?

"I may have a little job for you." King Edward said. "I shall tell you more when The Earls of Lancaster and the March arrive."

The King walked around the table and approached Savage, looking him up and down. The dishevelled knight felt uncomfortable under the King's gaze, which seemed both appraising and critical. As he got closer, King Edward's nose wrinkled and a look of evident displeasure creased his face as if he had just drunk sour milk.

"My God you are filthy," he said. "And you stink. I'm going to order you a bath."

The King walked to the door, opened it and spoke in a low voice to someone outside. He closed the door then returned to the table and drank a long draft of wine. Savage could hear the ice rattling in the goblet and his parched throat lusted for the taste of anything but the brackish water that was all he had had to drink during his years of captivity.

The doors opened again and in strode another tall, broad-shouldered man dressed in dark colours. He was older than the King, but not much, and his clothes were just as sumptuous.

"Ah! Speak of the Devil and he shall appear: My Lord Lancaster." The King announced. His tone of voice held a hint of what to Savage sounded like displeasure. The newcomer showed no signs of deference towards the King. There was a distinct resemblance between the two men, both in height and facial features. This was not surprising, given that they shared a grandfather. Lancaster had gone completely bald though. He looked at Savage for a long time without comment, then turned to King Edward.

"He doesn't look like much." Lancaster said.

The King sighed and rolled his eyes. "He's been in a dungeon for the last five years. What do you expect?"

"Will he be any use to us? Look at the state of him!" Lancaster returned. "He looks wretched."

The King simply shrugged and looked disinterested. There was clearly no love lost between the two men. Savage wondered just what the nature of their relationship was. The situation was now getting beyond belief. Not only was he in the presence of the King, here also was the Earl of Lancaster, chief of the Council of English Barons and the second most powerful man in Country.

The door opened again and another man in his early thirties entered. He too was richly dressed in linen and furs. His straight brown hair was combed and cut fashionably long. He wore a long, drooping moustache and his two ice-blue eyes regarded Savage coldly from beneath hooded lids. Savage deduced this must be Roger Mortimer, first Earl of the March and one of Lancaster's chief rivals to power. While the king had regarded Lancaster with coldness, the look he shot at Mortimer spoke of vicious, unbridled hatred.

"Where am I? How long have I been a prisoner?" Savage croaked.

"You could at least have given the man a drink." Lancaster scolded the King. He poured out a goblet of wine. "Ice?" he asked.

"Why not?" Savage shrugged. He had not had iced wine since his time in Outremer. God alone knew what was about to happen next so he decided he should make the most of things.

The Earl of Lancaster opened a heavy wooden chest that sat on the table. It was lined with straw and packed with shaved ice, gathered from the top of a welsh mountain and sent post-haste to the royal table. Lancaster spooned a couple of ladles of ice into the wine and then strode over to hand it to Savage.

"You are in Goodrich Castle in the shire of Hereford. It is the thirteen hundred and fifteenth year after the birth of our Lord. You have been a prisoner here for the last five years. You're a lucky man Savage: if we had not happened to be stopping here on our journey south and heard about an Irish prisoner-and a Knight Templar to boot-you would be remaining so for a very long time to come. I gather you removed the Sheriff's foot during your arrest. Pimlott survived but now gets around with a wooden peg-leg. He is more than happy to leave you here to rot."

Savage took a gulp of the wine. After years of drinking nothing but stagnant, brackish water the drink burned his throat and provoked a choking cough.

"What did they do with my brethren? Fourteen of us were imprisoned. Some died, I know, but the rest were taken away." He gasped when the cough subsided.

Mortimer gave a little chuckle. "Savage, the world has changed in the five years since you were locked away. Allow me to bring you up to date. As you are well aware, before you were imprisoned King Philip of France issued warrants for the arrest of all the Knights Templar throughout his Kingdom. The French Inquisition uncovered confessions of indescribable blasphemy being carried out by members of your Order and the Pope ordered the arrest of all Templars in the world."

"Lies! We are innocent!" Savage roared. "A man will admit to anything under torture."

Lancaster looked annoyed and waved a hand. "That is a question for philosophers now, Savage. The argument was concluded long ago. The World moved on. Those who make the world move dictate what are lies and what is truth. Your Order lost that battle and so the argument."

"Naturally, here in England we were less credulous of the fantastic claims of our French cousin and the hysterical demands his puppet Pope." The King interjected. "The Crown in England has always had an excellent relationship with the Temple of Solomon. Two thousand Templars formed the guard of honour at my own Coronation. We could not simply turn our backs such a noble brotherhood. Therefore we resisted the calls for your arrest as long as we could."

Lancaster continued the story: "However, since the fall of Acre there are no longer any Christian lands to defend in Outremer. The purpose your Order was created for no longer existed and you were difficult to defend. The Order of the Temple was dissolved and its possessions handed over to the Order of Saint John."

"The Hospitallers!" Savage groaned. "What happened to all my brethren?" He demanded.

"In France they were not so lucky. After such terrible confessions of guilt hundreds were burnt at the stake." The King said. "Here in England things were different. Torture is against the law in this country and so it is no co-incidence that there were no confessions to heresy here. Eventually the Holy Inquisition requested that Templar prisoners be extradited to France where they could be questioned 'properly'. Obviously we refused, so the Holy Father decided to send the Inquisitors over here, and unfortunately circumstances arose that meant it was finally necessary to accede to some of his demands."

"In the world of politics, Savage," Lancaster peered down his nose at the bedraggled knight before him, "it is not always possible to stick to principles. Sometimes certain values have to be sacrificed in order to attain other goals. We could not afford further war with France, not while we had a war on our doorstep with the Scots. So a marriage between King Philip's daughter Isabella and King Edward was arranged to cement peace between our nations. The peace depended on the marriage. King Philip needed the Templar's money. We needed the Peace."

"And the price was the Templars?" Savage hung his head.

"If I'd known then what a bitch she was I would have saved us all a lot of bother and jilted her at the altar." The King growled. "But Philip of France became my Father-in-law. Wives and in-laws, Savage, are the nemesis of all men's happiness. Don't you agree?"

Savage felt a sudden stab of guilt so severe as to almost make him wince.

"Your majesty," Mortimer said, with all the respect of someone talking to a mangy dog in the street, "we would all prefer that you didn't refer to the Queen of England as a bitch."

King Edward glared at Mortimer. "What better way is there to describe a woman who whores herself in the beds of other men?"

"Perhaps," Mortimer rejoined, "if you paid more attention to your wife than you do to Syr Hugh Despencer she might not feel the need to seek solace…elsewhere."

Mortimer bared his teeth in a grin so provocative it left Savage in no doubt just whose bed the Queen was currently sleeping in. What amazed him was how Mortimer thought he could get away with such audacity.

For several seconds it looked very like Mortimer and the King were about to come to blows.

"Gentlemen let us not let domestic matters confuse the issue here." Lancaster interjected with a reproachful glance in the directions of both Mortimer and the King. "We reached a compromise. We did a deal with both the Pope and the King of France." The King said. "English Templars would not be punished for the guilt of the Order as a whole, provided they made a public rejection of all heresy and asked for the Church's forgiveness. They were then allowed to retire to a monastery on a rather generous pension of four pence a day."

"None of my brothers would accept such terms." Savage argued, but his voice lacked conviction.

Lancaster chuckled. "Nearly all of them did. Three years ago Pope Clamant ordered the final, complete dissolution of the Order of Knights Templar, and the Knights Hospitaller completed their acquisition of all Templar properties the year after. To bring a close the matter, King Phillip had the Grand Master of your Order, Jaques de Molay, slowly roasted over a fire in Paris last year. The Order of Knights Templar is gone forever, and will soon be forgotten. A mere jotting in the margins of the history chronicles."

Savage hung his head. There was so much to take in. That the Order had ceased to be was simply stunning. All those centuries of warfare, the countless men who had dedicated their lives to the Order. The castles they built, the churches they founded, the wars they fought, the lives lost. All gone. And for what? For the Hospitallers and the lying, greedy King of France to steal their wealth? He grunted, sourly. The Good Lord had led them all on a merry dance of fools.

"So what is it you want of me?" He asked after a few moments.

"I believe you are Irish?" Lancaster said.

Savage nodded. "My Father had a manor in the Earldom of Ulster. I grew up there. Its years since I left though." His childhood seemed so long ago now, almost like a dream.

"If you were free, would you return there? You must want to inherit the estate?" Lancaster questioned.

Savage shook his head. "There's no longer a manor to inherit. The plague took my parents years ago and my older brother inherited the land. While I was serving in Cyprus with the Templars I got word that he had been killed in a hunting accident. As he died without an heir, the Church seized his estate. I have nothing to go back to."

"Well perhaps we can give you a good reason to go home." The King grinned like a wolf. Savage got the distinct impression he might not like whatever he was about to propose.

Chapter 6

The door of the room opened and two servants staggered in, awkwardly carrying a large bath tub between them. They placed it before the open fire that roared in the massive dog grate and procession of maid servants streamed in with pails of steaming hot water. The conversation in the room halted while they tipped the pails into the bath until it was brimming with water. After the last bucket was added the servants withdrew and closed the door behind them.

"This is for you. I suggest you get undressed." The King smiled. "No need to be shy. I'm sure you're not, though. Not after all those years spent in an all-male Military Order. You should have no difficulties being naked in front of other men."

Savage shook his head. "Templars are forbidden to see their brethren's naked flesh. It stops sinful thoughts. We are forbidden to wash more than necessary and must never change our underwear." This rule had caused Savage to suffer painful groin boils in the sweltering heat of Cyprus, and he was often disgusted by his own smell.

After years in the filth of the dungeon, he itched to feel the soothing caress of the warm water. He stripped what remained of his filthy garments off and jumped into the tub, immersing himself totally and ducking his head to soak his hair and beard. The hotness of the water stung his skin but the feeling of warmth was absolutely heavenly.

As he lolled his head back in the water, he became aware that the King and the other two Lords had gathered around the bath.

"We have been having a little bother with our friends in the North." The King said.

"In Ulster?" Savage asked.

"Not the north of Ireland: the north of Britain." Lancaster interrupted tetchily. "Robert Bruce, the self-appointed King of Scotland, continues to rebel against England. He besieged the Crown's last remaining Scottish castle at Stirling last year, the King here lead an army north to relieve it and Bruce slaughtered us at Bannockburn."

The King shot a spiteful glance towards Lancaster. It was obvious the memory was still a raw wound. "They fell on us like cowards and brigands!" He roared. "Ambushed us in a bog and slit our horses' bellies! Chivalry and Honour mean nothing to them. Nothing!"

Lancaster remained placid. "After such a humiliating defeat, the Barons of this land felt that the King was being poorly advised. Lord Mortimer and I were appointed to the onerous overseers and advisors to the King."

All became clear to Savage. The King had never been popular. Compared to his iron-willed, warrior father, Edward was far too swayed by handsome young men. While he showered them with gifts and affection, they usually wormed their way into positions of power and authority. The Barons of England hated this.

From his prison cell, Savage had overheard the guards speaking in hushed tones about the battle at Bannockburn. It had been a disaster for the English: thousands of English knights were killed and the Scots had escaped, well, Scot-free.

After that, the Barons of England must have decided that enough was enough. He had clearly not been deposed, but evidently King Edward the Second was now little more than a figurehead, a lapdog of the two men who were the real power in the land: His cousin Thomas, Earl of Lancaster and Roger Mortimer, Earl of March.

"Robert Bruce knows no boundaries. His greed is voracious." Mortimer growled. "After victory at Bannockburn he presses us and harries our borders in the north. His ally, that treacherous bastard King of France, has attacked our domains in Aquitaine and Bordeaux. King of Scotland is not enough for Bruce. A land of Bogs and Mountains? Not him. He wants England."

"What's all this got to do with Ireland?" Savage wondered. He looked down at the water he sat in, suddenly realising that the cloud of black speckles slowly spreading around him were drowned lice from his hair and beard.

"Ireland is the back door to England." Lancaster explained. "The English Border with Scotland has a string of heavily fortified castles along it, garrisoned with thousands of men. Fighting their way South would be costly for the Scots. If they went west instead and took Ireland, then an alternate invasion route opens up for them. Ireland gives us soldiers and grain. Taking Ireland will cut that off and if Ireland falls, the next step would be Wales."

"You can be sure the Welsh will be quick to jump on Bruce's wagon." The King said. "They still smart from my royal father bringing them to heel. They hate me because my father named me Prince of Wales."

"Bruce is planning to invade Ireland and put his brother Edward on the throne there." Lancaster said.

"That's madness." Savage stated. "Ireland has no King. The country is a mish-mash of little kingdoms and petty earldoms, constantly at war with each other. Parts of it are under English Law, parts of it are under Gaelic Law, some of it has no Law at all."

"Actually Ireland does have a King. Me." King Edward said.

"With respect, Sire, you are King of England, your other title is Lord of Ireland" Savage said. King Edward's eyes flashed with a look that suggested that if the reins of power had been more fully within his grasp, the bedraggled knight before him would be flogged for such insolence. There was not just anger in the King's eyes though. Edward seemed to be flicking his eyes over Savage's naked body in the water in a way he might look at a choice piece of roast venison he was about to devour.

"Many in Ireland believe they owe you no allegiance," Savage continued, feeling discomfited by the King's gaze, "and not just among the native Irish either."

"I am well aware of that. There are many in England who believe that also." The King finally tore his eyes off Savage and directed a bitter glance towards Lancaster and Mortimer who ignored him.

"You are right, Savage, and that's a worry for us." Lancaster said. "We must know if we can rely on the Irish to fight the Scots. Bannockburn bled us white. Our armies are depleted and we cannot afford to fight a war on more than one front. Currently we are fighting in France. The Scottish border is heavily fortified but if we move troops from there to strengthen Ireland we could be leaving the direct route to England wide open."

"Bruce's brother Edward is offering himself as an alternative King to the people of Ireland." Mortimer said. "He presents himself as fellow Gael who all on the Island can unite behind."

Savage could not hold back an ironic laugh. The Bruce family were no more Gaelic or celtic than King Edward was, or any of the Barons of England, Scotland or Ireland. They were all the descendants of the Norman knights who had crossed the channel with William the Bastard, later named "Conqueror". Most of them were related to each other, if not by blood, then by marriage. All of them still spoke French as their first language.

"That might work with the gaelic irish," Savage mused. "The anglo-irish knights and barons of Ireland though: They won't fall for that sort of nonsense. They may not think much of the King of England but why would they support Bruce?"

"That's a good question." King Edward re-joined the conversation. "We suspect that many of the nobility in Ireland are indeed sympathetic to Bruce's cause. The key question is how many of them, and why? Our spies tell us Bruce has obtained something-we don't know what specifically-that has somehow gained at least promises of allegiance from them. It seems this treasure is some sort of holy relic Bruce obtained from the Templars."

Savage frowned. There were family allegiances between the Irish and Scottish nobility, particularly in Ulster, but blood ties usually broke when self interest intruded. Ireland's current interests, both trading and military, lay with England, not Scotland. Whatever Bruce had must be very special.

"We want you to go home to Ireland." Lancaster said. "If you agree to work for us there then we will grant you a Royal Pardon. Your guilt will be expunged and any penance for your heresy and association with the Knights Templar can be put off to a time that will be more convenient to you, perhaps when you retire, for example."

"What is this work?"

"Travel to Ireland and deliver a warning from the King to Richard de Burgh, the Earl of Ulster, about the impending Scottish attack. Bruce will strike Ulster first. The sea crossing from Scotland is only 12 miles. What we need to know is how sure we can be of his Earldom resisting the Scots. If they land unopposed, Bruce will have a bridgehead in Ireland and the way to Dublin will be wide open. Ireland will be as good as lost. Earl Richard did good service fighting the Scots with the King's Royal Father. We have a different King now though, and De Burgh has married his daughter to Robert Bruce. We need to know if family ties will prove more powerful than loyalty to his King. De Burgh assures us of his loyalty but is he actually intending to switch sides and let the Scots walk in? What about the knights and barons of his feudal levy? If they intend to join the Scots side, then De Burgh will have no army to fight with anyway. This is crucial information to us. We cannot afford to commit to troops to Ireland to fight the Scots there unless we absolutely have to. That is what we want you to find out."

"I'd like to get out." Savage said, suddenly feeling vulnerable in the water surrounded by these three wolfish men. He needed to play for time to think about what they were asking him to do.

The King and the two Lords shrugged to show they did not care what he did. Savage raised himself from the water and stepped out of the tub. He stood shivering and suddenly very conscious of his nakedness as he bent to pick up the pathetic remnants of what remained of his clothes.

"My dear Syr, please forget about those rags." the King lifted a large fur rug and passed it to Savage. "Wrap yourself in this. We will make sure you get new clothes."

As he released the fur onto Savage's shoulders, the King let his hand fall on the knight's arm, letting it trail a little too long on the sinewy muscles of his bicep.

"He's in surprisingly good shape, considering such a long stay in prison," he said.

Mortimer and Lancaster now also cast their eyes over Savage's body, but their gazes were more curious and lacked the hunger that was in the King's eyes. Savage's flesh was a ghastly grey and spoke of someone who had not seen the light of day for years. He was gaunt, his cheeks hollow and his body had not a spare ounce of fat, but he did not have the usual withered, enfeebled look of a man who had been incarcerated for years. Instead, the grey skin was pulled taut over wiry, sinuous muscles so the knight's body looked like a skinned rabbit.

"After five years in a dungeon, most men are feeble wretches, hardly able to stand by themselves." Mortimer said. "How did you manage to avoid that?"

"I walked. Constantly. Up and down the cell," Savage replied. "All day, every day. I pulled myself up on the window bars, stood on my head, anything to keep myself fit." Uncomfortable with the men's scrutiny of him, Savage wrapped himself the fur.

"You want me to be a spy? A cloak and dagger man?" his voice betrayed his distaste.

"Sometimes we must all do things which we find a little unpleasant." The King said with a nasty smile. "If you are successful you will be rewarded well."

"Why me?" Savage asked.

"You are Irish, so you will draw less suspicion." The King explained. "Normally a messenger from the King delivers his message and leaves straight away. You, however, have family ties to Ulster. You have a reason to stay around for a while. As a Knight Templar, you were trained in the use of codes and ciphers. You can send back messages to us in secret writing so that if they are intercepted by prying eyes, their import cannot be divined. In short: you are perfect for the job. When we stopped here on our journey and heard that there was an Irish Templar in the dungeon we couldn't believe our luck."

"And if I refuse?" Savage asked, a little half-heartedly.

"You can go back and rot in prison." Lancaster stated. "Alternatively you can hang. Your only way out of jail is by Royal Pardon and the only way you will get that is by agreeing to work for us. The choice is yours."

Savage shrugged. "What choice do I have? I'll do it."

"Excellent!" The King beamed. "Guards! Guards!" He banged the table loudly. The two soldiers who had dragged Savage up from the dungeon entered the room and stood stiffly to attention.

"By the way, Savage" Mortimer said. "Just in case you are thinking that once you are out of England you are out of our influence. We have other agents in the country, and we are very sure of their allegiance. They will be told of your mission.

If you decide to abandon it and disappear into a bog somewhere, they will find you and you will die as the traitorous dog you are."

His threat hung in the air like a noxious fart for several seconds before the King interjected. "I'm sure it won't come to that. Guards: Take Syr le Savage to the kitchens and get him a good dinner, then make sure he gets a haircut. Arrange a room for him and I'll send the Royal Steward to make sure he gets some new clothes."

Savage suppressed a smile at the look of astonishment on the face of the guard with the broken teeth.

"Don't just stand there man! Get on with it!" Lancaster thundered.

"This way…em, Sire." The guard held the door open. Savage gave him a provocative grin as he was ushered out the door.

"One last thing, Savage." The King called after him. Savage stopped and turned to face him again. "Do you know who Hugo de Montmorency is?"

Savage's face lit up with an expression of cold rage. "He is the Judas bastard who betrayed us at Garway."

"That's one way of putting it." The King replied. "He did indeed see the error of his heretical ways and informed Sheriff Pimlott of the gathering of Templar conspiracists at Garway that lead to your arrest. After renouncing the Temple, he was welcomed into the Order of St. John, the Knights Hospitaller. He has done rather well for himself. Hugo de Montmorency is now Knight Marshal of the Order of St John in Ireland. I believe he is currently advising the Earl of Ulster on defensive tactics and we don't trust him one little bit. Perhaps this extra piece of information will whet your appetite for this task."

Savage nodded, then he turned once more and left the room.

The door closed behind them, leaving the King, the Earl of Lancaster and Earl Mortimer alone.

King Edward mused: "We've probably just sent him to his death. If Montmorency recognises Savage and our suspicions are correct, he'll kill him. If De Burgh is in league with Bruce, he will also get rid of him."

Lancaster shrugged. "Does it matter? If they kill him then we'll know where they stand straight away. In the meantime, if he can find out any information of use to us it will also be helpful. I should not need to remind you Gentlemen that we are desperate. He will probably end up dead either way. Who cares as long as we get what we need?"

Chapter 7

Richard Savage stood on the Forecastle of the Mary. Below him, the prow of the ship sliced cleanly through the grey-green water. The boat surged up on the waves then dipped into the troughs, throwing up a spray that spat cold, salty drops across his face. Astern was the open sea, before him lay the coast of Ireland.

A fortnight of proper food and rest, the attentions of the Royal Steward and the King's personal surgeon had effected an enormous change in Savage. The hungry gauntness of his cheeks had begun to fill out and the grey dungeon pallor of his skin was now tinged with pink. His ragged clothes were gone, replaced by a fine pair of soft buckskin hunting boots that came up past his knees, woollen leggings, a dark green tunic and a heavy black woollen hooded cloak. His unkempt beard had been trimmed to a respectable goatee and while the Royal Barber had wanted to cut his wild mane of hair into a fashionable shoulder-length bob, Savage had insisted on a close crop. Old habits died hard: while a Templar he had not been allowed to grow his hair. Besides, long hair was a paradise for lice.

He had boarded the ship in Bristol and paid the reprobate captain for his passage in gold. The crew had looked with greedy eyes at his purse, but the presence of his sword, kidney dagger and the Royal Seal on the scroll he carried had been enough to deter thieving hands during the journey.

The voyage had taken the best part of two days. Savage had spent the first day in the grip of abject terror. He had never liked sailing, but after being so long in the dungeon his previous unease had changed to an irrational panic. The sky seemed impossibly big and the sunlight hurt his eyes. He was painfully aware that the boat was merely suspended over unknown black depths. At any second he expected the ship to split asunder, plunging into the water, sinking down to a freezing, completely inescapable death.

When evening on the first day had arrived and this still had not occurred, it began to dawn on Savage that he could either spend all the rest of journey huddling down beneath the deck, or he could get over it.

After that revelation he began to find the experience enjoyable, even exhilarating. He spent most of the second day up on the bow, watching the waters skim by beneath, enjoying the wind in his face and the feeling of speed and freedom that came with it.

The Isle of Man had just been retaken from the Scots but the seas around it still had to be skirted with care. The Mary was a Cog: a squat, clinker-built cargo ship with a square-rigged sail and castellated platforms were built onto her prow and stern. This particular cog spent its time shuttling across the Irish Sea between Bristol and Dublin, Bristol and Drogheda or Bristol and Carrickfergus. She ferried wine, furs and other luxuries on the way out and returned with a hold of grain, wolf skins or the big shaggy hunting dogs Ireland was famous for breeding.

After pitching and rolling on the open sea, whipped by wind or huddling for shelter under the canvas tarpaulin that provided the only cover on board, Savage was looking forward to getting onto dry land.

The swell of the sea was calming as they surged up the sea lough towards Carrickfergus, the Capital of the Earldom of Uladh, or "Ulster" as the Normans had named it.

As the Mary approached the harbour, Savage could already smell the stench of the town. Carrickfergus was cloaked in a misty shroud of filthy smoke and noxious fumes. Its air was thick with the miasma of wood fires, the hoppy fragrance of beer malting, the smell of cooking food and the odours that arise from so many people living packed close together. While it was not as bad as the reek of the dungeon he had spent the last five years in, after several days in the clear fresh air of the open sea the smell was a touch overpowering.

Carrickfergus Castle, a massive stone fortress, loomed menacingly over the harbour. At the sight of it Savage mused how ironic it was that his return to Ireland should be at Carrickfergus. Twelve years before, he had sailed out from that very harbour, vowing never to return. He had travelled far: to the very ends of the known world, and now here he was back in the same place.

As he gazed down into the dark waters of the lough he wondered what ghosts were waiting to rise up to greet him from the murky depths of his past. He had forsaken much when he had left home to join the Templars.

The memory of a smiling young woman surfaced in his mind and he felt the old pangs of regret. He closed his eyes tight shut to dispel the memory. Where had that come from? He thought he had managed to successfully push it out of his mind during the years in prison. He had made his decision and accepted the consequences. There would no going back.

Except that now he had come back.

He had no illusions about how dangerous his task was. Ireland was a rat's nest of intrigue, alliances and counter-alliances. Nothing here was as it seemed and nobody could really be trusted.

And where did his own allegiance lie? A Scottish invasion would be a disaster for the people of Ireland, but he had abandoned the island years ago. What was it to him? Then again, what was Edward of England's cause to him either? Now the Order was gone, was there anything left for him to follow?

At the very least, he consoled himself with the fact that he was now away from England and the reach of Sheriff Pimlot. He could still simply forget about his mission and disappear, but then he would have to deal with the other royal agents Mortimer would send after him.

Lancaster had told him the names of some of the other agents. Two were knights: De Sandal and Talbot. There was a third person called either Le Poer or Powers but all he had been told about him was that he would contact Savage when the time was right. Until he came up with a better one, his immediate plan was to deliver the message to the Earl, then try to make contact with Talbot or De Sandal to get an idea of how the land lay.

The Mary hove around the mouth of the harbour to tie up at the quay. Around it the busy harbour was full of vessels of all sizes and descriptions. Crews bustled away either embarking or disembarking cargoes. Among the more mundane ships such as merchants' trading galleys up from Dublin or the cogs loading up with corn bound for England, Savage spotted a Portuguese galley that was probably trading pottery and wine and a boat that looked very like a Hebridean warship. The sight of the Scottish vessel immediately made him uneasy.

"You'll be leaving us then." The Captain grinned at him. The man was an experienced old sea dog who had spent years navigating the Irish Sea. The long, ragged scar that slithered down his left cheek was a testament to the fact that crossings were not always as uneventful as the one they had just completed. Attack from pirates was an occupational hazard for sailors and from the demeanour of the Captain and crew of the Mary, Savage suspected that they were not averse to supplementing their income with a bit of piracy themselves.

Savage nodded. "I have a message to deliver to the Earl." He explained.

"Well he won't be too hard to find." The Captain replied, pointing at the massive bulk of the castle that overlooked the harbour. "That's his house."

Savage began collecting his belongings.

"Will you be wanting us to wait on you for the return journey then?" The captain enquired.

Savage shook his head. "I'll arrange my passage back to England when I've completed my business here. If you're still in port I'll bear you in mind."

"We're leaving soon as the cargo is switched. You're not the first Royal Emissary we've brought to Ireland lately, you know." The Captain said. His grin had a nasty edge to it. "Never brought any of them back, though. The last one was about a month ago. He just vanished. Like a ship in the fog. He got off our boat right here in this harbour and we never heard of him again."

Savage fixed the Captain with a steely glare, but did not respond. Slinging his bag across his back, he scrambled up onto the Quay and set off along the harbour towards the castle.

From the battlements of the fortress, a black-cloaked figure watched his approach with interest.

Chapter 8

Carrickfergus castle was built on a rocky outcrop with an ancient and dark history. Carraig na Feargus –"the Rock of Fergus" jutted out from the shore into the cold, choppy waters of a wide, deep sea lough in north east Ireland. It was named after Fergus MacErc, an ancient King who met his end when his ship floundered on the rock during a storm.

The massive, squat stone fortress had been constructed so skilfully on the promontory it looked like it had been carved out of the black rock rather than built on it. An unmistakable symbol of Anglo-Norman power, the square keep and imposing curtain wall of the castle dominated the town and the whole lough. No matter where you stood on the lough shore you could not miss the ominous facade of the stern fortress.

The double-towered front gate was newly built and a portcullis hovered over the entranceway like a row of jagged teeth from some savage beast. As he approached up the hill from the harbour, it reminded Savage of the maw of Hell that he had seen used as a backdrop for a mystery play, "the Harrowing of Hell".

A sullen Irishman stood on guard at the castle gate. Savage knew he was Irish from the clothes he wore. His upper body was covered by a long, saffron coloured padded linen tunic that reached down to his knees –the léine croich: a sort of cloak-cum-armour worn by Irish warriors. This was decorated with stripes and heavily pleated to protect from sword cuts. The léine was belted in the middle and a wicked looking Irish knife hung from the broad leather belt, along with a pouch to hold his belongings. His hair was shaved at the back and sides but grew long at the front in the Irish style and as Savage approached, he lowered the spear he carried so that its tip faced the new comer.

"Who might you be?" the Irishman wondered, regarding Savage with a laconic eye. The man was a member of the Bonnaught of Ulster : locally recruited Irish soldiers who made up the Earl of Ulster's garrisons. Though hardy, reliable warriors, Savage recalled from the days of his youth that these men had an attitude to authority that could best be described as "sceptical".

Savage produced the scroll that bore the heavy seal of the Lions of England and showed it to the gate guard. "Richard le Savage," he introduced himself, "Emissary of the King. I have an urgent message for the Earl."

"Really?" The gate guard seemed unimpressed. "Which King would that be now?"

Richard Savage was well aware that in Ireland 'the King' did not necessarily mean Edward Plantagenet, but could well refer to any one of the number of rulers that were scattered around the various Provinces or petty kingships. He was also well aware that the gate guard was being deliberately obtuse.

"King Edward the Second: King of England, Wales, Scotland and Lord of Ireland." He elucidated.

The gate guard raised a sceptical eyebrow and smirked. "I hear Robert de Bruce has taken away at least one of those titles." He said.

Savage felt a frisson of anger. Apart from the fact that the man was being deliberately provocative, to further annoy Savage they were carrying out their conversation in Irish, a language that Savage was out of practise in. He consoled himself that at least it was not English, a tongue he found particularly uncouth.

Suddenly a commotion erupted from within the castle. Behind the guard, through the castle gate, Savage could see a riderless horse standing placidly in the cobbled courtyard that lay between the outer curtain wall and the older inner wall. The irate owner of the horse had just burst out into the courtyard from the gate in the inner wall. He wore the tattered, dirty russet cassock of a pilgrim. His wildly bearded face was flushed a deep scarlet and his brows knitted in a terrible glower. To Savage's surprise, the pilgrim leapt athletically straight onto his awaiting horse without the use of the stirrups.

"I go!" He roared, as he grabbed the reins of his horse. "I leave this den of sin as Lot left Sodom! The Earl will have to account for all this before his Maker!" With that, the horse clattered out of the courtyard at a brisk gallop, forcing Savage and the gate guard to leap aside.

While the guard was distracted, Savage strode quickly past him.

"Hoi!" the guard protested, but Savage just marched purposefully on across the castle courtyard. The guard wrestled with the dilemma of whether or not to stay at his post or chase the newcomer but quickly decided that he would be better remaining at the gate.

The Earls bodyguards were more than capable of protecting him from any threat.

Savage did not need a guide to tell him where to find the Earl. It was the last day of April -the Eve of the Mayday Holiday- so the Earl of Ulster would be in the great hall of the castle, hearing legal cases from his tenants and vassals and listening to requests for aid from the common folk. The great hall and the keep were at the heart of the castle, inside the old inner wall that had been built over a century before by Sir John de Courcy, the first Norman knight to conquer Ulster.

Savage entered the gate in the old wall and headed for the hall.

On either side of the door to the hall stood a heavily-armed galloglaich, mercenary warriors feared for their prowess and ferocity in battle. Obviously the local militia were only relied on so far. The galloglaiches wore heavy chainmail armour, and each bore a pole-axe that looked big enough to split a man in two. Their long blond hair and the two pairs of light blue eyes that coolly regarded the approaching Richard

Savage from under their helmet visors bore testament to the mercenaries' Norse fore-fathers, the Fionn Gall. As Savage neared the door the pole-axes clattered together in a cross that barred his progress further.

A third man stepped forward. He was in his mid-thirties and was richly clad in expensive, colourful robes. He had a pleasant smiling face and long fair hair. From his belt hung a heavy bunch of huge iron keys.

"Greetings Sir," The man said in welcome French. "I am Henry De Thrapston: Keeper of this Castle and the Earl's Treasurer. I am afraid you cannot go any further until we know who you are and what your business is."

"I am Richard le Savage." Savage replied to the courteous greeting in like terms. "I am here as Emissary for the King of England with a message for the Earl of Ulster."

Henry De Thrapston raised his eyebrows. "A message from the King, eh? We were beginning to think he'd forgotten about us out here. But tell me;" he continued, scratching his blond beard in interest. "You say your name is Savage. That's a local name. Have you any relatives around here?"

"My father held a manor on the Southern Lough Shore."

"I thought I detected a hint of a local accent." De Thrapston grinned. "I knew your father - a long time ago. You must be John."

"Richard." Savage corrected.

"Richard? I thought you'd gone into the Church." De Thrapston said, looking genuinely puzzled.

Savage quickly looked away to avoid de Thrapston's eyes. He did not want to pursue that topic any further in case it led to dangerous questions about the Templars. He changed the subject: "Sir Henry this message is of the utmost importance: Life or Death. I must speak to the Earl as soon as possible."

De Thrapston nodded. "I mustn't delay an Emissary of the King with idle chatter. No offence, but you know the rules: I must ask you to surrender all weapons before entering the great hall of the castle."

"No offence taken." Savage said with a confident tone he did not feel as he handed his sword and dagger to De Thrapston. "Murder so often comes as the smiler with the knife beneath his cloak."

De Thrapston handed Savage's weapons to one of the soldiers who took them off to the castle armoury. The Keeper of the Castle then led the way into the great hall. It was a long, narrow building with woven rush matting covering its floor and exquisite, expensive tapestries hung on the walls. The hall's two large windows provided ample illumination so no torches were required.

At the far end of the hall was a raised dais, on which sat an ornately carved wooden chair. On the chair sat Richard Og De Burgh, the Red Earl of Ulster.

Immensely rich and exceedingly powerful, Richard De Burgh ruled everything east of the Bann river from Coleraine in the North to Dundrum in the South East, as well as vast estates in Connaught in the West of Ireland. Now in his fifties, the chestnut hair that hung down his back in two long braided plaits was streaked with grey, as was his beard. He wore leggings and jerkin made from the finest of English wool, but he was also clad in the Irish style of a saffron kilt that hung down to his knees and was wrapped over his left shoulder where it was fastened with a large gold Celtic brooch. The kilt was woven to a local pattern, but the wool it was made from was of the utmost quality from the sheep of the Cistercian Monasteries in the North of England. The original colour of de Burgh's hair was only one of the reasons why the Poets and Bards of Ulster had dubbed him the "Red" Earl. Red was the colour associated in the Celtic legends with violence and death. He had dark, starkly arched eyebrows and when angry had a stare that could wither grass at one hundred yards. At the present moment, however, he was highly amused at something.

Standing behind the Earl was a tall, thin man who was not smiling. With close-cropped black hair and beard, this man was wrapped in a long, black cloak which had a white equal-armed cross on the right shoulder.

Savage stiffened in surprise. He had not expected to run into Hugo de Montmorency quite so early on his return to Ireland. To his relief, Montmorency showed no signs of recognising him. Five years in a prison must have changed him.

Two more armed galloglaiches stood on guard before the dais.

"Sir Richard le Savage," Henry De Thrapston announced. "Emissary from King Edward of England."

"Forgive my merriment, Sir Richard," The Earl said in ringing tones, "but I've just had a visit from a local parson."

"I think I was almost run over by the man on my way in, Sire." Savage said.

"He's a local character, one of those itinerant preacher types that seem to be about these days. A very hot-headed shepherd." The Earl replied. "Perhaps that shows the strength of his convictions but a lot of folk think he's just a wandering madman. He came here to request - nay demand - that I ban the 'heathen and pagan practices'" The Earl shouted these words in what must have been an imitation of the departed priest "which the people will carry out tomorrow to celebrate the May Day, or Beltane as they call it here. Fool. What does he want: a riot? The people would go mad! Then he started ranting about the tournament we are holding, complaining that the Pope has outlawed jousting and melees."

"People need the chance to enjoy themselves sometimes. Priests would have us on our knees praying all the time." Savage said.

"Indeed." Said the Earl. "'Who will rid me of this turbulent priest?', eh, Montmorency?" This last quote was directed at the Knight Hospitaller standing behind him, who merely gave a dry smile.

"The man is a heretic." Montmorency said. No further explanation as to what exactly the Hospitaller's opinion of what should be done with him was required.

"Now." The Earl became serious. "What business does the King have with us? Forgive me if I seem discourteous, Sir Richard, but you don't look much like an envoy of a King."

As part of their job involved crossing enemy battle lines, Heralds tended to advertise their identity. So richly and sumptuously dressed were they that they could usually be seen coming from a mile off, which was a distinct advantage when there were archers around who could shoot an arrow through your eye from a distance not much short of one.

"You are referring to my humble dress, Sire," Savage said. "This was so as not to attract attention to my mission. I don't usually work as an emissary. I was chosen for this mission because I am from Ulster myself and the King knew I was returning here to visit my homestead."

The Red Earl narrowed his eyes. "You're not a cloak and dagger man, are you?" He inquired, his voice laden with distaste.

"No." Savage shook his head. "Nothing so exciting. But my message has to remain secret until you decide what action to take on it." With that Savage reached into his pouch. Instantly, the two bodyguards standing before the dais drew their daggers, then relaxed when all that Savage retrieved was the parchment scroll with the large red wax seal on it. He handed this to De Thrapston who, on seeing the imprint of the Lions of England on the seal, carried it reverently down the hall to the Red Earl.

Earl De Burgh broke it open, unrolled the scroll and, to Savage's faint surprise, began to read. Reading was a skill looked down on with disdain by the ruling classes and looked up to in awe by the lower classes. Virtually no members of either rank could do it. The Red Earl was obviously an exception, but from what Savage knew of him, De Burgh was an exceptional man.

"I'm honoured that the King has deigned to write to me," The Earl announced, but his voice betrayed the fact that magnates as powerful as Richard De Burgh by and large were not exactly knocked head-over-heels in awe by letters from Royalty. De Burgh was virtually a King himself; He was certainly as rich as one. "He instructs me to pay heed to the message delivered by his special emissary, Sir Richard Savage, and to treat it with the urgency and importance it deserves-"

Savage was startled. "Sir, the message is a secret one, for your eyes only." He protested.

"Don't worry." The Earl replied. "Everyone here is completely trustworthy."

Savage glanced at the black clad Knight Hospitaller and doubted this.

Earl de Burgh carried on reading: "'By the time you read this message, the Scottish Parliament will have gathered at Ayr, a stone's throw across the sea from your Earldom. Our spies tell us that under cover of the gathering of the Parliament, Edward Bruce is gathering an invasion fleet that will set sail for Ireland as soon as the Parliament finishes. Your Earldom is closest to Scotland and first in line for attack. This attack is imminent. Your King is warning you so that you can look to your defences and raise the feudal levy. Your Earldom of Ulster is all that stands in the way of disaster. We expect you to do your duty to God and to your King. Edward Rex. '"

There were several moments of silence in the Hall as the echoes of the King's words died away. The Earl stood up slowly and deliberately and looked Savage in the eye.

"Sir Richard," He said in a low, even tone. "I would not be so churlish as to blame the messenger for the portent of the message which he bears, so I absolve you of any blame. However, is the King not aware that my own daughter is the wife of Robert Bruce? Is the King asking me to believe that my own kinsfolk are plotting a war against me? This is a terrible insult!"

"Sire," Savage protested, "The information is from highly reliable sources. The invasion plans are set. The army is ready. Edward Bruce has struck a bargain with Thomas Dun, who has gathered together half the ships in Scotland to carry the invasion force across the Moyle Sea to Ireland. For all we know they have already set sail."

"Thomas Dun?" Montmorency sneered. "The man is a pirate. If the tale is true then we will have nothing to worry about. Dun will just steal Bruce's money and he'll see neither height nor hair of any ships."

"Sire," Savage ignored the Hospitaller and addressed the Earl. "You led Irish troops on two of the King's Royal Father's campaigns in Scotland. You received the surrender of the Scots yourself. Your Earldom sends supplies to the King for his wars in France. Bruce is determined to stop Irish aid to England in her Scottish wars. I urge you to take heed of the danger-"

"The marriage of my daughter and my sister were arranged to reconcile our houses. The King need not concern himself. We will not be attacked." The Earl stated. "And even if we are, we are ready. The Bonnaught and my galloglaich troops are one Hell of a standing army who can fight off ten times their number of Scots while the feudal levy of knights is gathered. I've also commissioned Montmorency, here to organise new defence plans for the Earldom which he is implementing as we speak. Sir Hugo is Knight Marshal of the Order of St. John here in Ireland. He is well learned in the latest arts of warfare from their experience defending the Holy Land."

"It isn't very long since the Saracens retook the Holy Land that the Hospitallers were supposed to be defending." Savage said.

Montmorency's eyes narrowed. "The loss of the Holy Places came through the sins of the crusaders, the Templars in particular." He hissed. "No amount of tactics can prevail when God himself has turned against you."

"Knight Marshal Montmorency is one of the finest strategists I have met." The Earl said and then smiled. "He is also a damned fine chess player: the only man to beat me in the last five years." He gestured towards a long table that ran along one of the walls of the great hall. Savage glanced over to see that a chess set was sitting on it. From the arrangement of the pieces it was evident that a game was underway.

"Montmorency and I have an on-going rivalry on the chessboard" the Red Earl explained. "As it happens, that very chess board was a gift from my son in law, Robert Bruce, two Christmases ago. Have no fear, Sir Richard," The Red Earl reassured. "We appreciate your concern for our wellbeing-and I'm sure that that is what concerns the King and not the possible loss of a valuable source of supplies, soldiers and tax revenue -but be certain that if the worst comes, we shall be ready. We always are."

It was clear that this was to be the last word on the matter.

Suddenly the Earl asked "How's your jousting?"

"Pardon?" Savage was somewhat taken aback.

"Your jousting." The Earl repeated. "Tomorrow is the May Day Holiday and we're holding a tournament. It will take place after church."

"I was hoping to visit my old family Manor..." Savage protested.

"Sir Richard, you are now my guest." The Earl said. "It would be churlish of me to let you rush off without entertaining you. You must stay here tonight. Tomorrow after church you can compete with the best of us in the tourney. Then tomorrow night I am having a feast here in the castle. You must come to that too. Even King's emissaries have to take a holiday some time."

"But I have no armour with me," Savage tried one last excuse.

"Don't worry about that," De Thrapston, the keeper of the castle spoke up, clapping Savage on the shoulder, "We'll soon sort you out with something."

"Yes, you do that Henry." The Earl assented with a smile, the thunder clouds of his anger now totally evaporated. "Now show Sir Richard to his lodgings. He can have the room in the North Tower."

"Thank you." Said Savage. "Your hospitality is most generous."

Generous, and undeniable. Savage was under no illusion that he had any choice in this matter. A vague feeling of foreboding crept into his chest as he wondered just how long he was going be a 'guest' of the Earl of Ulster.

"I seem to remember that your father was a fearsome man in the tournament." De Thrapston boomed. "I'll look forward to seeing if you're a chip off the old block."

"Indeed." Montmorency gave a sly grin. "I'll look forward to meeting you out there myself."

De Thrapston led Savage out into the courtyard. As the young knight followed the Keeper of the Castle dark, heavy rainclouds were gathering over Carrickfergus. He looked up at the stark, solid walls of the castle keep and could not help feeling a pang of unease as he noted just what a good prison it would make.

Chapter 9

After Richard Savage left, silence descended on the hall of Carrickfergus castle. A bright shaft of late afternoon sunshine poured in through one of the tall windows and the Earl watched little motes of dust spinning around in the column of light.

Eventually he said: "I don't think there will be any more vassals with requests today. Shall we resume our game?"

The Earl and the Knight Hospitaller left the dais and seated themselves at the chessboard.

"So: another dancer joins the carol." The Earl switched from French to English. "What do you make of this King's Envoy, Montmorency?"

The Hospitaller did not reply, but instead glanced nervously at the Earl's bodyguards who hovered a little way off.

"Don't worry about my galloglaich guards. They can't speak English." The Earl said. Montmorency visibly relaxed.

"I think this is a dangerous turn of events. It couldn't have come at a worse time." The Hospitaller mused, stroking his beard and studying the chess set on the board before him. The pieces were carved from walrus Ivory and represented viking warriors. King Robert Bruce had got the set from the Western Islands of his realm where the ancient influence of the Norse was still strong.

"Do you think the King suspects anything?" The Earl wondered aloud.

"Who can tell?" Montmorency moved the mounted warrior representing his knight to a bare three squares from the Earl's King. "I think we should not take any chances."

The Earl grunted at the audacity of the Hospitaller's move. "I don't intend to. What way is the wind blowing, Montmorency?"

Montmorency looked up at the Earl with hooded eyes. "If Bruce's fleet is ready to sail, then in a matter of days you will see yourself."

The Earl regarded the Hospitaller from under lowered brows. "It is not in my nature to wait and see. I expect you, Montmorency, to tell me these things. You are loyal to your Order, your Religion, not mortal Kings. That is why I trust you in this venture. Now tell me where things currently stand."

Montmorency sighed and shrugged. "Things hang in the balance. War can have all sorts of unexpected outcomes. However, with both France and Scotland against them, England's cause looks increasingly desperate. King Edward is weak and unpopular. He is a blasphemer and a sodomite. His barons could depose him at any minute. Success by the Scots in taking Ireland will be the final straw for him. It is only a matter of time then before King Robert Bruce rules all these Islands."

"What about here in Ulster? I've spent so much of the last few years embroiled in the damnable Gordian knot of Connaught politics that I've lost touch. What do people here think?"

"A lot of the nobility are for the Scots, but not all. Significant numbers still remain loyal to the catamite King of England. Some of them could cause real trouble."

"What do you think we should do?" The Earl took Montmorency's knight with his rook.

"If you decide to take the Scottish side and things go the way I expect, then those who remain stubborn in their support for Edward of England will have to be … removed." Montmorency did not seem too annoyed at the loss of his knight.

"Is anyone of significance against the Scots?"

"Several noble families and some of the Gaelic kings." Montmorency quickly moved his own rook up the board to take the Earl's. "The De Verduns, the Logans, the Mac Cartney and Mac Innis clans. Your Seneschal too."

The Earl rolled his eyes, both at the loss of his piece and the news. "Thomas de Mandeville is a loyal vassal. We fought together in Scotland and Gascony. If it comes to that it will be a shame."

"We all have to make sacrifices to achieve our goals." Montmorency said. He moved his bishop directly into the path of the Earl's king. "Perhaps if you were to declare your hand it may make some change sides. Publicly say which side you support."

The Earl snorted and ignored Montmorency's bishop. He could see the second knight lurking to take his Queen the minute he took the piece. "And risk losing everything? I don't think so, Montmorency, not till I'm surer of how things will turn out. Certainly not with Le Bottelier arriving here later."

The Hospitaller became excited. "The Justiciar of Ireland is coming here? This is a perfect opportunity to tip the balance! The King of England's representative in Ireland-the highest authority in the land-will be under your roof, in your power. It could hasten what we are trying to do!"

The Earl sighed and fixed Montmorency with a withering glare. "We? What I am trying to do, Montmorency, is survive. There was a time when I followed quests and kings and believed in causes, but those days are over. I did not spend thirty years building up vast estates to have them all blown away by the winds of Chance. When this war is over, regardless of who wins it, I intend to still be Earl of Connaught and Earl of Ulster, with my fortunes intact. And while I reign here, I want my future grandson on the throne of Scotland. Besides, Edmund le Bottelier will be very well guarded. He is also the only man in Ireland with enough soldiers at his command to challenge my power."

There were a few moments silence, then the Earl continued. "Perhaps things will be clearer after I speak to Dame Alys."

The Hospitaller's eyes narrowed and his nostrils flared slightly. "Why do you have dealings with that woman? The Bible is very clear on the matter: 'Maleficos non patieris vivere'. Witches thou shall not suffer to live."

"The Bible also tells us to love our enemies, not slaughter them with the blades of our swords, Montmorency. How does your military Order of warrior monks get round that particular principle of our Lord, Hmmm?" The Earl said.

"There is no dichotomy. Love our Christian enemies, kill all those who do not adhere to the true Faith. 'Tradideritque eas Dominus Deus tuus tibi percuties eas usque ad internicionem non inibis cum eis foedus nec misereberis earum.'" The Hospitaller said. "'Utterly destroy them. You shall make no league with them, nor show mercy to them.' It's all in the book of Deuteronomy, and in a hundred other places as well."

"The Bible sets no bar against Astrology, Montmorency. The Pope himself has his own Astrologer." Earl de Burgh said. "Dame Alys Logan is the best star gazer in Ireland."

"Astrology is not all she is adept in." The Hospitaller spat. "The woman is a witch, a mistress of the Black Arts. She worships the native demons of this land and has been seen around the town at night casting her spells."

The Earl smiled and took a sip of wine. "Then I'd rather have her on my side than against me. Sometimes, Montmorency, I cannot fathom you. On the one hand you rant and rave about the Scriptures, while on the other you urge me in the coming war to take the side of Robert Bruce-a usurper King-against the legitimate King Edward of England."

"Better a man like Bruce than the sinner King of England." Montmorency said.

"The Pope himself excommunicated Bruce for murder."

"The Holy Father is not infallible, regardless of what Thomas Aquinas wants us to think," said Montmorency. "God has shown his approval of Bruce's cause."

"Ah, yes. This mysterious 'treasure' he is supposed to have that you are so keen on." The Earl said.

"Supposed? I have seen it with my own eyes!" Montmorency hissed.

The Earl shook his head. "Trinkets like that don't impress me. Like I said before, once there was a day when I followed quests and believed in miracles, but that day is long past." With that he moved his bishop to midway up the board, taking Montmorency's rook in the manoeuvre. As he lifted the piece he examined it with interest. The rooks in the set were carved to resemble Viking beserkers with wide, staring eyes, gnawing frenziedly on the rim of their shields.

"Such a savage chess piece," The Earl said. "Montmorency, regardless of what my future plans are, what I really don't need right now is a King's Envoy rooting around in my business, reporting back God knows what to his Master. We can't do anything about it tonight though. The King will have informed the Justiciar of Savage's coming here and Le Bottelier will be expecting to meet him."

Montmorency gathered his cloak around him and leaned over the table as he moved his bishop back out of harm's way. He looked like a huge crow waiting on a branch for a dying man below. "He will be competing in the melee tomorrow. The tournament is a violent, dangerous sport. That is why the Holy Father banned it. Accidents happen."

The Earl's eyes flashed as he swiftly moved his queen right across the board to two spaces from Montmorency's King. "Let's make sure one does, eh? Checkmate."

Chapter 10

After leaving the great hall, De Thrapston led Savage to his lodgings. This was a tower on the inner wall that was much smaller than the Castle Keep, but just as thick-walled. The Keeper of the Castle kept up a pleasant, friendly chatter the whole way, his voice loud and booming in the courtyard.

"You've come at a very busy time for us. With the May holiday tomorrow and the tournament we have so many people coming to the town from all over Ireland. The Justiciar himself is due to arrive anytime. Then there's the May Day- or Beltane as the natives call it- feast tomorrow night. There is so much to do!"

"The Justiciar of Ireland is coming?" Savage tried his best to hide his interest.

"Yes. The Highest Power in the land- bar the King that is- is coming here for the tournament. His son Guilleme is competing." De Thrapston grinned. "It's a great honour but obviously means a lot of work for the likes of me."

There was no way into the north tower from ground level, so Savage and de Thrapston had to climb a stone staircase up to the battlements. Soldiers of the Garrison were stationed at various watch-points around the walls, and Savage immediately noted that the only one positioned on the battlements leading to the North Tower was standing right outside the one and only door to the fortification.

The soldier stepped respectfully aside to let them past, then retook his place, avoiding eye contact and staring out to sea instead of at Savage or De Thrapston.

"Here we are: your accommodation." De Thrapston smiled and held open the door. Savage entered the chamber and turned to face De Thrapston.

"What about my weapons?" Savage demanded. "They weren't returned to me after I left the Hall."

De Thrapston smiled disarmingly. "Oh don't worry about those. You won't need them this evening. I'll make sure you get them back before you leave."

"All the same, I'd prefer to get them now." Savage said.

The Keeper of the Castle's smile faded. "That won't be possible."

"I'm a prisoner, then?"

De Thrapston's smile returned. "Of course not! My dear Sir Richard: let's not fall out about this. I have my orders to follow as do you. Consider the situation: You have arrived unannounced at a time of great uncertainty. The Earl just needs to be sure about you and your intentions before you are likely to be fully trusted. Now, I suggest you get some rest." He glanced down at Richard's clothes. "I can bring something more suitable for you to wear if you like."

With that he closed the door. Savage was still looking at it as he heard the sound of a key being turned in the lock.

"God's balls!" Savage spat the worst curse he could think of.

He looked around his new lodgings. The room was round like the tower and the stone walls were hung with heavy warm tapestries. There was good clean straw on the floor and a large bed surrounded by heavy woollen curtains. Everything had the air of a rather comfortable bedroom, except for the fact that both of the windows had bars across them and the door was locked. Was this a prison made to look like a comfortable lodging, or lodgings that sometimes served as a prison? Was he once more a prisoner? Everything had been done so politely and with the minimum of fuss that it was hard to tell what was going on.

Then again, Savage mused, this was Ireland. On the one hand there was an ancient well-respected tradition of hospitality, on the other it was common practise that if you intended to kill someone, you made sure that first he was well at ease. It made it less dangerous to the attacker that way.

Savage looked out through one of the windows. Immediately outside was the sea and to his left he could see the edge of the turf ramparts that protected the town. The coast disappeared northwards. Along it, waves broke on the pale yellow sands of a beach. Directly below his window was a twenty foot drop onto the unforgiving black rock of Fergus.

He turned away from the window and sat on the bed. What was he going to do? He knew he had to do one thing as soon as possible: he had to get a report back to England about how the Earl had received the news of Bruce's intentions. However, how he was going to get to speak to any of the contacts Lancaster had given him from inside a locked room presented a significant problem.

The arrival of the Justiciar offered a glimmer of hope. If anyone could be trusted it would be him. Edmund le Bottelier ruled the Norman lands in Ireland in the name of the King of England. He had to collect the taxes and keep the peace. It was as simple, and as difficult, as that. At all costs Savage had to try to speak privately to the Justiciar at the feast the next night.

If he lived that long.

There was something odd about the room. Despite the glass in the seaward window and the locked door the smell of the sea was strong: too strong to be coming through the slight crack at the bottom of the door and there was a definite cold breeze coming from somewhere.

Savage got up and licked his finger. Holding it before him he felt one side colder than the other and turned to examine the wall on the cold side. A heavy tapestry draped the stones from floor to ceiling. The cloth had been woven to depict a scene of a King seated in regal splendour upon his throne. "Hic sedet Arturus" was the inscription above it. The light breeze seemed to be coming from behind the tapestry.

Savage braced himself, putting one foot behind him so he could either spring forward or backwards depending on what lay behind the arras, then swept the tapestry aside.

He smiled. The King on his throne was an appropriate motif for what lay behind the tapestry. Into an alcove in the wall was built a latrine, its wooden seat hovering over a sloping gap in the floor that opened out onto the rocks and the crashing waves that waited below.

Savage sighed and returned to sit on the bed. There was nothing left to do but wait for whatever the evening would bring.

Suddenly he heard commotion outside. The sound of horses' hooves clattered across the cobblestones of the Castle courtyard outside and Savage rose to see what was going on. The second window in the room faced into the inner courtyard of the castle. It too was barred but gave a good view of what was happening below. Being on the sheltered side of the room, it also had no glass so he could hear what was going on. Into the courtyard clip-clopped an old destrier that was long past its time to be sent out to pasture. Its thin mane and tail hung limp, its muzzle was almost white and its back was bowed.

To Savage's surprise, mounted on the warhorse's back was not a knight but a woman and a little girl. The woman was quite tall and dressed in a black cloak that covered her from head to foot. Despite the late afternoon sunshine, she wore the hood of her cloak up, hiding her face from view. The girl looked about ten or eleven, had long, curly blond hair and wore a dress that looked like it had seen better days. She was mounted on the warhorse saddle behind the woman. To the further surprise of Savage, a scrawny grey cat also sat perched on the horse behind the saddle.

With a deft hand, the woman brought her mount to a halt outside the Great Hall. As Savage watched he saw De Thrapston approaching her from the Hall doorway.

"Dame Alys. So good to see you!" The Keeper of the Castle greeted her. To Savage's ears there was something reserved, almost careful in the normally boisterous De Thrapton's tone of voice. The Keeper of the Castle proffered a hand to help the woman dismount. She ignored it and climbed off her steed with the easy grace of one used to being in the saddle. Once on the ground the woman swept back her hood to unleash a tumble of long black hair. Her skin was white as snow and she looked to be in her late twenties or early thirties. The girl jumped down too and they were both followed by the cat which leapt lightly off the horse to curl itself round the calves of its mistress.

Savage's brow furrowed as a memory from the long distant past resurfaced in his mind: De Thrapston had called her Alys. Could it be the same Alys he had known all those years ago?

"Please come into the Great Hall." De Thrapston said. "The Earl is waiting for you."

The woman lifted down a small leather chest that had been strapped behind the saddle of her horse then began to follow De Thrapston towards the Hall doors. Suddenly, she stopped and looked over her shoulder for a second as if somehow aware that she was being watched. In that instant Savage saw her dark, arched eyebrows and the flash of a pair of grey eyes that left him in no doubt.

"Alys de Logan." Savage breathed. "I'll be damned. After all this time…"

The woman turned away again and followed De Thrapston into the Great Hall. The girl and the cat slipped in behind her. Savage left his vantage point to return to his seat on the bed, slowly shaking his head at this turn of events.

If she was going to be at the banquet tomorrow it would certainly make for an interesting evening. This was one reunion that Savage did not relish the thought of.

Chapter 11

Seventy miles to the North-East across the sea from Carrickfergus castle lay the coast of another Carrick: this one a Scottish Earldom. On the beach there, as the sun began to slip towards the horizon, a short, stocky, black-haired man stood, gazing at the fog-obscured view before him.

The bay was long, sweeping and edged by a wide beach of pale blond sand. White-topped breakers rolled in to crash on the shore, breaking around the prows of hundreds of boats that were beached along the water's edge, their prows rising up like the heads of huge sea-horses. Beyond them, mostly obscured by the heavy sea mist that clung to the water, the vague ghosts of many, many other ships moored in the deeper waters of the bay could just be discerned. The true numbers of the fleet was obscured by the thick fog. The ships were a miscellany of maritime life: everything from humble fishing curraghs to massive galleys, virtually every serviceable ship in Scotland had been gathered in the bay. The unmistakable purpose of such a congregation hung in the air as an unspoken threat.

"Its like looking into the future, isn't it?"

A voice made the black haired man turn. Approaching along the beach, his feet ploughing through the deep sand, was another man. He was very similar in appearance but younger and fair-haired.

"Only this view is clearer, brother." The black haired man gave an ironic smile. Despite being in his middle age, his hair and beard showed no signs of grey. "Have you ever seen such a fleet?"

"Thomas Dun has done well." The blond haired man said. "He has gathered nearly four hundred ships for us."

The Black haired man nodded with satisfaction. "Well Edward: the time for departure nears. Soon you will be a King like I am."

"Aye." The blond haired man grinned. He too gazed out into the fog, but his eyes were not focussed on the wraith-like shadows of the ships. They sought a further goal: the unseen shore that lay beyond the horizon. "Edward Bruce, Earl of Carrick. King of Ireland here-after. I like the sound of it already."

"Let's not count our conquests too soon." Robert de Bruce, King of Scotland (for that was who the Black haired man was) cautioned. "We both have many battles to fight first. You must conquer Ireland, I must subdue our rebellious Western Isles."

"We will prevail, Robert. Look how far we've come already. God is with us. How can we doubt that now? He has sent us a sign of his approval." King Robert's younger brother said.

Robert de Bruce grunted. "He didn't always seem to be on our side, Edward. You forget the early days: when we lost at Kildrummy and our brother Niall was hung drawn and quartered by the bastards. They did the same to William Wallace. Remember how they hung our sister, lovely sweet Mary, in a gibbet on the walls of Roxburgh castle as food for the crows? In a gibbet, Edward. Let us never forget, never forgive that. Remember when they slaughtered us at the battle at Methven and I had to flee for my life and hide out on that godforsaken island off the north of Ireland ..."

"Speak of the devil!" Edward de Bruce cautioned his brother to silence as he spotted three figures approaching along the sand. Two of them were wrapped in dark woollen cloaks and underneath wore chainmail shirts. They bore a definite facial resemblance, but one of them was clearly much older than the other. The elder man's hair and beard had turned iron grey as he approached his fifties. His long hair was braided.

His companion was in his mid-twenties and his still jet black hair was coifed long in the latest French style. Both possessed the same pale blue eyes but while the elder man's bore a genial spark the younger man's emanated an arrogant, challenging stare. With them was a blond haired man with a full, bristling beard clad in the colourful, traditional wrapped apparel of a Scotsman, albeit a very wealthy one. This man led the way.

As they approached, a flock of black-headed terns in their path took to flight as one and wheeled around overhead, their high-pitched indignant cries filling the air.

"Ulick Ceannaideach. Cheiftain of the Clan Ceannaideach. My loyal servant!" Robert Bruce greeted the Scotsman in Gaelic and allowed the man to begrudgingly kiss his hand. "And Sir Hugh Bysset! Laird of the Irish Glyns. Hugh: is this your nephew John too?"-Bruce switched to Norman French- "Old friends, I'm glad to see you. I trust your crossing was an easy one?"

"Easy and short, Robert." Hugh Bysset, the Lord of the North Irish Counties responded, before suddenly remembering: "Sorry: Your Majesty. Last we met you were just a cousin, and one in trouble at that."

"Indeed Hugh!" Bruce grinned. "We were just talking about how you saved my hide when I was on the run from the English after Methven. I won't forget the danger you put yourself in by harbouring me in Rathlin Island castle."

The older Bysset chuckled. "Sure wasn't I the one that King Edward Longshanks ordered to hunt you down? Who was I in danger from? Myself?"

Both men laughed heartily. Bruce shook his head. "I often think of that summer I spent in that beautiful castle on Rathlin Island."

Bysset threw back his head and laughed again. "Aye, Robert. I'm sure you do. It was falling down! The rain used to come in through the roof in rivers and the island was about as far from civilisation as you can get. No need to be polite. It was a shit hole."

Bruce returned the knowing smile. "Yes, but a safe shit hole. We had a few good nights there, I remember."

Hugh Bysset nodded. "We did, when I brought a few wenches over to the island…"

"-And the Uisce beatha they distil on your lands," Bruce shook his head. "I had a few sore heads in those days on Rathlin."

"Have you heard the legend about you now, though?" Said Bysset. "You disappeared and could not be found, despite Longshanks having both sides of the Irish Sea combed for you. The common folk say that after the massacre at Methven you hid out in a cave for a year. While there you saw a spider trying to spin a web. You broke the web and the spider spun it again. You broke it again and it spun it again. No matter how many times you broke the web, that wee spider just kept re-spinning it. From this, you learnt that no matter how many times you are knocked down, you get back up and try, try again. This inspired you to carry on your fight against the English. Now Rathlin castle was bad, Robert, but it was far from a cave."

"Good story, though, eh? Appropriate anyway. I wonder where it came from?" Bruce winked. "Anyway, how are things in Ireland? Will my Brother be welcomed with open arms?"

Hugh Bysset frowned. "I wish I could say that, but the ground is far from sure. Some support you, some don't. On the one hand I bring a letter for you from Domnall Ui Neill, King of Tyr Eoghan, pledging his support for you. It's signed by thirteen other Chieftains. The De Lacys might support you also. On the other hand I've also brought a couple of people with me to show how precarious things are…"

"What about these English dogs?" The Ceannaideach Chieftain interrupted in Gaelic, uncomfortable at being excluded from the conversation in a language he did not understand. "When do we question them?"

For the first time the young John Bysset seemed interested in the conversation and echoed Ceannaideach's query with a questioning glance towards the King of Scotland.

Bruce laid a re-assuring hand on Ceannaideach's muscle-packed shoulder. "Ulick I know you are keen to use your special talents. We will go and question them straight away." He signalled to his brother Edward and the Byssets to follow him as they set off up the beach towards a forest of tents that lay between the beach and the walls of the town of Ayr.

As they walked, several blazes of light appeared in the distance. Through the fog, they appeared to be igniting up in the sky somewhere.

"The Beltane fires." Bruce commented in Gaelic. "Tonight begins the Feast of Beltane. On the hilltops all around here the traditional Beltane-eve bonfires are being lit. There will be feasting and the cattle will be driven between the blazes to purify them. Hugh, I'm sure if we could see through the fog to your lands in Ireland we would see the same fires being kindled."

"Oh yes, the natives-" Bysset checked himself as he caught a withering glance from Robert Bruce "-we will be lighting them on our headlands and hilltops tonight too. It's been the tradition since time immemorial."

"This is why the coming war is so necessary, Hugh." Edward Bruce joined the conversation, putting one arm around Bysset's shoulders and another around Ceannaideach's. "We are not two people, but one. We are separated by sea, but we are one people, with one culture, one language and shared traditions. Six hundred years ago, we Scots left Ireland and crossed the Moyle Sea to forge this country. Now we shall return to join our own folk, to help them throw off the yolk of their foreign Overlords. This is not about Ireland and Scotland, it is about uniting Greater Scotia."

Ceannaideach nodded enthusiastically. Bysset shot a raised eyebrow towards King Robert Bruce. Either Bruce did not see it, or he chose to ignore it.

"Who are these men you have brought to us?" Robert Bruce asked as they approached one of the large leather tents. Two heavily armed highlanders stood on guard at the entrance.

"One is a sea captain." Bysset said. "He is little more than a pirate, but the most recent cargo he ferried across the Irish Sea to Ulster is very interesting: an Envoy of Edward of England. We don't know if this sea captain is working for the English Crown or not but it will be worth finding out whatever information he has. He had just left Carrickfergus for England when one of my warships intercepted his boat and brought him here. We thought it prudent to stop him potentially returning a message to the English."

"Who's the other one?" Said Edward Bruce.

"Raymond de Sandal. Bachelor knight from the North coast of Ulster. His family own the castle that guards the bridge at the town of Coleraine. We've received information from the Hospitaller that he has been actively working as an agent of the English crown in Ireland."

Robert Bruce nodded. "What about this Envoy of the King of England? What's King Edward up to? Does he know how close the invasion is?"

"The Earl has kept the Envoy in Carrickfergus castle, no doubt until he knows more about what the man's mission is." Bysset said.

Bruce frowned. "Ah, my always-scheming Father-in-Law, Earl Richard de Burgh. Is there any chance that soon he will declare openly whose side he is on?"

"The army is ready to sail. His time for prevarication is running out." Edward Bruce growled.

"You know the Earl as well as I do, Robert," Hugh Bysset said. "Trying to discern what is going on in his head is like trying to count how many ships there are out in that fog."

"What about the Holy Secret we possess?" Said Bruce. "Does that not influence him in any way?"

Bysset shook his head. "What do you think? Spiritual matters do not impress the Earl any longer. All he cares about these days is keeping his estates and wealth intact, and sheltering the ambitions of himself and his family."

The Bruce brother's exchanged glances.

"He won't be happy to hear what the Parliament has just approved then." Edward Bruce said.

Bysset looked puzzled.

"Gathering of the Parliament here at Ayr was a cover for mustering our invasion army," Robert Bruce explained. "However, there was also legitimate business for it to discuss. As the Earl of Ulster's daughter has not seen fit to provide me with a son yet, I need to make provision for who will succeed me if I'm killed. I have currently no male heir, so Parliament has approved my Brother Edward as my successor to the Throne."

Bysset frowned and shook his head. "The Earl certainly won't be pleased to hear that."

"How long are you staying?" Robert Bruce quickly switched the subject. "We will feast tonight. You are both welcome."

Hugh Bysset shook his head. "There is a tournament at Carrickfergus tomorrow. John here is competing and there will be a feast at the castle tomorrow night. We must be there or people will ask questions."

Robert Bruce nodded his approval. "Very prudent. However do not forget we are counting on you to pilot the invasion fleet to a safe landing place in Ireland. Now, let us have a talk with our guests, shall we?"

The two highlanders on guard stood aside to let them enter the tent. Just before they opened the tent flap, Robert Bruce laid a hand on Ceannaideach's chest. "Ulick. These men are yours to question, find out what you can. The sea captain probably knows nothing so concentrate on the knight."

Ceannaideach nodded. Hugh Bysset noticed that almost unseen, the scotsman was drawing a dagger from up the sleeve of his tunic.

The tent flap was dawn aside and they all entered. Ceannaideach signalled to the two highlanders to follow them in too. The inside of the tent was gloomy in the late afternoon murk but they could see two men, trussed up uncomfortably with their hands bound behind their backs to their ankles. They both lay on their sides. One of the highland guards kindled a torch and hung it in a bracket to give more light to the scene.

"Up dogs!" Ceannaideach roared in English. "Kneel before your King!"

The command was useless as neither man could move of their own accord, so the highlanders dragged both up into a position where they were resting painfully on their haunches. One of the men was the weather beaten Captain of the Mary. He looked at the men before him with a defiant, almost sceptical gaze. This was probably not the first time he had been in such a position. His companion was a young man with dark brown hair. He would probably have been described as good looking, if his nose had not been recently smashed and his right eye blackened.

"What does Edward of England know of our plans?" Ceannaideach growled. "You might as well tell us everything right now and save yourselves a lot of bother."

"I don't know what you are talking about." The Sea captain said. "I am a merchant. I don't know the King's mind."

Ceannaideach took a step towards him and grabbed him by the hair. The knife in his other hand flashed briefly in the torchlight as its point entered the captain's skull to the right of his nose. Ceannaideach flexed his wrist and with a brief sucking noise the captain's eyeball was flicked out of its socket. The ruined orb stuck the leather tent wall with a wet thump, then began to slide down towards the ground, oozing a ghastly trail of blood and slime behind it. The whole thing was done so quickly that the eyeball had reached the round before the Captain started screaming from the pain. Edward Bruce looked on with grim approval. Hugh Bysset flinched at the sudden violence. His nephew John's face took on with an expression of gloating enjoyment.

"I'm not here to piss about," Ceannaideach shouted, "Tell us!"

"Shove your face in a turd you son of a whore." The sea captain managed to gasp through the pain and shock.

Ceannaideach smiled, but it was not a pleasant smile. "You must have seen enough of the world, old man."

With grim slowness he pushed the dagger back into the Captain's empty eye socket. The sound of metal on bone was audible as he scraped the point against the back of the man's orbit, locating the remnants of the optic nerve. The Captain screeched and tried to draw away but one of the highlanders stepped forward to hold the back of his head.

With a steady hand and agonising slow pace, Ceannaideach continued to apply pressure to the blade. Above the cries of the man the crack of bone splintering could be heard. The Captain's screams suddenly became impossibly high-pitched as the knife entered into his brain, an inch at a time. Ceannaideach's face bore a look of steady concentration as deliberately controlled the speed of the blade as it penetrated further and further into his victim's skull. The Captain's cries changed from squeals of pain to strange shouted gibberish. His body bucked and shuddered but the highlander kept him in a merciless grip. Eventually, when the knife had gone in about five inches, the Captain stopped making a final gurgling noise and his body slumped into a limp deadweight. The highlander let go of him and the body slid backwards off Ceannaideach's blade to crumple on the ground.

Hugh Bysset grimaced with displeasure. The strong smell of urine pervaded the air in the tent and at first he thought it came from the captain's corpse as death relaxed all the muscles in the body, then he spotted the steaming pool that surrounded Raymond de Sandal. The young knight's face was a mask of terror as Ceannaideach turned his attention to him.

"Now, laddie," Ceannaideach growled. "Why don't you go easy on yourself and tell us what we want to know?"

De Sandal looked desperately at the two Byssets, his eyes beseeching for mercy. "Help me! SyrHugh: our fathers are friends! John: we've fought together! Hunted together!"

John Bysset returned Sandal's desperate pleading with a wicked smile. "You have chosen your side in this war, Raymond, and you have chosen badly. We cannot help you now."

The elder Bysset avoided Raymond's eyes and looked down at the ground. "Tell them what they want, lad. It will be quicker."

With the fading of his last hope, something died in Sandal's eyes. He hung his head in dejection. "Sir Roger Mortimer, Lord of the March, employed me to send regular reports to the king about what was going on in Ulster." He said n a monotone voice. "They know about your plans to invade Ireland but with most of the English army fighting in France the King is gambling that he can rely on the Irish Lords to repel the invasion. Last week I received orders from Mortimer that I was to make contact with a knight called Richard le Savage who would soon be arriving in Ulster as Emissary of the English King. The superficial reason for Savage's visit is to bear a message from the King to the Earl, but his real mission is to act as a spy and try to determine which nobles can be trusted to fight for the English Crown. The Justiciar will be informed and those deemed untrustworthy dealt with. I was to give Savage whatever help he needed." De Sandal sighed.

There were a few moments silence. "You have no doubt already told the King what side we are on?" Hugh Bysset asked.

De Sandal shook his head. "I did not know until now. You are a friend of my father's: you hid your treachery well." A spark of bitterness entered his voice.

"You are scum, De Sandal." John Bysset spat. "A spy. A dirty cloak and dagger man. What way is that for a knight to behave?"

"Better than one who betrays his rightful King and the land of his birth." De Sandal raised his head and met Bysset's glare.

John Bysset's nostrils flared. His eyes blazed and he spat into the upturned face of de Sandal, then slapped the back of his hand across his face, knocking his sideways.

Hugh Bysset turned to Robert Bruce. "Robert: this young man could be useful to you. I know his father and the whole family are all great warriors. Perhaps you should offer him the chance to join our cause? Perhaps if he knew about the Holy treasure you have…"

"It's too late." Edward Bruce growled. "The game has already begun. The dies are cast. Sides have been chosen. Kill him."

Ceannaideach grinned and held the hilt of his dagger towards Edward Bruce. "The pleasure is yours Sire."

Edward Bruce hesitated, looking down at the knife with a slightly appalled expression on his face.

"Let me do the honours." John Bysset stepped forward and grabbed the dagger from Ceannaideach. He pulled De Sandal's head back by the hair and swiftly drew the blade across the Irish knight's throat, opening up a wide, gory tear. Air wheezed from De Sandal's cut windpipe and hot blood from the severed arteries shot up in a fountain to splatter Bysset's chest and face. With an annoyed grunt he shoved the dying knight away from him so he collapsed sideways to gurgle and choke his last few seconds of life away on the ground in a swift-spreading pool of blood.

Hugh Bysset sighed. "There was no need for that." He said.

Edward Bruce glared at him. "He chose his side. He had to die. Everyone who opposes me will meet the same fate."

Both men locked gazes for several moments until King Robert stepped between them. "Come, men. Let us not fall out over a couple of dead spies. We have bigger challenges to face and another spy to deal with, probably a more dangerous one. I do not like the idea of this Richard Savage being in Ulster at this time. If he finds out who our supporters in Ireland are and he tells the Justiciar it could totally destroy our invasion plans."

"So what do want us to do?" Ceannaideach asked.

"I want him found and I want him dead." Robert Bruce ordered.

Chapter 12

As time crept past, Richard Savage grew more and more bored. After considering several escape plans, searching the room for potential weapons and thinking through how he could defend himself against possible attacks, he was left with very little left to do but lie on the bed. At one point he even dozed off.

As it began to grow dark, the sound of footsteps approaching on the battlements outside roused him.

Savage leapt off the bed, grabbed the heavy earthenware water jug from the wash stand and hid behind the door.

As the key rattled in the lock, Savage raised the jug up above his head. The door swung open and a tall figure entered the room.

Savage stepped out from behind the door and brought the jug down as hard as he could on the back of the man's head. To his dismay he saw just too late that the man wore a heavy conical iron helmet and the blow he intended would shatter his skull simply caused him to stagger forwards. The jug smashed into a thousand shards, Savage cursed his own impetuousness and the newcomer cursed loudly in Irish. The man was a good head taller than Savage and he had shoulders like the crossbeam of a ship. His hair was long and blond his helmet was that of a galloglaich mercenary.

With his only weapon smashed, Savage now had to fight him with just his fists and feet.

He planted his foot in the man's back, sending him flying forwards onto the bed. The galloglaich hit the bed head first. With surprising agility for such a big man, he tumbled forward head over heels over the bed to land like a cat back on his feet.

Savage ran forward, jumped up onto the bed and swung a kick at the man's head. The galloglaich ducked. The blow missed, but then Savage leapt onto him, using his body weight to push the man down towards the floor.

The galloglaich went down as far as his knees under the weight of Savage, who clung onto his upper body with one hand and his knees and at the same time ripped the man's helmet off with his free hand. At least things were a bit more even now. He was about to use the helmet as a club when, with enormous strength, the galloglaich powered himself back up to his feet again, lifting Savage with him and then dumping him backwards to bounce off the bed and crash against a table that sat against the wall. The table collapsed under the impact and Savage landed on the floor.

"Look if you don't want any supper just say so!" The man shouted in a peeved tone of voice.

Savage scrambled to his feet and glared, puzzled and panting at him. He was in his thirties, had the long blond hair and pale blue eyes common to the galloglaiches, but also wore a long, drooping moustache in the Irish style. He was not approaching for further attack. Was this some sort of ruse?

"Supper?" Savage asked.

"I'm here to bring you down to get something to eat. Are you coming or not?" The galloglaich said.

When Savage still did not move the galloglaich shrugged his shoulders and turned to leave.

"Wait: I'm coming" Savage decided that trick or not, he stood a better chance of getting away if he was at least out of the locked room.

"Good. There's someone I want you to meet." The big galloglaich said over his shoulder.

The two men crossed the battlements to the staircase, then descended to the deserted castle courtyard.

"It's very quiet." Savage said.

"Aye." The galloglaich said. "The Earl's gone out of the town to meet the Justiciar who's riding up from Dublin. Most of the guard and the rest of the nobles are with him."

They walked past the great hall towards the castle buttery, a low building built against the inner castle wall between the hall and the kitchens.

"So do you always attack everyone who walks into your room?" The galloglaich asked, a faint smile playing on his lips, "Are you one of those mad bastards that just wants to fight everyone?"

"I thought you'd come to kill me." Savage replied.

The galloglaich stopped, turned and looked Savage straight in the eye.

"Let's get one thing straight, friend." He said. "If I'd come to kill you, you'd be dead."

Savage met his gaze, then the galloglaich turned and led him the rest of the way to the Buttery.

In the gathering gloom of evening, the Buttery had been lit with a couple of pitch torches that were placed on brackets. The room was little more than a long vault and being a store room for provisions, the walls were lined with casks containing ale, wine, salted meat and fish. To help keep the stone room as cool as possible, there were no windows.

An attractive young serving girl was busy hanging up legs of smoked ham on hooks high up the wall.

In the middle of the room a table had been set up on which waited a couple of trenchers of bread, a large hunk of cheese and a frothing jug of beer, along with three cups.

A man stood beside the table. He was in his forties but showed no sign of middle-aged spread. Instead he was lean and wiry, with the hardened look of one who spends most of his time in harness and on campaign. He was wrapped in an un-ostentatious brown woollen cloak, his beard was trimmed and like Savage his hair was cropped short.

The galloglaich grunted an order to the serving girl who quickly left the room, closing the door behind her.

"Good evening Syr Richard." The man at the table said in French. "Welcome to Ulster."

Savage acknowledged the words with a nod.

"I am Thomas de Mandeville, Seneschal of Ulster." The man continued. "MacHuylin here tells me you arrived today with a very interesting message for the Earl from our King."

"The message I brought was for the Earl. If he wishes to share it with you I'm sure he will." Savage said.

"Syr le Savage, I salute your strong sense of duty, but you may as well know that MacHuylin has already told me the content of your message." De Mandeville said. "I am merely interested in verifying it and to get your opinion."

Savage looked at the Galloglaich, MacHuylin, who returned a broad grin. "The Earl's bodyguards might not understand English, but they know enough French to get the gist of your little talk today."

"So the Earl cannot trust his own bodyguards?" Savage shook his head. "I'm sure he will be interested to know that."

MacHuylin's eyes narrowed. A spark of anger ignited in his eyes.

The Seneschal raised a calming hand. "Steady on: The Earl can trust MacHuylin's galloglaiches with his life." He stated. "I am Seneschal however. I am responsible for the security of the Earldom. It is my duty to know what is going on everywhere."

"We protect the Earl, but we work for the Seneschal." MacHuylin said. "Have done for generations."

"I am surprised the Earl has not already told his Seneschal the content of my message, especially given its implications." Savage said.

"So am I." De Mandeville responded. "Surprised, and a little concerned."

Both men looked each other in the eye for a long moment. Finally Savage nodded his head. "Alright. I told the Earl that the Scots are preparing to invade Ireland. They will attack Ulster first. The invasion is immanent."

The Seneschal poured three cups of beer from the jug. The golden liquid splashed around the vessels and a hearty foam welled up to froth over the rims. He passed one cup to Savage and one to MacHuylin before lifting one himself and taking a reflective sip.

After a few moments he asked "How did the Earl react to this news?"

"He was annoyed." Savage said. "He refused to believe his son-in-law Robert Bruce would be planning anything against him." With that he took a thirsty swig of his ale, draining most of his cup in one swallow. The taste of the ale was rich and full, and its heady aroma awakened memories from his childhood. He gave an involuntary appreciative sigh. It was a long time since he had tasted cuirm, the barley - brewed Irish beer.

"Good stuff, eh?" MacHuylin chuckled. "That's from the Earl's own brewery. I wouldn't knock it back like that if I were you. Its strong stuff, especially for an Englishman's stomach."

"Syr Richard is a local man, Connor." De Mandeville said. "I'm sure he drank enough of it when he was growing up." In answer to Savage's surprised look he added "As I said, it's my job to know what is going on in the Earldom, who everyone is and where they come from. I have been asking around about you since MacHuylin here told me about your arrival."

Savage looked at MacHuylin. "And what exactly is your job?" He asked.

"Connor MacHuylin is captain of the Earl's troop of galloglaiches. A fine body of men known as 'The Route'." The Seneschal explained.

"So you're a mercenary?" Savage found it hard to keep his distaste from his voice.

The galloglaich was unperturbed. "The best that money can buy," he grinned.

"MacHuylin's Route has formed the core of the Bonnaght of Ulster-the closest thing we have to a standing army-for the best part of the last century." De Mandeville explained. "I'm not sure the term 'mercenary' does them justice."

"Let's call it a bond of mutual self-interest that has traversed several generations." MacHuylin said. "My great, great grandfather came here from the Hebrides to fight for the Ui Neil Kings. When the English arrived he soon realised that real military power was in the Earldom of Ulster. We've been fighting for whoever ran the armies in this part of the world ever since. For the past hundred years that has meant someone from the de Mandeville family: Earls come and go, but family ties are more secure."

Savage had heard of "the Route" when growing up but had never had contact with any of them. They were a ruthless clan of warriors originally from Scotland whose heritage was a mixture of Norse and Gael. The one thing they excelled at was war, and for most of the last few centuries they had made their living hiring their swords to whoever could afford their blood money.

"You see what I mean?" MacHuylin addressed De Mandeville. "The Earl is ignoring the danger."

"To be fair, he is not completely ignoring it." Savage interjected. "He may dismiss the possibility, but he says the Earldom's defences are ready to repel attack. Montmorency the Hospitaller is seeing to that."

Both the Seneschal and the galloglaich gave a derisive grunt. De Mandeville shook his head as he pushed the bread and cheese in Savage's direction. "I'm sorry Connor, but I simply refuse to believe the Earl would betray the King and the rest of us, regardless of his family connections. We spent four years together fighting the Scots. It makes no sense for him to side with Bruce against the Crown now. Montmorency on the other hand, is another matter. I trust him about as far as I can throw him."

"That's something we can all agree on." Savage said, as he cut himself a hunk of cheese and took a bite. "I have my own reasons not to trust him, but why do you not? The Earl seems to hold him in high esteem."

The Seneschal grunted again. "Perhaps I sound like the fox in the fable who claimed the grapes he could not reach were sour," he said, "but I am Seneschal in Ulster and he is interfering in my business. I am responsible for the defence of the Earldom. Montmorency has wormed his way into the Earl's favour through weasel words and stories of his military prowess that no one here can verify. He is supposed to be a strategic expert, but so far his suggestions for defensive changes have been questionable. In my opinion they actually leave us more open to attack. His latest bright idea is to remove MacHuylin's galloglaiches from the Motte at Donegore and replace them with a force of kerns from Syr Hugh Bysset's lands in the Glens."

"Well now you can see why." MacHuylin said. "With us away from Donegore the Scots can walk straight in, seize the strongest fort outside Carrickfergus and the way both North and South is wide open for them."

The Seneschal sighed and rolled his eyes. "Connor: Are you asking me now to believe that as well as the Earl and Montmorency, Hugh Bysset is also involved in this Scottish conspiracy?"

MacHuylin shrugged. "Who knows who can be trusted?"

Savage felt a strong urge to place his faith in the Seneschal and reveal to him the full extent of his mission. There was something inherently dependable and honest about the man's demeanour that prompted trust. Something however stopped him. This was Ireland and the old maxim still applied: trust no one.

"What about the Keeper of the Castle?" Savage asked. "Do you think he's trustworthy?"

"De Thrapston is a sound enough fellow." The Seneschal replied. "Loyal as a lapdog to the Earl but without an ounce of guile in his body: He doesn't have the intelligence for it. He does whatever the Earl asks him to, and will pass on to Earl Richard everything you say to him. Who knows what the Earl will tell Montmorency, so if I were you I would be careful what you say to him."

Savage took another bite of cheese and they all took another swig of beer.

"I know one man we definitely can trust." De Mandeville stated. "The Justiciar. He will be at the tournament tomorrow and the feast tomorrow night. We need to make sure Savage here talks to him."

MacHuylan nodded in agreement. "What do we do with him in the meantime?" The galloglaich tilted his head towards Savage.

"Syr Richard, I'm afraid you must go back to the tower." De Mandeville said. "The Earl has left specific instructions that you be not allowed to wander and we must respect that until we know for definite what is going on."

Savage sighed at the thought of going back to the locked room, but realised that at these men could help get him access to the Justiciar if he went along with their plan.

"I must go and ride out to meet the Earl. The Justiciar will be here soon and they will be wondering where I am." De Mandeville stood up and finished his beer. "If I cannot speak to the Justiciar alone I will try to contrive a situation where you, Syr Richard and the Justiciar get to meet, either at the tournament or the banquet. In the meantime, be careful and please try hard to keep yourself alive.

Chapter 13

Mayday dawned. The Sun awoke above the horizon and ascended into a cloudless sky. The air was fresh and alive with birdsong and the promise that all the hardships, frugality and darkness of winter were now at an end. With the new born spring, life had returned to the earth.

Savage had spent a restless night. MacHuylin left him back to the tower and he had gone to bed but every noise outside, no matter how slight, had woken him and sent him leaping to his feet, ready for an attack. By morning he was groggy and foul tempered.

Even if he had wanted to, Savage could not have slept long. The castle's denizens were awake from first light: It was a holiday and there was so much to do. To his surprise, Savage awoke to the sound of music. Looking out his window he saw a group of minstrels were playing happy tunes down in the courtyard.

The hammers of the armourers were already beating a ringing tattoo as harness and weapons were prepared for the jousting tournament. Lances were being nailed, helmets polished, bright shields strapped and swords ground on huge, whirring grindstones not, as in preparation for battle, to sharpen them for the kill but to make sure they were blunt. This was a Tournament, not War: It was important to avoid unnecessary deadly wounding. Prepared arms were being mounted onto pack horses and donkeys for transport out to the tournament field.

At his door Savage found some Mayflowers had been pushed into the keyhole. He had not noticed them the night before and concluded that they must have been placed there by some well-meaning servant to keep away evil fairies. Savage sniffed them, before taking a couple and pinning them to his tunic.

Before long Henry De Thrapston arrived. Whistling cheerfully, the Keeper of the Castle unlocked the door and looked in. He was accompanied by two soldiers.

"Morning Syr Richard!" He said with a cheery grin. "I hope you are ready for the tournament. Wash, breakfast then church. Then we shall go to the lists."

Savage did not reply. De Thrapston's bonhomie was beginning to grate with him. In sullen silence he followed De Thrapston and the soldiers first to the Castle wash house where big wooden tubs were filled with hot water. Quite a few folk had already washed themselves and the water was grey and starting to get tepid. Savage did not mind though. He now welcomed any chance to clean himself. He had been in a dungeon for years, and before that the Templars, who had been forbidden to wash or even change their underwear, something Savage had always found quite hard.

The Great Hall was a hive of activity and packed with people breaking their fast at the long tables. Savage and De Thrapston took seats on one of the long benches and a serving woman placed a trencher of white bread with some fish on it before each of them, along with a mug of ale.

Savage devoured it all, then De Thrapston led the way to the outer Castle courtyard where people were gathering for the journey to church. Horses' hooves clattered on the stone flags as knights, ladies and the barons of Ulster congregated. The Earl was mounted on an impressive black charger. On a grey palfrey beside him sat his wife, the Countess Margaret. Despite her fifty years of age, Margaret was an alluring woman and her grey hair leant her an air of grace rather than making her look aged. Behind them like a malevolent raven was Montmorency in his black Hospitaller cloak. Beside them was the Seneschal, Thomas de Mandeville, who gave a discrete nod to Savage.

De Thrapton led the way to a waiting brown pony. "This one is for you." He announced, before climbing up onto the white horse that waited beside it. Mounted on another white mare was a blond haired, small woman with a very pretty face.

"Allow me to introduce my wife, Edith." De Thrapston said "Edith: This is the man I was telling you about."

"I'm honoured to meet you, Madam" Savage said, taking her proffered hand and kissing it.

Edith De Thrapton smiled at him but did not speak.

Once everyone in the procession was mounted, the great castle gates swung open and the lords and ladies rode out and down the hill into the town.

The procession was led by a phalanx of armed galloglaiches, followed by the Red Earl and Countess De Burgh. It was a magnificent sight. Horses and riders blazed with embroidered gold and crimsons and their banners bore their heraldic crests, each family had their own, each family member had their own variation to denote their status in the clan. A couple of fantastically dressed heralds flanked the procession, carrying brightly hued banners that flowed in the wind.

Carrickfergus was abuzz with excitement. The townsfolk were all clad in their best clothes and the market was already doing a roaring trade. The taverns were open and already the sound of singing could be heard coming from them. The whole place was fizzed with the jolly holiday atmosphere.

The townsfolk, also wending their way to Saint Nicholas' church, cleared the way for the riding nobility. Savage noted that the betting was already going furiously. People in the street pointed excitedly at one knight or the other as they rode past and money stakes were exchanged over who was going to do well in the tournament.

Any game had winners or losers, Savage mused, and at least all the common folk were going to win or lose were their pennies. The knights taking part would be playing for honour or injury, or worse.

"There was a woman at the Castle last night," Savage asked De Thrapston as they rode. "Was that Alys de Logan?"

De Thrapston raised his eyebrows. "You know her? Yes it was. She is the Earl's astrologer."

"I knew her when I was growing up." Savage explained. "Our fathers were good friends and we often visited the Logan manor."

"Well you'll probably find she's changed a lot since then." De Thrapston replied. "Some say she's a witch."

Savage snorted. "That's one way of putting it. She has a temper I know that."

"No, really, I mean it. One that casts spells I mean. She has been seen around the town after midnight, sweeping with her broom and chanting spells. That big cat of hers is strange too. They say it is her demonic familiar. She also has a tongue that can cut corn. Young John Bysset must have the heart of a lion for taking her on."

"Who is John Bysset?"

"He's a knight from the Glens, nephew of the Lord of Twescard." De Thrapston explained. "Ambitious sort of a fellow. Currently he is courting Dame Alys. You'll see them both later at the tournament: He's competing."

"I can't wait." Savage grunted. "There was a little girl with her."

"That's her daughter." De Thrapston confirmed. "Odd child. Wicked tongue like her mother. Goes everywhere with her, like the cat."

"Alys is married? If Bysset is courting her-" Savage asked, his voice had tone that was a mixture of confusion and consternation.

"Was married. About ten years ago." De Thrapston grunted. "Poor bugger didn't last more than a couple of years. Accident apparently but I wouldn't be surprised if she didn't poison him. She's a widow now. Somehow survives alone down in that tumbledown castle of hers at Vikingsford. The daughter is supposed to be the product of that marriage, but who knows? Some say the devil himself is her Father."

They arrived at Saint Nicolas Church. All the nobility began dismounting.

"You can sit with us." De Thrapston offered.

"No." Savage stated.

"You can't sit on your own, Syr Richard." Edith de Thrapston said. "Do join us."

"I won't be going in at all. I no longer go to church." Savage responded. "I will wait outside during the Mass."

Both De Thrapstons looked shocked, Henry was particularly uncomfortable. Savage enjoyed his indecision, knowing he wanted to attend church but also that he would not let Savage stay outside alone in case he absconded.

A galloglaich was standing close by, listening to the conversation. He pulled off his helmet and Savage saw it was MacHuylin.

"It's all right, Syr Henry." MacHuylin said. "I'll keep an eye on him. You go on in."

A smile of relief spread across De Thrapston's face and he and his wife followed the rest of the nobles into the church, from where the sound of singing could already be heard.

"Not going to church? You'll get a bad name." The galloglaich said. "You're not religious?"

Savage gave a small, bitter laugh. "Not any more."

"They won't be long anyway." MacHuylin said. "Nobility barely stay til the Mass is said."

Waiting on their horses, they lapsed into silence. Savage felt unable to talk much. Tension was tightening his throat and he felt it hard to concentrate on anything but the coming competition. A familiar sense of anticipation was building within him about the tournament. It was not war, but it was the closest thing to it without anyone getting killed. The combat would be real enough, but the weapons blunted. In his breast was a strange mixture of excitement, relish and dread. He looked forward to the chance to use the skills he developed through years of training, but after so many years fallow, wasting away in a dungeon, would he still be able to fight?

After a short time MacHuylin gave a derisive grunt. "Well here comes someone who will disagree with you on Religious matters. There's no doubt what this man believes anyway."

Entering the churchyard through the lych gate was the preacher that Savage had seen storming out of the Castle the day before. MacHuylin gave a little whistle through his teeth and the galloglaich troops standing guard outside the church all became alert to the newcomer. The ones still mounted drew their horses into a barrier before the church door while the rest hefted their axes into a ready position.

"This man is a religious lunatic." MacHuylin explained. "He's an itinerant preacher, a member of one of those religious orders that make their own rules and are always attacking the church. You know, the sort who think we should all be equal, with no lords or kings. Everyone should share the earth together and all that shite. His accent says he is from Dublin, but he's been wandering around Ulster for a year now, disturbing the peace and stirring up the common folk with his mad notions. I'd say he's coming here to disrupt the service, shout abuse at the nobles and cause a commotion. He's done it before."

MacHuylin addressed his men: "Don't let that man into the church. We don't want the Earl disturbed in his holiday prayers."

The galloglaich soldiers grinned, anticipating the prospect that soon they would liven up their boring day by giving this man a good kicking.

As the preacher approached, he slowed and looked with disdain at the ranks of armed men who arrayed themselves to block his path.

"So, the Earl's lapdogs wish to stop me entering God's house to hear the Mass on a holy day?" He spat. "Who do you think you are to say who can enter church and who can't? The Lord's own appointed angels?"

"The Angels of Death, maybe," MacHuylin said. "Move on now, Father. You don't want to get yourself hurt now, do you? Not on a holiday."

"And who is this? It must be Saint Peter himself. " The Preacher's voice was heavy with sarcasm. "Why no: It's only Connor MacHuylin, the Earl's chief lapdog."

"I prefer the term guard dog, Father." MacHuylin growled. "And you should fear my bite."

The Preacher glared at them all through long, dirty hair that hung over his face, then spat into the dirt. "Curse you and all those who oppress the poor and the meek! The Judgement Day is coming, when the Lord will bring his vengeance down upon you. The Lord you serve is nothing to the one I serve. You can break my bones, but you cannot break my spirit."

"I'll be happy with your bones." MacHuylin replied.

The Priest gave an incoherent roar and swayed slightly, but did not advance. Savage wondered if the man had been drinking.

"And who is this?" The preacher suddenly locked his eyes on Savage. "Another lackey of the Earl?"

"Never you mind who he is. Move along," MacHuylin's voice was losing his patient tone.

Savage raised a restraining hand towards MacHuylin. There was something about the priest's challenging glare that provoked Savage. He wanted to meet the man's challenge and show he was not afraid. "I am Richard Savage, Emissary of King Edward." He said.

"A pox on all Kings!" The priest roared. "The Earl is Satan's slave but the King is the very Devil's whore! No wonder you cower behind the protection of the galloglaich. Do you fear me? You should."

Savage jumped down off his horse and strode forward towards the priest. "Watch it: He's not wise." MacHuylin warned. Savage, his own anger growing in his breast, ignored him.

"Now you listen to me, Priest." Savage jabbed a provoking finger on the man's chest. To his surprise, the Priest grabbed it and held his hand.

"No you listen to me Syr Richard Savage" The Priest roared, "You son of a whore, son of the Widow, for the good of your soul."

Both men's eyes met. Savage could hear the galloglaich soldiers coming forward and he held his hand out behind them to tell them to stop.

"What did you just say?" He breathed.

"I said you are a whoreson of the Widow" The Priest said in a low voice, his mouth breaking onto a mischievous grin. "A heretic dog of the Temple." He winked, then raised his voice again so the galloglaich could hear him. "Your lord is nothing compared to mine. Jesus overthrew the mighty Julius Caesar, what is King Edward of England compared to him? That is the key. Your Master the King is worthless shit who will be swept away by the coming tide. I, Guilleme le Poer, say take this message to him." He stepped close and pushed a piece of parchment into the fold in Savage's tunic as he whispered "and take this one also from another of his lapdogs, now push me away and hit me a thump." With that the Priest spat directly into Savage's face.

Savage did not need to be prompted. He shoved the Priest away from him and caught him a glancing blow across the side of the head.

MacHuylin had seen enough and signalled the galloglaichs forward. As they advanced purposefully, the priest stumbled backwards towards the lych gate, shouting curses and waving his fists at them. Before they reached him he took to his heels and ran out of the churchyard.

The galloglaich troopers broke into laughter that disguised their disappointment at missing out on the chance to teach the priest a violent lesson in manners.

"Let him go." MacHuylin ordered. Behind him the doors of the church were opening and the people were already starting to leave. The galloglaich soldiers began preparing for the Earl leaving the church.

Savage retrieved the piece of parchment the priest had pushed into his tunic and took a surreptitious look at it. There was a message written on it, but the words were indecipherable: a strange mixture of letters that did not spell any recognisable words or phrases. The work of a madman? Perhaps. Julius Caesar was dead before Jesus Christ was born, so what did the priest mean by saying Christ overthrew Caesar?

Suddenly all became clear.

The message was cipher text, encrypted using the Caesar's Cipher technique. Julius Caesar had used it to encrypt messages to his Legions. The message was hidden by taking each letter and substituting it with the one that came three after it in the alphabet. To decrypt the message you did the opposite. Looking again at the message, sure enough he quickly saw that the first letters spelt out his name. This was a secret message for him.

Before he could get further, he spotted out of the corner of his eye Henry De Thrapston approaching. With him the black cloaked figure of Hugo Montmorency.

Quickly he pushed the message back into his tunic.

"You did not attend Mass, Syr Richard." Montmorency stated. "I hope we will not be meeting in a church court some day."

Savage did not reply, but simply met the Hospitaller's glare with a cool gaze.

"One place we will definitely be meeting soon is in the tournament. The state of your Soul it is not something to take lightly, Savage." The Hospitaller said. "The tournament is no place for someone used to the soft life at court. You will get hurt."

He turned his horse and rode off towards the lych gate.

Henry de Thrapston appeared beside Savage. "Don't mind the Hospitaller, Syr Richard. He loves his religion the way some men love gambling or hunting. It is his passion. Take heed when I say religion, mind you, not God. There is a difference, I believe. Anyway, now I've made my peace with my God, let's go and get armed for the Jousting."

Chapter 14

The service ended, the congregation of Saint Nicholas' Church erupted into an excited, bubbling throng. Their duty to Christianity complete, they burst eagerly out of the church to begin the May Day Beltaine festivities. Outside in the churchyard, people milled around, chatting or greeting old friends who they had not seen during winter.

Many visitors had come to town for the jousting tournament, staying with relatives, in hostelries or-if members of the nobility-in luxurious tents erected near the tournament field. Savage noticed one man in particular who exited the church alongside Earl Richard and the Countess Margaret. He was a rather tall, long-limbed, middle-aged man with a ring of long grey hair hanging around his head, the crown of his head being completely bald. He had a small grey beard, a hooked nose and a combination of small but protruding eyeballs and highly arched eyebrows that gave him the look of being constantly surprised about something. He was dressed in a gold embroidered tunic and long, sumptuous green robes with fur trimmings.

Savage turned to the Castellan, de Thrapston. "Is that the Justiciar of Ireland, Edmund le Bottelier?" He asked.

"Indeed it is," De Thrapston replied. "He's here to watch his son competing in the tournament."

The Justiciar of Ireland ruled Norman lands inside The Pale in the name of King Edward.

"I must speak to him," Savage said, earnestly. "Can you arrange it?"

Henry De Thrapston was taken aback at Savage's intensity but replied "I'll see what I can do. Look out: here's your friend." He nudged Richard in a conspiratorial way.

Savage turned to see Alys De Logan walking past, arm-in-arm with a younger man dressed in clothes so fashionable as to be almost ridiculous. Behind them traipsed the same little girl who had been with her at the castle the evening before. To Savage's critical eye the man's tunic was far too short for decency. The trend for shorter and shorter men's tunics had evolved while he had been in prison, and it was definitely a mode that he did not approve of. In Savage's opinion if he really wanted to look at men's arses he could go to the bath house. The young man's leggings were also a silly bright yellow colour and his shoes were so pointed that they caused him problems walking. His ridiculous appearance was enhanced when Dame Alys mounted onto the same old warhorse Savage had been her on the night before, making her higher in the saddle than the man beside her.

Both Alys and the young man were sharing some private joke and laughing as they walked their horses towards the lych gate of the church. As they neared Savage, Dame Alys caught sight of him and the laughter dissolved in her throat. Her face fell into a look of scorn.

"Why, Syr Richard le Savage." She said. "I hoped you were dead."

De Thrapston, sensing the tension, gave an uncomfortable laugh. "You mean you thought he was dead, Dame Alys."

"Did I?" Alys regarded Savage with a withering stare.

"Alys. Hallo," was the best Savage could muster. His face was turning a deep crimson colour.

"Who is this, Mother?" demanded the little girl, regarding Savage with a look that was withering for one so young. She had the fine features of Alys but her bright green eyes had something else in them: an aggressive arrogance that provoked irritation in Savage.

"He is no one, Galiene." Alys de Logan spat the words with venom.

"Is this the famous Richard Savage we have heard so much about?" The young man with Alys seemed very excited. "You did not tell me you knew an Emissary of the King, my Dear!"

Alys de Logan made a particularly unladylike derisory grunt while continuing to look at Savage with a clear mixture of disbelief and disdain. "An Emissary of the King? What games are you playing at now, Richard?"

"Syr Richard is here to warn us all of the dangers of the Scots invading us. Complete nonsense of course." The young man said. His watery blue eyes held a glare of challenge and his wide grin was more like a wolf's when it sees his prey than warm and friendly.

There was something about the man that Savage instinctively did not like. He seemed to exude arrogance the way fat men sweat. Savage narrowed his eyes. "News travel fast here." He said, shooting a reproachful glance at De Thrapston. "Including news that was supposed to be a secret."

"Ulster is a small place, Syr Richard. It's hard to keep secrets here." The young man said. "I am Syr John Bysset. Heir to the Lordship of the Glens and Dame Alys's betrothed."

A small, bitter smile crept across Savage's face. "That is something we have in common, then." He said, delighting at the look of confused consternation that spread across Bysset's face as he looked to Dame Alys for explanation.

"Childish as always, Richard." Dame Alys sighed. "Syr Richard is referring to a time very long ago, when I certainly must have been very young and very foolish. The world has moved on considerably since then. I am no longer the child you knew, Richard. I have no doubt you probably are, though."

"We grew up together." Savage commented for the benefit of de Thrapston and Bysset.

Bysset looked genuinely annoyed, which pleased Savage. "You must tell me all about it, my dear." He growled.

De Thrapston did not like awkwardness and decided to step in. "Come: we must go to the tournament field, Syr Richard. We must get ourselves armed."

"Surely you are not competing in the tournament?" Bysset's expression became a mixture of disbelief and delight.

Savage nodded.

"You should watch yourself, John." Alys de Logan commented. "'Savage by name, savage by nature'. That's what we used to say about Richard when we were growing up."

"And I used to call you-" Savage began.

"Shitty skitters, I remember it well." Alys cut him off. "Richard was always so immature and found the fact that I had freckles hilarious."

Bysset regarded Savage with undisguised contempt. "How gallant of you, Sir." He sneered. "I doubt, however, that a fat lazy courtier will survive very long in the melee at the tournament today. Be warned, Savage: We are frontier lords here, used to real combat. You won't last five minutes." With that, he climbed on his horse and started towards the lych gate away from the church. Dame Alys gave Savage a final cursory glance before following Bysset at a more sedate pace on her tired old warhorse. The little girl, Galiene, mounted behind her, watched Savage with a hostile glare as they rode away. Behind them both Savage saw the same grey cat from the night before still sat in the back of the saddle.

"Betrothed?" De Thrapston gave a low whistle. "You didn't mention that! I take it you did not part on amicable terms?"

Savage shook his head. He was not prepared to say any more on the subject.

"Well take heed of Bysset's warning and be careful today; especially of him" De Thrapston commented. "He's one of the best jousters in Ulster, and a great horseman. Arrogant little shit, though."

Both men laughed.

"You've annoyed him too." De Thrapston continued. "He is going to be Dame Alys's husband and he's the sort of man who will now see you as a threat, regardless of how long ago you were involved with her, or how badly your betrothal ended, or even the fact that she now evidently despises you. That all won't matter to him. He will be out to get you."

"Was it that obvious she despises me?" Savage asked. He was finally starting to warm to De Thrapston. He seemed a genuine kind of man.

"Syr Richard, if she had spat in your eye it would not have been more obvious." De Thrapston smiled. "However, the course of true love is never smooth. Anyway enough of hearts and flowers. It's time for combat."

Chapter 15

They rode out of the churchyard and into the town's
Market place, where the crowds of people started to divide.
The nobility began making their way to the tournament arena
while the ordinary townsfolk headed for the countryside. Only
one generation removed from the land, they instinctively made
for the meadows and woods to perform the rites their forebears
had executed since time immemorial.

Beyond the town walls a huge Maypole had been erected
and a raised area prepared for the performance of Robin Hood
plays. The northern clans of the MacArtaines and Ui Cahans
were starting a hurling match in the meadow near the town
ramparts.

A cheer erupted suddenly and everyone turned to see a
group of Mummers who seemed to appear from nowhere.
Outlandish yet familiar, these strangely costumed figures were
the focus of affection for everyone. As Savage watched, the
bizarre leaf-clad Twig and the ominous Hobby Horse skipped
around the market place, prodding young women and sending
little children scurrying in delighted terror. Gleefully the
townsfolk followed the Mummers as they danced up the,
pursued all the way by the ranting protestations of the itinerant
preacher, Guilleme le Poer. The priest ran after them, shaking
his fist and quoting Holy Scripture. Savage wanted to speak to
him again but among the crowd it was impossible.

A more serious mood descended on the knights who rode
to the Lists, the tournament arena. This had been erected
beyond the town ramparts in a wide, flat meadow beside the
little infirmary run by the Franciscan Friars. An area one
hundred yards long and roughly oval in shape had been
enclosed by wooden stakes and roped off. This was where the
action would take place. Around it, wooden scaffolding had

been constructed to provide tiered seating for the audience. A canopied seating platform had been put up for the most important people watching. All around, heraldic banners and flags danced in the light breeze. Flowers, great bunches of whin bush and other greenery were garlanded everywhere in honour of May.

A small village of tents was erected at one end of the arena near the infirmary. Here, knights from all over the country had taken up residence. Servants were cooking food, wine was being opened and the holiday atmosphere bubbled everywhere.

One tent was much longer and taller than all the others. De Thrapston steered savage towards it. As they pushed aside the flaps and went in, Savage saw that it was filled with weapons and armour.

"This is the arming tent." De Thrapston explained. "Most knights will have their own armour but the Earl has furnished this tent from his castle armoury so anyone competing can get any pieces of harness they might need, anything they have forgotten or replace broken weapons or armour. The tournament will be rough, after all. Take your pick. Arm yourself. This is the best equipment money can buy."

Savage walked around, inspecting the equipment. Coats of mail hung on racks, swords lay in bundles, sheaves of spears and lances stood upright. Helmets sat like rows of severed heads on the ground. De Thrapston noticed a puzzled expression on Savage's face as he examined the war gear.

The tent flap opened and MacHuylin entered.

"Are you competing today?" Savage said.

MacHuylin laughed. "Fighting is my job. It's what I get paid for. The idea of doing it for fun on my day off does not appeal to me. No, watching nobles smash the shit out of each other while I sit back and watch, sipping some excellent French wine is more my idea of a holiday. Found anything you like?"

Savage frowned. "This armour is brand new, in great condition, but it's all a bit old-fashioned. It's all chainmail and leather. Is there no plate armour? Look: the spear heads and dagger blades are long and thin. They're designed for penetrating mail. Against modern plate armour they'll bend instead of going through it."

De Thrapston and MacHuylin exchanged knowing smiles. "What age were you when you left Ireland, Syr Richard?" The Castle Keeper asked.

"Eighteen,"

"Your training in arms would have been in the knightly skills your father taught." De Thrapston surmised. "I'm guessing you never fought in a real war here."

Savage shook his head. "There was peace when I was growing up."

"Well, Syr Knight," MacHuylin explained. "Modern plate armour is useless in Ireland. Same with heavy war horses and long lances. Half this country is a bog, the rest is forest. You need to be light and manoeuvrable, or you get killed very quickly. The Irish don't fight like you Normans. Their knights have no stirrups. They ride towards you, throw their spears and ride away again. If you chase after them on a heavy warhorse, laden down with your plate armour, you'll soon find yourself bogged down, stuck and sinking in a marsh. Then they come back and cut your throat at their leisure. Same with the woods: no room to charge, so you need light horses and light armour."

With the help of De Thraptston and MacHuylin he dressed himself for the tournament. After stripping off his clothes, Savage first put on a shabby leather tunic, stained with rust, polish and oil from armour. He pulled on a pair of linen trousers, then struggled into chausses-chainmail leggings-putting one hand on MacHuylin's shoulder to stop himself falling off balance as he did so. On top of everything went the hauberk, the long chainmail shirt that reached to his knees.

"Is there no plate armour at all?" He asked again.

"There might be but you'll regret wearing it. No one else will be wearing any plate." De Thrapston said. "You'll be lumbering around, weighed down by the weight and everyone else in the Melee will be scampering around you."

"It's what I'm used to fighting with." Savage was implacable. De Thrapston shrugged and began rooting around in a pile of assorted armour pieces.

"What about some weapons?" MacHuylin said. "You pick up lances and shields in the arena but you need a second weapon. An axe? A warhammer? No you'll probably want a sword."

Savage began looking through the swords that were stacked on a table.

"Here we go!" De Thrapston suddenly announced, dragging a rusted breastplate out of the pile he had been searching through. "It's a bit worse for wear I'm afraid…"

"It'll do." Savage responded and de Thrapston strapped the two pieces of the breastplate onto Savage's torso, one half protecting his chest, the other his back.

Once it was on, Savage returned to his quest for a weapon. The swords to him all seemed quite short and axes he had found unwieldy: devastating if it hit its mark but highly likely to throw you off balance if it missed.

Suddenly his eyes lit up. Leaning against the wall of the tent was a massive Sword of War. A huge weapon that had to be used with both hands, its blade was nearly as long as he was tall. He had learned how to fight with these weapons in the Templar training yard but had never had the chance to use one in anger.

"Good choice." MacHuylin said, as Savage lifted the weapon to inspect its long blade. "That one is German, but it's modelled on the claidheamh mòr, the Scottish Great Sword."

"You can't use a shield with that." De Thrapston warned. "You need both hands to swing it."

Savage nodded. De Thrapston noticed that Savage's eyes took a faraway look in them as he held the sword before him, both hands on the blade, point downwards, the great hilt forming a cruciform shape. At the sign of the cross De Thrapston instinctively crossed himself.

Savage hesitated, then coldly, deliberately spat on the blade.

There was silence. Savage turned to see MacHuylin and De Thrapston both regarding him with serious gazes.

"You are shocked at such blasphemy?" Savage said. "Shocked that someone would spit on the sign of the cross?"

De Thrapston shook his head. "No. I know what it means: you were a Templar. That is what the Knights Templar did when preparing for battle."

MacHuylin looked at Savage with a new respect.

Savage was surprised they knew the pre-battle ritual. "It is misunderstood." He said. "We were taught to do it to become used to doing it. It's what the Saracens would make us do if we were captured. Others saw that as blasphemy. They used it against us when the Order was suppressed."

De Thrapston stepped forward and laid a hand on Savage's shoulder. "I always had respect for the Knights of the Temple. The suppression of the Order was a travesty."

"If you were a Templar," MacHuylin said, "I'd say you'll be useful in a fight."

After he had picked up a helmet, Savage was ready. They all then left the arming tent to go to De Thrapston's own tent so he could get ready too. Once inside the tent, De Thrapston was helped into his armour by his wife who fussed around him, her small frame racked with concern.

"Normally a knight would have a squire to help him into his arms," De Thrapston said, a little sheepishly. "My squire is my son Hubert, however. He graduated to knighthood last year and he is away fighting for the King's armies in Gascony."

"You will look after Henry today, won't you?" Edith de Thrapston begged Savage as she tightened up the straps on the back of her husband's hauberk. "He is not as young as he used to be."

"I fear he'll have to look after me." Savage replied. "I'm a bit out of practise."

De Thrapston chortled. "I don't think that will make any difference. You'll be a formidable opponent."

"Opponent?!" Edith De Thrapston took a sharp, fearful intake of breath and glanced apprehensively at the heavy pack of muscles set around Savage's broad shoulders.

"Opponent?" Echoed Savage. "I had no idea."

"Standard Tournament rules: Tenans and Venans," De Thrapston explained cheerily. In a tournament, the Tenans were the home side, the challengers who would meet all comers. The Venans were the visiting knights who would meet the Tenans challenge. "Tenans will be knights ofUlster, the Venans all visitors." De Thrapston continued. "In the Mélee, the local knights will joust against everyone else. Naturally, I'll be jousting for the Earldom. I know you were born here, Savage, but the Earl has commanded you will be on the other team."

"You'll go easy on him, won't you?" Edith entreated Savage. "Henry can be so rash, and he doesn't know his limitations."

Savage grunted. "Don't worry. He'll probably knock me off my horse before I get near him."

Edith De Thrapston did not reply. For all his protestations she saw the flash of danger in Savage's unsettling eyes. Without further words, she pulled the brightly embroidered surcoat that bore his family coat of arms over her husband's head, then gave him a quick kiss on the cheek. For a second the De Thrapstons stood, locked in a tender moment as they caught each other's gaze.

Savage stood apart, alone. He breathed a heavy sigh, trying to dispel the nervous butterflies that were dancing about in his chest.

Now De Thrapston was armed, they went outside to pass the time until the hour for them to compete arrived. Servants of the De Thrapstons had set up three chairs outside the tent and laid refreshments on a small folding table.

Everywhere there was an exciting buzz of activity. In the arena the seats were rapidly filling with eager spectators. Mild cheers arose from the few actually watching the single combats that had already begun. These fights were between Bachelors, young knights in their first year of knighthood, and not many were interested in them. These were the warm up for the main event, the Mélee.

"Wine?" asked De Thrapston, pouring himself a large goblet of the ruby liquid.

"Ale, please," said Savage.

"Want to keep a clear head, eh?" De Thrapston said, pouring out some ale for Savage. "Sensible fellow. I'll stick to my glass of strong red wine though. I find it's always good to have something in your stomach to steady the nerves and deaden the pain." He grinned. Savage smirked at his black humour and Edith tutted loudly.

"Don't jest, Henry." She scolded. "It's tempting fate."

"You can't change your Fate, my dear." De Thrapston said, his always-present grin fading slightly. "We're all part of a tapestry that's been woven by mightier hands. When your thread's snipped you have to go."

There was a moment's silence. The noise and bustle seemed to be getting more intense. In the arena a particularly exciting single combat was proceeding to the jubilant cries of onlookers. Several wrestling matches had started behind the stands between members of the merchant class of the town. These were as avidly supported (and speculated on) as the chivalric combat going on in the arena itself. Everywhere music was played, accompanied by raucous singing and the various different instruments, voices and tunes mingled to create a glorious cacophony. Monks were gathering in the herb garden of the infirmary, pretending to work while all the while trying to catch a glimpse of the sports they were forbidden to watch.

Suddenly a hand bell rang.

A groan of horrified disgust ran through the throng in the tent village. Savage and the De Thrapstons turned to see two figures approaching, swathed in ragged clothes and wrapped in grubby bandages that extended over their hands and heads so that not an inch of their skin was visible. Both rang hand bells to attract attention to themselves as they passed by. All the people in their way leapt aside in terror, clasping handkerchiefs or sleeves to their mouths and noses, afraid to even breathe the same air.

"Lepers?" Savage asked, taken aback. "Here?"

"Yes." De Thrapston confirmed, his face twisted into a grimace of disgust. He pointed across the field to a cluster of buildings that huddled together outside the town walls. "That's the Franciscan friary." explained the Keeper of the Castle. "They run a infirmary which has a small leper hospital attached to it."

"Are there many there?" Savage asked. He had seen the ravages of the terrible disease during his time in the East and had a good idea what horrors lurked beneath the bandages on the two unfortunates. Leprosy was a dreaded disease, believed to be spread by just touching the infected person, or breathing the same air as them.

"A few. I don't really know. I don't make a habit of visiting it myself." De Thrapston told him. "They shouldn't be out though! Contagious creatures like that. I blame the Hospitallers for bringing it back over here from the East."

"Is someone taking our name in vain?" The voice of Hugo Montmorency made them turn around. The Hospitaller, John

Bysset, Alys De Logan and another man were approaching. All the men were armed for the tournament.

"Get out of here!" Bysset yelled in an arrogant roar. "You shouldn't be here among decent people! Clear off you damned infectious beasts!"

If this show of bravado was meant to impress Alys, she looked nonplussed.

The lepers stumbled off through the tents and disappeared. Bysset clapped an unwelcome hand onto Savage's shoulder.

"Well, Syr Henry?" He addressed De Thrapston. "What sort of opponent do you think Savage here is going to make? He'll not worry us, will he?"

"I'd say he'll give us some bother." The Keeper of the castle replied.

"The fat, lazy life at Court is hardly the best preparation for combat against real fighting men." Montmorency sneered.

"I'm sorry- where are my manners?!" De Thrapston interjected. "Allow me to introduce Syr John Talbot." He said, gesturing towards the third newcomer whom Richard had not met before. "He's on our team."

Savage saluted him and Talbot returned the gesture. He was in his thirties, had a long scar running down his left cheek and was very tall, with rather long arms. In close combat he would have a long reach. Savage took a mental note of the blue and green colours of Talbot's heraldic surcoat, so he would know to beware that reach if he met him in the arena.

"I'm honoured to meet you." Talbot said. "I hear you are from the Court of King Edward." Savage nodded and Talbot continued: "In that case I am sorry, Syr, that the first time we meet is as opponents."

"In whose favour will you be fighting today, Syr Richard?" Bysset demanded.

"I'll be fighting for no-one's honour but my own." Savage answered.

"My dress has two sleeves." Edith De Thrapston announced, unfastening both of the said articles and taking them off. A lady's sleeve showed her favour for a particular knight.

"Today I shall have two champions." Edith smiled, "my husband and Syr Richard."

"I hope I will not dishonour your favour, Madam," Savage said, slightly abashed at having to accept the charity of the older woman, but appreciative of her well-meant gesture.

"And you must wear mine, John." Alys de Logan spoke, taking off her sleeve.

"You're sure that there's no-one else you'd rather give it to, my Dear?" Bysset swaggered, "There's poor Syr Richard there with no-one's favour to wear but an old married woman's! Whatever will people say?"

They all laughed, except Savage.

"Syr Henry: we need to organize ourselves for the tournament." Montmorency addressed De Thrapston. "Syr Richard, if you don't mind, we'd like to talk tactics."

This was Savage's cue to leave. "I'll go and join my own team." He said.

"You'll find them at the south end of the lists." Montmorency informed him. "Oh, and watch out for any invading Scotsmen, won't you?" He added with a chiding laugh.

"I'll see you all in the arena." Savage said. He turned and went to find the knights he would be fighting with.

The Venans knights from out of town had gathered at the southern end of the arena. Savage introduced himself and was told that he would fight in the vanguard. Briefly the tactics were outlined: There were fifteen knights on each team and the two teams would line up at opposite ends of the arena, facing each other. The opposing teams would then attack each other in a confusion of combat known as a Mélee. At each team's end of the arena was a tall pole surrounded by a small roped-off corral area. The idea was either to beat your opponent senseless or, if he surrendered, take him to the corral where he was honour-bound to stay, either until the end of the tournament or until one of his team rescued him. To prevent the latter, two of Savage's team were assigned to stay back and guard the corral once prisoners had been taken. This rear guard consisted of two Dublin knights, Tristan FitzPatrick and Magnus FitzGerald.

The man who was to lead the side was the Justiciar's son, William le Bottelier. He wore magnificently burnished armour that reflected the sunlight like a dazzling steel mirror. The Bottelier Arms were proudly emblazoned on his surcoat, as they were on the horse he led by the reins.

Servants brought the other knights' horses forward and they all mounted, struggling to fit themselves into the heavy wooden war saddles that would hold them upright on their steeds. The knights then hung their shields around their necks by the strap.

"Right," William Bottelier said, tersely. "Let's show this lot what we can do."

Squires brought forward each man's weapons. Savage slung the big sword of war across his back by a leather thong. Each knight then rode his horse forward and collected a lance from a stand, before forming up at their end of the lists.

Trumpets blared and a hush descended on the crowd. A herald stepped out into the middle of the arena, just in front of the canopied stage which held the most prestigious spectators: the Red Earl and his wife the Countess Margaret, the Justiciar Edmund Bottelier and the Seneschal Thomas De Mandeville and his wife Elizabeth. In a loud, ringing voice the herald announced the rules of the tournament. No missiles of any kind, neither arrows, darts or throwing knives, were to be brought into the arena. No short swords, knives, daggers or stabbing weapons were allowed and all blades must be blunt. The penalty for breaking any of these rules was death.

The knights donned their final pieces of armour. They drew on heavy, chainmail gauntlets then pulled padded leather skullcaps onto their heads. Over these they put cumbersome, flat topped iron helmets which had a slit to see out of and holes punched in the front to allow breathing.

The herald left the arena and it was almost time to begin.

As he breathed in through the grill of his helmet, Savage could taste the acrid taint of iron in the air on his tongue. For him, this was the worst part, the last few seconds before the Mélee began. There was nothing else to occupy the mind, nothing more to prepare, nothing to do but wait for what was to come.

He surveyed the opposition who were lined up facing them one hundred yards away at the other end of the arena. Montmorency was in front, the leader of the team. Dressed in black armour, the Hospitaller's surcoat was a simple white with a black cross on it. Behind him lined out the other fourteen knights that made up the Ulster team. In garish red armour was John Bysset. Beside Bysset Savage recognised John Talbot's green and blue surcoat. Savage also recognised the coats of armour of Patrick De Lacy, a Copeland and two more Byssets, Hubert and William. Alain FitzWarin was there, as of course was Henry De Thrapston. The identity of the other six knights he could not be sure of.

The warhorse shifted beneath Savage. A massive creature, the knight's charger was itself a weapon, used for battering and crushing enemy troops. Weighing close to a ton, the horse was trained to respond to the rider's vocal commands. In the clamour of war when the hands were occupied with fighting a knight could not always grip the reins. Savage had been assured by de Thrapston that this horse, Curoi, who was from de Thrapston's own stables, was excellent and reliable. He hoped de Thrapston was right as his own personal safety now depended on it. De Thrapston had told him that Curoi was so intelligent he understood commands shouted in French or Irish.

Savage had replied that he did not care if the horse understood Arabic, as long as it did what he told it to.

The heralds raised their trumpets. The knights lowered their lances into charging position. Last minute nerves sloshed around Savage's stomach like cold soup. The heralds sounded loud blasts. The crowd erupted into bloodthirsty cheers.

The Mélee began.

Chapter 16

On the hill above the Tournament arena, another group of men were also preparing for combat. At the edge of the tree line where the meadowland swept steeply upwards to become heavily wooded hillside, sixteen men were changing out of linen shirts and pulling on chainmail armour, coifs and padded leather jerkins while they made final checks of their weapons. Spears, knives and swords were sharpened and crossbows test-fired. Their leader was tall and muscular, his chest and arms crossed with scars that told of previous battles. His hair was long and dark brown, tied back out of the way behind his head.

"Look at them: Their Lordships playing at war." He spoke in gaelic, his voice heavy with contempt as he looked down on the knights lining up for the tournament below. "We'll give them a real one soon enough."

"King Domnall: Why don't we attack now while they're at play and kill as many of them as we can?" One of the warriors asked as he struggled to pull on a blue hooded tunic over his chainmail. "I don't like lurking around up here. They say these woods are haunted."

Domnall mac Brian Ui Néill, King of the Clan Eoghan, smiled. "Diarmuid, if they are, it's the ghosts who should be scared of you, not the other way round. I admire your courage and fighting spirit, though. But even though you are my best warriors, hand picked for this mission, there are far too few of us to take on fully armoured knights. No, men, we've been given a special task by King Robert of Scotland, crucial to the success of the coming invasion that will sweep these foreigners off our land and into the sea. That's why we're here, and that's why I, your King chose to accompany you on this dangerous-but glorious-mission."

"Why do we have to wear this foreign war gear?" Another of the warriors grumbled, a trickle of sweat running down his face. "It's too heavy. We won't be able to run or move. If we're killed wearing this no one will know we are warriors from the Kingdom of Tyr Eoghan. There won't be much glory in it for us."

King Domnall chuckled. "That, Aodh, is precisely the idea. If we are caught or killed, no one is to know who we are or where we came from: That would destroy the surprise. When the Scottish army lands on the Eastern shores of Ulster our army will attack from the West at the same time. We want them as unprepared for that as possible. But do not worry about Posterity, my fine warriors. That's why we have brought this man along with us."

The King slapped a large hand on the shoulder of the pale, thin man standing beside him. Like the others he had crawled into chainmail and hooded tunic but his slight frame barely filled the armoured vest, leaving it hanging in folds around him. Clearly no warrior, he had a steel helmet on his head that was too big for him and sat at an awkward tilted angle, making him look ridiculous.

"My King, I was wondering what use I will be on this mission." The man said, pushing the helmet back so he could see properly. "I am your chief Poet. I'm no use in a fight."

"And I don't want you getting into one, Suibne." The King replied. "Men, our task is to sow terror and confusion throughout the Earldom so they're in disarray when the Scottish army arrives. That job starts today. King Robert has agents down at the Earl's Jousting tournament. Their job is to kill a few of the key people who are likely to get in the way of the Scots. We will provide cover for them and make sure they escape. Your job, Suibne, is to witness everything that happens, and record it in poetry for posterity. If King Domnall Ui Neill falls today disguised as a foreigner and miles from his home, I want to make damn sure everyone knows what happened. So if there is any fighting, Suibne, you hide. Watch what happens, but don't get involved. You're no use to anyone if you don't survive to tell the tale of what we did and the part we played in Edward Bruce's war for our freedom."

Suibne the poet sighed and was quiet for a few moments.

"King Domnall," He eventually said. "As your Court Poet, by ancient rite I have a certain…license to say what others dare not. That is true isn't it?"

The King nodded, but his grin became fixed. He was not the sort of man who appreciated any form of contradiction of his authority. People did what he told them and that was the way he liked it.

"Well using this fool's pardon," Suibne continued, "I feel there are a few things I should ask."

"Go on." King Domnall said, his tone of voice suggesting more threat than encouragement.

"Why are we in league with the Scots?" Suibne the Poet asked. "If Edward Bruce succeeds won't we just swap one lot of foreign overlords for another lot?"

King Domnall shook his head. "Surely you know that our enemy's enemy is our friend? Besides, the King of Scotland holds the most Holy treasure, the sacred vessel. Is that not an unmistakeable sign that God favours King Robert Bruce? If God is on his side, do you want to be against God? Let's not forget too that the Scots speak our language, share our culture. They're our cousins, not strangers. Edward Bruce is Earl of Carrick: The heartland of Alba's ghaeltacht. This will be the foundation of a great Gaelic alliance that will sweep the English out of this Island. Perhaps more."

Suibne gave a sly smile. "True, my Lord," he said, "Edward and Robert de Bruce have Gaelic blood on their mother's side, but on their Father's side? They're no different from our own French-speaking foreign overlords down there."

King Domnall grunted. "Well I'd rather have an overlord that was half a Gael than all English. We and the Scots have much in common. Hundreds of years ago, before they went across the sea to claim Alba, the Scots lived in Ireland. Their Stone of Destiny is Irish sandstone, taken by the Kings of Dal Riada across the Moyle sea to their new Kingdom when they founded Scotland. Now they are returning to their former home to help their cousins."

Now it was Suibne's turn to laugh. "I know that very well, my King." He said. "As Court Poet, part of my training was to learn the history and lineage of the Ui Neill Kings, stretching right back to Niall of the Nine Hostages himself, and even beyond to the time before time and the coming of the Milesians to Ireland."

"So you know I speak the truth." King Domnall stated.

"But those Scots you speak of have always been our enemies, my King. The Ui Neill's have fought their Kingdoms of Ulidh and Dal Riadh for centuries. It was your noble ancestors who drove them out of this island to Scotland. Now you are inviting them back."

King Domnall took a step closer. His muscular frame towered over the much smaller poet and he glowered down at him.

"Suibne MacDunlevy," The King growled in a low voice. "As you say, your position as Court Poet keeps you safe from harm. Ancient rite states that the king cannot harm his Bard, and his Bard is free to speak his mind. So he acts as the King's conscience. I cannot touch you if you displease me. But if you really displease me, I can always remove you from your position as Court Poet, and then-" he said with a thoroughly unpleasant smile "-then you will be fair game."

Suibne swallowed hard. The King held his gaze for a few seconds, then he turned to his warriors to see that they were now all prepared.

"Right men." The King said. "Let's get back into the trees and wait for the killing to begin."

Chapter 17

Spurs dug into horses' flanks. Steeds surged forward. Starting at a slow trundle, the chargers soon reached full thundering gallop as the knights rushed towards each other. In the crash of metal on metal, the whinnying of horses and screaming of battle cries they crunched together.

Montmorency and John Bysset both charged towards Savage.

Savage knew Talbot's reach advantage would be dangerous if he got close, so aimed at him with the lance. At full gallop, he veered past Montmorency and Bysset, whose lance missed him by inches.

Talbot saw him coming and levelled his lance at Savage's chest. At the same time he grasped his shield handle, raising it to cover himself. Savage also grabbed his shield but pushed it away from himself as Talbot's lance struck, masterfully deflecting the harmful point. His own lance point struck Talbot's shield dead centre. Talbot was carried clean off the saddle and flipped head over heels off his charger's back. Savage's lance shivered then shattered at the impact, leaving him with a four feet long stump in his hand.

Savage roared "Arretez!"

For his size and considering the momentum he had gathered, Curoi reared to a halt amazingly quickly, so quickly that Savage nearly fell off.

Grabbing the reins he pulled the horse around through a full turn so he was facing back the way he had come. Montmorency and Bysset had also halted their charges and turned around and both were now charging at him again. Either they were out to get him or they saw him as a threat to their team. Montmorency had obviously been lying when he mocked Savage.

Savage could not fight both of them at once. Neither had he time to speed out of their way.

Talbot, dazed from his tumble, got to his feet but suddenly staggered backwards into the path of Montmorency. The Hospitaller's horse smashed into him and Talbot disappeared beneath the hooves. Savage, dismayed, hoped Talbot's armour would save him from serious injury. He had seemed a decent man.

Savage dug in his spurs and Curoi began lumbering forward. Montmorency and Bysset's rapidly approaching lance points were converging on Savage's chest. Suddenly Savage dug his spurs in deep and screamed the order to charge, "Foncez!"

The horse started violently to a gallop and Savage slipped between the lances, escaping through the tight gap between Bysset's and Montmorency 's horses.

Amid curses, his attackers reined their chargers to a halt, both stopping simultaneously. Montmorency turned his horse left. Bysset wheeled his horse right. They collided in mid turn and Montmorency was knocked off his mount.

Savage saw none of this as it happened behind him, but laughed with glee at his success in evading them. He slowed his horse, but did not see another of the Tenans team, Henry Copeland, closing rapidly on him from behind. Henry Copeland's lance had been shattered in another combat and he now brandished his second weapon: a morning star. This horrific instrument was a wooden stick with a chain attached, on the end of which was a lethal iron ball. Copeland swung it around his head then struck at Savage as he rode past.

The ball impacted Savage on the back, just below his ribs, smashing the plate armour and sending a sharp pain through his body. The force of the blow knocked him forward and only for his automatic reaction of grasping his horse's neck he would have fallen off.

Copeland slowed his charger and turned around to attack Savage again, this time from the front. Savage heaved himself back into an upright position, the shattered back plate armour falling off as he did so. He saw Copeland coming and realised he had no time to draw his sword. Copeland swiped once more.

Savage held up the broken lance stump in line with his face where the morning starwas aimed. The chain hit the lance and the iron ball chain harmlessly wrapped itself around it. Savage wrenched the lance and tore the morning star out of Henry Copeland's hand. Unwrapping the morning star would take too much time so Savage dropped both lance and star and grabbed Copeland's knee as he rode past. Savage heaved upwards and Copeland, completely surprised by this unexpected move, toppled sideways off his horse.

The pain from Copeland's attack provoked Savage's anger. He dropped his shield to hang from its strap and tore the thongs off his sword pommel and ripped it from its place on his back. The fallen Copeland, struggling to his knees, only had time to raise his shield to protect his head before Savage began a vicious rain of blows on him from above. The massive sword blade crashed relentlessly onto the upheld shield. Copeland was unable to raise himself any further. With a crack Copeland's shield gave way and came apart. The bindings unravelled and handles fell off, leaving Henry Copeland totally unprotected. He howled with dismay and looked up in horror to see the terrifying sight of Savage on his horse above him, the huge sword raised to bring down another deadly blow.

Copeland screamed out his surrender.

Savage accepted Copeland's surrender. He led his prisoner to the corral where the battered remnants of the heraldic crest on his shield were hoisted onto the tall pole to show everyone he had been captured. Seeing that it was one of the Tenans who had been captured, the local crowd jeered.

Savage charged back into the thick of the fighting.

The frantic combat continued. Pieces of shattered lances and broken armour littered the ground. Swords flashed in the sunlight as they hacked up and down. Helmets were hewn and sheared. Knights sported wounds and bright red blood splashed across their armour. Men on horseback fought other riders or mercilessly swung at men on foot. Dismounted knights fought each other or did their best to knock riders off their steeds. Casualties mounted, as did the numbers of prisoners taken.

At length the heralds' trumpets blasted out the signal to cease hostilities and a rest period was called. Both teams withdrew to their own ends of the field.

The hot, stifling helmets were torn off with gasps of relief and the panting knights, their hair matted with sweat, eagerly glugged down fresh, cold spring water that was brought to them in jugs by servants. Field repairs on battered armour were attempted, while physicians did their best to treat minor wounds and abrasions. Dismounted knights took the chance to catch riderless chargers.

Squires evacuated incapacitated casualties from the middle of the tournament arena. John Talbot was severely dazed and did not know where he was. He was helped off to his tent to receive the attention of a physician. Two other unconscious knights were also carried out of the lists. One, Magnus FitzGerald from Dublin, had incurred a potentially dangerous wound when a lance had pierced his armour. Alain FitzWarin retired from the fray with a broken arm.

The Venans team had taken three prisoners: Henry Copeland, William and Hubert Bysset. The home team likewise had three prisoners. Both teams were now down to ten a side. Savage listened while William Bottelier gave a brief rallying speech.

"Men," he began. "We are doing well. It's pretty even at the moment so our first aim is to free our three captured team members so we'll gain the advantage of numbers. I expect every one of you will do your best but if we put in that little bit of extra effort we'll have the beating of this lot. Watch each other's back. We can't afford to lose any more men so if you see one of our lot in trouble, help him if you can. You all know what we have to do, so let's do it.'"

The knights all nodded grimly. Glad of the brief respite, they took the opportunity to get their breaths back while the spectators took the chance to relive their bladders, place more bets and get some food and drink either from their hampers or from the various merchants, hawkers and vendors in the arena.

All too soon the trumpets announced that the contest was about to begin again. The knights lined up once more at opposite ends of the arena. Spectators took their seats, their excitement barely contained as they began shouting and cheering even before the action began.

The second blast from the trumpets unleashed the full roar of the crowd and the knights surged forward to do battle once more. Screaming bloodthirsty battle cries they converged in the centre of the arena, swinging great blows at their opponents.

Suddenly in the thronging battle a horse stumbled and everyone went down, each charger tripping over its neighbour. Horses screamed and armoured knights were sent tumbling as a horrified gasp burst from the crowd. Savage saw the calamity but with Curoi charging at full speed and he could not avoid it. His charger fell and he was launched forward over Curoi's head. Feeling his body turn right over in the air he clenched his teeth in expectation of the bone breaking impact.

By sheer chance Savage landed on the soft flanks of a fallen horse. The mount gave a startled whinny and thrashed beneath him, bucking him off. His fall but not his bones broken, he struggled back to his feet.

Utter confusion reigned. A tangled mass of bodies-horses and men-writhed on the ground, attempting to extricate themselves from each other. Savage stumbled out of the mess and looked around desperately for Curoi. The horses got to their feet, all except three who would never rise again. There was a chorus of moans from the injured men who could not get up either.

One of Savage's team, his shoulder dislocated in the fall, lurched out of the arena for medical attention.

The battle erupted once more, this time on foot. The danger was heightened as confused, riderless horses cantered aimlessly among the fighters. Swords, maces and blunted axes battered against shields, helmets and armour as the struggle for supremacy continued. Savage caught sight of Montmorency and Patrick De Lacy frog-marching a dazed William Bottelier - clearly beaten into submission- away from the fray towards their prisoner corral.

Savage abandoned the search for Curoi and set off to attempt a rescue. Adrenaline raced through his veins as he ran across the arena, dodging horses and avoiding fighting knights. The strange exhilarating ecstasy that takes over fighting men, excited by the mixture of fear, anger, injury pain and hair's breadth escapes from death, ignited in him. Without thinking he screamed the old Templar battle cry: "Baussant!"

Montmorency 's head whipped around at the sound, just in time to see the on-rushing figure of Savage before he crashed into him. The impact knocked the knight Hospitaller sprawling onto his back. Savage kept going and ran over the top of him, planting a mailed foot directly on the Hospitaller's chest on his way over, pausing only slightly to kick the Hospitaller's dropped sword out of range of his grasp.

William Bottelier took the chance of having one arm freed and shoved De Lacy away to free his other. De Lacy went after Savage with his sword. Bottelier grabbed Montmorency's fallen sword from the ground and began attacking the fallen Hospitaller on the ground.

Savage was just turning to face the danger when De Lacy caught him a powerful blow across his right shoulder. Savage staggered at the impact but his chest plate held. He struck back, swinging the great sword of war towards De Lacy's torso. De Lacy jumped back to avoid the blow, but the length of the blade was such that he could not get far enough away in time. The blade smashed into De Lacy on his left side, somewhere near the ribs. He gasped as the wind was driven from his lungs. Savage took advantage and struck again, swinging overhead and hitting De Lacy on the helmet. De Lacy went down, dazed and winded. He dropped his weapon and vaguely raised his hands to show he surrendered.

Montmorency was a fearsome warrior, but unarmed and on the ground, Bottelier had total advantage and soon forced him to surrender.

Bottelier and Savage led their prisoners back to the corral.

"What was that battle cry you were shouting, Savage?" Montmorency hissed.

Savage ignored him.

When they got to the prisoner corral they found Henry De Thrapston, who was feeling very silly. He had attempted to rescue one of the Byssets only to have been captured himself by John De Logan, the knight who was guarding the corral for the Venans team.

"Come on," Bottelier shouted to Savage. "We have them!"

"I'll come too," De Logan said. "They don't have enough men left to try to rescue any of our prisoners."

He was right. Of the original thirty men, only thirteen were still capable of fighting. Five of the Tenans team knights were left, who were struggling with five of Savage's team. Savage, Bottelier and De Logan would make an extra three man advantage.

Despite aching muscles they charged back into the fray, screaming like furies. Almost immediately one of their team mates fell and their advantage was cut by one. John De Logan attacked his assailant while Bottelier joined Tristan FitzPatrick in his battle against another Ulster knight. Savage joined John

De Logan and they were both soon knocking their opponent backwards.

Suddenly Savage was knocked to the ground. John Bysset had rendered his opponent unconscious and dashed over, dealing Savage a powerful blow with his deadly mace. Savage hit the ground and turned over onto his back to see Bysset standing over him, swinging the mace down at him. Desperately, Savage rolled to his right. The mace head sunk into the turf with a soft thunk. While Bysset freed his mace Savage frantically scrambled to his feet.

He had just made it when Bysset took another huge swipe at him. Savage brought both hands up, inverting the pommel of the sword of war so the mace shaft hit the sword blade and blocked the blow.

Savage spun round in the opposite direction, the great sword sweeping an arc with him. Bysset saw this and blocked with his shield.

Bysset struck again, swinging his mace at Savage's head. Savage blocked the blow again but this time only succeeded in slowing the blow down before it hit the faceplate of his helmet. The heavy iron head of the mace smashed the helmet in, thumping into his left cheek and bursting a gush of blood from his nose and split lips.

Savage staggered backwards, hundreds of little twinkling stars spinning before his vision. Bysset went for him again. Savage managed to dodge sideways and Bysset missed. The weight of his miscarried blow set him off balance and made him stagger.

Savage took advantage and sprang away from his opponent to take up a defensive stance facing Bysset, ready for his next assault.

Suddenly there was a bang and Savage felt something strike his chest. The impact made him stagger backwards. Confused, he looked about him. No one was near enough to strike him. For a second he wondered if he had imagined it. Perhaps the blow to his head had be fuddled his senses?

He looked down: An arrow was lying at his feet, its shaft broken and the long, thin head-designed for piercing chainmail-was bent almost double from the impact with his plate armour.

Savage looked about wildly. Someone had shot at him.

This was completely against the rules of the tournament. No darts, arrows or shooting weapons were allowed, on pain of death. There was no one in the arena could have shot at him, and surely no one in the seats would have. A brief movement caught his eye and he saw a figure up on the roof of the stands where the spectators sat. Savage shaded his eyes with one hand to get a better look and got a brief glimpse of a man on the roof. He was wrapped up in a large heavy cloak and was slinging a bow over one shoulder. Within seconds the man had disappeared out of sight.

At that moment, Bysset attacked him again. Savage caught sight of a movement out of the corner of his eye. Instinctively he leapt backwards and put enough distance between himself and Bysset's mace that the intended blow glanced off his chest plate.

Savage growled and swung his great sword overhead, smashing it down onto Bysset's upraised shield. Savage felt cold rage flowing through his veins. His nostrils flared and his eyes took on an empty aspect. He now intended to finish this.

Bysset desperately tried to defend himself as Savage commenced a merciless onslaught of blows that forced him staggering backwards. Savage struck again and again, smashing with his sword until Bysset's shield fell apart. Savage continued to rain blows on Bysset, striking now at the helmet. He kept on hitting until the helmet burst asunder to reveal Bysset's startled, blood-streaked face.

As this final blow landed, however, the disintegration of Bysset's helmet caused Savage's sword to twist and fall out of his grip.

Bysset, despite his glazed eyes, saw Savage had lost his weapon and raised his mace.

Savage had only one weapon left.

He slammed his mailed fist into Bysset's handsome face, smashing his nose, splitting his lips, breaking one tooth and knocking another out completely. Bysset fell to his knees, his eyes rolled wildly then he pitched forward, unconscious, landing face first in the dust.

The immediate danger removed, Savage's own fatigue and grogginess took over. His muscles ached. His back and shoulder hurt from the blows he had received. His face was numb and he could taste blood in his mouth. Encased in his armour, he was unbearably hot. His vision swam and he staggered, about to fall.

William le Bottelier suddenly appeared beside him and grabbed his arm, steadying him. Savage could hear excited cheers from the spectators.

"It's over Savage!" De Logan exclaimed. "We've won!"

Savage's eyes closed and he collapsed.

Chapter 18

Slowly, painfully, Savage opened his eyes. His head was sore and his body ached. For a second he wondered what he was doing lying in a hammock in a tent but then the memories of the tournament flooded back.

He was back in Henry De Thrapston's tent, still clad in the battered remnants of his armour, the hilt of his sword still grasped in his right hand.

"So here is the King of England's lion!" The voice of William Bottelier burst through the tent flap as he entered. With him was his father, Edmund, the Justiciar of Ireland, and the Seneschal of Ulster, Thomas De Mandeville.

Savage struggled to raise himself but the Justiciar waved his hand.

"Don't bother getting up De Courcy," He said, smiling. "You deserve a rest after your exploits today. How are you?"

"A bit groggy," Savage mumbled through bruised lips.

"You did magnificently." Edmund Bottelier praised. "When you rescued my son it turned the whole Mêlée around. The Ulster Tenans team did not stand a chance after that. Look." He pointed at the sword still grasped in Savage's hand and addressed the other two: "They couldn't even take his sword from him when he was passed out."

"Where's Henry De Thrapston?" Savage asked. "Is he alright?"

"Oh he's alright." The Seneschal commented. "He's getting stuck into the wine with the rest of the losing team. They're drowning their sorrows."

"What about that man Talbot?" Savage wondered. "I saw him get hit by Montmorency's horse."

Everyone nodded seriously.

"He took a nasty blow, but the physician says he should recover," Thomas De Mandeville said. "He's resting in his tent at the moment. I see you've won yourself another lady's favour," he commented with a sly smile. "Edith De Thrapston will be jealous."

Savage was initially perplexed as to what the Seneschal was talking about, but then he saw that wrapped around the pommel of the sword in his hand was the ragged green sleeve of a woman's dress. It must have become entangled on his weapon when he was battering the helmet of one of his opponents.

"Although not half as jealous as John Bysset will be." De Mandeville added. "That's the favour Alys De Logan gave him."

Savage's face flushed.

"Get some rest. We'll see you later." The Justiciar said as they all began to file out of the tent. "Well done Syr Savage." He stopped and pressed a hand on Savage's shoulder, locked eyes and added in a low voice "Seneschal de Mandeville and I have spoken. You and I will talk seriously later, once you have a chance to recover from the tournament."

Savage nodded to show he understood.

They all left and a fussing physician arrived. He was a small, fidgety, nervous man who helped Savage out of his armour and examined his injuries. Savage's shoulder was badly bruised, as was the point below his ribs where the morning star had hit him. His left cheek was battered and swollen and his lips were split, but his nose was not broken. The physician applied compresses of lavender and sage that were held in place by bandages around the body. After he had administered his treatments he left, telling Savage to rest.

Stiff and sore as he was, Savage did not feel like resting. Now he was alone, he reached into his undercoat and retrieved the encrypted message the mad preacher Le Poer had given him earlier.

It took some time, but luckily Savage was not disturbed for long enough to work out the hidden meaning of the message. It read:

"Sir Richard Savage. King Edward, your King, sends you greetings and urges that you report to him on the situation in Ireland as soon as you can. The Scots Parliament has gathered at Ayr and a very large fleet has been assembled there also. The King requires whatever information you have that may be of help. Sir John Talbot of Carrickfergus is a trusted knight who can safely relay messages. I will tell you all I know when we meet later. Guilleme le Poer."

Carefully and deliberately, Savage tore the message into tiny, irretrievable pieces. He then got up, dressed and left the tent, deciding he would pay a visit to John Talbot. Hopefully he was not too badly injured.

The people in the tent opposite De Thrapston's gave him directions to Talbot's tent and he set off, weaving his way between the tangle of colourful marquees and busy, happy people. At last he came to the tent bedecked with Talbot's blue and green heraldic colours.

Savage swept open the tent flap to enter.

"Someone's killed him." A harsh, Northern Irish voice stopped Savage in his tracks.

Crouching just inside the tent was Connor MacHuylin. He seemed to be examining the ground. Savage looked past him to see John Talbot lying in his hammock. Talbot's eyes were open, as if staring at the roof of the tent, but he was most definitely dead. Bright crimson blood still oozed from a stab wound to his heart and dribbled from a long, smile-like gash beneath his chin. His white shirt was soaked in gore and the blood was still dripping from the hammock into a dark puddle on the ground beneath.

"There's tracks here at the tent entrance and from these footprints I'd say there was two of them." The Irishman announced, rising to his feet. Savage found himself looking up at MacHuylin who was about a head taller than him.

"How do I know you didn't do it?" Savage challenged.

The galloglaich glanced at Savage with a look of annoyance similar to one he would give to a pestering fly or midge.

"Wise up." He said, brushing Savage aside and leaving the tent.

"What's going on?" Savage persisted. "Who killed him?"

MacHuylin turned to face Savage. "I think we'd better start trying to find that out, don't you? I saw Talbot take that tumble in the tournament and came to see how he was. I found him like you saw him. Now: While we're standing here blethering, whoever killed him is getting away. Are you going to help me or are you going to get in my way?"

"We should ask the people in the tent opposite if they saw anyone enter or leave this tent except you." Savage suggested.

"Bit of a hero today, weren't you, Savage?" MacHuylin commented as he marched off to the tent opposite. Sitting outside it where the wife and manservant of one of the knights in the tournament.

"Hallo there," MacHuylin began. "Have you been sitting here long?"

"Since the Melee finished." The woman replied.

"Did you see John Talbot being brought back to his tent?" The Irishman inquired.

"Yes." The woman said.

"Was he left alone?" Savage asked.

The woman and manservant both nodded. "The physicians and servants all left him alone."

Savage interrupted, "have you seen anyone else go into the tent apart from this man?" He demanded, pointing at MacHuylin .

"Indeed." The woman replied. MacHuylin smiled at Savage.

"Who was it?" MacHuylin demanded.

The woman's face twisted with disgust and fear. "Two lepers!" She said.

"Lepers?" MacHuylin echoed, surprised.

"Yes! In his tent!" The woman's expression showed she was obviously shocked. "He must have given them short shrift though, because they came out quickly and hurried off."

"Did they, now." MacHuylin scratched his chin.

"There's a leper hospital at Franciscan friary." Savage said. "I saw two of them earlier."

"I know. I do live here you know." MacHuylin said. "We'd better get over there quickly."

Savage nodded. "Raise the alarm." He told the woman and her servant. "Sir John Talbot's been murdered."

They started to run, Savage's aching muscles complaining the whole way. Quickly they sped across the field towards the infirmary and climbed the short rise up to the wattle-walled garden where herbs, vegetables and plants grew. In the early May sunshine the monks' garden was a heady mixture of aromas from herbs and flowers and the gentle buzzing of bees gathering pollen. The harmonious singing of the friars drifted from the small chapel. As MacHuylin and Savage entered the garden several grey-cowled monks instantly pretended to be at work.

"Where's the hospital?" MacHuylin demanded of one or them. The monk pointed meekly towards a low building that was joined to the small chapel.

As MacHuylin and Savage strode purposefully towards the door, a tall, gaunt monk came hurrying across the garden towards them. His eyes were red-rimmed and they stared from his skull-like, completely bald head which was pale and emaciated from self-starving and mortification of the flesh. He looked like he had just crawled out of one of the graves which huddled around the back of the infirmary.

"What's going on here?" the monk demanded. "Who are you and what do you want?"

"I'm Richard Savage and this is Connor MacHuylin, Commander of the Bonnaght of Ulster." Savage said. "Who are you?"

"I'm Abbot FitzGerald." The monk replied indignantly, as if Savage should have known. "I'm in charge here."

"We want to go to the Lazar house." MacHuylin told him.

"We don't let anyone into the leper colony because of the danger of infection." The abbot stated, putting himself between them and the door.

"You let them out though." Savage argued. "What about the danger of them infecting others then, eh?"

The Abbot was most indignant "We do not!" He roared. "Do you think we're irresponsible? We can't just let dangerously ill and highly infectious people out to wander around when there are so many people about. What do you think we are? Fools?"

"Well some of them have been wandering about amongst the tournament over there." Savage insisted. "I saw them with my own eyes."

"Well they weren't from here'" The Abbot replied angrily.

"Come now, Abbot'" MacHuylin growled. "What other leper house is there in Carrickfergus? People at the tournament saw lepers. Now are you going to let us in?"

The Abbot hesitated, then said: "Wait here. I'll check for you."

He disappeared through the door.

"Do we believe him?" Savage wondered aloud.

"I don't know. I don't know why they would let them out, particularly on a day like this." MacHuylin mused. "I, for one, don't really fancy going in there. Leprosy is a horrible disease."

The Abbot soon returned. "I've spoken to the monks who tend the lepers." He told them. "They assure me that no one entered or left the Lazar house today. You can come in and ask them yourself if you wish."

Both MacHuylin and Savage hesitated. Neither had any desire to enter a leper house.

"I don't know who it was you saw," The Abbot said to Savage, his voice softening "but those two lepers were not from here."

MacHuylin shrugged and he and Savage turned to return to the tournament field.

"If they didn't come from here, where on earth did they come from?" MacHuylin wondered. "Itinerants maybe? Just arrived in Carrickfergus?"

"If they were lepers at all," said Savage. "They could have been disguised as lepers."

"Fake lepers? Why?"

"To hide their identities," Savage said. "The lepers I saw earlier, presuming that they were the same ones, were totally swathed in bandages. You could not see an inch of their faces or hands."

"No-one's going to look too closely at a couple of lepers anyway," said MacHuylin . "A very good disguise."

"Wait." Savage stopped. He whirled round and began striding back towards the infirmary door. The Abbot had been in the process of closing it but seeing Savage coming back he once more he stopped.

"'Those two lepers', you said?" Savage glared at the Abbot. "Neither of us mentioned how many there were, but you seem to know there was two."

A look of either fear or anger flashed across the Abbot's face, Savage could not decide which it was.

"What is all this nonsense?" The Abbot shouted. "Look: if you don't believe me then look for yourself. We have nothing to hide. This is a house of God."

"That won't be necessary." MacHuylin added. "Savage: I'm not going into a house of lepers."

"Can't you see he's counting on us being too scared of the disease to look for ourselves MacHuylin? It's like the disguise: No one is going to want to look in a Lazar house any more than they would look beneath a leper's bandages."

A look of dawning realisation mixed with anger crossed MacHuylin's face.

"I think we will look round the hospital after all," Savage flashed an aggressive smile at the Abbot.

Chapter 19

Still clad in his black robes and armour, Hugo Montmorency stalked through the tournament campsite like a raven. Eventually he arrived at the large tent of Sir Henry Copeland where the members of the defeated home team who still could walk unaided had gathered to lick their wounds.

Montmorency swept open the tent flap and entered. There was a welcome coolness inside the spacious tent. The air was filled with the mixed tang of the seat of horses and men and the aroma of damp grass. The beaten knights were sitting in chairs or reclining on the ground, half clad in armour or stripped to their linen undergarments. Some sported black eyes or other facial bruises and their hair was matted with sweat into unflattering arrangements. A large jug of consoling burgundy wine was being passed around.

Montmorency hovered on the edge of the circle of knights, listening to the conversation.

"We would have had them but for that man Savage." Sir Henry Copeland stared into his cup of wine, shaking his head a little. "He's quite a fighter."

"He made the difference between the two teams today." Patrick De Lacy agreed, taking a long drink. "I heard he is originally a local man: Why wasn't he on our side?"

"He grew up in Ulster but left years ago." Henry de Thrapston explained. "He works for the King now."

John Bysset stood up and grasped the wine jug in a bad tempered grab. Half his face was now hidden behind a swathe of bandages that were packed with herbs. Some green juice was seeping through the linen. "That's what I don't understand." He grunted. "A King's Emissary shouldn't fight like that. They avoid fights, make peace, that sort of thing. Savage fought like a hardened warrior."

"That's because he is one." Henry de Thrapston smiled. "He was a Templar."

An awed hush fell over the knights.

Montmorency's eyes glittered and he stepped forward. "How do you know that?"

"When we were arming him, he spat on the cross his sword formed: The old Templar battle ritual." De Thrapston said.

The mood of the assembled knights lifted perceptively. "We shouldn't feel so bad then. I don't mind losing to Knight Templar!" De Lacy grinned and refilled his goblet of wine. All the other knights laughed and the conversation started to bubble.

Montmorency laid a hand on John Bysset's arm. "We must talk. Come."

The Hospitaller led the young knight out of the tent. They made their way in silence through the campsite until they came to Bysset's tent where they entered. Bysset dismissed the servants waiting inside with a derisory sweep of his hand.

"I have word from Scotland," Montmorency said once they were alone. "The invasion fleet is ready and the landing site has been chosen. They will sail from Ayr and land where we were suggested: Vikingsford sea lough, near Laharna."

Bysset nodded seriously. "Good. It's the best place to land a large force near Carrickfergus. If they sail down the Antrim coast and round the Maiden islands they won't even have to enter Carrickfergus Lough. They will be out of sight of the Castle the whole time and none of the garrisons will be any the wiser that the ships have landed."

"Unless a coast guard sees them," Montmorency said.

Bysset chuckled. "That Antrim coast and the Glynns are the lands of my Uncle Hugh. He will play the same trick he played when he was supposed to be hunting for Robert de Bruce. Be assured: there will be no coast guards, or if there are, they will be looking the wrong way."

"The landing site is not in your Uncle's fiefdom though. Vikingsford lough is De Logan land, watched over by the castle at Corainne point," Montmorency said. "We need to secure and fortify the site before the fleet sails. We need to clear the beaches to make sure that the Scottish army can get ashore as quickly as possible. How goes your wooing of Dame Alys?"

Bysset smiled again. "We are betrothed. Soon we shall be married and then the lands will be mine."

Montmorency shook his head. "We have no time to wait for that now. The invasion is immanent. Betrothal will have to be enough. Now we must remove Dame Alys from the chessboard. That will not be hard. Everyone knows she is a witch. We will construct a suitable cause and then have her arrested. As you are engaged to marry her it will not seem strange that you take control of her lands and Corainne castle while she awaits trial. With her out of the way we will be free to prepare the beach and harbour for the invasion."

"What about the girl? Dame Alys's daughter Galiene?"

"Kill her." Montmorency said. "The offspring of a witch is a witch too. We don't want to leave a legitimate heir to the castle now do we?"

Bysset nodded once more but looked slightly uncomfortable. He involuntarily touched the parcel of herbs that was bandaged to the right side of his face."

"Just what is that?" Montmorency asked.

"It's a poultice of herbs," Bysset explained. "Dame Alys made it for me. She said it would reduce the damage done in the tournament to my face."

A flash of pure anger crossed Montmorency's face and he ripped the bandages off Bysset's head, revealing the bruised and swelling cheek that Savage had smashed with his fist.

"Witchcraft! Potions! You young fool: you must have nothing to do with that woman's evil concoctions. She could be casting spells on you that twist your resolve and jeopardise this whole adventure. Trust in God alone."

Bysset looked at the ground, his face reddening with anger. He bit his tongue though, knowing he could not beat the Hospitaller in an open fight.

"What about the Earl?" He asked, his voice thick with suppressed rage. "Is he with us or against?"

Montmorency shook his head in disgust. "The Earl still prevaricates. He is waiting until he is sure which side will win, then he will join that side. He has no backbone any more. No faith. We can no longer afford to wait to see which way he jumps. We must take action ourselves. He is a fool anyway: God has already shown us which side he favours. He has given such a clear sign."

"The Grail...." Bysset's eyes took on a faraway look. "Will King Robert bring the Holy Treasure with him to Ireland?"

Montmorency shook his head. "King Robert is not coming with his brother Edward to Ireland. He is sailing to the Western Isles to subdue rebels there."

Bysset looked crestfallen. Montmorency laid a consoling hand on his shoulder. "Do not fear, John. You may get your chance to see the Holy Treasure yet. The Scots need someone who knows the waters to guide their ships safely around the Maidens Islands into Vikingsford Lough. That man is you."

Byssets eyes lit up and the smile returned to his face.

"Once we have dealt with Dame Alys and secured her castle, you must travel to Scotland and return at the head of the invasion fleet." Montmorency continued. "I am sure King Robert will reward your vital service with a sight of the Holy Vessel that bore our Lord's blood."

"And what of Syr Richard Savage?" Bysset asked. "We were supposed to have killed him by now."

Montmorency grinned like a hungry wolf. "He was lucky in the tournament. Who would have thought he was wearing plate armour? Otherwise the arrow would have gone straight through him. Our agents got Sir John Talbot though so it has not been a completely wasted day. Do not worry: this news of Savage being a heretic Templar is a stroke of luck. We can use this against him and arrest him too, along with the witch."

"You will need to be careful: There is still a lot of respect for the Templars. You saw how the other knights back in the tent reacted there now," Bysset said.

Montmorency shook his head. "By the time anyone tries to do anything about it I shall have transferred both Savage and Dame Alys out of the country and into the hands of the Holy Office of the Inquisition."

Chapter 20

At the Friary, the Abbot shook his head and began to close the door. "Really this is most ridiculous. I gave you the chance to look around here and you declined- "

MacHuylin stretched out a large hand, preventing the door from closing. "We're coming in." He stated.

"You dare speak to me like this?" The Abbot raged. "I am a man of God."

"Aw shut up." MacHuylin replied as he and Savage pushed their way through the door past the protesting friar.

"This is an outrage!" The Abbot shouted, mucus bubbling on his lips and spraying with every word.

"Have you something to hide, Abbot?" Savage demanded. "I am an emissary of King Edward of England. I have authority to go wherever I feel I have to." He added. MacHuylin raised a sceptical eyebrow that Savage hoped the Abbot did not see.

The Abbot's demeanour changed. In an instant the cast of rage left his face and an obsequious smile sneaked across his lips.

"Not at all," he said. "I merely am indignant at this intrusion. This is the property of the Church. As for the King - well, you hardly expect the authority of a devil worshipping sodomite to be recognized here, do you?"

"You watch your tongue, monk." Savage said.

The Abbot continued, non-plussed, "We have nothing to hide here. We are simple men of God. We live in peace, doing our best to worship our Saviour and trying to help those less fortunate than ourselves. You may search where you please."

"Right. We'll start in the Lazar house," said Savage. "Lead the way, Abbot FitzGerald."

The Abbot nodded and preceded them across a short, barren hallway to a door which opened into the hospital. This was a long room with seven beds on each side and aromatic herbs hung around the walls. There were only three patients. One, a peasant woman with a fever, tossed and turned in her sweaty bed. A couple of beds away lay a gaunt-faced man whose leg had been amputated. The operation had perhaps been futile as he looked like he was not long for the world. On the other side of the room was a bearded man with an arm in splints and his chest bandaged, lying on a bed beneath a big wooden crucifix that hung on the wall.

There was a door at the other end of the infirmary and the Abbot led the way to it. This door was adorned with a crucifix and black crosses were painted on the walls around the door, each one a magic talisman to try to contain the dreaded disease that lurked on the other side.

"The lepers stay in there." The Abbot announced. "I have already done my duty and spent the allotted months that all we Franciscans must spend tending the lepers, so you'll understand why I do not accompany you inside."

"Aren't they a bit close to the other patients?" asked MacHuylin.

"This door is seldom opened." The Abbot revealed. "There is another door at the other end of the lazar house which opens into an enclosure for them to go outside if they wish."

Savage turned to MacHuylin. "You don't need to come in as well." He said. "I've no wish to place you at any more risk than necessary."

"Fair enough," MacHuylin consented, not without some relief. He was willing to fight anyone on earth if needs be, but there was something about the silent, invisible nature of the disease that appalled him.

Savage took a deep breath to try to dispel the nervous feeling in his chest. He pulled his cloak up around his mouth and nose in case he might breathe in the contagion in the air, then he disappeared through the cross-marked door.

MacHuylin waited, watching the silent Abbot out of the corner of his eye, his hand never far from the hilt of his dagger. He had no intentions of underestimating how dangerous the Abbot might be. Irish monks regularly took up arms and it was not uncommon for monasteries to go to war against each other.

Almost immediately, Savage returned, his face now angry. "Just what are you playing at, Abbot?" He demanded. "There's no lepers in there. The place is empty!"

"You merely wished to see the lazar house." The Abbot smiled provocatively. "You didn't say anything about any lepers."

"Don't play games, monk," Savage's ire was raised and MacHuylin noted how intimidating the flashing green eyes of the knight became when employed in an unflinching stare. There was murder in those eyes.

"Why didn't you tell us there were no lepers here?" MacHuylin inquired.

"You didn't ask." The Abbot replied. "Lepers are free to roam the countryside as long as they stay away from crowds and outside towns and villages. The last two staying here left several days ago. Perhaps if you would like to come back next week, we might have some more by then."

Savage took a deep breath and rolled his eyes, trying to contain his anger. "Alright. Now we'll search the monks' cells."

The Abbot shrugged nonchalantly. "Very well." He sighed. "But I don't know what you expect to find here." He led them back out of the infirmary and across the peaceful garden.

They walked around the chapel, hearing the melodious singing wafting from it, until they came to the door of the monks' accommodation building. Inside, they searched the cells one by one. Each was virtually identical: A bare stone room with either one or two hard and very uncomfortable looking beds. Some cells had small tables and the occasional one had a little footstool. Lucky monks had a window. The only decoration was a simple wooden crucifix, hung on the wall of every cell.

By the time they had completed their fruitless search, Savage's anger had faded to disappointment.

The Abbot smiled triumphantly. "Now I hope you are satisfied." He said. "I'm sorry it had to go this far, but I understand you have a job to do. Perhaps you would like to share our evening meal, just to show we follow our Lord's example and forgive our enemies their trespasses against us?"

MacHuylin shrugged. Savage shook his head. "We need to go. There is a banquet at the Castle tonight." He said.

The Abbot smiled. "I'll show you the way out."

He strode off, back the way they had come through the accommodation building.

"Hold on." MacHuylin stopped and pointed to a short corridor leading off to the right of the main passageway. "You didn't take us down there."

Savage's interest was reawakened. "What's down there?" He asked the Abbot.

"Just another monk's cell. Same as all the others." The Abbot smiled, trying to be as nonchalant as possible. Both Savage and MacHuylin noticed a flicker of concern flash across his face.

"All the same, Abbot, we'd like to take a look." Savage said, pushing the grey-cowled friar aside to stride down the corridor. At the end of it was a door, the same as all the other cell doors. Eagerly he pushed open the door and went inside, closely followed by MacHuylin and the Abbot.

"Looks like the Abbot was right," MacHuylin said. It did look just like the others: Two beds, a small table and a window.

"Yes, but what's missing?" Savage said.

kno

"W
the
"A
fl
p

li
o

a
j

MacHuylin Immediately dash
pinned the Abbot up against the
trouble monk," he spat, befor
disgust and running after
"Empty words!" th
Out of the doors
garden towards the
in the gates and
disappear ov
"We
gate. Th
garde

"They knocked the stool over, spilled ...
What is that anyway, Savage?" He repeated his query.

"Hashish," Savage replied. "At least I think it is."

"What?" The galloglaich had never heard the word.

"I can scarcely believe it, Connor," Savage shook his head. "But I think that there have been members of the cult of Assassins here."

He looked at MacHuylin, a light of sudden realisation dawning in his eyes. Through the window came the sound of a horse whinnying and the clatter of hooves.

"That bastard monk has been keeping us busy," he roared, "while whoever was living in this cell gets away!"

ed out of the cell. Savage
wall by the throat. "You're in
e releasing the friar with a look of
MacHuylin.
Abbot shouted after him.
they dashed and charged across the
friary gates. They tore open the little door
rushed out, just in time to see two riders
r a small hillock to the North West.
eed horses." Savage said and re-entered the friary
e Abbot was just coming out of the door into the
n.

"Where are your stables?" Savage demanded.

"We don't have any-" The Abbot began.

MacHuylin's fist smashed into the monk's cheek, opening the skin and sending him reeling backwards to collapse unceremoniously onto his backside in a vegetable patch.

"Balls," the galloglaich said. "We don't have time to piss about any more: Tell us where the horses are or I'll break your god-damned neck."

The Abbot-under no illusion he did not mean it-waved in the general direction of the side of the infirmary. Savage and MacHuylin ran round the building and sure enough they found well equipped stables with a variety of steeds inside. By luck, a couple of novices were in the process of saddling four of the horses.

Without any explanation, the young monks were thrown aside and MacHuylin and Savage leapt onto a horse each. Within seconds they were at full gallop, tearing across the monastery garden, ploughing up herbs, flowers and vegetables as they went.

Hooves thundering, they left the Friary gates and charged over the hillock to the north-west. Once over the rise, they saw the two riders ahead starting to climb up the steep Knockagh hill which rose up behind Carrickfergus.

The riders were wrapped in green cloaks. Every so often they turned their heads to check on MacHuylin and Savage's progress. At such a distance it was impossible to make out any features, but they could see that both green-clad riders had black beards and long curly black hair.

"You recognized something in that cell, didn't you?" MacHuylin shouted as they careered across the countryside. "What's going on? Who are the cult of Assassins?"

"I'll tell you later." Savage shouted back. "It's complicated. I can scarcely believe it myself."

The riders ahead were fleeing directly up the hill towards some woods that covered the summit. MacHuylin and Savage pursued them doggedly, their horses' hooves throwing up lumps of brown earth behind them. Savage's horse was already tiring, and he began to fear he would not be able to keep up.

"Looks like they're heading for Doagh Manor," MacHuylin deduced. "If they go into those woods the only path which goes through the trees leads there."

"There's no other way through?" asked Savage.

"Not on horseback. At least not without a great deal of trouble," MacHuylin shouted back. "The undergrowth's too thick."

Desperately they drove their horses on in an attempt to catch up on the fleeing riders before they reached the woods. The wind roared in their ears as the hooves of the horses beat a thunderous tattoo across the turf. The ground rushed past beneath in a green blur. Savage pushed aside thoughts of what would happen if his horse set a foot wrong and stumbled.

The two riders up ahead disappeared amidst the trees. The pursuers spurred their own horses up the last hundred yards of the hill until they too reached the woods.

Without slowing they dashed into the trees. The narrowness of the dirt path forced them immediately into single file, MacHuylin first. At full gallop the ride through the woods was heart stopping. As the path twisted and turned the riders could see no more than ten feet in front of them at most. They ducked beneath branches and leapt fallen logs as thorns and briars grasped at their cloaks and breeches.

Suddenly they burst into a small clearing. MacHuylin reigned his horse to a halt without warning.

Desperately Savage's horse swerved around MacHuylin's to avoid a collision before stopping also.

"What in the name of God's guts are you doing?" Savage demanded. "They're getting away!"

MacHuylin held up a hand. "Listen," was all he said.

Savage did just that. He noticed what MacHuylin was getting at. He could hear the panting of their horses and the sound of their own heavy breathing. Apart from that there was only the frantic chirping of disturbed birds. No hoof beats. The men they were chasing had stopped also.

"They must be hiding somewhere," said MacHuylin.

Without warning the undergrowth came alive and men came pouring into the clearing from all sides. Savage did not have time to count but a cursory glance told that there were at least fifteen of them, on foot and all armed.

"It's an ambush!" shouted MacHuylin, ripping his sword from his sheath.

"Get out of here," Savage shouted. "Back the way we came!" Even in full armour he would have hesitated to take on all fifteen of their attackers. Without either chainmail or a weapon there was only one option: Flee.

MacHuylin wheeled his horse to head back to the track and Savage did likewise. The ambushers closed in on them. Savage noticed that while they bore a variety of weapons from long knives and clubs to spears, they were all dressed alike, each wearing a dark blue tunic.

MacHuylin slashed aside a spear with his sword then brought his weapon down on one of the attackers, who countered with a blow with a long Irish knife. The galloglaich spurred his horse and it bolted forward, its powerful legs pushing aside two more of the blue-clad ambushers.

Savage followed him. One of the attackers stepped forward and thrust at him with a stabbing spear. Savage spotted the attack and arched his back so that the spear missed its target and went behind him. He grabbed the shaft of the spear with his left hand and tugged it, pulling its owner closer to him. Savage lifted his right foot out of the stirrup and drove it down onto his attacker's chest, sending him flying away from him but leaving the spear still in Savage's grasp.

MacHuylin brought down his sword in a wide arc which caught a club wielding ambusher on the side of the neck, striking his head clean off. The severed head tumbled off into the undergrowth while the decapitated body staggered wildly backwards, blood shooting from the severed neck arteries in a hideous fountain.

Undeterred, five attackers crowded together to block the mouth of the path out of the clearing. With a frightening whoop, MacHuylin spurred his horse again and leapt clean over them, sending them cringing down to avoid the flying hooves.

Savage hurled the spear at the men. It missed but made sure they stayed crouched. Then he followed MacHuylin and spurred his horse to jump.

The palfrey, more tired than MacHuylin's steed, did not leap as high. One of its rear hooves caught an ambusher on the forehead, stoving in his skull with a horrific crack.

Now on the woodland path again, Savage and MacHuylin drove their horses back through the trees every bit as furiously as they had come, but now as the hunted, not the hunters.

Savage heard the unmistakeable click and snap of a crossbow firing, almost immediately followed by the sickening thwack of the bolt striking flesh somewhere nearby. He sucked in a breath, expecting the onslaught of pain from somewhere in his body.

Instead, his horse gave a startled squeal and reared up on its hind legs. Looking round, Savage saw the feathered end of the crossbow bolt embedded in the horse's flank. The palfrey wheeled around wildly, just as the sound of two more crossbows fired. The whirling horse saved Savage as the bolts aimed at his body struck the horse in the neck and stomach instead. With a blood-flecked whinny the steed collapsed sideways, throwing Savage off the saddle into the undergrowth.

Savage landed heavily, thorns from the brambles piercing and tearing at his skin.

"Connor I'm down!" He shouted. "Leave me and get away yourself!"

He did not know if MacHuylin heard him, but he could hear the hoof beats of the galloglaich's horse receding through the forest. Behind him, his own horse screamed and thrashed, flailing hooves in every direction. He could also hear running footsteps and the crashing sound of men wading through the undergrowth as the pursuing ambushers approached.

Savage looked through the brambles towards the path. The pursuers were nearly on him. Desperately he crawled further into the thick undergrowth, burying himself in the undergrowth away from view.

"Find him!" he heard one of the pursuers shouting. Lucky for him, the thrashing of the dying horse made the men following him pause, afraid of being struck by the flying hooves. Through the bramble branches Savage could see five men approaching along the woodland path, two with loaded crossbows, two with spears and a tall, big framed man with long brown hair who appeared to be their leader.

"Kill that thing." the leader ordered, pointing at Savage's horse with his sword. The two spearmen drove their weapons into the animal's chest and belly, skewering the points home into heart and vital organs. The poor creature screamed once more and tried to squirm away from the agonising spears. Within seconds it gave a final grunt and died.

"He's in the undergrowth somewhere." The leader directed, and the spearmen began prodding the bushes on Savage's side of the path with the bloodied spear tips, jabbing them randomly but methodically into the brambles.

Savage lay under the thorn branches, considering what options he had. There were not many. Every time he moved the bramble bushes rustled and waved, giving away his position. If he stayed where he was, given the meticulous nature with which the spears were prodding the bushes, it was only a matter of time before one of them struck him. That left the option of surrendering.

"You two make sure you have a clear field of fire." The leader of the ambushers shouted at the crossbowmen. "Shoot the bastard as soon as he stands up."

There goes that option-Savage thought to himself.

There was something odd about this situation: The ambushers all spoke in Irish with local accents but they were not dressed like Irish warriors. Instead, the blue tunics and chainmail coifs were more common to war gear from the Island of Britain. Crossbows were not Irish weapons either. Could they be mercenaries?

The stabbing spears were getting steadily closer to where he lay. If he did not do something soon he would be dead.

The big leader held up his hand. "Quiet," he ordered. "I think I can hear him breathing". The spearmen froze. Savage could see they were watching the brambles, straining their ears for any sign that would give away his position. Desperately he held his breath. The frantic ride and ambush had left him panting however and within seconds his lungs were burning.

Mercilessly the ambushers stood still as statues and continued to wait. Savage could hold on no longer and his breath exploded from his mouth.

Through the brambles he saw the pursuers' eyes light up as they pinpointed his position and began moving towards him, weapons raised for the kill.

Suddenly, a piercing screech echoed through the trees. It was a weird, chilling sound like a cross between a woman wailing and a baby crying that rose and fell on the wind, somehow expressing a terrible sense of the utter desolation of bereavement, and the loneliness that was to come for those left behind.

The pursuers all stopped dead. Savage was surprised to see terror in the eyes of the Spearmen.

"The Banshee!" one of them whispered.

Chapter 22

News of Syr John Talbot's murder spread like a wild fire through the tournament arena and the tent village around it. Tightly-controlled panic ensued. Murder was a far from unusual occurrence in Ireland, but what gripped everyone's thoughts straight away was the question if this was an isolated killing, or possibly the herald of a sudden massacre? A gathering of great nobles in one place was such a tempting target for so many enemies and the killing could be the start of a surprise attack, either from without or within.

The Justiciar had ridden north from Dublin with a bodyguard of one hundred hobelars, the light cavalry Ireland had become famous for. Immediately the word of the murder was heard, the captain of his guard hurried Edmund Bottelier unceremoniously into his spacious tent. The now-dismounted cavalrymen, swords drawn, formed a ring of steel around the tent. In a similar way, the Red Earl had retreated to his arming tent while his galloglaiches blocked entry to anyone.

Around the arena, men grabbed their weapons and prepared to defend themselves and their families from whatever attack might be immanent.

As time passed and no wide-scale attack emerged, people began to relax slightly. The Justiciar sent messengers summoning the Earl, the Seneschal and the other important nobles of Ulster to his tent to hold council.

When everyone had arrived, the council began. The Justiciar sat in a chair, sipping from a goblet of wine. The Earl sat on a seat beside him. Thomas de Mandeville stood opposite them. At first, the Seneschal of Ulster had been unsure where he should put himself, for it was unusual for him to find himself in the situation that he did now, where the Earl was not the most senior person in the room. Richard de Burgh may have been the richest, most powerful baron in Ireland, but as representative of the King of England, the Justiciar still outranked him.

Montmorency was perched on the edge of a table. John Bysset stood beside him and sitting next to him was his uncle Hugh. Beside them was a fat middle-aged man fantastically clad in a red and yellow tunic who could easily have been mistaken for some sort of minstrel or troubadour.

"Well, now," the Justiciar said. "I've been to many tournaments where someone got killed, but not usually in such a cold-blooded, deliberate way. You men represent law and order here: What the hell is going on?"

There was silence. The Earl shrugged. "Who knows? Men get killed every day in Ireland."

"I want Syr Talbot's killer found, Richard." The Justiciar continued. "These are uncertain times. I believe a messenger brought a message from the King, warning of a Scottish attack. I hope this is not the start of something worse."

John Bysset gave a loud tutt. "Hardly," he sighed. "Talbot was a notorious womaniser. He was probably killed by some jealous husband he cuckolded."

"Or maybe it was a woman," Montmorency added, his eyes glittering with an idea that had evidently just occurred to him. "Some bitter woman he jilted probably killed him."

"Edmund, this is Sir Johan D'Athy." The Earl of Ulster referred to the fat man dressed in red and yellow. "Johan is the Sheriff of Carrickfergus County. I have already charged him to find Talbot's murderer."

At the mention of his name, D'Athy puffed up his chest like a multi-coloured balloon. "I'll have the bastard strung up by tomorrow morning, Sire." He said.

The Justiciar raised a sceptical eyebrow. "I'm sure you will," he said. "Whether the particular bastard you string up will be the same one who carried out this murder will remain to be seen."

D'Athy looked somewhat deflated by the Justiciar's sarcasm.

"So who do you think could have done this?" Le Bottelier asked. "Apart from jealous husbands, who else could have killed Talbot. What about the Clan Eoghan?"

The Seneschal stroked his beard at the mention of an old enemy. The gaelic kingdom that lay to the west of was always trying to push the boundaries of the Earldom of Ulster back towards the sea.

"It's possible," he said. "King Domnall Ui Neill never misses a chance to hit us. But why? Why randomly kill one man?"

The Earl snorted. "You know as well as I do Thomas what the Irish way of warfare is: An ambush here, a murder there. If you cannot beat someone in open battle then try to wear them down, pick them off whenever they get the chance. Ui Neill could have a man in among the gaels at the tournament."

Montmorency shook his head. "The Clan Eoghan is too weak to move against the Earldom of Ulster."

"Will there be many gaels at the feast tonight?" the Justiciar asked.

"Some." Earl Richard replied. "All trusted allies. Muircetach and Thomas Ui Cahan, the princes of the Ui Cahan clan, Deidre and Emer their wives. A few of the MacCartain clan. MacHuylin's clan. We have nothing to fear from any of those folk.

"Let's not take any chances," the Justiciar said. "I will add my one hundred cavalrymen to your castle garrison. They can all stand guard while the banquet is held. But setting the native Irish aside, what about the message Savage brought? Do you think this could have anything to do with the Scots?"

The Earl of Ulster looked annoyed at the suggestion. "Not this again." He groaned. "Do you really believe that Robert Bruce, my own son-in-law, would be planning an attack on my lands and I would not know about it?"

The Justicar did not reply for several seconds. Finally he said, "Have you heard the news from Scotland? Their Parliament is sitting at Ayr right now."

The Earl looked puzzled. He shook his head.

"The Parliament's decrees have already reached me in Dublin via the King's spies. I'm surprised you have not heard" The Justiciar said. "King Robert Bruce has named his brother Edward as his successor to the throne."

The Earl's jaw dropped. His astonishment was undeniable. "What?" He growled.

"I'm sorry that you heard it this way, Richard," Edmund Bottelier continued, his tone softening somewhat. "But if your daughter gives birth to a son, he will not be the next King of Scotland. The Scots Parliament has dubbed Edward Bruce heir to the throne." He paused for a few seconds, then added: "And Ireland."

"Ireland?" Thomas de Mandeville said. "I don't recall anyone asking us about that."

"No," the Justiciar said. "I somehow doubt Edward Bruce is expecting us to just hand the throne of Ireland over to him either. Their intentions are clear Gentlemen. Sooner or later the Scots will come to take what they want. Richard: I had begun to wonder if you knew about this but your reaction shows me that is not true."

The Earl clenched his fist and slammed it down onto the arm of his chair. "God damn him to Hell! The sly bastard." He hissed.

"You see now Robert Bruce's true regard for you and your family." The Justiciar said.

At that moment a commotion erupted outside the door of the tent. The Captain of the Justiciar's bodyguard was shouting "No one goes in or out during the council. Justiciar's orders."

Connor MacHuylin's voice could be heard responding "Get out of my way you arsehole."

The Earl stood up. "That's the Captain of my Galloglaich troop," He explained. "He really should be in here."

The Justiciar nodded and Earl de Burgh swept the tent flap open. "MacHuylin: By God's bones, man! Where the hell have you been? Assassins running around killing folk and the chief of my bodyguard is nowhere to be seen! I could have been murdered in my seat at the lists for all the good you would have been. I suppose you've been off swiving with some wench in the woods, eh? Well it's not good enough."

"You know this man, sire?" The Justiciar's captain asked.

"Of course I do. Let them in you idiot." The Earl grunted and the Captain stood aside.

MacHuylin was out of breath from his frantic horse ride from the woods. He nodded to the assembled men in the tent. "Earl Richard," he panted. "Savage and I were chasing John Talbot's killers-"

"You know who killed him?" Johann D'Athy asked.

MacHuylin shook his head. "We didn't see their faces: they were disguised as lepers. Hiding out at the friary."

"What nonsense is this?" Montmorency objected. The Justiciar held up a hand to silence him.

"There were two of them. They got away on horses." MacHuylin continued. "We chased them up the hillside. It looked like they were heading for Doagh. When we followed them into the Earl's hunting woods there were more of them: soldiers waiting to cover their escape. I got away but they must have got Savage."

"Is he dead?" John Bysset asked, eagerly.

MacHuylin shrugged. "I turned round and he wasn't there any more. They meant business. Well-armed and wearing chainmail."

"Who were they?" the Justiciar demanded.

Again MacHuylin shrugged. "I don't know. They weren't wearing any recognisable livery."

"English or Irish?"

"They weren't dressed in Irish clothes," MacHuylin said. "I reckon there was about fifteen of them. I'm going back to find out right now, though. This time I'll have my men with me."

"You do just that," the Justiciar responded. "Take as many men as you need. Savage must be rescued."

"If he's still alive." MacHuylin commented, as he turned and left the tent again.

"I'm going with him." Thomas de Mandeville said, following the galloglaich out of the tent.

"This is worrying news." The Justiciar commented. "Richard: You and I will talk more at length about this and other matters. These other men have important work to do. Montmorency?"

The Hospitaller hopped off his perch on the table to his feet. "Yes, my Lord?"

"I gather you have been asked to create defence plans for the Earldom. I urge you to work with the Seneschal to make sure that Ulster is well prepared to defend itself from attack, either from the west or from across the sea."

Montmorency bowed his head in obedience.

"Sir Hugh," le Bottelier addressed Bysset. "Your lands in the Glyns are closest to Scotland. Bruce will have to sail past your realm to strike. We will have need of your ships to patrol the seas, and your men-at-arms to watch from the coast."

"You can rely on us, Sire." John Bysset smiled.

"And you, D'Athy," The Justiciar finally addressed the Sheriff of Carrickfergus who immediately snapped to attention. "You work with MacHuylin to find out whoever killed Talbot. By the sound of it, it wasn't a jilted woman and this could be the start of something much more serious. Now go all of you."

Everyone left the tent except for the Earl and the Justiciar.

When they got outside, John Bysset pulled Montmorency aside and spoke quickly in a hushed, anxious tone. "The Earl did not take the news from Scotland well at all. What do we do now? This will turn him against us."

"Do not worry. I have been preparing for all eventualities," Montmorency hissed. "An unpleasant surprise awaits the Earl that will get him out of our way. All dies are now cast and the time has come to make our move. We will strike at the feast tonight."

Chapter 23

Beneath the brambles, Savage peered through the branches, trying to see what had made the terrible wail.

His pursuers, rooted to the spot, their faces white masks of terror, also looked around frantically.

Their big leader was far from pleased.

"What are you doing you weak-kneed cowards?" He shouted.

"That was the cry of the Banshee!" one of the spearmen groaned. "It means death!"

"What nonsense is this?!" King Domnall Ui Neill, the leader of the men roared. "Suibne, where are you? Tell these fools there are no Banshees here!"

"I've heard there is, my King." The voice of the poet came from the undergrowth beyond the clearing where Savage and MacHuylin had been ambushed. "The lore of the land tells us that these woods are haunted by the Banshee called Una."

"Damn you Suibne you've filled these men's head with fairy tales and nonsense!" The King shouted. "Are you men or children?"

"I'll fight a hundred knights in armour my Lord," one of the spearmen wailed, "but I'm damned if I'll fight a fairy. Certainly not the Death Fairy herself."

"There she is!" One of the crossbowmen squeaked, pointing down the woodland track.

Savage risked giving his position away by moving so he could look. To his astonishment, he could see the figure of a woman dressed in a heavy green cloak standing on the path. She had the long hood of the cloak drawn up over her head, hiding her face in shadow. One very pale hand was raised towards the men at arms, a long, slender finger pointing in their direction.

The awful wail emanated through the trees again, a howling, screeching keen that set the teeth on edge and sent a shiver down the spine.

"Shoot it for Jesus' sake!" King Domnall shouted. When nothing happened he turned round to see that all his warriors had turned tail and were running as fast as they could down the woodland path away from the apparition in green.

For a couple of seconds, he hesitated, then aware that he was alone with Savage somewhere in the bushes and an approaching Banshee, decided the best option was to follow his men. Taking to his heels, he ran off down the path.

Silence descended on the woods. Even the birds had been frightened away by the Banshee's howl.

Savage lay very still. He knew the legend of the Banshee well, the Irish death-fairy whose scream warned of impending doom. He no longer believed in God, devils and certainly not fairies, but until he knew for sure who this weird vision was he had no intention of revealing himself. It could be a ploy of the ambushers to find his hiding place.

"Richard Savage, I know you are here, hiding like a rat in the bushes somewhere."

To his surprise, the Banshee in the green cloak spoke in French. There was something familiar about the woman's voice. "They won't stay away for long. Come with me if you want to live."

Savage still do not move. The Banshee gave a shrug, evident even through the heavy folds of her cloak.

"Suit yourself." She said and turned to go. "Stay and die."

"Wait!" Savage called, cautiously raising himself from the brambles. "Who are you?"

The Banshee stopped and turned around to face him again. She pulled back the hood of her cloak and her long black hair tumbled down around her pale-skinned face.

It was Alys de Logan.

"Follow me," was all she said and started off down the woodland path.

Savage ran after her. They walked quickly down the path for a short while, then Alys took a sharp left turn, pushing aside thick undergrowth to reveal another, smaller path-narrow and barely more than an animal track-running off through the trees.

"It's a poachers' path," Alys explained. "This wood is part of the Earl's personal hunting forest. The ordinary folk are hung if they are caught hunting here so the poachers have these secret paths criss-crossing the woods. Those men who ambushed you aren't locals. They won't know about them."

Moving quickly, they set off down the little track, having to crouch low to avoid tree branches and thorns that grasped and tugged at their clothes.

"Who are they? What is going on?" Savage asked as they hurried along.

Alys de Logan gave him a sharp glance and touched her finger to her lips. "Keep your voice down." She hissed. "There are more of them in the woods and they'll hear you. These secret paths pass by sometimes within feet of the main pathways."

"How do you know about them?" Savage whispered. "Why are you up here anyway?"

"I come here often to gather herbs," Alys replied. "There are certain times when it's better to pick them. Mayday is one of the days some herbs are at their most potent. No doubt you have heard I am a witch."

"I was told that, yes." Savage said. "I was surprised I must say. What does your Father make of that? And your brother, Robert?" Savage was careful not to mention Alys's Mother, who had died giving birth to her.

"They're both dead," Alys said. "Plague."

Savage was taken aback slightly by her bluntness. "I'm sorry to hear that. Robert and I were good friends. Your father and mine were like brothers."

"Shht," Alys stopped and held up a hand signalling that he should both stop talking and walking. The little poacher's path had come to the edge of a clearing in the wood. Through the foliage Savage could make out the figure of a man standing in the clearing. He wore the same blue tunic as those who had ambushed him.

"Another one of them," Alys breathed, almost inaudibly.

Behind them, through the trees, the sound of shouting could be heard. King Domnall had obviously succeeded in rallying his men and the hunt for Savage had restarted.

"We have to get past this one if we're to escape," Alys whispered. "There's no way round the clearing."

Savage considered how they could do this quickly and quietly. Through the branches he could see the man was standing half turned towards them, a drawn sword in his hand. He was unaware of them watching him, but as soon as they stepped into the clearing he was sure to shout and all his friends would come running. Somehow Savage had to rush to him, cover his mouth and silence him before he had a chance to raise the alarm, all the while trying not to get impaled by the man's sword.

This would be difficult.

He cursed the fact he had no weapon. There was no choice though, so he stepped in front of Alys, putting a hand out to motion that she should stay back.

"I'll handle this." Savage murmured, stepping forward out of the cover of the trees. The man in the clearing saw him immediately, raised his sword and opened his mouth to shout a warning.

Something silver shot past Savage's head from behind him and hit the man in the clearing with the solid thunk of a blade striking deep into flesh. The man's mouth was open but no sound came out: his breath stopped in his throat by a throwing knife that was now embedded up to the hilt just below his adam's apple. His eyes bulged and he grasped at the knife hilt, trying desperately to suck air in through his blocked windpipe as he sank to his knees.

Alys de Logan pushed past Savage and reached the man as he started to fall forward. She grabbed him by the hair and pulled his head back, swiftly drawing another larger knife across his throat beneath the chin, severing the large veins and completely cutting his windpipe. Immediately she pushed him face down to the ground where he coughed and gurgled slightly as his lifeblood bubbled out into the grass. Very quietly, but very quickly, the man died.

"I'm not the little girl you left behind here any more, Richard," Alys said as she drew her throwing knife out of the dead man's throat and wiped it clean on his cloak.

"So I see," Savage said, shocked but impressed at the speed and ruthlessness with which she had dispatched the man.

"These days, Richard, a woman on her own has to learn to look after herself. Come on: The path continues over here."

With the sound of King Domnall's men approaching behind them, Savage hurried after Alys as she set off down another little poachers' pathway on the other side of the clearing.

"For your information I am not a witch- at least not in the ignorant way people like you would define it," Alys said as they hurried through the trees. "With my father and brother dead I was left alone. I had to find some way to hold on to the family estate. That's not easy for a woman on her own, you know. I had to fall back on my natural talents and use the gifts God gave me to survive."

Savage stopped, his face betraying dismay. "You became a prostitute?"

Alys flew around to face him. "No," she spat. For a second her hand hovered worryingly in the vicinity of her knife hilt. "Trust you to immediately think of that! I mean my intelligence, not my body. I am clever, so I've had to make the most of that."

She started off down the track again. Behind them, the voices of their pursuers were receding.

"It sounds like we're losing them." Savage said as they hurried along.

"We must keep going. My horse is not far," Alys replied. "After my father's death I needed a way to bring in money to keep the estate going. I learned the art of Astrology. Casting horoscopes for wealthy clients like the Earl brings in a good income, but not enough. I also have to fall back on the lore my wet nurse taught me when I was a little girl. She was a 'Wise Woman'. Folk who were sick paid her for a charm or potion to cure them. Now they come and see me when they need a remedy."

"Or a curse. Sounds like a witch to me," Savage said. He was familiar with the sort of "cunning folk" she referred to: Every village had one-usually old-woman who knew what herbs cured what diseases or cast love spells or divined where stolen or lost property could be found. As far as he was concerned it was peasant superstition.

"Well you would think that way with your 'convictions', Richard," Alys said with a bitter sneer. "Tell me: Did you ever find the Holy Grail?"

"What?"

"The Grail. I seem to recall you jilted me to go and seek the Grail or some such nonsense."

"Alys, I left Ireland to join the Order of Knights Templar," Savage was indignant. "I went to fight for Christendom. I believed in what I was doing. I was sincere, not like most of the freebooters who went to fight in the East. I really believed that Christian order had to be defended from heathen chaos." He shook his head, amazed himself at his own naivety.

"I'm sure we're all so grateful," Alys mocked. "And what about me? Was I not worth fighting for?"

"You're still bitter about it, even after all these years?"

"Have I not got a right to?" Alys spat back, flames of rage blazing behind her eyes.

Savage shrugged, feeling very uncomfortable.

"I was in love with you Richard," Alys hissed. "You knew it. I thought you loved me."

Richard was quiet for a moment. He scratched his head awkwardly and looked away, avoiding her glare. "But I did-" he began.

"Did you?" Alys cut him off. "Did you really? Well you had a strange way of showing it! How do you think I felt Richard? Eh?"

Savage sighed and rolled his eyes.

"How do you think it feels when the person you cared for more than anything, who you would have died for, who you would have given the world for, chooses the world rather than you?" Alys said.

Savage was astonished to see a strange liquescence in her eyes. In all the years they had spent together in their youth he had only seen her shed one tear, and that was when she had broken her arm while out riding. Even that had been quickly dashed away by her angry hand.

"We were to be married," she continued, "but you had to go and save Christendom, or find the Holy Grail or whatever it was that was more important than getting married to me."

There were a few moments of bitter silence as they continued to walk. The denseness of the trees and undergrowth was beginning to thin as they approached the edge of the forest.

"Why didn't you marry someone else?" Savage finally said. "Get yourself a rich husband and you won't have to fiddle about with potions and star gazing any more."

"Oh I've tried that, don't you worry," Alys responded. "Edward FitzPatrick. A man supposedly from a good family with a reasonable fortune. Actually a complete waster: Little more than a drunk and a philanderer who was just after my manor. Thankfully he died within a year of our marriage." She caught sight of the look on Savage's face. "And no, Richard, I did not kill him. He fell off his horse coming home drunk from one of his mistresses and broke his worthless neck."

"You had a child with him before he died though: The little girl. What age is she? Eleven?"

"Ten." Alys retorted quickly, glancing away from him and to avoiding his eyes. "Galiene: she is my only help and succour in this world. I've brought her up to look after herself."

"What about this John Bysset fellow?" Savage asked, his voice betrayed more interest than he effected.

Alys looked at the ground. "Sir John is courteous and attentive to me. He has his own fortune so has no need of my lands, so I can be sure he is interested in marrying me for myself. He may be rather full of himself but why should he not be? He is young and fit-good looking too-and still is, despite your efforts in the tournament today."

Savage was surprised again to see what looked like the hint of a playful smile on the corners of Alys's mouth. "How is he?"

"His face is a mess. But it will heal quickly. How long it takes his pride to recover is another matter." Alys said, her face softened as she broke into a sunny grin. "John is of the opinion that punching someone in the face as you did is the action of a common thug and very un-chivalrous."

"And you agree?" inquired Savage.

Like a ray of sunshine between clouds Alys's smile faded and the usual hard hostility returned to her eyes. "I'm only a woman, Richard. What would I know about your silly little boys' games?"

They emerged from the trees into the edge of a wide, sweeping meadow that lead downhill towards the sea. They were now on the other side of the woods from where the tournament arena was, but in the distance they could see the turf ramparts that surrounded the town of Carrickfergus, and the Castle brooding on the rocky promontory, giving it the appearance of being built in the sea itself.

Alys de Logan's old warhorse was tethered to a tree nearby. There were no sounds of pursuit coming from the woods.

"It looks like we've escaped." Savage said as they finally stopped beside the horse. "Have you any idea who they were?"

Alys shook her head. "They're Irish, but they dressed like English men-at-arms, that's all I can say. I was up here late last night-"

"On May Eve? In the dark?"

Alys scowled. "I'm a witch, remember? There are certain rites we must perform. May Eve- Beltaine -is one of the holiest nights of the year. Herbs gathered on May Eve are extremely potent. Anyway, I saw them last night in the woods, huddled round a little campfire. I heard one of them telling the story of Una the Banshee who haunts these forests, which is how I had a fair idea they would be frightened by the appearance of a 'Banshee' today. He was talking in Irish. If pushed I'd say it was a Tyr Eoghan accent."

Savage nodded. "Lucky for me some folk still believe in fairies. I want to thank you for saving my life."

Alys turned to look him in the eye. For a second he held her gaze as neither said anything.

"Don't be under any illusions, Richard," Alys finally broke the silence. "My father loved your father like a brother. I did it for his sake, and for no other reason. This changes nothing between us."

"For whatever reason you did it, I'm grateful," Savage said.

Again their gazes locked, perhaps for a few seconds too long. Then Savage looked at the shaggy old horse and smiled.

"By the Good Lord," He said, "Is this Cernach, your father's old war horse? He must be long past retirement age now."

Alys swung herself nimbly into the saddle and looked down at him. "It is Cernach. A woman like me cannot stretch to afford a new horse, so he must serve me as he did my father."

There was a loud meow from the long grass and Alys' large cat ran out from the long grass and leapt up onto its mistress' lap.

"What an extraordinary animal." Savage commented. "I've never seen a cat so tame. It's almost like a dog."

Alys smiled and stoked the cat, which purred and stretched luxuriously. "Lu is very familiar with me."

"You call him Lu?" Savage asked, stretching up to stroke the animal himself. "After Lugh the old pagan Irish Sun God?"

The cat hissed and spat at Savage's approaching hand. A mischievous smile spread across Alys' face that all of a sudden made her look about fourteen years old. "No: After Lucifer. And he does not like anyone but me."

"Should I ride in front then?" Savage said. "The cat can sit behind you."

"You, Sir Richard, will not be riding anywhere." Alys said. "I share Lu's aversion to being close to you and anyway I am going home to my castle. It's about four miles back to Carrickfergus in that direction. You will walk."

Chapter 24

"My Lords, the time has nearly come…"

The Scottish Lords kneeling before the altar of Alloway Kirk were surprised to hear their King's voice interrupting the service. A spear of late afternoon sunshine lanced through the one tall window to light the altar and the squat, powerful figure of King Robert Bruce, who now stood beside it, bathed in the warm russet glow. The priest who had been reciting the liturgy bowed his head and quietly withdrew to stand beside a door in the nave.

They were hearing mass. The tiny little chapel was so small only ten of them could gather there, and that was the way Robert Bruce wanted it. Their knights and men-at-arms all waited in the graveyard outside. Inside, the barons had heard confession and the time had nearly arrived for the Eucharist when the King had suddenly stood up.

"I must depart for the Western Isles." King Robert announced. "It is time that rebellious part of my realm accepted their rightful King. My ships and my army wait for me at Tarbert. We sail in the morning. You, my brother Edward, must return to Ayr and await young Sir John Bysset's return from Ireland to guide your ships across the Moyle sea. This is the last time we shall all be together for a long time. We go to war, so perhaps for some of us this is our last meeting."

The faces before him were grim, determined.

"Now I must lay out my plans." The King continued. "Ulick."

The Chieftain of the Clan Ceannaideach looked up, expectant.

"Yours is the most important mission." Bruce said. "You must take the Holy Treasure to its place of safety on the mountain of the Noquetran. Guard it there with your life."

Ceannaideach's disappointment was obvious on his face. "Sire," he protested, "I want to fight! I want to go to Ireland!"

Bruce laid a hand on the kneeling lord's shoulder. "I know you do, Ulick, but someone must guard the Treasure while the wars are raging. It is the most precious thing we possess, and all our hopes depend on it. I cannot risk it falling into the hands of our enemies so until the battle for Ireland is won, it must remain here in safety and I need my most trusted, most valiant warrior to guard it."

Placated by the King's words, Ceannaideach's back straightened and his chest swelled noticeably with pride. Some of the other Barons hid knowing smiles with bowed heads: Violent maniacs like Ceannaideach had their uses, but the war in Ireland would require strict discipline, obedience to orders and skilled martial arts, something Ceannaideach could easily disrupt and put the whole enterprise at risk.

"Neil and Thomas, I want you to go with my brother to Ireland." Bruce addressed Sir Neil Fleming and Thomas, the Earl of Moray.

Edward Bruce scowled and rose to his feet.

"Robert. I do not need nursemaids."

The King smiled. "Edward I know you do not. We have fought together many times. I know how capable you are, but you go to conquer Ireland. The battles you will have to fight will be hard, so I want my most trusted barons to be at your side. Neil and Thomas have led our troops through our greatest tests. I want them to go with you to Ireland."

Fleming and the Earl nodded their acceptance. Robert Bruce and his brother locked challenging glares for several moments, then Edward finally sighed and nodded too.

Suddenly the door of the chapel opened. All heads turned to see a tall, black haired man in the doorway. His beard was trimmed close and he was wrapped in an expensive woollen cloak. On the right shoulder of the cloak was emblazoned a purple lion, rampant on its hind legs. At the sight of this badge a murmur of disquiet ran through the church. All the Scots stood up, recognising the emblem of the noble Irish family of De Lacy.

Several of the Scots barons' hands fell instinctively to where their swords would have been. This was a church, however, and none of them were armed.

The newcomer smiled, and deliberately placed his hands on his hips, pushing aside his cloak to reveal the broadsword strapped around his waist.

King Robert Bruce was as surprised as his barons by the arrival of the newcomer, but he did his best to appear unruffled.

"Sir Walter de Lacy." The King said. "What brings one of Ireland's most powerful barons to a wee Scottish Kirk? And you come armed into a Church, Sir? Surely you have nothing to fear in a house of God?"

De Lacy laughed. "Oh really? I seem to recall you murdered Red Comyn, the only man who could challenge your right to the throne, while he was praying in Church. I don't intend to let that happen to me."

"What do you want, de Lacy?" Bruce's demeanour of pleasantry dropped from his face like an ill-fitting mask.

"That is a good question, King Robert." Sir Walter De Lacy said. "You and I cannot be said to be on the same side. Indeed I fought against you in the Old King Edward's wars in Scotland. However, I have received an unusual offer from Domnall Ui Neill, King of the Clan Eoghan, of Tyr Eoghan in Ireland. He is no friend of mine either-we've been fighting each other since the day we were born-and yet now he offers me peace and an alliance. He says we have a common cause, and that cause is the one of your brother, Edward, who is proposing himself for the vacant High Kingship of Ireland."

"What do you think of this proposal?" Edward Bruce interjected.

De Lacy smiled again. "Well, it's an interesting offer. Particularly-as you know doubt are well aware-as I am currently caught between Scylla and Charybdis. That damnable Roger Mortimer, Earl of the March, claims my lands in the Ireland. Not content with swyving the English Queen behind King Edward's back, he wants my lands in Meath, and has come to Ireland with his own army that now sits encamped on the Southern borders of my lands. I cannot match his strength, but I have nowhere to go: To the north-east is De Burgh's Ulster, to the north-west Tyr Eoghan. Both are my enemies. Now Domnall Ui Neill tells me that your brother is coming to our Island and that you are looking for local support."

"A baron like you, with castles and knights at his command? We would welcome you with open arms!" Edward Bruce's eyes were eager and bright.

De Lacy held up his hand. "To come over to your side would be a huge step for me to take. I must betray my country, my King, even some of my family."

"You would be well rewarded," King Robert stepped forward. "We need men like you. Name your price."

De Lacy smiled. "Judas wanted thirty pieces of silver for his betrayal. My fee is somewhat larger: I want Ulster. Generations of De Lacys were Earls of Ulster before the damned de Burghs usurped my great-grandfather. If I join you, and you win Ireland, I want Ulster back."

The Bruce brothers exchanged glances.

"Sir Walter, A moment if you please while I consult with my brother." King Robert said and he and Edward Bruce walked behind the altar where they could talk privately.

"We've already promised Ulster to Domnall Ui Neill," hissed the King.

"Ui Neill's gaelic ceithernn troops are all very well but De Lacy can give us armoured knights: Heavy cavalry and crossbows. Without that sort of military might we don't stand a chance of taking Dublin." Edward Bruce whispered. "If he joins us who knows what other Irish Barons will come on side too? We need him Robert."

"What do you want to do?"

"Let us agree to his terms. Let them both think they are going to get Ulster, then we will sort it out when we've won the war. Besides-" Edward winked at his brother "-who knows if they'll both survive the war? If needs be we can make sure one-or both-of them don't."

A wicked grin crept onto Edward Bruce's face, then immediately disappeared as both men returned to join De Lacy at the altar.

"Sir Walter," King Robert held out his hand to de Lacy, "we accept your price. Will you join us?"

De Lacy hesitated. "King Robert. I said this was a big step for me." He stated. "Despite my personal difficulties, before I betray everything I hold dear, I need to be sure of the justness of your cause." For the first time the Irish Lord's confident demeanour seemed to slip and he looked unsure of himself, almost sheepish. "The messenger King Domnall Ui Neill sent to me was accompanied by a knight Hospitaller called Hugo de Montmorency. He said God has shown his support for your cause by delivering into your keeping the most holy of treasures," De Lacy's voice became hoarse.

There was silence in the chapel. All eyes were on De Lacy and the King.

"King Robert," De Lacy continued, "if this is true, it would be the proof I need to convince me that joining your brother's side is the right thing to do. When my great-grandfather lost his lands in Ulster he joined the Crusade against the Cathar heretics in southern France. It was rumoured that the heretics held the very same Holy Treasure in their possession. He fought many battles, killed many men, women, even children in that great struggle. His one aim was to find it and recover the Treasure for the true Faith. He never did. He died a bitter man, terrified his blood-soaked soul would burn in Hell forever for his atrocities. If it is true that this Treasure is indeed real, and that you bear it, then joining your army would be a way for me to atone for his sins. It would prove to me the justice of your cause. How would God allow an un-righteous King to bear this Holy Vessel?"

Both Bruces were surprised to see the glimmer of tears in the eyes of De Lacy.

Robert Bruce stepped forward and laid his hand on De Lacy's shoulder. "Sir Walter, you have come at exactly the right time. Come and kneel with the rest of us, and behold what enfolds."

The King nodded to a priest who was standing beside a door in the nave of the church. The cleric opened the door and as the last rays of the setting sun flooded in, the King, his brother, Sir Walter de Lacy and all the barons fell to their knees.

For a few seconds there was silence, then the ethereal sound of women singing came in through the door. The little cruciform chapel filled with the sweet, heavy smell of incense as a group of six nuns, their white robes pulled over their heads to hide their faces, came through the door and processed towards the altar. It was they who sang the almost angelic air.

Behind them, through the opened door, came a priest bearing a pure gold candlestick that was inlaid with black enamel. A large altar candle glowed on the candlestick.

Next through the door came the priest who had been saying mass. Before him, in both hands, he reverently bore something that was covered in a cloth of pure white heavy silk.

A murmur ran through the nobles and all of them made the sign of the cross.

The procession came to the altar and came to a halt. The priest place the silk-covered object on the top of the altar, then raised the cloth so all in the Chapel could see it. He beckoned to King Robert Bruce who stood up and respectfully approached the altar.

"Behold: The Holy Grail." He said.

Chapter 25

The sea breeze whispered through the grey wispy strands that were all that remained of Edmund le Bottelier's hair. He took a deep, appreciative breath and scanned the view.

It was magnificent.

The Justiciar of Ireland stood on the rooftop of the Carrickfergus castle keep, overlooking the town, the mountains, the shining waters of the lough and the distant misty hills of Holy Wood on the far shore.

Briefly he considered composing a few lines of verse on the scene (a flair for poetry ran in his family) but his contemplation was disturbed by the arrival on the rooftop of the Red Earl of Ulster, Richard de Burgh.

"Ah, de Burgh," Bottelier welcomed him. "Thanks for coming. I thought this would be the best place to meet. We can speak freely up here."

The Earl nodded his agreement. On the rooftop there was nowhere for eavesdropping ears to conceal themselves: No tapestries or curtains, no furniture. No-one could hear their words but the seagulls.

"Richard, I want some honest answers," the Justicier said. "I need you to tell me the truth. This is just between you and me, so tell me what you really know about the plans of Robert Bruce and his brother. I give you my word it will go no further. We've known each other for years. You know you can trust me."

At first, the Earl did not reply, then he said: "Why do you think I would know any more than you?"

"Oh come on de Burgh!" Bottelier responded with anger. "I'm Justiciar of Ireland for God's sake. I'm the highest authority in this island, bar King Edward. Do you think I'm stupid? Do you think I don't have my own spies, telling me what is going on? Your daughter is married to the Scottish King! Half the nobles who owe you allegiance have family ties in Scotland. Are you telling me you know nothing and expect me to believe it?"

"Edmund," The Earl soothed. "I've spent most of the last four years in Connaught trying to stop the bastard Fitzgeralds stealing my lands. What I know about Ulster is rumour and hearsay."

"Richard, if the Scots invade, and they are driven back into the sea, it's going to look very bad for you when the King starts to ask questions in the aftermath," the Justiciar said.

"Edmund," the Earl regarded the Justiciar with a cool gaze, "if the Scots invade and are successful, then it's going to look very bad for your prospects as representative in Ireland of the King of England."

Le Bottelier sighed and looked once more at the view. "Do you think I'm not well aware of that? And right now, Edward Bruce is not the only threat to my position as Justiciar. That damned Roger Mortimer-when not in bed with the King's wife-is poisoning the barons and the Royal court against me, saying I am useless, not in control of the country and rubbish like that. He wants my job and I'm damned if he will get it."

De Burgh scratched his beard. "Interesting," he commented. "Why would Mortimer want to be Justiciar of a land that could fall into the hands of the Scots?"

"He intends to lead the battle against them. To be the hero of the day, then who will oppose him when he shouts to be made King of England?"

"So he is looking out for himself. As we all must in these times,"

The Justiciar tutted and shook his head. "Is this really the Earl of Ulster who forced the Scots to surrender in Edinburgh eight years ago? Now you talk of self-interest, of looking after yourself. What of Honour, Richard? Loyalty?"

The Earl grunted. "Loyalty, Edmund? Who is there to be loyal to these days? You talk about Edinburgh. It was different then. Loyalty to the old King Edward was easy. He was a great soldier, a stern king, and if you stepped out of line you knew about it pretty quick. We were loyal to him but he was also loyal to us: If you were a good soldier he looked after you. If you did him good service he made sure you were not forgotten. But his son? This weakling 'King' Edward? He can't even control his own barons, the very men who are supposed to be there to keep him in power. He flew like a rat from the battlefield at Bannockburn without so much as breaking a lance. He forgets the military service I did for his royal father. It seems these days all you need to be in the royal favour is to be a young man with a pretty face."

Le Bottelier sighed again. "Richard, we are supposed to be loyal to the Crown, not the man who currently wears it. Think of what it represents: Common Law, Justice, Freedom. The Magna Carta. In this world it is those things that are important. They are precious in the midst of all this…."He struggled for the words and waved his hands in general annoyance. "Chaos. Disorder. What sort of a world is it where a man declares himself king, as Robert Bruce has done? Now his brother declares himself king of Ireland. Where will that leave us all? I'll tell you: Driven into the sea. If they win, do you think the Scots will let us stay here? Don't fool yourself. Bruce and his allies will send us to our graves or out of Ireland. There will be no mercy, no forgiveness. This will be a fight to the death for whoever rules this land, Richard."

The Earl was looking out at the horizon, but his gaze was unfixed as if he was staring at something beyond sight. "So once again we fight for Ireland. This Island is like a beautiful, cold hearted woman, Edmund, you know that? The Gaels, the Scots, the Norse, us: Whoever comes here falls in love with her. But she doesn't love them. We all get jealous of whoever else wants her and we end up fighting over her. But she doesn't care. She's like the sort of woman who likes to see men fight over her. She doesn't give a damn if we all kill each other and the last man standing dies of his wounds. This damnable Godforsaken country..." he trailed off, his curse lacking conviction.

Before the Justiciar could reply the noise of clattering hooves and raised voices came from below. Both men looked over the edge of the parapet and saw horsemen arriving in the castle courtyard below. They were muddy and their horses looked tired, thirsty and wind-broken. They had obviously been ridden far and hard. One of the men bore the red cross and black eagle badge of the De Burghs on the shoulder of his cloak.

"That's strange," The Earl frowned. "That's Eamonn Albanach, my Seneschal from down in Connaught. What's he doing up here?"

The men entered the keep below.

"I believe I know what you are up to, Richard." The Justiciar resumed their conversation. "I think you are playing along with both sides, letting both the Scots and the King think you are on their side until you see who is more likely to win. If I'm right, you are playing a dangerous game."

The Earl looked at the Justiciar with undisguised anger. "You think I am some sort of politician?" he growled. "I've always supported the King, but times are different now. This King is far from popular. The Church is against him. Most of his most powerful barons-men like Mortimer-are openly hostile to him and could overthrow him at any moment. He has problems in Wales. His army was devastated by the Scots last year. He's not exactly what you would call a good horse to back. Anyway, who is there worth fighting for in this? All I know is that when this war is over I intend to still rule my lands. Connaught especially. The land down there is rich and beautiful. Ulster is a spider web of alliances, counter alliances, marriages of convenience and constant plotting. If necessary it can go to Hell, but I'm damned if I'll let go of Connaught."

"So there will be war?" The Justiciar smiled. "You know they are coming? Are those killings related to it?"

Before the Earl could answer the door to the rooftop burst open and the Seneschal of Connaught appeared.

"I gave orders that we were not to be disturbed!" De Burgh shouted.

"Sire: I bring grave news that cannot wait." The Seneschal was out of breath and the expression on his face showed he was not jesting. "I've ridden night and day from Connaught. Your lands are under attack. The Fitzgeralds have invaded. They burned Cong Abbey and are besieging your Castle at Ashford."

"The treacherous bastards! They wait 'til I am gone to make their move." The Earl strode to meet the Seneschal and guided him back towards the door. "Tell me everything!" he said.

With that the Earl and the Seneschal of Connaught left the castle roof top.

The Justicier of Ireland returned his gaze to the sea with a care-worn look on his face.

Chapter 26

As it turned out, Savage did not have to walk all the way back to Carrickfergus.

Shortly after Alys plodded off towards Vikingsford on her old warhorse, MacHuylin and several of his galloglaichs burst out of the woods, swords drawn and murder in their eyes. This dissipated at the sight of Savage.

"You're alive? Good man," MacHuylin said. "Any sign of those bastards who ambushed us in the woods?"

Savage told his story.

"So they were Irish?" The galloglaich said. "I don't like that one bit. Clan Eoghan bastards I'll bet. And that witch woman Dame Alys was up here too? Do you think that was co-incidence?"

"She killed one of them." Savage replied. "I doubt she's in league with them."

"All the same, she's trouble that one." MacHuylin said. "I'd stay away from her if I were you. Her and her weird daughter."

The rest of MacHuylin's men emerged from the woods and they all concluded that whoever had been lurking in the trees was now long gone. They re-mounted their horses and rode back to Carrickfergus Castle.

Trotting into the castle courtyard, Savage saw Thomas De Mandeville inspecting a horse in the mouth. Beside him stood two other men, one young and raven haired who had the look of Gaelic nobility and another tall and blond-haired with the same piercing blue eyes as MacHuylin.

At the sight of him, the galloglaich let out a yelp of surprised joy and leapt off his horse. Both men embraced each other in huge bear hugs.

"Aegus! I didn't know you were coming! How are you lad?" MacHuylin said, then turned to Savage who was dismounting at a more careful pace. "This is my cousin Aengus Solmandarson from the Hebrides. Aengus, meet Richard Savage, knight of this shire."

Savage and the Hebridean saluted each other.

"Any friend of Connor's is a friend of mine," Aengus commented in his strange, lilting accent. The family resemblance to MacHuylin was undeniable: The same broad shoulders and blond hair that spoke of their Norse ancestors. Savage remembered the longship he had seen in the harbour on his arrival the day before and reasoned that it must have belonged to this man. The Hebridean galley, a superb warship developed from the Old Viking dragon boats, was another inheritance the peoples of the Western Isles owed their Scandinavian fore-fathers.

"So what brings you to Ireland?" MacHuylin addressed his cousin.

"Aengus has brought news from Scotland. Bad news." The Seneschal said.

"Aye," the Hebridean said. "Robert Bruce is sailing our way with an army. He intends to conquer the isles."

"Any word of what his brother Edward is up to?" Savage asked.

Aengus nodded. "He was still at Ayr yesterday, but from the number of ships and men-at-arms he has gathered round him I doubt he is just there for the meeting of the Scottish Parliament."

"Do you think he will join Robert in raiding the Western Isles?" De Mandeville asked.

Aengus shrugged. "I don't know. Wherever it is they intend to go, they're ready for a fight when they get there."

"The Earl has had bad news too," De Mandeville said. "The FitzGeralds have attacked his lands in Connaught. He leaves first thing in the morning for the south to drive them out."

"Do we go with him?" MacHuylin asked.

De Mandeville shook his head. "The Clan Eoghan would love that. Soon as we're gone they'd be over the border. Then there's Edward Bruce and a few thousand men and ships a stone's throw away on the other side of the Moyle Sea. I don't think it would be a good idea. But we shall talk about this later. I need to hear just what went on in the Friary too. However, right now we need to get ready for the banquet."

"The feast is still on? After all that's happened?" Savage was astounded.

"Why not?" De Mandeville grinned. "The Earl rides to battle in the south in the morning, who knows what we face here in Ulster. We could all be dead soon so we may as well enjoy ourselves while we can."

He patted the glossy flanks of the horse. "Couldn't interest you in a good horse, could I Savage? She's a real beauty."

Savage shook his head. "Hopefully I'll be going back to England soon, so unless she's also a very good swimmer ... " He shrugged.

"Oh well. You've missed a real bargain," De Mandeville said. "Never mind; I think I'll be able to talk MacArtain here into buying her. You take a good look at her Congal." He laid a hand on the shoulder of the black haired Irishman. "Feel free to take her for a ride."

While the English aristocracy took their horse trading very seriously they could not match the sheer passion with which the Irish nobility entered into the activity. It was ingrained in their way of life and Thomas De Mandeville was no exception.

"Now let's go and get washed. The water should be heated by now and I'd like to get into a bath before half the castle has been in it before me," the Seneschal said. They left the Gaelic lord looking at the teeth of the horse and headed towards the castle wash house.

Chapter 27

Peter, the porter of Corainne Castle, watched the approaching horsemen with suspicion.

His mistress, the Dame Alys, had arrived on her worn out old horse a short time before and announced she was going upstairs to prepare the herbs that she had picked. As far as he knew, she was not expecting guests.

He saw the thick smoke rising from the roof of the castle and crossed himself. This meant that his mistress and her daughter were brewing their potions. Peter had served the Logan family since he was a child and it saddened him to see Alys reduced to selling remedies and spells in order to make ends meet and hang on to the castle. He worried about the danger she put her immortal soul in by meddling in those black arts. It was such a shame to involve the little girl in the Devil's work too.

Peter's official title was porter, but the mistress of the crumbling castle could only afford two servants, him and the old woman who cooked, so his role also covered butler, castellan, stable hand, bailiff and any other job that needed doing. He did not mind though: with so few dwellers living in the castle and only one horse, he was not kept very busy. Besides, he was an old man now and the truth was he had no family to look after him or other home to go to. He had served the mistress's father, and now he would serve her until he finally gave up his ghost.

Corainne "castle" was actually little more than a fortified tower. It sat on the end of a long, sickle-shaped promontory that jutted out into the lough of Vikingsford at one end of the natural harbour. It had one four-storey stone tower where Dame Alys and Galiene lived and a courtyard surrounded by a wooden palisade. There was a little wooden lookout tower above the gate, which was where Peter stood watching the approaching horsemen.

They were armed, that much he could tell. He could see the glint of the late afternoon sun on chainmail and weapons, and that was never a good sign. There were thirteen of them. Two were dressed in black with long black cloaks flowing behind them like the wings of ravens. Nine were dressed in leather and chainmail and carried poles, staves and spears, one was very brightly dressed and the last one had a light blue cloak.

Peter reached out and yanked a string that ran up from the little lookout tower to a bell that hung on the wall of the main castle tower. If these men meant trouble, there was little an old codger like him could do to stop them, but at least he could warn the mistress of their coming.

He saw Dame Alys looking out of the top window of the tower and knew she now was alerted, then turned his attention back to the approaching horsemen. As they drew nearer he made out the white, equal-armed crosses on the shoulders of the men in black cloaks. He relaxed slightly. Those men were a knight and a sergeant of the Order of St. John. Knights Hospitaller. Men of God would not be here for mischief.

The man in the blue cloak spurred his horse forwards so he led the troop. Now he was closer Peter recognised who it was and relaxed completely.

"Ach, Sir John, is it yourself?" Peter smiled as John Bysset reined his horse to a halt outside the gates. Sir John had become a regular visitor to the castle lately and Peter and the old cook knew he was wooing their mistress. While he was happy for her-Sir John came from a wealthy family who could give her the comfortable life she deserved-he worried a little about what the future would hold for him. He reckoned that Sir John would not be a very sympathetic master, certainly not the sort who would continue to employee an old servant who could no longer work for his keep.

"By sweet Jesus you've been in a fight, I see," Peter said, seeing Bysset's split lips, bruised cheek, swollen nose and blackened eyes. "Is that from the big tournament in Carrick? I bet you gave as good as you got though!"

Bysset grunted and glared at the old servant from under lowered brows. "Open the gate. We have business with your mistress."

"Certainly sir, certainly." Peter hurried as best his old bones would carry him down the ladder from the lookout tower. His arthritic hands and his withered arms shook as they strained to lift the heavy wooden bar from the gate, then he swung the gate open.

The horsemen entered the courtyard and dismounted.

"Where is your mistress?" demanded a fat man in a tight-fitting yellow and red tunic.

"Who are you, Sir?" Peter asked, not liking the man's haughty tone.

"I, villain, am Sir Johan D'Athy, Constable of Carrickfergus." The fat man was indignant.

John Bysset raised a conciliatory hand, his face took on a friendly smile. "Now, let's not all fall out," he said. "Peter, where is Dame Alys?"

Peter pointed to the tower with the smoke rising from the chimney. "She is in the top room, brewing her potions."

The friendly expression dropped instantly from Bysset's face. "Right. Seize him," he commanded and two of the men-at-arms grabbed Peter, each holding him by one arm.

"What is this?" Old Peter was incensed.

"So we catch your black mistress at her spells, eh?" Hugo Montmorency, the Hospitaller knight, said. "We are here to end her Devil's work and arrest her for the murder of Sir John Talbot earlier today."

"Murder?" Peter was incredulous. "My mistress helps people, she does not murder them!"

"What is going on?"

The sound of a woman's voice made them all turn round. Alys de Logan was looking down from the top window of the tower.

"Don't say a word." Montmorency growled in a low voice to Peter.

"Dear Alys! It's me," Bysset smiled.

"They've come to arrest you mistress! Run!" Peter shouted. He suddenly stopped, his eyes widened and he looked down at the hilt of Montmorency's kidney dagger that now protruded from just below his rib-cage. Dark red blood dribbled out around it onto the ground. With eye-dazzling speed the Hospitaller had drawn the knife and driven it up under the old man's ribs to puncture his heart. With a heavy groan the porter slumped in the arms of his captors, who promptly let go and he fell face first into the mud of the courtyard.

Bysset swore as Dame Alys disappeared from the window.

"Go!" Montmorency commanded the men-at-arms. "Get her. Kill the child."

D'Athy nodded in agreement and waved them in the direction of the tower. The door of Corainne Castle was on the first floor, reached by a wooden ladder and the men-at-arms rushed straight to it.

The ladder forced them into single file and the first one had got about half way up when John Bysset shouted a warning. The man looked up just as a large iron cooking cauldron, still brimming with steaming liquid, came careering down from a third storey window of the tower directly above the ladder.

The man-at-arms did not have time to react as the heavy cooking pot smashed into him, landing on his head and spraying the men behind him with boiling liquid. All three men who had started their ascent of the ladder came tumbling off it. The first man, who had borne the brunt of the pot's impact, collapsed and slithered off to land in the mud where he lay, unmoving.

"Get that bitch away from that window, damn it!" D'Athy screeched. Montmorency signalled to the Hospitaller sergeant, who un-strapped a crossbow from the saddle of his horse. He slipped his foot into the stirrup at the bottom of the weapon and with both hands cranked it into the firing position. Releasing his foot from the stirrup, he raised the crossbow and aimed it at the window from which the cooking pot had come.

"Next time she shows herself, shoot her." Montmorency ordered.

While the Hospitaller covered them, D'Athy's remaining men-at-arms recommenced their ascent of the ladder to the door, this time keeping a cautious eye on the open window above their heads. Nothing more fell from above.

Soon the first man reached the door. He and the second man clambered onto the ledge on which the door sat and forced it open.

The men at arms streamed into the tower. While the sergeant with the crossbow still covered them, Bysset, D'Athy and Montmorency all followed them up the ladder into the tower. Once they were all in the crossbowman lowered his weapon and began climbing up after them. He got half way up when a heavy wooden chair came clattering out the window above to thump into him. The impact of the falling furniture snapped his forearm and swept him off ladder, his crossbow discharging as it tumbled from his grasp. The crossbow quarrel shot straight into the wall of the tower, ricocheted and embedded itself with a soft thump in the body of the prostrate man-at-arms who had been hit by the cauldron. If he was not already dead, he certainly was now.

Montmorency looked out from the door at the carnage behind him and swore. He turned to Bysset. "What can we expect from her now? Will she have any more surprises for us?"

Bysset shrugged. "She's resourceful, I'll give her that. She's obsessed with hanging onto what she sees as her birth right, so I'm not surprised she's putting up a fight. But she's just one woman and she's trapped upstairs now. There's only one way up and down this tower and it's by that spiral staircase over there. Things should be easy from now on."

"What is upstairs?" Montmorency asked.

"There's a sitting room on the next floor," Bysset replied. "What's on the top floor I don't know. She never let me up there. I assume it's her bedroom and some sort of brew house where she concocts her spells."

Montmorency gave a derisory snort. "You mean to say you have been wooing her all this time and not seen her bedroom?"

Bysset glared at the knight Hospitaller. "Coming from a man like you who has vowed celibacy-"

The Constable stepped between the two men. "We have urgent business, gentlemen," he reminded them. "Come. Upstairs. Let us end this nonsense now."

They were standing in a sort of store room area that occupied the first floor of the castle. In the right hand corner was the entrance to the spiral staircase that led to the upper floors of the tower. The men-at-arms rushed towards the stairs with D'Athy following at a discrete distance.

They climbed two turns of the spiral and came to the door leading to the second storey of the tower. The first man-at-arms tried the handle.

"It's locked." He reported.

"She must be in there. Break it down!" shouted D'Athy from further down the staircase.

The first man-at-arms man to reach the door took a step back on the stairway then smashed his shoulder into the door. The wood was rotten and the impacted forced the lock from the wood with a soft crackle. The door sprang open and the man tumbled forward into the room. The next man on the stairway ran in after him, his dagger at the ready.

With the tension in it released, a rope that had been attached to the inside handle of the door freed its hold on a large iron spade that was suspended in the air by another rope. The spade's weight now made it descend to the floor. As it did so, it pulled taut a third rope that tightened across the trigger of an ancient crossbow that was set up, cocked, on a table opposite the door.

The crossbow fired. At such close range the quarrel went clean though the chest of the first man through the door, shattering his heart on the way. The iron bolt exploded from his back and embedded itself in the shoulder of the man behind him, who screeched and dropped his dagger. Momentum carried the first man on across the room even as he died, blood fountaining from the wounds in his chest and back. He collided with the table the crossbow was on and crashed onto it, knocking it over and crashing to the floor where he expired with a final surprized gurgle.

The soldier who had first broken open the door stayed to the floor with both hands over his head. The man with the quarrel in his shoulder writhed on the floor and screamed in agony. Outside on the staircase, the rest of the men-at-arms ducked down.

"What in Hell's name is going on?" demanded John D'Athy. Being round the bend of the staircase he could not see.

"It was a trap," shouted the man-at-arms lying on the floor. "Crossbow set up to fire on anyone coming through the door. Adam is dead. Malachi wounded."

D'Athy turned to glare at Bysset who was behind him on the stairway.

"Did you not know about these tricks?" He demanded.

"Of course not," Bysset hissed. "She never mentioned them to me!"

"Is she there?" D'Athy shouted.

The man lying on the floor cautiously raised his head. All he saw before him was a comfortable sitting room with a big fireplace in the far wall. An embroidery frame with a half-finished tapestry on it sat near the window.

"No sign of her." The man on the floor reported.

"When you said she was resourceful, I didn't think you meant downright dangerous!" Montmorency, who was behind Bysset on the stairs, growled. "Constable D'Athy, I believe the Bible is very clear on this. It states in the book of Exodus that you should suffer not a witch to live."

D'Athy shouted to his men further up the stairway: "She must be on the top floor. Let's not take this bitch alive lads, eh? I hear she is a pretty one too. First man to get her can have her. We'll slit her throat afterwards."

The remaining men-at-arms recommenced their ascent of the stairway with renewed eagerness, pushing each other in the jostle to be first. The narrowness of the stairwell only permitted single-file but the men crowded together so that there was little room between them.

"Wait! One more thing!" Bysset shouted from below. "She told me there is a trip step on the stairway between the second and third floor."

The men-at-arms slowed their pace somewhat as they scanned the stairs above them as they made their way up.

The first man had made it about half way between the two floors when he shouted "Found it!" and pointed at the step three in front to him. Sure enough it was lower than all the other stairs, deliberately made so to catch the foot of anyone unfamiliar with the castle who may be rushing up the stairway in a hurry.

"Lucky you spotted that, mate," the man-at-arms second on the staircase said. "These steps are so steep if you'd tripped on that you might have brought us all down the staircase with you."

"Aye." The first man, pleased with himself, took a big step over the lowered stair, placing his foot on the step above.

There was a cracking sound as the step gave way beneath his weight and collapsed along with the two steps above it. With a cry of surprise the man-at-arms fell through the hole and tumbled down onto his comrades on the turn of the spiral below. One stone stair smashed directly onto the head of the man in front of D'Athy, stoving his head in with a wet crack and spraying the Constable with a sticky mess. The man-at-arms who had stood on the collapsing stair landed on the rest of his colleagues and everyone on the stairway went tumbling backwards. All of them toppled down the stairway, each man's weight knocking over the man behind and sending him tumbling until they all spilled around the corner back into the sitting room on the second floor.

"God's balls!" D'Athy roared as he picked himself up.

"She didn't happen to tell you about a collapsing stair as well?" Montmorency spat in Bysset's direction.

Bysset shook his head meekly.

The remaining uninjured men all got to their feet and began to ascend the stairs again, this time with a lot more caution. Once they had all negotiated the gap where the collapsed stairs had been, they gathered outside a door that lay at the very top of the stairway.

"What do we do?" A man-at-arms asked for guidance. "It could be another trap."

D'Athy nodded and turned to Montmorency and Bysset. "I don't want to lose any more men."

"I think it's time we used our guile," Montmorency said. "She is a woman after all so let's play on her weaknesses. Bysset here is betrothed to her after all." He laid a hand on Bysset's shoulder. "Go and talk to her. Convince her that you are not here to hurt her. I'm sure her affections for you must count for something. While you do that, I'll go and get the crossbow."

Bysset nodded and pushed his way past the men in front until he came to the door.

"Just keep her talking and away from that damned window," Montmorency hissed as he turned and ran back down the spiral stairway, his black cloak billowing behind him.

Bysset tapped hesitantly on the door. "Alys? Alys my love, are you there? It's me, John."

"Oh I'm here alright." Alys de Logan's angry voice came from behind the door. "Don't you 'my love', me! What is the meaning of this? You come here with armed men? I was a fool to ever trust you. You were only after my lands all along!"

Bysset shook his head, a useless gesture given that the door was closed and she could not see him. "No, Alys, it's not like that. The Constable just wants to talk to you about some silly gossip that is going around the town that you are a witch. I've come along to make sure you are alright."

"Talk to me?" Alys was incredulous. "He killed my porter!"

"Yes that was unfortunate," Bysset coaxed, "and I'm sorry about that. I truly am. I will get you another porter. But let's all sit down and talk this through and avoid any more unpleasantness, eh?"

There was silence and Bysset smiled. His charm never failed and he was getting through to her. He slid his dagger out of its sheath and slipped it into his belt at his back, then laid a hand on the door latch.

"I'm going to come in," Bysset said in a calm, re-assuring voice. "That's alright isn't it? There are no unpleasant surprises waiting for me are there?"

"The door is open," Alys responded in a quiet voice.

Bysset carefully pushed the latch and the door opened a crack. The men-at-arms around him moved away from the door. He stood to one side and pushed the door fully open.

Nothing happened.

Bysset looked into the room and saw what looked like a mixture of a bedroom and a kitchen. It was dark and gloomy, the windows letting in little light. There were two beds near the door and there were several tables stacked high with herbs and bottles of liquids. The room was divided by a set of heavy curtains that hung half way down the room. The curtains went right across the room from floor to ceiling and were divided into three. One had been pulled aside to show a large cauldron of steaming liquid sitting on a stone hearth near the chimney at the far end of the room. In another break in the curtains stood Alys de Logan.

"Where is Galiene?" Bysset asked.

"Not here," was the only reply Alys gave.

Bysset looked behind him and saw that Montmorency had returned, now armed with the crossbow of his fallen comrade. The Hospitaller nodded to Bysset and Bysset stepped into the room, his hands spread out before him showing he had no weapons.

"There, you see?" He cooed. "I've not come to hurt you. How could you think that of me? You know I love you."

Alys did not reply. She looked down at her feet and Bysset advanced further into the room. Behind him, Montmorency crept up the stairs and stood out of sight at to one side of the door. Cautiously he peeked around the corner and saw Bysset with his back to him and Alys standing in the gap in the curtains.

"Now!" The Hospitaller shouted. Bysset flung himself to the floor. Montmorency stepped out into the doorway and raised the crossbow. Dame Alys had no time to react before he fired the weapon directly at her chest.

To everyone's surprise, instead of a soft thump followed by a fountain of blood and a scream, there was a loud clang. The crossbow quarrel seemed to be embedded deep in Alys de Logan's breast, but her dress around it appeared oddly distorted and there was no blood.

For a split second, Bysset believed Alys had used her witchcraft to conjure up some sort of invisible shield that had saved her, then he saw her turn away and disappear, leaving the crossbow bolt somehow embedded in mid-air. He leapt to his knees, drew his dagger and tore the curtains aside.

He realised now how they had been tricked. A tall, perfectly flat, highly-polished sheet of metal, its centre now warped and distorted by the crossbow bolt, stood between the gap in the curtains, reaching from floor to ceiling. It was angled so as to reflect the part of the room hidden behind the curtains.

Montmorency had shot the reflection of Alys, not her.

The real Alys had actually been standing beside the big fireplace, hidden from them by the curtain. With a shout of rage Bysset hurled his dagger at her but Alys was already moving too fast for him. She darted to the wide fireplace and grabbed a rope that hung inside it. Without hesitation Alys leapt past the fireplace and into the chimney space behind it, quickly sliding down the rope. In the pitch black of the chimney she kept slipping down, sending up a billowing cloud of soot behind her.

D'Athy's men-at-arms and Montmorency rushed into the room above and they all ran to the fireplace.

The big chimney went right down the tower of the castle, stopping at every floor on the way to open into a fireplace. In seconds Alys had shimmied down the rope to the first floor, where she tumbled out into the storeroom, coughing and wiping the soot from her eyes.

The little girl, Galiene, stood beside the fireplace waiting for her. She too was covered in soot having climbed down the chimney ahead of her mother. She held a lit torch that she had taken from a wall bracket.

Alys quickly got up and grabbed the torch. Returning to the fireplace, she touched the flame to the rope she had descended. It had been carefully soaked in tallow and grease and ignited instantly.

In the room two stories above, Bysset, who had been just about to grab the top end of the rope and give chase, had to let go and spring back as the fire consumed it.

On the first floor, Alys and Galiene ran to the door and slid down the ladder out of the castle. Alys pulled the ladder down behind her.

"After them!" Montmorency shouted and the men-at-arms all turned and began descending the stairs as fast as they could without risking tumbling down the steep, spiralling stairwell. Where the steps had collapsed slowed them further as they negotiated the hole.

In the castle courtyard, Alys ran round whooping and screaming like a mad woman. She slapped the flanks of the horses that had been left un-tethered, waiting their masters' return. The frightened horses panicked. Some reared on their back legs and kicked other steeds, increasing the chaos. Alys pulled open the courtyard gates and the stampeding horses immediately dashed for freedom.

Montmorency and Bysset emerged on the first floor doorway to find the ladder gone, leaving a drop to the ground two and a half times the height of a man. Their were just in time to see their horses fleeing the castle.

Galiene and Alys grabbed the mane of a horse each as they galloped past and pulled themselves up onto their backs. As she rode under the wooden lookout post above the gate, Alys's big cat jumped down off the palisade and settled itself behind her in the saddle.

All the men in the tower could do was watch as Galiene, Alys, the cat and the rest of the horses galloped away.

Bysset swore and impotently kicked at a sack of grain.

"Well I never," John D'Athy shook his head in genuine amazement. "Who would have thought a woman could get the better of a company of men-at-arms?"

Bysset pulled Montmorency aside. "What do we do now?" He hissed.

"Don't start panicking," the Hospitaller growled. "You're worse than the horses. Alright she got away. So what? We've got what we came for: the castle. I doubt she has anywhere to go now anyway. A witch who is wanted for murder? She will be hunted as an outlaw. In the meantime you are now the master of Corainne castle."

Bysset's anxious face relaxed. "Aye, you're right. Alys has no family left. The girl and her lived here by themselves. Who will believe the word of a fugitive witch?"

Montmorency nodded. "D'Athy and I have to return to Carrickfergus. By now the Earl should have heard some rather bad news from Connaught. You get your men down here and start making sure that the harbour and the beach out there are ready to land Edward Bruce and his army."

Chapter 28

As Savage finished washing, Henry De Thrapston arrived at the castle bath house. He had broughtsome fashionable clothes for Savage to wear to the feast.

"My wife assumed you will not have brought any clothes suitable for a banquet," De Thrapston explained, "So I've brought you some more stylish items to choose from. We can't have you coming tonight dressed like you are going hunting.

"I'm not wearing any of those silly short tunics or pointy shoes." Savage grunted, surveying the clothes before him with suspicion.

Reluctantly he selected the longest green velvet tunic that De Thrapston had brought and grey woollen leggings. All of the shoes were simply too ridiculous for him to wear and he pulled his deerskin boots back on. Once he was dressed, De Thrapston accompanied him to the Great Hall for the banquet.

A transformation had occurred since Savage's visit the day before. As soon as the wooden doors were opened, the hall exhaled a breath of warm air. Charcoal blazed in the wide-chimneyed hearth in the west wall and in a brazier in the centre of the hall. Cressets and waxen torches were placed in the wall brackets, while the walls themselves were hung with glorious tapestries that came from as far a-field as Toulouse and Turkestan. Glittering with the brilliance of their embroidery, these seemed to be alive with the scenes of knights and ladies, hunting and jousting depicted on them. Servants had erected trestle tables: A long one across the top of the hall for the most important guests and one down each side of the hall for the rest of the feasters. A rich silk canopy was wafted above the top table. All three tables were covered with clean, white cloth and silver saltcellars, spoons and overlays sat on top of them.

Savage was impressed, and said so.

"Really," De Thrapston shook his head, "A few years away and you forget that Ireland is as civilised as anywhere else. Now," He continued in a serious tone, "The Earl has asked me to apologise to you, but your arrival was somewhat unannounced and the invitations for this banquet were made some time ago. I'm afraid that there isn't enough room for you at the top table. To make room for you someone else would have to be moved, which would cause all sorts of offence- you know how petty people can be. I'm sure you understand."

Savage understood perfectly. Messenger of the King he may be, but here in Ulster he was still Richard Savage, son of a poor knight from the Lough shore and therefore not fit to sit at the top table with the lords and ladies.

"Still, I must introduce you, you know?" De Thrapston continued, bustling Savage towards the top table.

Sumptuously clad barons and ladies, the cream of Ulster society, were settled at the tables chattering noisily while scarcely heeded musicians played in the background. Henry De Thrapston led Savage from one end of the top table to the other, introducing him to each of the nobles in turn.

At the right-hand end of the table, the seats of least importance at the top table, (yet more important than the rest of the seats in the hall) sat William De Sandal and his wife Patricia. They came from a powerful, wealthy family with lands in the north-west, right on the dangerous border between the Earldom of Ulster and the lands of the Clan Eoghan. Their castle, Mount Sandal, guarded a great fortified bridge across the Bann river at Coleraine. Most of their wealth came from the tolls they charged to cross the bridge into and out of the Earldom.

Beside the Sandals sat a lean, hungry faced man in his forties that de Thrapston introduced as Eamonn Albanach, Seneschal of Connaught. He looked desperately tired from his journey and the cup of wine that he cradled in his weary hands looked like it would send him over to sleep.

Next to Albanach was the Senshal of Ulster, Thomas de Mandeville and his wife Elizabeth. Sitting on the Seneschal's left hand side was Congal MacArtain. The MacArtain clan ruled the little kingdom of Iveagh, the Earldom of Ulster's closest neighbour to the south and ally in the on-going war with their common enemy: The Clan Eoghan of Tir Eoghan in the West. The MacArtains had fought for the Earl in the Scottish wars too. Congal was one of the younger sons of the MacArtain royalfamily.

"Did you buy that horse?" Savage asked.

"I did not," MacArtain grinned. "I'd know better than buy one of De Mandeville's nags!"

"Don't you listen to him, Savage. He's just trying to get me to lower the price." The Seneschal laughed.

The Earl sat beside the Seneschal and he greeted Savage courteously, apologising personally for there being no room for him at the high table. Savage was then introduced to the Earl's wife, Margaret. Savage noted that her eyes bore the same flashing glance as her husband's, which was not surprising, considering that both their great, great grandfathers had been the same man.

Next to Margaret sat Edmund le Bottelier, Justiciar of Ireland. "We'll have that talk later tonight, Savage," he said. "I'll send word to you after we eat."

Savage nodded, noting the Justiciar's brusque tone and the worried expression on his face.

Beside him sat the Constable of Carrickfergus, John D'Athy, still dressed in his ridiculous red and yellow tunic. He gave Savage a rather pompous Hallo.

"I'll be wanting a word with you too, Savage," D'Athy said. "I intend to get whoever killed Talbot and I hear you know something about it."

Beside D'Athy was Sir Hugh Bysset, the Lord of Twescard, the north-eastern county of Ulster and his wife Emer. Savage noted there was no sign of Hugh's arrogant young nephew John and silently hoped that it was due to injury from the tournament. Beside Bysset sat Hugo Montmorency, Irish Marshal of the Knights Hospitaller. He was locked in deep conversation with Bysset and barely glanced up to acknowledge Savage's presence.

The final places at the top table were occupied by allies from outside the Earldom. Muircetach and Thomas Ui Cahan were members of the family which controlled the lands to the north-east of the Earldom of Ulster. These two well-dressed noblemen were accompanied by their wives. Deirdre, who was married to Muircetach was disarmingly pretty while Thomas' wife Naimh had the oddest mouthful of teeth Savage had ever seen. The Ui Cahans and the Byssets had connections going back years. Brian MacCartan sat next to Niamh Ui Cahan and nearly at the end of the table sat Alain and Beth FitzWarin. The FitzWarins were another of the major families of the Earldom of Ulster, holding lands in Down and the Ards peninsula.

All-in-all, the top table had a representative of the top rank of Society, all except one very notable exception.

"I see the Archbishop is not here. In fact there don't seem to be any churchmen here except the local priest." Savage pointed out.

De Thrapston looked downcast and a little embarrassed. "The Earl and the Archbishop have fallen out again. They don't get on very well I'm afraid."

Savage nodded. The Earl of Ulster was well known for having a stormy relationship with the Church. Years before, a particularly stormy dispute between the Earl and the Bishop over authority and land rights had almost led to a small war.

"Let's go and take our seats." De Thrapston said, leading Savage towards the table on the left hand side of the hall.

"You're not sitting at the top table?" Savage wondered.

"I thought I'd keep you company during dinner." De Thrapston explained. "We couldn't have you sitting alone

amongst people you don't know, could we? I also have a
reason of my own for wanting to sit down here. We will be
sharing our table with one of the finest troubadours in Ireland.
I'm sure his conversation will be somewhat more interesting
than what they'll be discussing at the top table."

They both took their places on the bench. While the top
table had seats, with all the diners sitting behind the table
facing into the hall, the other two tables simply had long
benches on either side of them for diners to sit on.

De Thrapston proceeded to introduce Savage to his fellow
diners around him at the table. He slapped a hand on Savage's
shoulder.

"Everyone, this is Richard Savage, Emissary of Kind
Edward of England. My wife, Edith, you have already met."

"Madam," Savage said, taking her proffered hand and
bowing to kiss it.

"Please call me Edith." Edith De Thrapston smiled and
blushed to the roots of her hair.

"Sir Roger Blanquet," De Thrapston extended his hand
towards a brown haired knight who looked to be in his early
thirties sitting on the other side of the table. Blanquet nodded
coolly.

"Sir Raymond Jordan." A stocky middle-aged man sitting
beside Edith de Thrapston announced himself. The Jordan
family held lands further along the lough shore from
Carrickfergus. Once they had been one of the more important
of the Ulster families but now had fallen from the favours of
Fortune. Savage saluted him and the timid looking, mousy
woman sitting on the other side of him. She must have been his
wife, but Jordan either forgot or did not bother to introduce
her.

"Knew your father." Raymond Jordan said. "Remember
you as a wee runt of a boy. Bad-tempered little troublemaker
you were. Still: You've gone far."

"And this," de Thrapston said with a flourish towards the man sitting on the other side of Savage, "is none other than Guilleme 'the Rhymer' la Roche, the famous troubadour and poet who has travelled up from Dublin to entertain us tonight after dinner."

"The Rhymer" was dressed in a fine, part-coloured tunic that must have cost a small fortune. His long black hair was combed and straight. His long beard had similarly been combed straight and twisted into two long plaits that hung down to his chest. His face wore a strange little smile and his blue eyes sparkled with a look of what Savage could best describe as mischief.

There was something arrestingly familiar about the man.

"Please to meet you, Sir Richard." The Troubadour said with a tiny, almost imperceptible wink.

Savage smiled and tipped his hand to his forehead in salute as suddenly he recognised the man. His hair was a different colour, his beard clean and tidied and his rags had been replaced by fine robes and a fantastic hat, but it was definitely the mad preacher, Guilleme le Poer, who had earlier given him the encrypted message from the King.

"I look forward to hearing you sing for us." Savage said, "I hope it will not have too religious a theme."

Suddenly a blare of trumpets announced the arrival of the first courses of dinner. These were several fine soups, lavishly seasoned with spices. Servants swept through the hall, depositing large bowls on the tables for diners to ladle out their own portions into smaller wooden dishes. Savage was starving and eagerly tucked in. He had been very partial to spiced food ever since he had been in Cyprus.

"This must all seem rather shabby to you, compared to the grandeur of the Court." Edith de Thrapston commented, gesturing to their surroundings.

"I've no idea," Savage replied. "I never saw the Court. I will say that this castle would match the best in England.

Certainly the last one I was in, anyway. A little smaller maybe. I believe the King's Hall in Westminster is the most grand hall in all of Europe, though."

"Course it is." Jordan stated, as if he knew. "The King is better than everyone else so he has to have the best surroundings. And with a young French wife to keep happy, he has to keep up with all the latest fashions."

"From what I hear," Blanquet, the knight sitting beside Savage, piped in, "the King is not too concerned about keeping his French Queen happy. Not as keen as Lord Mortimer is anyway. The King prefers handsome young men to pretty French maids. "

Raymond Jordan erupted into an ecstasy of bluster. "Don't you start repeating scurrilous rumours here, Blanquet!" He bellowed. "We don't want to hear half-baked lies and rebellious talk, ruining our dinner, especially when we're in the presence of the King's own emissary."

Savage said nothing. He had heard a lot of the same rumours before he had ended up in prison.

"There's not a shred of evidence to support your ridiculous stories." Said the little wife of Raymond Jordan in what must have been the most timid scolding voice Savage had ever heard.

"The Duke of Lancaster, the Earl of Warwick, the very Archbishop of Canturbury, for God's sake, all testify to the fact that King Edward fancies boys, rather than girls." Blanquet said, spooning soup into his mouth.

"Lies!" Raymond Jordan looked positively distraught. "How, Sir, can you say such things about our own Sovereign Lord? And he a married man too! Call yourself a man of honour?" Raymond turned to Savage. "Sir; I must apologise for this man's churlish and treacherous talk."

"You ask him, he would know." Blanquet gestured to Savage, a mischievous grin playing across his lips. His evidently enjoyed baiting Jordan the way some men enjoyed baiting bears. "What about his 'favourite', Piers Gaviston? They were pretty friendly, weren't they?"

"I wouldn't know." Savage said. "I've only worked for the King for a matter of weeks. Before that, I was in prison. I've been in a dungeon for most of the last five years."

Savage quite enjoyed the stunned silence that interrupted the dinner table conversation for a few seconds. Raymond Jordan's wife actually missed her mouth with her spoon and dribbled soup down the front of her dress.

"Piers Gaveston's mother was burnt as a witch." Blanquet finally said, aiming a sideways glance at Savage. "According to Church Law, the offspring of a witch is automatically a sodomite. Therefore King Edward's favourite is a sodomite. Are you arguing with Church Law, Jordan?"

"Gaveston was over here a few years back," Jordan stated. "Came over to help sort out that trouble down in Connaught. Damn fine soldier. Virtually unbeatable at the jousting. Great storyteller. All round good chap."

The next course of dinner arrived. Fish of all types: Grilled, boiled, stewed or baked in bread, all served with deliciously subtle sauces. One thing Ulster was not short of was fish. The Earldom had rich fisheries on the river Bann as well as smaller fishing centres at Holy Wood, Rossglass and Tara in the Ards Peninsula. With the wine and the heady Irish beer the conversation flowed and everyone began to relax.

"You are not a supporter of the King, then, Sir?" Savage addressed Blanquet as he ladled some fish from a serving dish into his own wooden bowl.

The Irish knight smiled. "I reserve the right to criticize those who claim to govern us," Blanquet said. "Especially when they meddle in our affairs and involve us in needless wars that have nothing to do with us. The recent adventures in Gascony and the war against Scotland are good examples of what I mean. "

"It's our duty to support the King in his wars." Jordan said.

"Even if the quarrel is nothing to do with us here in Ireland or worse, could do us harm?" Blanquet asked, his smile now gone. "Look at the Scottish War: half the families in Ulster have Scottish ties, either by blood or marriage. We're torn between loyalties. And do you think Robert Bruce hasn't noticed our aid to the English? You can bet he's going to stop it pretty soon, and when his vengeance comes you know who's going to be first in line, don't you? Us."

"What about your duty to God, Sir?" Jordan insisted. "The King is divinely appointed by God. His will is the Will of God. The Pope excommunicated Robert Bruce. I know whose side I'm on."

Blanquet grunted. "God has other ways of showing his favour. I have heard it said that King Robert Bruce bears the Grail."

"Don't start that nonsense," Jordan growled. "The Grail is a myth."

"What was that?" Savage leaned forward, his eyes fixed on Blanquet. "Bruce has the Grail you say?"

"So I have heard." Blanquet nodded. "God has shown His favour of Bruce's cause by delivering the Holy Grail into his hands."

"Come, come," Henry De Thrapston interjected, wearing a placating smile. "Let's not ruin dinner by arguing religion and politics."

"There's nothing to argue." Jordan stated with a sniff. "I am right and he knows it."

The meal continued, with servants struggling into the hall, laden with venison, poultry, peacocks, boar and various pies.

As the other diners began a lively discussion on the relative merits of the food, Savage leaned closer to the "poet", Guilleme the Rhymer.

"Why exactly are you impersonating a famous troubadour?" He whispered.

Guilleme smiled. "The real Guilleme the Rhymer happens to be a friend of mine. The King gave him twenty marks last Christmas for performing for him in London. Thankfully none of these folk have ever met him though."

"What are you doing here? Isn't it a bit of a risk?"

"It is my job to gather information for the King without being noticed. Feasts like this are an excellent opportunity to hear all sorts of interesting things," 'the Rhymer' whispered, nodding in the direction of Blanquet. "What better disguise at a feast for me than a famous poet from out of town?"

"Well I hope you can sing," Savage commented. "How did you know the Caesar cipher, by the way?"

"You are not the only former Templar in the employ of the King, brother." Guilleme smiled. "I was in the Order's Commandery of Perigord when the arrests began. I escaped. Just made it to the English dominions in Gascony with the Inquisitors hot on my heels."

Their conversation stopped as the end of the meal arrived and Henry de Thrapston stood up to announce that the entertainment would begin. 'Guilleme la Roche' bowed and joined the musicians at the top of the hall.

This should be interesting-Savage thought to himself.

Several other poets joined 'La Roche' and they began to sing. To Savage's surprise, 'La Roche' had an impressive voice. On reflection it would have been stupid for le Poer to disguise himself as a troubadour if he could not in fact sing, but he was so good Savage began to wonder if 'La Roche' was a disguise of Le Poer, or vice-versa.

As the poets sang and he listened to the rich, intricate lines woven by the bards, Savage began to feel for the first time as if he had come home. The Red Earl was a great patron of poets and his Court was always blessed with visits from the best of them. Whether de Burgh's patronage was motivated by a love of their art or to annoy the Church (who wanted them wiped out as remnants of paganism) was a matter of debate.

After so long away, Savage had some problems re-adjusting his ears once more to the subtleties of the Irish language, but he listened enthralled to the rhythms of the words and gleaned the sense of the story. The Irish sang in the same style as the Norse: Each singer singing in a different voice and key that all melded into a beautiful harmony. The poets sang a haunting romantic tale of a warrior and a princess who fell in love, but she was betrothed to theKing who the warrior served.

As the song ended, Savage turned to De Thrapston. "Was Alys de Logan not invited tonight?" he asked.

De Thrapston nodded. "She was. I don't know why she didn't come. John Bysset is not here either. Maybe they had more pressing business. Marriage planning and all that."

General singing soon began around the tables and it was not long before the tables were cleared, taken down and taken out of the hall, while the musicians began playing carols and dancing songs. The minstrels played brass stringed harps and lyres with stunning dexterity. No one could play music like the Irish. Even the English conceded this. The English and Welsh played in a slow, deliberate way. Irish musicians were quick and lively, their fingers dancing over the strings like sunlight sparkling on water. Even with such rapid finger work, the rhythm was maintained with unfailing discipline and despite a thousand embellishments the integrity of the tune was fully preserved throughout the song.

Dancing soon began. Savage was surprised to find himself a bit of a celebrity, with lots of the young and some of the older ladies at the banquet beseeching him to dance with them. While flattered at this, he found himself more than a little abashed. He soon found himself quite out of breath as he rediscovered the wild abandon with which people entered into dancing in Ireland. Soon the whole hall was dancing, with the exception of Montmorency and John D'Athy who seemed to be deep in earnest conversation about something.

After a few dances, the day's exertions in the tournament began to get the better of him and Savage took a seat at the side of the hall. What he needed was some more beer to ease the stiffness of his muscles and the aches from his bruises. A pretty serving girl brought him a draught of cuirm from the Earl's brewery and Savage quickly sunk it, enjoying the feeling of warmth that it spread throughout his body. His face flushed as he watched the dancers twirl and leap before him.

MacHuylin appeared beside him. Sweat was glistening on his forehead from dancing.

"You're not dancing, I see." He commented.

"Too tired." Savage shook his head. "You're doing alright, though. You haven't sat down since the music started. You seem to have quite a harem of admirers."

"A ha-what?" Asked MacHuylin.

"A harem." Savage explained. "It's what Saracen kings call the place where they keep all their wives. I mean that there's a lot of women seem very fond of you."

MacHuylin grinned wickedly and smoothed his droopy moustache. "Ah, well, you can't blame them for that, can you? I'm a good looking man. Have you no lady friends yourself?"

Savage shook his head.

"Oh sorry, I forgot," MacHuylin said. "Your fancy woman isn't here tonight."

"My what?" Savage was confused.

"De Thrapston says you're soft on the witch, Alys de Logan." MacHuylin grinned. "Well rather you than me, my friend. That woman is nothing but trouble. She's already put one husband in the grave."

"I am not soft on her!" Savage was indignant.

At that moment an attractive woman in her early thirties danced up and tugged MacHuylin's arm.

"Come on, Connor," she implored, "come and dance."

"Oh well, duty calls." MacHuylin winked at Savage and swept off to re-join the dance.

Savage took another swig of ale and reasoned that he should really be make better use of his timeby having another talk with 'Guilleme la Roche' or Le Poer .

"More ale, Sir Richard?"

A voice interrupted his thoughts and he looked up to see a beautiful young serving girl with long, braided blond hair and eyes the colour of cornflowers, a brimming jug of ale in her slender arms. Savage was so disarmed by her wide white smile that the most intelligent thing he could think of to reply was "Um ... Yes please."

The young woman obliged. As she carefully re-filled his cup with sparkling golden liquid, she said "His Excellency, the Justiciar sent me over to ask you to meet him outside. On the battlements of the sea wall."

Savage looked round and saw Bottelier was standing at the far end of the hall beside the doors. The Justiciar nodded to him then left the hall.

Savage set down his beer and set off down the hall after him. The whirling dancers impeded his progress but after a few detours he made it to the doors and left the hall also.

Outside, the sun had long set and Savage's sight was swamped by the dark. A chilly breeze-Winter's last breath-gripped him and made him shiver. On his right were the lights from the castle kitchens where the cook was vomiting profusely out the door.

Savage looked around, trying to locate the steps leading to the battlements. To his surprise he saw the Constable, John D'Athy and six men-at-arms approaching from the castle courtyard.

"Just you stop right there, Savage." D'Athy called.

"I'm on my way to meet the Justiciar." Savage stated, noting that the men with D'Athy were all armoured and armed, one with a sword, two with spears, one with an axe and two Flemings had loaded, cocked crossbows.

"You're going nowhere, Savage." D'Athy replied. "I have just been informed that you were involved in Sir John Talbot's murder today. On top of that I also hear that you are a Templar, and therefore a fugitive heretic. You are under arrest."

Chapter 29

"If he moves, shoot him." D'Athy directed the Flemish crossbowmen.

Savage quickly assessed his options and realised he had none. The door of the hall was closed behind him, the courtyard was open and the Flemings were professional mercenaries. If he tried to run he would be shot.

Savage raised his hands to show surrender.

D'Athy grinned. "That's more like it. Your accomplice Dame Alys had less sense. Men: Take him to the tower."

"What do you mean?" Savage said. "What have you done with Alys?"

"Take him to the North tower!" roared D'Athy.

"The Justiciar is waiting to see me." Savage said.

"Do you think I will let you near the Justicar so you can murder him too?" D'Athy said.

"What? This is ridiculous!" Savage shouted.

"Take him to the North Tower." D'Athy repeated. "If he tries shouting for help, kill him. If he tries to run, kill him. He can stay a prisoner in the tower while I go to fetch the Inquisition."

With that, D'Athy stalked off towards the castle gates.

"Come," one of the crossbowmen ordered in his heavy Flemish accent.

Savage sighed and realised he would have to comply. The men-at-arms shepherded him to the stairs that led to the North Tower.

As they jostled him along the battlements, Savage saw the figure of the Justiciar standing on the battlements of the sea wall about sixty yards away, his shape outlined against the sky in the bright moonlight.

"Shhh!" One of the Flemings touched his finger to his lips and raised his crossbow, warning Savage to not try crying out.

They arrived at the door of the tower where Savage had spent the previous night. The door was opened and one of the men-at-arms shoved Savage into the room. The door slammed behind him and the key turned. Tonight there was no question if the room was a prison or not.

Savage swore and swung a futile kick at the locked door. They had not bothered to give him any light and he was glad he was familiar with the room layout from the night before. Moonlight streamed in from the two windows, giving some illumination as Savage stalked around the room once, trying to work out what to do. He walked to the barred seaward window and looked out. The black sea churned below the window, waves crashing against the dark, unseen rocks. Far to his right he could make out the battlements of the sea wall and the figure of the Justiciar still standing there waiting for him to arrive.

"Sire! Over here! In the tower." He shouted.

It was useless: the Justiciar was too far away to hear him over the whooshing rush of the waves.

He sighed and cursed the fact that he was once more a prisoner. What had D'Athy done to Alys? He could not simply sit here and wait for D'Athy's return.

Despite his situation, Savage was able to manage a grim smile. It was a stroke of luck that they had decided to imprison him in the same tower as the night before. Then he had worked out an escape plan, and this was the perfect time to implement it.

He went to the bed and quickly stripped it. All in all there was a coversheet, a blanket and two warm woollen sheets beneath. He twisted each one and tied the opposite corners of one to another until they made a rope, just short of four times the length of a man.

One end of his make-shift rope Savage tied to an iron torch bracket on the wall. He then swept aside the tapestry of King Arthur to reveal the wooden-seated privy. Down the hole and through the sloping gap in the wall he threw the other end of the rope. It would be a tight, very unpleasant squeeze, but he could make it out of the tower by climbing down the latrine to the rocks below.

He wrapped the rope round himself once, then stepped up onto the ledge of the latrine. He raised the wooden seat and placed his right foot down into the hole. Bracing his back against the wall, he placed his left foot into the latrine also and began to shuffle down into the hole.

Fortunately this was an aristocratic privy with a long drop into the sea, and thus was kept well flushed by buckets of water to stop any unpleasant odours seeping back into the room above. All the same, as Savage descended into the green-coated closed funnel of the latrine and the stench of urine became overpowering, he was glad he wore the clothes De Thrapston had lent him and not his own.

It was a tight squeeze. His body filled the shaft completely and his face was mere inches from the disgusting slime that coated the stone walls. To his alarm the shaft also seemed to be narrowing as he descended. The lack of space was making it hard to breath.

Savage pushed himself down a few more feet and he could his feel his feet come free of the bottom of the latrine shaft into fresh air. This would be the tricky part. Once he got out of the latrine shaft there would be nothing but sheer wall descending twenty or so feet. If he was not careful and used the rope to slow his descent he would just plummet to the jagged rocks below, smash himself on them and roll broken and helpless into the sea that licked hungry waves across them.

He raised both arms above him to take a good grip of the rope then shoved his weight downwards, propelling his body into the bottom of the latrine shaft.

He stuck.

To his horror the bottom of the shaft was not wide enough to allow him out. His legs and stomach went through but his chest was squarely lodged in the narrow shaft, suspending him with his bottom half dangling in thin air. To make matters worse, the width of the shaft was like a vice around his chest. He could not breathe in.

Panic gripped Savage. Unable to breathe in, he could not call for help. With his feet hanging in mid-air there was nothing he could get purchase on to push himself back up. He would die stuck at the bottom of this stinking shit hole. Lack of air was already prompting a flurry of black specs to swirl round his vision.

A spark of anger flared within Savage. Of all the indignities he had faced, this was the final straw. There was no way he would let himself die this way. Not if he could do anything about it.

He closed his eyes and tried to think. The answer came to him and he knew there was only one way out. He had to do it quickly or he would pass out. He also knew that if it did not work then he was dead.

It was against all nature. Every instinct in his body demanded he conserve the air that remained in his lungs as long as possible and hang on to each life giving breath. With concentrated effort, however, Savage relaxed his body and deliberately breathed out, expelling the air from his lungs and reducing the circumference of his chest.

It worked.

Savage dropped down through the hole and his body fell into space. By luck his shoulders lodged at the bottom of the shaft and stopped him tumbling straight down onto the rocks below.

Now his chest was free he could breathe deeply again. He sucked in a couple of lungfulls of air, not minding now that it stank of piss and his face was closer than ever to the ordure covered walls of the latrine shaft.

Savage pushed his arms straight above him, taking as strong a grip on the rope as he could while at the same time relaxing his shoulders so that they would fit through the gap at the bottom of the shaft.

In a few seconds he was free of the stinking latrine and hanging from his rope against the exterior wall of the castle. Above him was the tower where he had been prisoner, below him was fifteen or so feet of sheer stone wall and below that a short, steep bank on rough stone rocks against which the sea crashed violently. Even at that height above it, Savage was already getting splashed by spray from the waves breaking on the rocks.

Quickly, he descended down the remaining length of the rope. The last few feet he had to be careful. It was dark and finding a footing on the uneven, slippery rocks tricky. Eventually however he found himself hanging at the end of his rope and his feet were still not on the ground. He just had to let go.

Savage fell a couple of feet then hit the rocks. His left foot hit a solid flat rock but his right landed on a sloping, slippery rock and he fell heavily, cracking his knee off a stone and banging his backside off the wall. He managed to steady himself, just as a wave crashed onto the rocks beneath him and soaked his legs in spray. The constant washing of the waves over the rocks at least meant he was not currently standing in a heap of shit from the latrine above.

It was dark, but a bright, almost full moon bathed everything in its baleful light and sparkled silver across the sea before him. The warmth of the day had gone and a strong wind churned the water into choppy waves. Savage was standing on the rocks of the promontory that the castle was built on. Behind him the sheer walls of the castle towered up into the night. To his right the castle extended out into the sea lough, while far to his left the castle met the shore and the walls of the town of Carrickfergus. In front of him was the sea.

Now he was out of the Castle, all he had to do was get to a ship, then get out of this country and away. There was nothing he could do about the situation and there seemed to be no one who could be trusted. If he stayed here much longer he would end up dead. It was time to look after his own interests and get out of Ireland.

Chapter 30

Alys de Logan shifted uncomfortably in the undergrowth and wished she could get a better view of what was going on in her castle. Galiene crouched, silent, beside her. It was dark now but there seemed to be no let-up in the activity that had started soon after they made her escape in the late afternoon.

At first, she had been surprised they were not pursued. After a frantic ride inland away from the castle as fast as their stolen black horses could carry them, they soon came to realise that no one was chasing them.

Wary of a trick, they continued on at a slower pace, constantly looking over their shoulder but soon became convinced that-even allowing for the time it would take to round up the stampeded horses- no one had bothered to come after them.

If they were not chasing them, what were they up to?

Eventually they slowed to a halt and Alys tried to think what she should do-what she could do. She could ride to Carrickfergus and appeal to the Earl, but the men who had come to arrest her had included John D'Athy, Constable of Carrickfergus. He worked for the Earl. Would she just be riding into a trap?

The memory of John Bysset's smiling face, beckoning to her with one hand, a look of appealing fondness on his face while his other hand reached for his dagger made her clench her fist in anger. How could she have been so blind, so stupid as to let someone like him worm his way into her affections?

It was as she had secretly suspected but never wanted to admit to herself: Bysset had only been after her land. She had been a fool to ever think that a young handsome knight like Bysset would have actually been interested in an impoverished widow like her.

Alys sighed and again considered what to do. Nothing came to mind. She and her daughter were the last of her family. There was no one left who would take them in. While the local people came to her for potions and charms, they still regarded her with suspicion because she was a witch. The townspeople of Carrickfergus avoided her altogether. As a woman on her own, and a witch too, she was outside society.

Over the years she had learned to survive on her own. She took pride in the fact that she had held on to the family castle and lands and managed to scratch a living, however meagre, by using her own talents, knowledge and ability. But now she had lost her home and she had lost everything. The precarious grasp with which she had managed to hold on to the coat tail of society had been ripped away and she was alone.

A single tear welled up in Alys's right eye and trickled down her cheek as she gazed into the middle distance.

"Why are you crying, mother? It was only a castle. At least we are alive."

Alys turned to see her daughter looking at her with her solemn, bright green eyes. She wondered at the strength of the child that could go through such an experience as they just had, but seemed so unperturbed. What she described as 'only a castle' represented her daughter's entire hope for the future. The child knew this, but was able to shrug it off. Her despair was quickly replaced by a deep sense of pride in her daughter, coupled with anger at what had been done to both of them. She quickly dashed the tear away. She wanted her castle back God damn it and by Christ she was going to get it.

The first step would be to get back to Corainne and see just what was going on. What was so important that they needed her out of the way, that they had accused her of murder and witchcraft?

"I don't know why I'm crying, Galiene," she said, "when what I should be doing is seeing just what John Bysset is up to. Come on. Let's go back."

"Are you sad because of Sir John?" Galiene asked.

"A little. But I am more angry that I let him trick me into thinking he liked me."

"I never liked him. He always looked at me in a funny way."

Alys stopped and turned to face her daughter. "You know what?" She said. "I don't think I ever really liked him either. I suppose I was as bad as him. He was only after my land, and I was only after his money. Let that be a lesson to you."

It took them longer to get back than it had to get away. Their escape had been by the most direct route: The track that led inland from the harbour of Vikingsford and up into the woods that separated it from Carrickfergus. Now they were fugitives, Alys decided that the most sensible ploy was to take the smaller paths that shadowed the main track way but were behind the tree line and so out of sight. Most of the paths were too narrow or overgrown to ride at any sort of pace, so they had to dismount and tie their stolen horses to a tree. They could come back and get them when they needed them. The big grey cat leaped down and followed at their heels as they set off on foot through the trees.

It was a good decision. The main road to Vikingsford soon became very busy.

The sound of drumming hooves made them halt and they crouched down behind a large holly bush near the edge of the track. A few moments later, the Constable D'Athy and the Hospitaller Montmorency, having recovered their stampeded horses, galloped past on the main track, full tilt in the direction of Carrickfergus.

Once they were past, Alys and Galiene resumed their journey homeward. Shortly the sound of hooves again interrupted their progress. This time there was much more of them on the road. Again Alys and Galiene ducked under cover and watched a troop of about twenty men-at-arms, all dressed in the livery of the Byssets, thundering down the track way, this time in the direction of Corainne castle.

Twice more before they reached the castle they had to halt their journey as bands of men in various liveries and none galloped past on the main track, all going in the same direction as them. Two open wagons stacked high with wooden stakes, shovels, wood chopping axes, adzes and other tools bounced past, trundling their way to the castle as well.

Finally Alys and Galiene arrived at the edge of the woods. There was nothing now but open groundbetween the tree line and the castle of Corainne. Beyond the castle was Vikingsford lough, a long, narrow natural harbour of the sea surrounded by low hills.

Having run out of cover to hide in, Alys, Galiene and the cat sat down to watch what was going on as the afternoon wore on towards night.

The little castle had become a hive of activity. The men who had passed them on the track were all hard at work. Most of them were on the short rocky beach beside the castle, clearing all the gorse and driftwood into big piles. Were they planning a bonfire? If so, it was a day too late. The Beltaine fires from the night before were now all just smouldering embers.

Another group of men were in the woods near them chopping down trees. These were carried back to the castle where they were worked into sharp topped palisade stakes, planks and logs. A group of men had begun digging trenches along the inland side of the castle. The castle itself seemed to being stripped down of all unnecessary furniture and clutter. As Alys watched she saw her flock of chickens being slaughtered. She winced as soldiers carried the corpse of her faithful old porter Peter out of the castle and dumped it unceremoniously on the dung pile outside. More soldiers pulled down rotten and crumbling parts of the palisade wall that Alys had neither the money nor the manpower to repair and strengthened the gaps with new wood. They dismantled the rickety old platform above the gate. Horses dragged four large trees from the woods and soldiers manoeuvred them up into upright positions in pits on each side of the gate, forming the base of a new, much stronger gate tower. As Alys watched, she realised that what she had originally thought were trenches were defensive ditches. The earth dug out of them was being mounded behind them to form a new earthen outer wall for the Castle.

As the sun set she spotted the sail of a small ship coming up the lough towards the castle. It beached itself in the shallows and Alys saw John Bysset come swaggering out of the castle courtyard. She ached for a bow or crossbow at that moment to cut him down with but she had nothing and just had to watch as he paddled out into the water and hauled himself onto the boat. Sailors on the ship used long poles to shove the vessel back out into the deeper water. Once re-floated, it turned round and sailed off back up the lough, finally disappearing out of the lough mouth into the open sea.

Darkness fell but the work continued. Torches blazed in all rooms of the Castle tower and the big piles of driftwood and gorse were set ablaze, giving light so work on the entrenchments and defences could continue into the night.

At length Alys sighed and stood up. Her castle was now stronger than it had ever been and it was garrisoned with a troop of soldiers. There was very little she would be able to do right now to get it back. She needed to think, to form a plan. She was one lone woman against a knight, his soldiers and the Law. She needed allies but there was no one who would help her.

Alys narrowed her eyes. There was one person who might help, but he had let her down before. Could she put her faith in him now?

Chapter 31

Savage picked his way carefully along the bottom of the castle wall.

If he was to get away, he had to edge his way along the ledge of rock at the bottom of the castle wall until he reached the shore. Extreme caution was required. Green slippery seaweed coated the rocks that at any moment his feet could slide on, sending him tumbling into the sea below. The hungry waves smashed high up the rocks and an especially big one could crash over him and suck him into the sea's freezing black maw.

A movement ahead made Savage pause.

He strained his eyes in the dark. To his surprise, about thirty feet away there were some other people on the rocks at the base of the castle wall like him. The moonlight showed a couple of skin boats had been pulled up onto the rocks and a group of about ten men in heavy cloaks were gathered at the bottom of the wall. What really stunned Savage was that about halfway up the wall was another man, dressed completely in black, who was climbing up the sheer stone wall like a human spider.

He had no idea how he was managing it, as the blocks of the wall were smooth and well pointed, leaving little or no purchase for someone to climb, yet this man was doing it.

The moonlight glittered briefly on steel. The men at the bottom of the wall were armed. Whatever they were up to, it was probably not good.

As he was unarmed, dressed in a tunic and supposed to be escaping from the castle, Savage decided that it would not be prudent to try to go past these men. He would have to go the long way round and climb his way right round the castle to the harbour side. What would make it even trickier was he would have to go round the exposed end of the fortress that jutted furthest out into the sea. The waves there were bound to be bigger and have a higher reach. It was however preferable to trying to get past a bunch of armed men.

He was just about to set off when to his dismay he saw another band of men huddled at the bottom of the wall in the other direction also. This group was much larger than the other, and another black clad man was in the process of a similar seemingly impossible ascent of the sheer castle wall, this time on the seaward wall.

There was only one sort of warrior Savage knew of who could attempt that sort of climb: An Assassin.

Incredible as it seemed, he had suspected since that afternoon when they had found the strange cells at the Friary that there were members of the Saracen Cult of Assassins at work in Ireland.

When a Templar, he had been taught about the various Saracen regiments, warriors and battalions he was likely to face in battle. Savage recalled Gaston, the grizzled old Templar sergeant who delivered the lecture on the Assassins. Gaston had only one arm, the other lost in battle and his iron grey hair hung down over half his face to hide the fact that he had lost an eye as well. He had fought in Acre, Egypt, Cyprus and even the pagan forests of Eastern Europe.

"The Assassins are the one enemy you should fear." Gaston told the ranks of eager young volunteers in his soft West Country burr. "Because they don't fear death. They are trained for murder, and they don't care if they die in their attack. That is the one enemy you can never completely guard yourself from. You can't hide from them either. There is a famous tale the Saracens tell of a Caliph who became an enemy of the Old Man of the Mountains, the Assassins commander. He knew assassins would be sent after him so the Caliph hid himself away in a tall tower, on top of a high cliff.

There was only one narrow pathway up to the tower and one door to the tower and the Caliph knew he could keep it watched at all times so he would see if they came for him. He thought he was safe, but he was a fool. They didn't take the path: They climbed right up that cliff and right up the tower and climbed in the top window. Six died in the climb but the one who made it cut the old Caliph's throat as he lay in his bed. The Old Man of the Mountains teaches the Assassins all sorts of tricks for climbing, and they have special hooks and shoes for it. Can climb anywhere they can. Add to that the fact that they don't care if they die, so they don't care if they fall off, and pretty much any wall, tower or cliff is not a problem for them. No lads, you can't hide from these buggers and you should be scared of them."

"You tell us we should fear them, and we can't hide form them, so what should we do about them then?" Savage had demanded.

"You should kill them." Gaston growled. "Bunch of bloody fanatics they are. It's the only thing you can do with the bastards. Kill them any chance you get."

Now, as he watched the two men scaling the seemingly impossible climb of the castle wall he was sure that they must be members of the sect of Assassins. It was these men who had murdered John Talbot, tried to murder him and had escaped from MacHuylin and him at the friary.

All of them could not be Assassins, though. Otherwise they would all be on their way up the wall together. No doubt the rest of the men huddled at the bottom of the wall were the same Irish troops who had ambushed MacHuylin and him in the woods so the Assassins could escape.

Irishmen he could explain, but what where two Assassins doing in Ireland? He had to admit, this question genuinely intrigued him. Who was their target now?

It must be the Justiciar. Savage thought of le Bottelier standing waiting for him on the seaward battlements while these men sneaked silently into the castle and stuck a knife in his back.

On top of that there was Alys. D'Athy said they had dealt with her in some way. Could she be imprisoned somewhere, awaiting the Inquisition? Or worse? Could he really just leave her again and save his own skin?

In that instant he came to a decision. Even though he had just successfully broken out of the castle, he must now somehow break back in and raise the alarm.

To Hell with D'Athy and whatever he was up to, the Seneschal and the Justiciar were the real law in the land and he would have to trust they would back him against whatever D'Athy's mad claims were. He had to get back into the castle.

His exit route was not available: The end of his makeshift rope of blankets hung too high up for him to reach.

As he watched, the assassin to his left, in the shoreward side, reached the top of the wall and disappeared over the battlements. Seconds later he re-appeared and threw a rope down. Immediately one of the armed men at the base of the wall began scaling it.

It would be risky, but Savage realised his best chance lay with letting them all scale the rope into the castle then hurry past to get to the front gate and re-enter that way. Hopefully they would not have time to kill the Justiciar by then.

One by one, the attackers went up the rope and climbed onto the battlements. To Savage's relief they all went up and left no one behind on guard.

As soon as the last man began his ascent up the rope Savage started picking his way carefully across the slippery rocks towards the shore end of the castle. He got right to the curve of the base of the gate tower before finally running out of footholds. Here the rock fell away into a steep incline that ran down into the sea.

Savage had to lie prone and crawl his way round to the front of the tower as the waves lashed him, threatening at any minute to pull him down into the sea below. Finally he came to the edge of the wall. The castle was separated from the land by a deep ditch dug across the front of the twin towered gate, the only side not surrounded by sea. As the tide was in, the ditch was flooded with seawater but it was also spanned by the lowered Castle drawbridge.

The ditch was too wide to jump but Savage heaved himself off the wall and landed on the side of the drawbridge. On the landward side of the drawbridge, the Justiciar's troop of cavalry were lounging around, forming an armed barrier between the town and the castle in case anyone intended attack. Little did they know the attackers had already outflanked them from the sea.

"You. What the Hell are you up to?" demanded a voice from the gateway as Savage pulled himself to his feet. He looked up to see the gate guard who had challenged him the day before standing in the castle
gateway, his spear again levelled in his direction.

At the same time, a shout of surprise came from above them, on the first floor of the castle gatehouse. Almost immediately the shout changed to a scream of agony that ended abruptly.

They were taking the gatehouse. Savage guessed what their next move was and he knew he had to get inside as fast as possible.

"The castle is under attack!" He shouted at the cavalrymen. "The Justiciar is in danger!"

He did not have time to see if they heard or heeded him as he raced across the drawbridge into the castle gateway, which was a long, narrow passage about fourteen feet deep.

The gate guard, not knowing what was going on but assuming Savage was a threat, lunged at him with his spear. Savage managed to grab the shaft and deflect the blow but the guard followed him and they stood facing each other in the gateway, the guard looking for his chance to stab again.

Above their head came a sudden loud squeaking of wood and metal and Savage dived forward into the entranceway of the castle. Surprised, the gate guard looked up to see the heavy portcullis of the castle, dropping from the roof with a roaring rattle of heavy iron chains.

The portcullis was an emergency gate: In the event of sudden attack it was designed to be released to drop into the Castle entrance and seal it in less than a second. It was made of heavy wood and iron, with large spiked feet to drive into the ground. The gate guard had no time to react before one of them thundered down into him, the massive weight of the portcullis smashing his body into a crumpled bloody mess before he could even scream. Savage, just inside the gate, was sprayed with his blood.

He got to his feet to see beyond the portcullis the Justiciar's cavalry had heard the commotion and were running towards the drawbridge to see what was going on. It was no use though. The dropped portcullis now blocked their entrance to the castle.

The attackers had taken the castle gatehouse, dropped the portcullis and now Savage was sealed inside the castle with them, while all of the Earl and the Justiciar's soldiers were locked outside.

Chapter 32

Edmund le Bottelier stood on the battlements of Carrickfergus castle, looking out at the silver wave-tops, iridescent with moonlight against the black sea. It was a beautiful sight, but he had no desire to stand out in the cold much longer. Where the Hell was Savage?

Below him in the dark shadow of the castle he could make out nothing save the obsidian silhouette of the wall falling away beneath him to merge with the rock and the plumes of blue-white froth thrown up where the cold black sea lashed into it. Looking into the dark waters gave him a strange chill in his stomach and he turned away.

Suddenly an arm slipped round his throat, squeezing his windpipe and cutting off his startled cry.

Strong arms wrenched him around to face away from the sea. Standing before him was a human figure swathed in black. No features could be seen except two glinting eyes that reflected the cold moonlight. The silver light also glittered on the blade of a curved knife, the point of which was aimed at the Justiciar's ribcage.

Le Bottelier knew he was about to die as the arm tensed to punch the blade into his heart. A flicker of annoyance flashed through his brain that he had to go this way, murdered in the dark by persons unknown.

The knife shot forward.

It stopped dead, its point inches from the Justiciar's flesh. A big fist was clamped around the wrist of his assailant, stopping its murderous progress.

Standing behind his assailant, le Bottelier saw the Earl's big galloglaich, Connor MacHuylin who seemed to have appeared from nowhere.

MacHuylin spun the knifeman around and head butted him full in the face. The man gave a startled cry and toppled over. MacHuylin was about to attack again but the man scrambled off the battlements and disappeared into the dark. The man holding le Bottelier threw him to the floor then leapt off the battlements into the courtyard after his companion.

"You all right?" MacHuylin asked.

Shouts came from below and both of them saw Richard Savage pounding across the cobblestones of the outer courtyard.

"We're under attack! They've seized the gate! The Justiciar is in danger!" Savage yelled.

MacHuylin and the Justiciar dashed down the steps from the battlements, the galloglaich bounding recklessly ahead to meet Savage at the bottom. There was no sign of the Justiciar's assailants. They had simply vanished.

"What's going on?" The Justiciar demanded.

"Assassins. They're in the castle." Savage was out of breath and gasping. "Those Tyr Eoghan ceithernn we ran into in the woods today too. They've scaled the walls and taken the gate house. They've dropped the portcullis."

"God damn it! My men are outside." MacHuylin swore, then looked puzzled. "What are 'Assassins' anyway?"

"Saracen fanatics specially trained to murder. I think they're after the Justiciar," Savage said.

Edmund le Bottelier finally caught up, puffing, with MacHuylin.

"Thank God you're alright, Sire," said Savage.

"Thanks to this man here." The Justiciar said, laying a hand on MacHuylin's shoulder. "If he hadn't arrived when he did I'd be a dead man."

"Lucky I had just popped outside for -ahem," the galloglaich coughed and looked awkward, "a moonlight stroll on the battlements when I saw them grab the Justiciar."

Savage suddenly noticed that the little wife of Sir Raymond Jordan was hovering, uncertain and worried near the bottom of the steps. He smiled, realising just what sort of "moonlight stroll" MacHuylin probably had intended. It was certainly not one Sir Raymond would have been happy with.

"They just appeared from nowhere, and then disappeared again like ghosts." MacHuylin commented.

Savage nodded. "They're trained to get in and out of anywhere. Hide in shadows. They've no fear of death either."

"What on earth are Saracens doing here?" The Justiciar said, looking around nervously. "We should get back into the hall. It's well lit and we can defend it 'til my soldiers get the portcullis up. God know who is scurrying around in the dark out here."

"We need weapons." Savage said.

"All weapons will be in the armoury. If I was attacking a castle, that's where I'd go straight after taking the gate." MacHuylin said.

All three men exchanged glances as they realised the implications of what had just been said. All the guests in the great hall would have been disarmed on the way into the feast and their weapons locked in the castle armoury. All the soldiers were locked outside and there were two assassins and at least twenty armed attackers inside the castle. The nobility of the Earldom of Ulster and several surrounding Kingdoms was unarmed and at the mercy of the killers at loose in the castle.

Savage heard a noise and looked up to the battlements. More men were clambering over the top of the battlements into the castle. Moonlight shimmered on iron sword blades.

"How many of them do you think there are?" MacHuylin asked.

Savage shrugged. "Can't be sure. It was dark but I'd say about twenty."

"There's more than that in the hall." MacHuylin said. "They have the swords but we have the numbers. De Thrapston will have the key of the armoury."

"To the banqueting hall," Savage said. MacHuylin grabbed Jordan's wife gently but firmly by the arm and they all dashed across the outer courtyard to the great hall of the castle.

Behind them they heard the clatter of armed men running down the steps from the battlements.

At the hall they burst in through the doors. MacHuylin closed the door over behind them but held it open a crack so he could watch what was going on outside without making a target of himself.

Savage and the Justiciar pushed their way through the dancers to the dais at the top of the hall where the musicians were playing.

"Stop playing." Savage ordered and as puzzled musicians complied, the dancers came to a disappointed halt.

"We are under attack." The Justiciar announced. "Armed men have taken the castle. My troopers are locked outside so we must deal with this ourselves."

General uproar ensued. The Earl strode through the crowd of dancers to the dais, his face a mask of cold rage.

"Who has attacked my castle?" He demanded.

"They don't wear any livery, Sire," Savage said. "But I believe they are from Tyr Eoghan. There are Muslim Assassins with them too."

"What?"

"It's true. They very nearly killed me," The Justiciar said. "Lucky for me that galloglaich of yours, MacHuylin, was out on the battlements at the same time."

"How dare they attack my castle?" The Earl said. "I'll have their heads for this." He swung round and seemed to be scanning the room, looking for someone.

"Where the Hell is Montmorency?" The Earl shouted.

The Hospitaller was nowhere to be seen in the hall.

"He can't help us now." The Justiciar said. "We must get to the armoury and defend ourselves. The portcullis is down so no one will be able to get in to help us."

The Earl nodded, the reality of the situation dawning on him.

Henry de Thrapston and Thomas De Mandeville joined them at the dais. De Thrapston rattled the huge bunch of keys that swung from his belt. "You'll need these," he said.

"Right. All the women stay behind. "The Earl ordered. "All the men follow me. We'll go to the armoury and get our weapons, then I want these bastards cleaned out of my castle. De Thrapston: Leave the key of the hall with my wife Margaret and she can lock the ladies in when we have gone."

The Keeper of the castle nodded.

"Sire, with respect I would prefer it if you and the Justiciar stayed behind in the hall." The Seneschal said. "For your own safety. It's you two they are probably after."

"Stay in here with the women?" The Earl growled. "While there are Tyr Eoghan men running around my castle? What do you take me for?"

"All the same Sire, I would be happier knowing you were safe in here." The Seneschal insisted.

"It's you they're after." Savage said. "It will be easier for us if we can concentrate on getting the castle back without having to look out for you as well."

"He has a point, Richard," the Justiciar nodded enthusiastically. "This is a young man's game: We're past our fighting days now."

"Speak for yourself." The Earl said, then caught sight of Countess Margaret, regarding him with a pleading look. De Burgh gave a heavy sigh. "Alright, I will stay." He said, as he led the way to the door. "There should be some guards around. Where are they?" He wondered aloud as they went.

"I was arrested earlier by the Constable and locked in the north tower." Savage explained. "There were Genoese crossbowmen left on the battlements to guard the tower. They're probably already dead. The Assassins would have killed them as soon as they got over the wall."

The Earl and the Justiciar both tutted and shook their heads. "That bloody fool D'Athy." The Earl said. "What is he playing at? Those mercenaries were expensive. With any luck he's got himself killed too."

"What's going on outside, Connor?" The Seneschal asked when they reached MacHuylin at his vantage point beside the door.

"Not much." The galloglaich said. "About fifteen of them came over the wall and down the steps after us. They must know there's a lot more of us in here because when they saw us going into the hall they stopped and headed through the gate into the inner courtyard."

"The armoury is in there. Next to the keep." De Thrapston said.

De Mandeville looked round and did a quick head count. "There are about forty men here. They may be armed but if we rush them at once we should be able to take them."

There were general nods of agreement but everyone realised that unarmed and un-armoured, some of them would also probably die in the attempt.

Savage saw a light coming from the open doorway of the kitchen near the hall.

"Let's got to the kitchen first." He said. "There'll be knives in there. Meat Cleavers, heavy ladles, pots, stools: grab anything you can find that you can use as a weapon."

"Right," MacHuylin swung open the door. "Go."

The men all piled through the doorway and ran the short distance to the kitchen. Savage hung back momentarily while De Thrapston locked the door of the hall behind them, then they both ran to meet the rest in the kitchen. It was empty except for the cook, who was lying insensible on the ground, face down.

"Is he dead?" The Seneschal wondered.

"Dead drunk, probably" MacHuylin grunted and stepped over the prone figure.

Everyone began ransacking the kitchen: turning over baskets, opening chests and grabbing carving knives, table knives, cleavers and anything that could possibly be used to inflict some damage on the enemy.

When Savage arrived he feared he was too late to get anything of use. Then he spotted the long iron meat spit that hung over the fire. He lifted this from its stand and hefted it in both hands like a spear. MacHuylin grabbed a huge meat cleaver and a small iron cauldron. De Thrapston had a carving knife. De Mandeville lifted two table knives. When the kitchen had been stripped of all dangerous implements, they prepared to make their move towards the armoury.

The band of men ran out of the kitchen and made for the gate in the inner curtain wall. Almost as soon as they were out of the doors there came the dull snap of crossbows shooting and two men screamed and fell, their improvised weapons clattering across the cobblestones.

Savage glanced around and saw figures on the dark battlements, two of them with crossbows. They were reloading.

"Keep going. Make for the gate!" He shouted. They could not afford to lose any more men. They may have started out with more men than the attackers but the odds were already shortening. Once the crossbowmen reloaded, they would become shorter still.

The castle was oyster shaped and built in two concentric circles. Off-centre, like a pearl at the heart of the fortress, was the big square keep that stood as a citadel: the point of final refuge if all the outer defences fell. Around it was wrapped the inner curtain wall. Circling all of this was the newer, much longer outer curtain wall that enclosed the courtyard, stables, great hall, kitchens, garrison quarters and various other buildings and guard towers. Savage and the rest of the men were headed for the armoury, which was within the inner wall. Once through the gate, they would be out of sight of the crossbowmen on the battlements and no longer a target for them.

They arrived at the gate to the inner courtyard without incurring further casualties and poured through. Then they halted.

Arrayed before the doors of the armoury were fifteen armed men. They wore no livery and were armed with a variety of spears, swords and axes. Their bulky shapes betrayed the fact that they had armour on beneath their plain blue tunics. Four of them were trying to break down the locked doors of the armoury.

"Who are you?" The Seneschal demanded. "What do you want?"

In answer, the men-at-arms launched a volley of spears. MacHuylin pushed the Seneschal aside, knocking him to the ground and diving after him as the iron tip of a spear sailed past, cleaving the air where De Mandeville had stood an instant before.

There were more cries of pain as the spears found other targets amongst the tightly packed ranks of the men from the hall.

With a roar the men-at-arms followed up the spear volley with a charge.

A big man came running at Savage, his sword raised above his head for the kill. Like the rest of the attackers, he clearly did not expect Savage or any of the men from the hall to be armed and they came at them without heed to their own defence.

Savage took full advantage and rammed the meat spit into the man's unprotected face. His battle cry was cut short as the point of the spit smashed through his open mouth into his skull, exiting the back of his head and taking his helmet off to bounce across the cobble stones.

Another attacker had a similar nasty shock as he ran into MacHuylin who swung his heavy iron cauldron left-handed in a scything arc that connected with his head, knocking him sideways. The galloglaich followed up with a swipe from the meat cleaver that went into the man's exposed throat. The blade dug deep, almost decapitating the man who collapsed like a scarecrow with the support sticks snapped, blood gushing from the huge wound in his neck.

"Back! Back!" One of the men-at-arms shouted in Irish and the attack stopped. Realising that instead of facing unarmed nobles they were in fact outnumbered by armed opponents, the men-at-arms sprinted off in the direction of the steps up to the battlements.

"Damn them to Hell. It's like fighting with shadows." MacHuylin roared. "Will they not stand still for one minute and fight us like men?"

"It's not us they are after." Savage stated as Henry de Thrapston ran to the armoury door to unlock it. Savage did a quick headcount: They had lost two men to the crossbows, a further three had been taken by the spear volley so that left…twenty?

"There should be more of us." Savage said. "There were forty in the hall, we left the Earl and Justiciar behind, we've lost five but there are only twenty men here."

In disbelief, everyone looked around, each man doing his own headcount.

"Not everyone has followed us out of the hall." MacHuylin said. "Cowards."

"Cowards? I hope so, Connor." The Seneschal said his face grim. "We left the Earl alone back there with them. I hope they aren't traitors."

"We have to go back." Savage said.

"No." De Mandeville said. "It's more important the castle is re-taken. You men arm yourselves and retake the gatehouse. Get the portcullis up and let the Justiciar's troopers in. Get me a sword and shield and I'll go back to the hall on my own and see what's going on. It was me convinced the Earl to stay behind so it should be me who goes back for him."

"Help yourselves, men." De Thrapston announced, swinging open the doors of the castle armoury.

They dropped their kitchen implements and armed themselves with real weapons. With a sword and shield in his hands, Savage felt less naked and he itched to get within striking distance of the enemy. Henry de Thrapston took the big key of the hall off his key ring and handed it to Thomas de Mandeville.

"Good luck." He said.

The Seneschal nodded. "And to you," he said, saluting them all. Then he turned to run back out of the gate into the outer courtyard.

Almost immediately they heard the sound of crossbows firing. After a heart-stopping second there came the clatter of the bolts hitting stone and they knew that they had missed their target.

"What now?" MacHuylin said, turning to Savage.

"The Seneschal is right. We need to get that portcullis raised." Savage said. "What's the best way into the gate tower?"

"There are towers on either of the gate with doors leading to the battlements so we could approach from either side." De Thrapston replied.

"Let's do both." Savage said. "We'll split into three groups: One needs to go after those crossbowmen on the battlements to the North. A couple of men will create a diversion and attack the gate from one side, while the rest of us go in from the other side. Any volunteers?"

"I'll go for the crossbows." MacHuylin announced. "Who's with me?"

William De Sandal, Eamonn Albanach and Congal MacArtain raised their hands.

"Good. Who wants to create the diversion?" Savage asked.

"I will." Raymond Jordan, now wearing an oversized helmet, said.

"And I'll go with him." Roger Blanquet volunteered.

"So will I," De Thrapston said.

"Alright. Get yourselves up onto the north battlements once MacHuylin is up the steps. The rest of us will head for the other battlements on the harbour side wall of the castle." Savage said. "The signal to start the diversion attack will be three slaps of my sword on my shield." He demonstrated, thumping the shield with the flat of his sword. It was a sound that could easily be mistaken for battle noise unless you knew what to listen for.

"Old Templar trick," Savage explained.

Now armed, they gathered at the gate that lead back out into the outer courtyard of the castle.

"When we go out, keep your shields high and make for the stairs to the battlements." MacHuylin said. "The most important thing is to try to spot where the crossbows are and goad them into shooting. When they do, be ready with your shield. Once they shoot, get the Hell up those steps as fast as you can go and get the bastards before they reload."

The men with him all nodded their agreement.

"Right. Let's go."

With that, they all charged back out through the gate, spilling into the outer courtyard of the castle. As he ran with them, Savage hoped for two things: Not to feel the piercing impact of a crossbow bolt and that the Earl and Justiciar were not already dead.

Chapter 33

Back in the banqueting hall, it had not taken long for the Earl and Justiciar to realise something was wrong.

Once De Thrapston turned the key in the door, locking them in with the musicians and the women, they both turned and strode back down the hall towards where the minstrels still sat, looking worried.

From behind several of the tapestries around the walls, men emerged. They had been hiding to avoid going outside with the rest. The Earl recognised Alain FitzWarin, Thomas Ui Cahan, Patrick de Lacy and various kinsmen of theirs, along with a couple of other local knights. All in all, there were ten of them.

"What's the matter FitzWarin?" The Earl said. "Too scared to go out and fight with the rest?"

FitzWarin gave a nasty grin. "That's rich coming from you. Shut your mouth de Burgh. Your time in power here has come to an end."

"Traitor," the Earl hissed, his voice dripping with contempt.

"Traitor?" FitzWarin shook his head. "To who? Not my family, my countrymen. To you, maybe. But then who are you to demand the loyalty of anyone?" He turned to Ui Cahan and said "Get that door open and go and get King Domnall's men and the assassins. We'll keep the Earl and the Justiciar here until you come back."

Ui Cahan nodded and he and three other knights ran to the hall door. They lifted one of the benches on the way and began using it as a battering ram against the stout timbers of the door.

"What are you going to do with us?" The Justiciar demanded.

"I would have thought that was obvious," FitzWarin said. "When the assassins arrive they will kill you. While they are at it we'll help the Tyr Eoghan warriors kill your women."

Most of the women in the hall (except those whose men folk were carrying out the coup) dissolved into frightened screams and huddled together in a clump near the dais on which the musicians sat. One however, did not join them. Countess Margaret de Burgh walked defiantly to the dais and stood between Alain FitzWarin and her husband the Earl. Her grey eyes held FitzWarin in a challenging glare.

"You need assassins to do your dirty work, Alain FitzWarin? You are a coward indeed." The Countess said.

FitzWarin returned her gaze with undisguised contempt. "We are unarmed, your ladyship. Perhaps you would prefer we strangle you and your husband like common criminals?" With that, he swept his hand in a scything arc, the back of it smacking into the Countess's right cheek, dealing her a blow that sent her sprawling sideways onto the floor.

"Bastard!" The Earl shouted and punched FitzWarin in the face, sending him falling backwards in turn.

Patrick de Lacy, a large boned young knight, stepped forward and launched a kick that sent the Earl sprawling onto the dais as FitzWarin rolled back up to his feet.

"Let's kill them now." FitzWarin shouted.

In the outer courtyard, MacHuylin, De Sandal, Eamonn Albanach and Congal McInnis ran towards the steps to the battlements, their shields raised in the hope of warding off the deadly crossbow quarrels. Jordan, Blanquet and De Thrapston ran with them, heading for the same set of steps. Savage and the rest of the men charged to the battlements steps on the opposite wall of the castle.

Within seconds of them emerging from the gate they heard the loud snap of crossbows being loosed. MacHuylin just caught sight of a shadow of movement on the battlements above and raised his shield in that direction. A crossbow quarrel clanged noisily off the metal boss, bucking the shield and sheering away at a right angle. To his left, Henry de Thrapston gave a cry and fell to the ground, clutching with his left hand at the feathered end of the quarrel that now protruded from his right shoulder.

"Now! Run! Before they reload!" MacHuylin shouted and he pounded up the steps to the battlements.

Outside the great hall the Seneschal stood, sword in hand. He saw how the doors bulged outwards with every blow dealt by the men inside. From the way the hinges were straining, Thomas de Mandeville judged that a couple more blows and the doors would give way. Quickly, he pushed the key into the lock and turned it so the door was no longer locked. The door rattled again from a blow from the inside. He waited a couple of seconds, until the men inside would be about to hit the door again, then pulled the latch lever and leapt aside.

The men inside swung the bench with all their might against the door. The unlatched door sprung wide open and they all shot through the doorway and sprawled out onto the courtyard, the four men falling to the ground tangled in the bench.

"What the Hell are you doing?" The Seneschal demanded.

The terrified look on the face of Thomas Ui Cahan as he beheld the Seneschal standing over him brandishing a sword told de Mandeville all he needed to know. Without mercy he chopped down. Ui Cahan raised an arm to protect himself but the sword clove his limb in two half way down the forearm, continued on its way and sliced deep into the prone man's chest. Ui Cahan gave a loud groan as his life blood gushed out onto the cobblestones.

The other three unarmed knights scrambled to get to their feet but before they could all rise de Mandeville had already impaled one of them through the back with his sword blade, making sure he would never rise again. The two who managed to get to their feet fled as fast as they could into the darkness.

De Mandeville rushed into the hall.

Savage and the remaining knights had no problems reaching the far wall of the castle. They quickly scaled the stairs to the battlements and made their way along them until they drew close to the first story doorway into the castle gatehouse. He had a lot of men with him, but the narrowness of the battlements and the door were designed specifically to negate an enemy's advantage in numbers. They were stretched out in single file along the battlements and would have to attack the doorway one at a time. As he neared the door and prepared for the attack, Savage fervently hoped that Jordan and Blanquet's diversionary attack on the far side of the gate tower would be a success.

MacHuylin was onto the first crossbowman while he was still cranking the handle to reload his bow. He had a man with him to protect him and he came at MacHuylin with his spear, intending to skewer the big man through the chest. With surprising dexterity for one so large, MacHuylin sidestepped the attacker so the spear point went into thin air instead of his bowels. He grabbed the spear shaft with one hand and head butted its owner, who staggered backwards off the battlement, stepping into thin air. With a startled cry he tumbled backwards and landed with a crunch on the cobblestones below.

The crossbowman had now managed to load the crossbow but was still raising it to shoot when MacHuylin's sword smashed the weapon from his hands. A second thrust went deep into his stomach and he collapsed onto the battlement ledge.

MacHuylin looked around to see the rest of the attackers disappearing into the darkness at the far end of the battlement, where it joined the north tower.

"Damn it why won't they fight?" the galloglaich roared. His blood was up, his eyes stared from his head and his lips were drawn back from his teeth. He had tasted blood and now all he wanted was more.

Eamonn Albanach laid a steadying hand on MacHuylin's shoulder.

"Come on. We've put them on the run." The Seneschal of Connaught advised. "It's more important we recapture the gatehouse now and get that portcullis open."

MacHuylin nodded and they made their way back down the steps.

Inside the great hall of the castle Thomas de Mandeville saw all the women were huddled at the far end of the room. A group of men were struggling in front of the dais on which the musicians were huddled. Alain FitzWarin had leapt onto the fallen Earl, raining punches down on the man on the ground. The hulking form of Patrick de Lacy loomed toward Countess Elizabeth, a wicked grin on his face as he cracked his knuckles. Behind them stood four other knights.

Without warning, there was a loud, discordant "bong" as one of the musicians stood up and smashed a harp around the back of Patrick de Lacy's head. The big knight staggered forward from the blow as the musician, Guilleme le Poer, grabbed a handful of the brass strings from the destroyed instrument that now were arrayed around de Lacy's head. Within a second they were wound around his neck and le Poer was throttling him. The wire of the strings bit into his hands but he held on grimly as de Lacy struggled and thrashed to get air. Behind him the other four knights closed in.

The Seneschal knew it was time to act and sprinted down the hall. He leapt onto one of the trestle tables that still stood and charged down its length. When he reached its end he jumped off and came on the four knights from above and behind, his sword slashing a vicious blow that carved a red stripe across the backs of two of them. As they screeched with unexpected pain de Mandeville kicked the third one forward onto his face and drove the point of the sword into the back of the fourth. As the man collapsed the Seneschal tugged the blade out of him and rushed onwards.

Alain FitzWarin sat astride the Earl on his chest, both hands locked around de Burgh's throat. Surprised by the sudden screams of his companions, he looked up just in time to see the blood-splattered Seneschal coming at him like an avenging fury.

"No, don't" was all he had time to say before de Mandeville's blade scythed through his neck and FitzWarin's decapitated head bounced across the hall floor.

Out on the opposite battlement to the one on which Savage prepared for the assault on the gatehouse tower, Sir Raymond Jordan and Sir Roger Blanquet waited to begin their diversion. Through the darkness came the clang of a sword being bashed against a shield boss, very deliberately, three times.

"Right" Raymond Jordan said, grasping the hilt of his sword and straightening his helmet. "That's the signal. Let's go."

He turned away from Blanquet to advance towards the gatehouse tower. Suddenly a strong arm snaked like a python around his neck and squeezed, cutting off his air supply. Another strangely scented hand clamped hard over his mouth. Whoever was holding him forced him to turn to face back along the battlements.

Now two figures stood behind him. One was Blanquet and another was a figure swathed in black who seemed to have appeared from nowhere. To Jordan's horror he saw a bright, curved knife, its metal blade glittering in the dark. Before he could react the knife was plunged into his chest, going in below his ribs in two quick stabs. First he felt as if he had been punched hard, then bright crimson pain exploded in his chest as his heart was pierced.

The arm around his neck was withdrawn and quick as a flash the knife slashed Jordan's throat, severing both windpipe and jugular. Hands then grabbed his ankles and heaved his rapidly dying body over the battlements into the maw of the black sea below, which hungrily swallowed him.

The two dark figures on the battlements looked around quickly. Blanquet nodded to them and one of them gave a low whistle. The door at the end of the battlements that lead to the gatehouse opened and men began running out of it towards them.

On the opposite battlements, Savage raised his sword and charged at the door of the gatehouse tower. He reached it in seconds and kicked it open, howling like a demon. Swinging the sword wildly, he plunged through the doorway into the tower, hoping momentum would carry him through. To his surprise his blade met thin air. Once through the doorway he stopped and saw the gatehouse was empty. Then he was nearly knocked off his feet by the rest of the knights who jostled in behind him, all equally amazed to find no one there to resist them.

"Where are they?" Brian MacCartan demanded.

Savage raised his sword and pointed to the opposite door of the tower which lay open. "They've run out that way." He said.

At that second MacHuylin barged his way into the gatehouse to see it was empty.

"Where the Hell were Blanquet and Jordan?" He shouted. "They should have been on the other side of that door."

"Let's see shall we?" Savage replied. "Some of you get the Portcullis up. The rest of you come with us."

As Brian MacCartan and a couple of other men began cranking the lever that inched the heavy portcullis back up laboriously to re-open the Castle gate, Savage, MacHuylin and the rest exited the tower by the opposite door and jogged along the battlements in pursuit of the castle's attackers. Halfway along the battlements outside Savage caught sight of a something at the base of the wall below and stopped.

"There's where one of them went." He said, pointing to the corpse of Raymond Jordan that lay sprawled on the rocks below where the sea had vomited it back up.

They recommenced their way along the battlements, hurrying yet cautious, aware that there was still one crossbowman lurking somewhere in the darkness.

From behind them came the sound of shouting. MacArtain had got the portcullis up enough for the Justiciar's troopers to scramble underneath and they were now pouring into the castle, filling the courtyard below.

"The tide had turned." Savage said. "The castle is ours again."

"Now let's hunt down those dogs down." MacHuylin said.

"Look!" Eamonn Albanach said, pointing upwards.

They followed his gaze and saw figures moving on the roof of the north tower that earlier had been Savage's prison. In the light from the torches in the courtyard below they could see a rope was tied to the flagpole on the castellated roof of the tower. The rope stretched downwards at a slant out of the walls of the castle. Savage followed its line to where it eventually met the sea and a boat that rocked on the waves. In the moonlight he could make out men straining at the boat's oars, pushing the boat away from the castle and keeping the rope taught. Down the length of the rope they could see men climbing down, their arms and legs locked around the rope and their bodies hanging down over the waves as they made their way to the boat.

"They're getting away!" Savage shouted. "How do we get up there?"

"Follow me." MacHuylin said, leading the way down the steps into the outer courtyard. They ran across into the inner courtyard and up onto the seaward battlements, approaching the tower from the opposite side from which Savage had gone in before. On this side the tower had a set of steps leading up from the battlements onto its roof.

By the time they arrived on the rooftop of the north tower none of the attackers remained in the castle. As they looked down they saw the boat that bobbed on the waves below was now jammed full of men. Three were still making their way down the rope. It would not be long until they too made it to the safety of the boat. Everyone in the tower knew that launching boats in the dark to try and catch them was futile. By the time anyone made it to the harbour, made ready a ship and launched they would be long gone.

"They've got away God damn it!" Savage growled.

MacHuylin reached inside his cloak and pulled out the big meat cleaver he had earlier taken from the castle kitchen.

"Not all of them." He said and chopped down on the rope, severing it from the flagpole. The rest of the rope went slack and dropped into the sea. The three men who had been climbing down it fell screaming, arms flailing, into the cold, black water.

Chapter 34

Savage spent what remained of the night asleep on the floor of the great hall. Despite the excitement of the previous day, he was untroubled by nightmares. He was too tired for any sort of dreams. As soon as he lay down and pulled a fur rug over himself, sleep triumphed and he lay oblivious to the noise around him as servants cleaned up the blood and aftermath of the battle.

He did not get the rest he hoped for, however.

Not long after dawn the doors of the hall were flung open and the chill, iron smelling sea air rushed in to bite and annoy exposed ears, noses and toes. Sir Thomas De Mandeville, the Earl, the Justiciar, Connor MacHuylin and Eamonn Albanach strode in. None of them had slept, but neither did any of them show any signs of grogginess. They had spent the night in conference, discussing the attack in the keep.

De Mandeville cleared the remaining detritus of last night's feast from a table and dragged it to the top end of the hall. He meant to make this his centre of operations for the day.

Savage rubbed raw eyes and vainly tried to brush the straw he had been lying in from his hair. For several moments he stared at the roof, wishing he could just roll over and sleep on, but he knew he could not.

The welcome sight of Henry de Thrapston, his arm now bandaged in a sling, entered the hall.

"I'm glad to see you are alright." Savage greeted him.

"Just a scratch, old boy." De Thrapston replied, but his weak smile and pallor, still grey from the pain of the physician's work to extract the crossbow arrow from his shoulder, belied his bravado. "This came for you. A messenger left it at the gate." The Keeper of the castle said, his voice shaky as he held out a roll of parchment with his good arm.

Savage raised an eyebrow and unrolled the letter. Immediately he recognised the jumbled nonsense of a message encrypted using the Caesar cipher. He looked around the hall to see if Guilleme le Poer was still around but there was no sign of him.

"The messenger who delivered this: What did he look like?" Savage asked.

De Thrapston turned the corners of his mouth down. "No idea. It was handed to the gate guard. You know what those fellows are like. The best I could get out of him was that it was a man. And an ugly one at that."

MacHuylin approached them.

"What's this? A love letter from the witch?" The galloglaich asked.

Savage frowned. "I don't know what it is yet. I am worried about Alys though: No one seems to know where she is and D'Athy said they had gone to arrest her yesterday. Any sign of him?"

MacHuylin shook his head. "He'll have disappeared down the nearest rat hole if he has any sense. Last night's events have brought the conspiracy in support of the Scots into the light. The knives are out. The Earl has ordered the arrest of anyone connected with the rebels who turned against him last night and anyone else likely to be involved. Hard questions are going to be asked, and not in a nice way."

Savage nodded. He had no doubt of the brutality that the galloglaich mercenaries would employ in any interrogation when given a free rein.

"He couldn't have arrested her." De Thrapston added. "She's not a prisoner in the castle or in the town prison. As Castellan I have authority over all prisoners of the Earl in either place."

"Maybe you should try her castle down at Vikingsford. They say that's where she brews her spells." MacHuylin said. "Good luck in finding her. Can you come and talk to the Seneschal and the Earl? They have some questions about what we found in the friary yesterday."

Savage accompanied MacHuylin up the hall to the table where Seneschal, the Earl and the Justiciar sat.

"MacHuylin tells me you might know who some of these murderers loose in the Earldom are." The Justiciar sat, arms folded. "Saracens or something? Sounds a bit far-fetched to me."

Savage took a moment to collect his thoughts, then asked "Have you ever heard of the Assassins, or rather the Hashishin?"

"What on earth's that?" MacHuylin screwed up his face in bewilderment.

"Not what: Who." Said Savage. "Hashishin is a Saracen word that means 'eater of hashish'. We call them 'assassins'. Far to the East, high in the mountains of Persia there is a valley. Young Saracen men, fervent in the Naziri branch of the Islamic faith, go on pilgrimage there. It's an awful place; dry as a bone, nothing but stones and dust and nowhere to hide from the scorching, blazing sun that bakes and boils the very brains in your skull. Only the hardiest and toughest make it to the fortress at the end of the valley, the castle of the Old Man of the Mountains. He is the head of the Cult of Assassins and is said to be immeasurably wise and centuries old. Personally, I doubt this. He's more likely to be the latest successor in a long line of Old Men of the Mountains. Anyway, when these pilgrims reach his fortress, the Old Man gives them food and water and reads to them from holy books. The most devout men then have visions of Heaven: A wonderful garden populated by beautiful women."

"How can they?" objected Edmund Bottelier. "The Saracen faith is false. How can heathens have visions of Heaven?"

Savage smiled and held up the pouch he had picked up from the floor of the cell in the infirmary. "That's where this stuff comes in," he said, passing the pouch to MacHuylin. "It's the dried leaves and tender parts of the hemp plant, called Hashish. It's a herb that alters your mind but much, much stronger than beer or wine. It alters the way you perceive things, gives you visions. If you were to eat some now you may well see visions of Heaven yourself, and I'm sure you're no saint."

"It's like the magic mushrooms that the hermit priests eat, then?" MacHuylin commented as he sniffed the herbs inside the pouch.

"Exactly," affirmed Savage. "The food the Old Man gives the pilgrims is laced with this. When they're out of their minds he leads them into a real garden he has within the castle and tells them they're in Heaven. In the middle of that burning desert the garden must seem wonderful and it's full of beautiful women. The would-be assassins of course believe that it actually is Heaven. From then on they become the slaves of the Old Man. They lose all fear of death. What have they to fear when they know for certain that Heaven exists? They have, after all, seen it with their own eyes. They live in the fortress and are trained in the art of murder, all the while being kept well supplied with hashish. They are taught that the way to ensure a permanent place in the heavenly garden is either to be martyred or to kill the enemies of God. The Old Man, either for political or religious purposes or just for plain old fashioned profit, sends these assassins out on murder missions. They're the most feared murderers in the World because they almost always get their target. The killer who does not care if he dies in the attempt is the hardest murderer to guard against."

"And it's all a sham. The visions are false." MacHuylin shook his head.

"The illusions of religion." Savage commented.

The Justiciar frowned at his cynicism. "Perhaps it's just God working in a mysterious way," he suggested. "But why do you think there are assassins are here in Ireland?"

"For a start, that." Savage said, pointing to the bag of hashish. "Then there's the cell in the friary. That woollen rug on the floor is a Muslim prayer mat. The designs on it were Islamic writing. Every day each Muslim must kneel on one of those and pray towards their Holy City. Remember also that the cell were we found this was the only room in the whole place without a crucifix on the wall. The Cross is blasphemous to Saracens because their Holy Book says that Christ did not die on the Cross."

A shiver ran through the assembled men at the heretical thought.

"I saw them climbing up the castle wall last night like spiders." Savage continued. "You saw them yourselves: They appeared and disappeared into the dark like ghosts. The only warriors I know capable of doing that are the assassins."

"Why on earth would Saracens stay with Christian monks though," MacHuylin asked, "and why would Christian friars keep them there?"

Savage shrugged. "That's a very good question. It's something to do with the Scottish invasion, but that makes it even more confusing. Why would Franciscan Friars be helping Robert Bruce? After all, he was excommunicated by the Pope. Something must bind them together. A common cause or an amazing treasure."

"And how did the Saracens get here?" The Seneschal wondered.

"Montmorency," the Earl stated. "He's Knight Marshal of the Hospitallers in Ireland. The Order of St. John has contacts in the East."

"The Hospitallers, like the Templars before them, are sworn enemies of the Assassins," Savage said. "Bruce must possess something very special if he can get members of both to work together."

"Let's start trying to find out, shall we?" The Earl said, clapping a hand on MacHuylin's shoulder. "Connor: I think you should take your galloglaiches out to the friary and bring Abbot Fitzgerald here. There are a few questions he needs to answer."

"Yes, Sir." MacHuylin grinned. Savage could sense the excitement and happiness in the galloglaich. Peace was not something that sat easily on the man. Now there was fighting and the prospect of coming war he could see that MacHuylin was in his element.

"Well I can't stand round here chatting," he said. "Not when I've got monks to harass." Still smiling, MacHuylin strode out of the hall.

The Earl waved a gesture that told Savage he was no longer required and he wandered back down the hall to re-join Henry de Thrapston.

"What about that message you were sent?" De Thrapston asked. "What was it about?"

"It's in code." Savage said. "I need a bit of time to work out what it says."

They sat down at one of the long tables and Savage began deciphering the message de Thrapston had given him. As the Templar cipher had been used again, he assumed le Poer sent it.

After some time, Savage eventually read out what he had decrypted from the message: "Sir Richard Savage: I have discovered the truth behind the murder of John Talbot, the disappearance of Alys de Logan and the coming invasion by Edward Bruce. If you want to know what I know, meet me alone this morning at Saint Nicholas Church, after the bell rings for the hour of Terce. Come alone or you will learn nothing."

Both men were silent moment.

"You're not going to go, are you?" De Thrapston asked. "To me it looks like a trap. You can see it a mile off. You could be going to your death."

Savage nodded. "It does look suspicious, but I have reason to believe I know who sent this message, and I trust them. I will go, but don't worry; I will be under the protection of the Cross." He smiled and patted the cruciform hilt of a dagger that was still strapped to his belt from the night before.

The Justiciar and Eamonn Albanach came striding down the hall and left through the main door that was now hanging at an angle after the battering it had sustained the night before. When they had gone, the Earl barked: "Thomas. Savage. A word in private if you please."

Savage exchanged a glance with the Seneschal who shrugged to show that he too did not know what the Earl intended.

They followed the Earl out of the hall into the cold morning light and up onto the battlements. It was clear the Earl did not want whatever was to be said overheard. He straightened his back and looked them both in the eyes in turn, then his shoulders sagged and he looked away from them towards the sea.

"Gentlemen, I have been a bit of a fool," The Earl stated, much to the surprise of both Savage and de Mandeville.

"I'm getting old and I'd lost sight of what really matters. All I cared about was hanging on to my wealth, my estates," de Burgh continued. "I have to be honest with you. I knew about the Scots' plan to invade Ireland."

De Mandeville visibly stiffened.

"I could not be sure how many of my barons would support the Scots, so I could not tell who was likely to end up victorious. You saw that for yourselves last night: FitzWarin,

De Lacy and Ui Cahan were all on Bruce's side. Who knows who else? I thought I could play along with both sides until it was obvious who was more liable to win."

De Mandeville shook his head in disbelief. "But Sire, we fought the Scots-"

"I know Thomas. I know." The Earl's fierce gaze softened. His voice cracked and it was obviously hard for him to get the words out. "But there is no fool like an old fool. While I thought I was being clever others with more devious minds than me were laying plans to remove me from the chessboard. They include my duplicitous son-in-law, his vicious bastard of a brother, and that snake Montmorency. It appears I am not as important a player in this game as I thought I was. Now I have been out-manoeuvred. Hubris, gentlemen, has been my Achilles heel. They have schemed with the Fitzgeralds to get them to attack my lands in Connaught, and now I have no choice but to go south to defend them, even though I know while I am gone the Scots will begin their invasion of the North."

"Why are you telling us this now?" Savage asked.

"Because I owe this man my life," The Earl replied, his voice hoarse. Humility did not come easily to him. "And I owe you an apology. Last night you had a choice, Thomas, and you chose to come back to the hall alone. You saved me and my wife. The least I can do now is tell you the truth and offer you the choice of what you want to do now. You are the Seneschal of Ulster. It is your duty to defend it from the Scots when they invade but as Seneschal you are my vassal. I will understand if you decide to either join the Scots or leave the Earldom to its fate and come south with me. I will hold neither against you."

"Leave?" De Mandeville spoke through clenched teeth. His eyes glittered with restrained tears. Anger and bitterness churned in his breast. "Where would I go? Where would any of us go?"

Thee Earl shrugged. "England? A man like you would be welcome in the King's army."

De Mandeville grunted. "The Irish call us English, but the English call us Irish. I don't belong there. My family has lived here for two hundred years. This is my home. No. I will stay and I will fight."

The Earl locked eyes with his Seneschal and saw the resolve that gleamed there like cold steel. He also saw the bitterness and anger at the betrayal he had worked on one of his oldest friends. De Burgh nodded.

"Very well." He said, laying his hand on de Mandeville's shoulder. "Then good luck to you. This I promise: If you can hold them, and if God allows me to beat the Fitzgeralds, I will return with the Justiciar and the army and together we'll sweep those Scottish bastards back into the sea."

"We'll do our best, Sire." De Mandeville said, spitting the word 'Sire' through gritted teeth in a way that showed he no longer felt any faith or allegiance towards the holder of the title.

"Good man. Obviously the Justiciar knows nothing of what I've been up to and I'd like to keep it that way. Syr Savage," De Burgh turned to Savage. "I said I owed you an apology."

Savage raised an eyebrow.

"I wanted you dead." The Earl smiled. "But you proved very hard to kill. I thought you would be a nuisance and might let the King know what I was up to. For that, I am now genuinely sorry."

Savage could not help a resigned laugh. "Apology accepted." He said.

"As I can't get rid of you I'd like you to work for me. The pay's decent enough-you can ask MacHuylin. What do you say? Will you do a job for me?" The Earl said.

"Within reason."

"Find that bastard Montmorency and cut his throat."

"With pleasure," Savage replied.

"Good." The Earl smiled. "Now: Let us plan for war."

Chapter 35

The promise of summer's arrival given by the warm sunny weather of May Day proved to be a lie. The morning dissolved into a steady November-like downpour of grey rain.

Richard Savage stood in the shelter of Saint Nicholas' lichgate with his hood up. The rain drizzled and dribbled around the graveyard, somehow seeming to wash the colour out of everything and dulling the distant final clangs of a bell that told the religious that the prayer hour of Terce had arrived.

Savage had arrived early and hidden himself in the alcove of the lichgate, but no one had come or gone from the church. Now the peeling bells attested that the appointed hour had come. Savage took a deep breath, steeled his courage and stepped out into the rain. He quickly crossed the graveyard to the church door.

From the other side of market place, Henry de Thrapston watched anxiously. Savage had ordered him to stay out of sight so as not to arouse the suspicions of whoever sent the invitation for Savage to come alone. With his sword arm in a sling, he would not be much use in a fight anyway.

The door opened easily and Savage took a cautious peep inside. With the grey steel of the rainy sky the church interior was gloomy and, as far as Savage could see, empty. He slipped into the small vestibule and closed the door as softly as possible.

Nothing moved in the church save the silent spiders calmly weaving their webs among the rafters. The only sounds were Savage's breathing and the rain drumming on the roof.

He carefully drew his dagger and held it, concealed but ready, beneath his black cloak. He took another cursory glance around, then flitted quickly up the main aisle towards the altar, moving from the cover of one row of stone pillars to another, watched only by the eyes of the Damned who gazed down forlornly from a big wall painting of the Last Judgement.

In the sanctuary behind the altar screen burned a single, tall candle which was set on the bare stone altar. It's melted wax dribbling down in miniature stalactites. The Sanctuary, the area behind the screen occupied by the altar, was well lit and mercifully free of shadows and niches in which a potential assassin could hide, so Savage slipped through the gap in the rood screen, the carved stone wall that had enough gaps carved in it to allow the poor at the back of the church to catch glimpses of the mystery of the mass.

Laid across the stone altar was a sword, its polished blade gleaming in the candlelight.

This was not especially strange. During the ceremony of making a new knight a sword was placed on the altar as a symbol of what the new member of the Order of Chivalry was expected to use it for: To defend Christianity. A new knight had probably been made that morning. Holidays were always a favourite time for young men to enter the brotherhood of Knights.

Savage ran his fingertips along the blade thoughtfully, pondering the horror of where that ideal had led to: The obscenity of countless hordes of people slaughtering each other in the East in the name of God. The Saracens had charged into battle yelling "Allahu Akbar!"-God is great- and the Crusaders had screamed back "Deus Le Vult!", God wills it.

A noise disturbed his thoughts. It was a strange sort of sound like a half-strangled hiccup. Savage froze, ears straining to catch any noise, eyes swivelling left and right. Trying to spot any movement.

Nothing.

Then the sound came again. This time Savage could tell where it came from: The small chapel in the eastern transept.

He sheathed his dagger and decided to take the sword from the altar; the heftier blade would be of more use in a fight. Carefully he left the sanctuary and crept down the aisle to the crossing of the church, the transept, where aisles led off east and west from the main body of Saint Nicholas' to small private chapels. Savage took a good look around before entering the east transept but could see no one. His nerves were starting to ache with anticipation. The constant watchfulness and expectation of attack was beginning to make him jumpy.

Savage entered the east chapel. In it the gloom intensified, despite it having its own window. There was a small altar and a large golden cross which, by a trick of reflected light from the window, appeared to glow in the dimness.

There was a figure before the cross, kneeling on the floor, head bowed in what appeared to be fervent prayer. Savage now realised what the noise he had heard was. It was being repeated constantly by the kneeling figure, but at a much lower volume.

It was sobbing.

Intrigued, Savage moved closer. Wondering if this was the person he was supposed to meet, but still wary of attack, he gave a slight cough to indicate his presence.

The kneeling figure froze, then turned his head to look at Savage, who saw that it was in fact the parish priest who had presided over Mass the day before. Now, he appeared gaunt, dark eyed, his bald head pale while tears streamed from his eyes.

"What do you want?" He demanded.

"What ails you, father?" Savage inquired. "Why are you crying?"

The priest stood up and approached Savage, a strangely forlorn look on his face. "We have been abandoned." He wailed.

Savage was puzzled. What did this man mean? Saint Nicholas was both a parish church and a pro-cathedral for the diocese of Down and Savage knew the Earl had chased the bishop out of the Earldom in a dispute over land, but surely the priest was not crying about that.

"By who?" He asked.

"By God!" The priest moaned, the wan light of despair in his eyes. There was something more there too. In the dim light Savage saw the gleam of fanaticism and further, he experienced that moment of realisation in which somehow he knew that the man he spoke to possessed a mind unhinged.

He decided to humour him.

"Abandoned by God?" Savage remarked. "That's a bit drastic isn't it?"

"It is true." The priest shook his head. "Because of our sins, because of our hypocrisy, because of our whoreing!"

"How do you know?" Savage asked, wondering if the priest was the one who had sent him the invitation. If so, he knew something and Savage had to find out what, regardless of the man's apparent insanity.

"Because I pray to him," The priest shook his head sadly, "And the only reply is silence. He ignores our pleas. This island is cursed because of the evils of the people -and they know!" Suddenly the fire in the priest's eyes flared again as he seized upon this topic with fervour. "Haven't you wondered why everyone here is so devout in their religion? It's desperation! They carry on their lives hoping God will recognize their cries once more. But he ignores us. He is blind to us now. We are beyond help. We lapse into strife, wars and chaos."

As if in echo of the priest's turmoil a loud rattle of thunder rumbled over the church. Savage started somewhat, but the effect on the priest was more dramatic. He flinched down to a crouching position, eyes wide with terror and pointing finger raised towards the roof.

"There!" He cried. "There is the voice of his anger. He roars his disapproval from the heavens! Ireland has been abandoned by God. Its people are wicked. Its churchmen conspire with heathen killers. Self-seeking greed rages throughout the land. The wolves of misfortune run wild across this country. We have been delivered into the hands of our enemies. The storm approaches. The Lord has let slip the Four Horsemen and their Apocalypse will be visited on the land. War, Famine, Plague and behind them the pale rider on the pale horse: Death! And Hell follows him!" The priest had risen once more to his feet as he approached his ranting crescendo.

"What did you say?" Savage seized the priest by the wrist. "What do you mean about churchmen conspiring with heathen killers? Do you know something about the Franciscans and the Saracen assassins?"

The priest frowned and looked a little confused, then a strange look of surprise came upon his face. Savage was about to press him further when he realised the priest stared not at him, but over his shoulder.

Instinctively he leapt sideways, just in time.

The blade of a knife, meant for his back, cleaved thin air instead. The weapon was propelled by a wiry, swarthy skinned man with thick curly black hair. Savage had been right. The man was a Saracen. An assassin was here in Ireland. It was a trap after all.

Savage now had the problem of staying alive long enough to let anyone else know. He brought his sword up and readied himself for defence. As he did so a second assassin entered the chapel, this one bearing a big curved sword, the deadly Saracen scimitar. His nose was swollen and both his eyes were blackened. This was obviously the assailant MacHuylin had head-butted on the battlements the night before. Both assassins were clad in long, hooded blue cloaks which were wet from the rain. There had been no need to disguise their dark skins in the bandages of lepers today as no one would look twice at anyone swathed in a cloak on a rainy day.

Savage realised he had been outwitted. He had expected someone to be waiting for him in the church, but the assassins had waited until he had entered Saint Nicholas' and was now trapped within. They had crept in after him through the only door in or out. Now he had to fight both of them.

"No!" The mad priest shouted, "You must not kill in the church. You must not shed blood in a Holy Place. I will not allow it!"

With a roar Savage swung the sword at the man with the scimitar. The assassin raised his own weapon to counter the blow and the swords met in a shower of sparks. To Savage's horror his blade snapped in two.

Another trick. The deliberately weakened sword had been left on the altar, design to tempt him topic it up and use it, and like a fool he had. He cursed himself for being so stupid, realising now that he had no time to draw his own dagger before the assassin with the knife struck.

Instead of drawing his weapon Savage smashed his fist into the knife wielding assassin's face then ducked beneath his companion's scimitar. As he did so, he threw himself sideways, ducking out of the side chapel into the transept of the church. The assassins rushed after him, pausing only to shove the priest aside.

Suddenly the door of the church banged open. Henry De Thrapston rushed in. To the astonishment of Savage, he was accompanied by Alys de Logan. Behind her was the dark eyed little girl Galiene.

"Good God!" De Thrapston exclaimed at the sight of the assassins. "You were right, Savage."

The assassins shouted "Allahu Akbar!" and charged up the aisle. The man with the knife went for Savage while the assassin with the scimitar charged ran past him to go for De Thrapston who was desperately trying to unsheathe his dagger.

"Galiene, stay back!" Alys shouted and stepped forward in front of her daughter. Fast as lightening she whipped the throwing knife from its sheath and sent it flying towards the approaching assassin. The assassin was too quick. He raised the blade of the scimitar in a sweeping arc that caught the throwing knife in mid-air. With a loud clang the blade was sent tumbling away from its intended target of the man's neck.

Savage jumped sideways to avoid the other assassin's knife thrust. He dropped to his right knee and swept his left leg around, connecting with the off balance assassin's shins and sending him toppling forwards. Finally with a spare second to draw his own weapon, Savage ripped it from it sheath.

Inside him, a calm voice said that they needed to capture the assassins alive, so they could be questioned, but all he could think of was that the other assassin was about to attack Alys and every second counted. Without further thought he drove the blade of the dagger through the fallen assassin's spine at the base of the neck, separating the bones there, killing him instantly. Old Sergeant Gaston would have been proud.

Fumbling with his left hand, De Thrapston had just managed to get his knife out of its sheath when the other assassin swung the scimitar at him. De Thrapston managed to block the blow but his smaller blade was unable to counter the weight of the sword and he went staggering backwards to fall on his backside. The only person standing between the assassin and escape via the door of the church was now Alys.

"Galiene run!" Alys shouted, deliberately putting herself between the assassin and her daughter. The assassin raised the blade to cut her down. Savage had scrambled to his feet but he knew he could not reach her in time.

The assassin brought the blade down but a howling, screaming creature came from nowhere and latch onto his sword arm, its weight making him miss his intended target of Alys's head.

It was the little girl, Galiene. Her legs locked round the assassin's torso, her fingers tore at the man's hair, his cheeks, his eyes. Her teeth sank deep into his forearm, cutting into the flesh and drawing blood up.

The assassin screamed, as much from surprise as pain. He quickly recovered though and grasped Galiene by the hair. Her strength was no match for his and his drew her teeth out of his arm, then violently tossed her away like a rag. Galiene tumbled before hitting the ground hard, her head giving a loud crack as it met the stone floor.

Enraged by the pain in his arm, the assassin momentarily forgot Alys, his intended victim and stabbed down at the little girl on the ground. The blade of the scimitar entered her flesh just as Savage hit him from behind.

He was running at full speed, bent over. Savage's shoulder connected with the centre of the assassin's back, sending him rocketing forwards. He released the scimitar and sprawled forwards, both hands out in front of him to break his fall. They both landed heavily but Savage's landed on top of the assassin, his weight driving the breath from the others body. Savage was up on his knees behind the assassin instantly. One hand grabbed a handful of the man's hair and pulled back his head, the other wrenched the blade of the knife across his throat.

There was a brief explosion of blood as the assassin's severed arteries spouted his lifeblood up the aisle but in a couple of heartbeats the torrent slowed to a steady gush. Savage let go of his hair and the dead assassin dropped face first into the widening pool of his own blood.

Savage got to his feet. His nostrils were flared, a pitiless snarl curled his lips and his eyes blazed in a cold, baleful glare. De Thrapston, a veteran of several battles, recognised the signs of the killing rage that descends on some warriors in the heat of battle. The Vikings thought these people were special individuals blessed with a divine rage. In reality they were just natural born killers.

A howl of anguish rent the air as Alys ran to the still body of her child. The sound seemed to break Savage's trance and a spark of humanity returned to his eyes. He seemed slightly confused, then ran over to where Alys was kneeling beside the little girl.

Alys moved quickly but purposefully as with expert hands she opened the insensible girl's dress to examine the wound the scimitar had inflicted. She listened to the girl's breathing, then lifted her eyelids to examine the pupils of her eye.

"Is she alright?" Savage asked.

Alys's head dipped and her shoulders seemed to sag. For a second Savage feared the worst, then he realised it was from relief.

"Yes, thank the Lord." Alys said. "She's had a bad knock to the head but I am sure she has just been knocked unconscious. She will come round soon and have a sore head for a few days. The sword wound has only pierced flesh. None of her innards have been hurt. With proper care it will heal." She took out a handkerchief and began to bind the wound.

"She's a very brave little girl." Savage commented. "Quite headstrong too, I'd warrant. She went after him like a leopard, even though you told her to stay behind you. Won't do what she's told and thinks she knows better. Sometimes a good thing." He gave a wry smile and laid a hand on Alys's shoulder. "She takes after her mother, no doubt."

"No." Alys dashed Savage's hand off her shoulder. She rose to her feet and turned to face him. Her face bore an expression that was a strange mixture of anger, defiance and also somehow relief. Tears were streaking down her face.

"Her father. She takes after her father, Richard." Alys said through gritted teeth. "Galiene is your daughter."

Chapter 36

Savage did not know what to do or say. He just looked from Alys to Galiene and back, his mouth open in astonishment.

Alys's shoulders dropped, her mouth turned down and she sobbed loudly, uncontrollably, dissolving into a paroxysm of tears. She leaned her head forward until it rested on Savage's shoulder.

Awkwardly, Savage put his arms round her. He could feel her tears soaking through his shirt as her chest heaved in massive sobs.

"You don't know what it was like Richard." Alys said through her tears. "Trying to hide the truth. Insisting Galiene was ten, not eleven. Bringing her up on my own, trying to hang on to my lands to give her some sort of future. Trying to explain to her why she didn't have a father like everyone else. All the while you were riding about the deserts of the East on some mystical quest."

Her anger returned. She raised her fists and began beating his chest with disconcertingly hard blows. Savage sensed she needed to vent her rage but her blows were hard enough to rock him backwards on his feet and he had to grasp her wrists to stop her. She went limp and collapsed against him again.

"And all the while, all that time, lying to myself." Alys continued. "Telling myself that you were not worth it. Knowing you thought more of some mythical holy relic than me. Telling myself and anyone who would listen that I hoped you got yourself killed but really hoping that one day you would come back. Because I still," She looked up at him, a look of sudden realisation and disbelief on her face, "still, despite it all, against everything in my head that tells me how stupid it is, how stupid I am, I still love you."

Savage was stunned. He looked down into Alys's eyes. Emotions he had not felt for years flooded into his chest and he felt confused, unsure, something seemed to grasp his throat that made it difficult to talk. He suddenly recognised in her eyes what he had been searching for all these years. Something deep inside him realised that he had gone to the ends of the earth in search of meaning, of mystery and something to give reason to his life. In fact those were the very things he had left it behind at home.

"For God's sake kiss her man." De Thrapston said with a weary sigh.

And he did. At first Alys responded fiercely, pressing her lips against his, then after a second or so she pushed herself away from him.

"Galiene," she said, her voice filled with concern as she turned to kneel beside the unconscious child.

"We need to get her to the castle." Savage commented. "The Earl has a good physician." He looked at the bodies of the dead assassins. "It's probably safer there, too." He added.

Suddenly a terrible wail echoed around the church as the priest rushed over to the corpse of one of the assassins and fell to his knees, beating the inert body with despairing fists. Appalled by the scene which had been played before him, he glared in horror at the blasphemous spectacle of spilt of blood in his church.

"You devil!" He shouted at Savage, pointing an accusing finger at him. "You will burn in Hell for what you have done. You have killed in a church."

"They deserved it." Savage said. "What did you want me to do? Turn the other cheek? We'd all be dead. I doubt God would disagree."

"This is blasphemy!" The priest raved. "King Robert Bruce may have murdered Red Comyn at the altar in Dumfries kirk, but God has shown his forgiveness for that deed. You are no Bruce."

Savage suddenly recalled the point his conversation with the priest had reached just before the assassin struck. He strode down the aisle towards the cleric, whose mad eyes still betrayed enough sense to show he realised he had perhaps said something he should not have. He began to back away but Savage grabbed him by the throat with one hand, pushing the point of his dagger into the man's cheek with his other. The blade dug into the flesh but not far enough in to draw blood.

"Steady on, Savage." De Thrapston called from behind.

"What did you say about Bruce?" Savage growled at the priest. "You knew about these Saracens being here, didn't you? Now you talk about Bruce? What is this 'sign' of God's forgiveness?"

Panic flooded into the priest's eyes as he struggled to pull Savage's hand away from his throat. "I don't know what you mean-" he began.

Savage thrust the point of the dagger harder and a little drop of blood welled up from the priest's cheek and ran down the runlet in the centre of the blade. "Surely you don't want me to offend God any further by spilling more blood in your church?" he said.

The priest looked at the dagger point that was an inch below his left eye. "God has delivered the Holy Grail into the hands of King Robert Bruce." He gasped.

"What?" Savage was astonished.

"The Grail. God has shown he favours the cause of Robert Bruce. He has allowed the Grail to fall into the hands of the Scottish King." The priest gasped.

Savage was so astonished he let go of the priest, who fell back and staggered off down the aisle, holding his throat. "The Grail. It is impossible." Savage whispered.

"Mother?" the soft voice of Galiene interrupted his thoughts. The little girl opened her eyes and looked around. "Where are those awful men?" she said.

"Hush Galiene," Alys stroked the little girl's hair. "They are gone. You are hurt."

"Come on. Let's get to the castle." Savage said. "I'll carry her."

He knelt down beside the girl and immediately she flinched away from him. "Get away from me," she squealed. Savage looked at Alys, unsure what to do now.

"Galiene, you are hurt." Alys stated. "We need to get you to the castle where a doctor will treat your wound. You cannot walk as you will bleed. Be a good girl and let this knight carry you. I know he doesn't smell too good but right now we need his help."

The little girl nodded but as Savage picked her up in his arms she continued to glare at him with a mixture of suspicion and hostility.

Alys laid a hand on Savage's shoulder and gave a little mischievous smile. "And when you are feeling a little better," she said to the girl, "Syr Savage has something important to tell you."

Chapter 37

As they made their way back to Carrickfergus castle, Alys recounted what had happened at her own castle the day before.

"I have no one else to turn to, Richard, so I thought of you. We went to the castle looking for you," she said at the conclusion of her tale. "They told me there that you had gone to the church."

"Lucky for me you did." Savage commented. "And if it wasn't for this brave little girl here, we'd both be dead."

He smiled down at Galiene who lay in his arms. The little girl immediately frowned and returned his gaze with one of irritation.

"Just what Bysset is up to down at your castle?" Savage said. "I think I should ride down there and see what's going on as soon as possible."

When they arrived at Carrick castle, the fortress seemed strangely deserted. There were only a few men-at-arms standing around the gatehouse. The courtyard was empty and most of the horses were gone. All the Justiciar's light horse troopers were gone and the fortress was a lot quieter without the associated hub-bub of gathered troops and nobles. It was clear that the Earl and the Justiciar had left Ulster and begun their journeys southward. Without the troops the great fortress seemed somehow naked, vulnerable and unprotected.

Savage passed Galiene to Alys and de Thrapston hurried them off towards the castle keep where he knew he would find the physician. The Earl may have gone, but his northern staff would remain behind to keep his houses running while he was away.

As they walked away the little girl, her face still white from pain, shot a hostile glance at Savage and stuck her tongue out at him.

The outer courtyard of the castle had been turned into a charnel yard. The bodies of the attackers killed in the battle the night before lay unceremoniously dumped on the rain-soaked cobblestones. Half a day after their deaths, they were starting to stiffen and their flesh had turned a ghastly pale colour as the blood settled to the bottom side of the corpses or drained out through their wounds.

Savage and de Thrapston had slung the bodies of the two assassins over the ponies they had ridden to the church on. Savage loosed the rope that tied them to the saddles and let the corpses thump onto the cobblestones of the outer courtyard, adding to the company of the dead already gathered there. As he did so, the clatter of hooves made him turn around.

MacHuylin and his cousin Aengus Solmandarson, flanked by his clan of galloglaich warriors, rode through the castle gate into the courtyard.

"You've been busy." MacHuylin commented, looking down at the bodies.

Savage rolled one of the corpses over with his boot so it lay on its back, showing the galloglaich the dark curly hair and swarthy skin of the man's face. "I was right about the assassins," he said.

MacHuylin regarded the corpse with interest. "So that's a Saracen, is it?" He mused. "You hear all sorts of wild stories: about how they have heads beneath their shoulders, wicked sharp teeth like lions, things like that. But really they just look like us. In fact," he smiled, "with those dark looks, are you sure they aren't Welsh?"

Savage shared his laugh as MacHuylin dismounted.

"Well I'll add one corpse to your two."
The galloglaich said. "The Abbot is dead."

Savage shot a reproachful glance at MacHuylin who held up his hands. "Don't worry, we didn't kill him."

Aengus dismounted and joined them. "Somebody else did that for us." The hebridean said.

The horse behind him bore the body of the abbot. He was lying on his back, arms and legs dangling down either side of the pony. In death he appeared even more gaunt than when alive and his skin was now of an unearthly pale pallor like the belly of a fish. The eyes that had been rimmed with raw red skin the day before now stared vacantly from pink sockets.

"We found him in his cell with his throat slit and he'd been stabbed in the heart." Aengus said as they examined the corpse.

"Just like Talbot," Savage commented. "Another victim of the assassins' knives. At least these two won't be killing anyone else." Savage gestured to the bodies lying on the cobblestones.

"I just hope that's all of them." MacHuylin said. "What on earth were Saracens doing here? How did they get here? Why are they killing people?"

"Good question," Savage said. "What about the rest of the friars?"

"They're all terrified." Aengus replied. "When we arrived they were cowering like frightened rats, wailing that the abbot's death was God's revenge for letting 'strangers' stay amidst them."

"The 'strangers' were these assassins." Savage explained. "The abbot was harbouring them and gave them their own rooms in the friary. Did the monks know anything about these 'strangers' ?"

"They insisted that they were forbidden by the abbot to have anything to do with the strangers housed with them." Aengus replied. "Apparently they were lepers, but they were not kept with the other lepers in the Lazar hospital. The monks suspected that their visitors weren't Christians, though.

They were never seen in the chapel for prayers and never attended the Mass."

"I think that confirms for me that the abbot was providing a safe house for them." Savage said. "The question is: why?"

MacHuylin grunted. "He's a Fitzgerald. Sorry, was a Fitzgerald. The Fitzgeralds have been sworn enemies of the Earl's family ever since his grandfather turfed them out of their lands in Connaught. That abbot's appointment by the Bishop of Armagh to the friary in Carrick is one of the reasons behind the Earl's current dispute with the Church."

"After we called there yesterday, they knew their hideaway at the infirmary was discovered, so the assassins must have decided to cover their tracks," Savage surmised. "They killed the abbot who knew who they were and who they were working with. We can safely assume that the rest of the friars knew nothing, as they claim. Otherwise you would have found a whole monastery full of corpses."

MacHuylin tutted. "Bloody heathen savages. These Saracens are barbarians."

His sentiment which was echoed by various nods, headshaking and "Ayes" among the rest of the galloglaich company.

"Actually, they look on us as barbarians," Savage said. "Their knowledge in medicine, geometry, geography, astronomy, arithmetic and natural philosophy far outstrips the most learned men in Christendom."

Surprised eyes fixed on from all around.

At that moment Henry de Thrapston returned from the keep. He was now accompanied by the Seneschal and Congal MacArtain. The three men strode across the courtyard to join the others.

De Mandeville viewed the various dead bodies and shook his head. "Well this is a right shambles," he commented.

Savage and MacHuylin gave their accounts of what had occurred that morning.

"I thought you said you trusted the person who sent you the message to come to the church?" De Thrapston asked.

"I thought I did." Savage replied. "It was encoded in a Templar cipher. The only person I know who would know how to use that is…." He trailed off, a memory of Hugo Montmorency in a white robe, its shoulder emblazoned with a red, equal-armed cross resurfaced in his mind and he swore quietly as realisation dawned on him. "Montmorency. It wasn't who I thought sent that message: It was Montmorency. He was a Templar before he betrayed us and joined the Knights of Saint John. He must be in league with these assassins."

"He seems to make a habit of betrayal," commented the Seneschal. "He's sold the rest of us down the river too. He's been working to lay the way for the Scots to invade us all along. And he's not alone. God knows how many of our friends and cousins here in Ulster are part of this damned conspiracy."

"Syr Thomas," Savage addressed the Seneschal, "We know the Scots are coming. Send out messengers, gather the feudal army here and prepare for defence. This invasion is immanent."

The Seneschal nodded grimly. "I agree, but you must realise Syr Richard, we need to be damn sure when and where a threat to us from Scotland will arrive before we move troops to meet an invasion. All our strength is directed westwards, towards our enemies in Tyr Eoghan. They'll seize upon any weakness of our borders and before you know it Ui Neill will come pouring across the Bann while our army has its back to him waiting for the Scots."

MacHuylin pointed at the corpses from the previous night's fighting lying across the courtyard. "If you ask me," he said, "Ui Neill is already here. Those are Tyr Eoghan warriors."

De Mandeville was silent for a moment. He scratched his close-cropped grey hair. All the men could see the strain on his face as he frowned, trying to work out what was the best thing to do. Finally he sighed and looked up at the clouds above as new drops of rain began plopping down from the sky.

"Right," The Seneschal finally spoke. "Gentlemen: we are now at war. Connor I need your galloglaiches to ride to the forts around the Earldom and tell them to prepare for battle. I want men up on the headland above the Rinn Seimhne peninsula at the head of Carrickfergus lough. It's only 12 miles to the Scottish coast from there and they can keep watch on anything crossing the sea. I will draft more detailed orders and muster the Bonnaught of Ulster. I'll send riders to tell the knights and lords of Earldom to muster at Carrickfergus with all the troops they can raise. The army will gather here. Anyone who does not come will be assumed to be a traitor. Henry?"

"Yes, Sire?" De Thrapston, the Keeper of Carrickfergus Castle answered straight away.

"How well provisioned is this castle?" De Mandeville demanded.

"I supervised the stocking of provisions yesterday," De Thrapston replied. "But I'm still re-stocking after the May Day feasting. I'm waiting for thirty crannocks of wheat to arrive from Dublin."

"Make sure it does arrive," the Seneschal pressed. "Send messengers after it -damn the expense. A castle is no use if there's no food in it."

The chilling portent of his words was not lost on any of them. If the Scots overran the army the castle would have to rely on its own strength. The garrison would endure the awful conditions of siege warfare.

"I'll do that," the Keeper of the Castle said, but as he did so he shot a wary glance towards the rain sodden sky. "Wheat is expense these days though. There was a bad harvest last year and if we have another wet summer famine will come."

"Syr, I think I should go down to Corainne and see what Bysset is up to at Dame Alys's castle." Savage said. "I believe it must have something to do with the Scottish conspiracy."

"Go." De Mandeville agreed. "But come straight back here once you see what is going on. I can't spare any men to go with you, though."

"I'll go with him." MacHuylin said. "He'll need someone to help if there's any trouble."

"Aye, right," Savage smiled. "Like in the forest yesterday when you left me to my death? Some help you were."

"I'll go with you too." Congal MacArtain announced. Savage and MacHuylin raised curious eyebrows.

The young prince shrugged. "I want to do something to help," he said. "There's nothing for me to do but wait for the army to gather and my father to march our clan north. Anything is better than hanging around here."

"Alright," Savage said. "We'll leave as soon as I check if Alys and Galiene are all right." He started to walk towards the inner courtyard and the castle's keep.

MacHuylin frowned. "What is it you see in that witch woman and her devil child anyway? Has she cast a spell on you?"

Savage stopped and turned to face MacHuylin again. His green eyes locked on to the galloglaich's. "Galiene is my daughter," he stated.

Savage was pleased to see a look of utter astonishment on the mercenary's face, but it was already falling into a smile as he turned once more to recommence his journey to the castle keep.

He entered the inner courtyard through to the sound of MacHuylin's hearty, gut-deep laughter echoing around the castle walls.

Chapter 38

Savage entered the inner courtyard of the castle and climbed the stairs to the first floor doorway into the castle keep. De Thrapston had said that he had put Galiene in the Earl's own bedroom, which meant he had to climb all the way up to the top floor.

He wound his way round and round, up the spiral staircase until he came to the door of the room at the top. Alys was standing outside the closed door, gnawing on the fingernails of her right hand. She looked distracted, she was pale, tired and her face was drawn with worry. When she saw Savage coming up the she first moved towards him, then stopped herself and avoided his eyes.

"How's she doing?" Savage asked.

"The Earl's physician is in with her now," Alys responded. "He's treating her wound. The man's little more than a quack: a leech merchant. I could see to her myself. I always have. I'll probably have to re-dress her wound when he is done."

"From what I know of the Earl, his physician will be the best in Ireland," Savage said. "You can't always do everything for yourself."

The old hostility sparked in her eyes and she shot him a spiteful glance. "I've had to up until now. There's never been anyone for me to rely on."

Savage rubbed a hand over his chin. His mouth was dry and in truth he felt more nervous and uncomfortable now than he had before riding into battle at the tournament the day before.

"Alys-" he began.

She held up a hand, "Listen Richard, I've been thinking about earlier. I've been up all night, I was over-tired and upset.

I'd just lost my home and I was worried about Galiene too. I let my emotions get the better of me. Don't put too much stock in what I said in the church."

"No," Savage took a deep breath. "I've been thinking too."

Alys opened her mouth to speak but Savage pressed a finger to her lips.

"Come, let us talk," He said. "I'm uncomfortable standing with you looming over me. Besides, these spiral staircases always make me a bit giddy."

Alys hesitated, then nodded her agreement. Savage brushed past her and they made their way on up the stairs to the door that opened onto the roof of the keep.

Immediately the door opened, a wind damp with the sea and the rain buffeted them and tugged at their hair and clothes. Dark clouds, heavy with rain, skittered across the sky, chased by the wind. Despite the weather, the brightness of the daylight after the darkness of the stairway made Savage frown. He walked out onto the roof of the keep to the crenulated wall. He gazed out over the dull green water of the lough, the harbour and the town. His stomach churned with mixed feelings and dread at what he felt impelled to say. He took a deep breath and turned. Alys stood looking at him. The expression on her face did not help his nerves.

"There was a time, Richard," Alys spoke first, "when I thought I knew what was going on behind those fierce green eyes. Now I have no idea. What is it you want? What are you looking for? What was it made you abandon me and go off to the East all those years ago? Did you ever find out?"

Savage shook his head. "No," he sighed. "But listen. Ten years ago we were both very young. My head was full of stupid ideas: Silly notions about adventure, questing to learn the secrets of life and God, saving Christian civilisation from the Saracens. Now I know these were just dreams, delusions. Mirages that lead men to nowhere but death. You ask me if I found what I sought, and the answer is no. I lost everything. I lost my faith in God. Worse, I lost my faith in man. Worst of all-" he looked straight into her cornflower blue eyes-"I lost you."

Alys seemed to catch her breath; her right hand went to her mouth. Then she frowned. "It's nice to know you chose a delusion before me," she said with bitterness.

"Will you listen to me for Jesus' sake?" Savage sighed. "Alys, I've come to realise, the quest I went on, I was looking for something that would give my life meaning, that would somehow say that this whole time on earth is not some sorry, pointless existence. I travelled from here nearly to the very centre of the world, to Jerusalem, and yet I realise now that it was a mistake. The very thing I was searching for all these years lay here all along. I had left it behind me. I thought I was seeking the Holy Grail, but all I was doing was running from the very thing I was looking for all along."

Alys frowned. "What are you talking about, Richard?" She said.

"You, Alys," said Savage. "I'm talking about you. I love you. I always have. I think I always will. I was a fool to think there was anything more important."

Alys looked confused, annoyed, then her brow creased and tears began falling from her eyes, spilling down her cheeks. She hung her head. "I never dared even hope-" she sobbed.

Savage strode across to her and clasped her in his arms. "I'm sorry, Alys. I'm so sorry for leaving you. I was a fool. If you will take me back, I vow I will never leave you again."

She looked up at him. "How can I believe you?"

Savage clasped her face between both his hands. With his thumbs he wiped away her tears then he kissed her. "You can't. It's up to me to convince you." He said.

"I want to believe you, Richard," Alys said.

Savage smiled and kissed her again.

"There's someone else you need to speak to," Alys said. "Galiene."

Savage nodded and they both left the roof. A couple of turns around the spiral staircase and they were back outside the door of the Earl's bedroom.

The physician was just leaving. It was the same small, fidgeting man who had attended Savage after the tournament the day before.

"She's a lucky girl," the physician announced in response to their anxious glances. "The wound is deep but clean. I've washed it and packed it with sage, then sewed it closed. I've given her a draught made from the seeds of poppies for the pain. It will make her sleep deeply but that will help her recover."

With that, he bustled on down the stairs. Alys led the way into the Earl's bedroom. The chamber was luxurious, with huge, arched windows in all four walls that reached from floor to vaulted ceiling. The view was fantastic. From the dizzying heights of the keep, they could look down on the lough and town. Nestled in the protective shelter of the castle was the busy harbour that was full of vessels of all sizes and descriptions. Beyond the harbour was the walled town. Savage was momentarily distracted by the view and he surveyed the higgelty-piggelty maze of timber frame buildings crammed inside the surrounding turf ramparts. It was a big town for Ireland, but tiny compared to anything in England. At the centre of the town the tower of Saint Nicholas Church rose above the houses like the hilt of a kidney dagger stuck into the land.

On the sumptuous, tapestry canopied bed lay Galiene. She was pale and her eyes were half closed. She looked like she was about to fall asleep. At the sight of Alys a drowsy smile came to her lips.

"Mother," she said.

Alys took Savage's hand and lead him over to the bed. The girl frowned at the sight of him.

"What's he doing here Mother?" Galiene asked.

"Galiene, I want to meet your father." Alys said.

The little girl looked really confused now.

"Mother you said my father was a worthless bucket of scum who left us alone in the world," she said.

Savage glanced at Alys, who shrugged.

"Well he is," Alys smiled, "but some people can change, Galiene. Maybe we should give him another chance."

Galiene looked doubtful. Savage sat down on the edge of the bed and took her hand. "I'm sorry Galiene," he said. "I'm sorry I left you. But now I have come back and I want to help look after you. I won't leave you again. I promise."

The girl frowned again. She was too sleepy from the poppy draught to pull her hand away. "Are you a knight?" She asked.

"Yes. Yes I am." Savage replied.

"Do you have a castle?"

Savage grunted. "No. I have nothing."

"Can you get our castle back for us?"

Savage patted her hand. "I'll try, Galiene. And if I can't, I'll get you a new one."

For the first time, the little girl smiled. "Good. Ours was falling apart," she breathed as the poppy drink finally overcame her senses and she slipped into sleep.

Alys sighed. "Poor thing. She needs some rest."

Savage stood up. "So do you. You look wretched."

Alys smiled, "complimentary as always, Richard. I admit it though. I'm tired."

"Get in beside her and get some rest. There's plenty of room for both of you." Savage said. "I'll make sure you aren't disturbed."

"What are you going to do?"

"I'm riding down to Corainne with MacHuylin to see what John Bysset is doing at your castle."

"Do you really think you can get it back?"

Savage sighed and looked her in the eyes. "I have to be honest with you, Alys. I don't know. War is coming. The Scots are preparing to invade and I think Bysset taking your castle has something to do with it."

"You will look after yourself won't you?"

"Of course I will," Savage said. "When you have rested and Galiene re-awakes, I want you both to get away from here. There will be fighting and when it starts it will be brutal and without mercy. We don't know who is on which side and anyone could be an enemy. I need to know you are safe while I am away. Is there anywhere you can go, anyone you know who you can trust?"

Alys shook her head. "No one."

There was a slight cough from the doorway and both of them turned to see Henry de Thrapston standing there, hovering awkwardly in the threshold.

"Syr Richard, MacHuylin is waiting for you in the courtyard," the Keeper of the Castle said. "It is time to go."

"Syr Henry," Savage stood up. "Do you know anywhere Alys and Galiene can go where they will be safe?"

"This is the strongest fortress in Ulster, my friend." De Thrapston said, patting the stone of the keep walls. "No safer place than here."

"Except last night…." Savage said.

De Thrapston nodded. "Granted. If the Scots invade we will evacuate all women and children anyway. They will all be sent south towards Dublin."

Alys shot a suspicious glance at De Thrapston. "You promise you will come back?"

Savage took both Alys' hands. "I will ride to Corainne and when I return if you have left I will meet you on the road to Dublin."

Alys frowned, not completely happy at the idea. Then she looked at the sleeping Galiene and realised she had her daughter's safety to think of also.

"You promise you will come for us?" She repeated.

"I swear." Savage stated.

She gave a little smile. "Swear by the Grail?"

"By the Grail," Savage kissed her, then left to follow De Thrapston down the spiral staircase.

"Come along Syr Richard." De Thrapston said. "Let's find out what is going on down at Corainne castle."

Chapter 39

Savage, MacHuylin and MacArtain rode north. Leaving Carrickfergus, they galloped along the coastline, riding along the golden sand of the beach along the lough shore. As they rode the rain finally ceased and the bright, early summer sun blazed down from gaps in the rapidly clearing clouds.

Several miles north of the castle, the shore became rocky and they cut inland, riding through a little village and scattering a bunch of chickens up into a clucking cloud of distressed feathers.

Out of the village they entered the wooded track that constituted the road to Vikingsford and Corainne castle. It wasn't long before their horses were labouring as they climbed the sharp rise of the headland that jutted into the sea, marking the mouth of Carrickfergus lough. From there the coastline turned sharply from an eastern to a northern direction.

"We'll meet my galloglaiches up here." MacHuylin said. "This headland above the Rinn Seimhne peninsula is so close to Scotland you could spit across the sea. This is where I sent my men after the Seneschal asked me to this morning."

"This war will be a cruel one," Congal MacArtain mused as they rode. "There's MacArtain family over in Scotland too, the branch of the clan who migrated with Fergus Mor a few hundred years back. They're Scots now, but still our blood."

"And yet you'll fight for the Earl-an English overlord-against them and Ui Neil, a fellow Irishman?" Savage asked.

"The Kingdom of Iveagh has fought with the Earl of Ulster for the last hundred years." Congal replied. "The Earl has been good to us, and in return we've fought in his battles for him. And his King's battles. We've fought in Flanders, Gascony and Scotland, all in the service of the Earl. Iveagh is a small kingdom, Syr Savage, and right now the

Earldom is the strongest power in this part of the world. Ui Neil may be a fellow Irishman but him and the rest of Clan Eoghan hate our guts. They'll wipe us out the first chance they get. We have a long, bloody history between us and the feud between our clans goes back centuries. The choice for us is easy. It's between survival and death."

"Wouldn't you rather have a Gaelic chieftain?" Savage asked. "Edward Bruce says he wants to unite Ireland and Scotland as Greater Scotia, to create a pan-gaelic alliance."

MacArtain threw back his head and laughed. "We're not soft enough to fall for that aul shite," he chuckled. "Some of Bruce's army may be gaelic clansmen but half of them are descendants of Saxons from the borders with England. Edubard a Briuis may like to pretend he uses the gaelic version of his name but we all know fine rightly his first language is French. Edward de Brus is no more Gaelic than you are. He's a Norman bastard like all your lot. No, 'better the devil you know', as they say. Don't get me wrong: We've no love for any of you and you don't belong here. We just hate them more than you. At least our Irish foreigners- Normans like yourself and the Earl-have been here long enough for us to half civilise you. You've adapted to our customs, you share our sense of humour. Your cousins that conquered Scotland are a different matter. But what about you? You work for the English King. I hear you have no lands here now. Why are you still here, getting caught up in this fight that isn't yours?"

Savage found he did not know what to say. Exactly why was he still here?

"Sure hasn't he got family ties here now?" MacHuylin interjected with a mischievous smile. "He's in love with the witch Alys de Logan and her wee girl is his daughter."

The galloglaich chortled to himself but neither Savage nor MacArtain shared his mirth.

"I won't have a word said against Dame Alys." The young Prince of Iveagh said. "My own sweet wife, Emer, was struck down with the melancholy madness after the birth of our son. Dame Alys tended to her, made her a concoction of herbs to drink every day. It wasn't long before she was back to her old happy self."

MacHuylin rolled his eyes. "Oh for Jesus Christ's sake! Herbs? She probably just needed a good ride," he muttered.

"What did you say?" MacArtain was indignant.

MacHuylin suddenly held up a hand. He reined his horse to a stop. Savage saw that he was no longer paying attention to them and was looking intently around. He too stopped riding. Congal MacArtain saw something had changed in the galloglaich's demeanour. He immediately forgot his anger and he too brought his horse to a halt.

"What is it?" Savage asked.

"Don't you smell it?" MacHuylin Asked. Savage and MacArtain exchanged puzzled glances. MacHuylin sat in the saddle with his head tilted back. He appeared to be sniffing the air.

"Blood," he said finally. Without another word MacHuylin swung himself out of the saddle and onto the ground. He began examining tracks in the mud. There were both hoof prints and footprints in the deep mire and to Savage it looked like a jumbled mess. MacHuylin seemed to be able to make some sort of sense of it.

"There was a fight here, and not that long ago." the galloglaich said. He pointed to the darkened colour of a puddle in the track way. "That puddle is darker than the others because there is blood in it."

Savage looked and sure enough the puddle was several shades darker than the others that had gathered on the track and more mauve than brown.

MacHuylin began examining the footprints in the mud, bent over almost double and with a look of pure concentration on his face. He followed the trail of prints to the side of the track and into the dense undergrowth beside it.

"God damn them to Hell." MacHuylin finally said in a flat tone of voice.

Savage and MacArtain dismounted and joined MacHuylin at the side of the track. Lying half-covered by undergrowth were the corpses of two men. Both wore the armour of the galloglaich but their helmets had been removed. Three arrows protruded from the chest of one of the men. His companion had several stab wounds to his chest and stomach. Both had had their throats cut. They lay in a large muddy pool of their own blood that was almost black.

"Are these your men?" Savage asked. His question was unnecessary as the blazing anger in the glare MacHuylin returned to him showed.

"It looks like someone didn't want an eye kept on the crossing to Scotland." MacArtain commented. "We'd better let the Seneschal know."

Savage shook his head. "Let's go on to Corainne. This must have something to do with what Bysset and Montmorency were up to there."

MacHuylin nodded. "I agree. With any luck we'll come across whoever did this to Niall and Tor. If we do I'll gut the bastards."

In grim silence, the three men remounted their horses and continued their ride up the hill. As they neared the top of the headland the woods cleared and they entered the high upland, the very north-east corner of the island of Ireland that was so scoured by wind and rain driving in from the sea that anything that was taller that the height of a gorse bush simply could not grow.

Eventually they reached the top of the headland. To their right sheer black cliffs dropped away into an angry sea. Ahead the ground sloped downwards towards the peninsula of Rinn Seimhne that wrapped itself round the inlet of Vikingsford.

Behind them was Carrickfergus Lough, its far southern shore where Bangor and the Holy Wood lay clearly visible in the summer sunshine. To the north east was the sea, the North Channel, a short stretch of water that divided Ireland from Scotland. Where they now stood the Scottish coast was closer to them than the village of Beal Feirste at the far end of Carrickfergus lough. A brisk wind whipped their cloaks and hair and the same breeze was rapidly clearing the thick sea mist that has risen with the earlier rain. They could see the west coast of Galloway, clear and visible on the other side of the sea, so close that they could make out fields and the lines of wall boundaries between them. It was twelve miles away, but from this height it looked close enough to swim to.

As the wind cleared away the fog more, it also revealed something else.

"Oh dear, sweet Jesus Christ."

Congal MacArtain breathed. All three of them stopped riding once again, this time to simply stare at the sight that lay before them.

As the fog rolled way, as the channel between the coast of Galloway and Ireland became visible, they could see hundreds and hundreds of ships, dotting the sea, all in a massive line.

Savage had never seen so many ships, even on Templar raids into Egypt. A huge flotilla of vessels was making its way across the channel from Scotland to Ireland, and on the closest ships they could clearly see the sun glittering on the arms and armour of the men who sailed in them. Their purpose was unmistakeable.

The invasion of Ireland had begun.

Chapter 40

"I can't believe I let you talk me into this," Savage muttered out of the side of his mouth.

"What's the matter?" MacHuylin asked. "Do you not think I could pass as a proud Scottish clansman?"

Savage and MacHuylin were walking right through the middle of the Scottish army. They had sent Congal MacArtain back to Carrick to warn the Seneschal of the arrival of the Scots but remained behind themselves. With the galloglaich sentries on the headland murdered it was up to them to try to learn as much as possible about what was going on.

As the young Irish prince had turned to ride off, Savage grasped the bridle of his horse.

"Will you do me a favour?"

Congal nodded.

"Find Dame Alys de Logan at the castle. Give her this message from me: Tell her to take Galiene and go south for Dublin straight away. I will join them when I can."

"I will," MacCartan said. "They will have to travel through Iveagh. I'll make sure she has safe passage through the kingdom."

With that he had ridden back towards Carrickfergus.

To get a closer view of what the Scots were doing, Savage and MacHuylin rode down from the headland by the base of the Rinn Seimhne peninsula to Corainne. Like Alys when she had been dispossessed the day before, they tied up their horses and crouched in the undergrowth at the edge of woods, thirty yards from the castle on the shore.

The first ship to arrive flew the banner of the Byssets. The large cog led the way around the tip of the Rinn

Seimhne peninsula and into the mouth of Vikingsford lough. It dropped anchor a little way offshore and curraghs set out from the castle to meet it. It was quickly followed by several sleek longships that rode straight up onto the beach like the Viking raiders who had given their name to the lough four centuries before. Heavily armed men leapt from these ships and ran up the beach to the castle.

Savage and MacHuylin, watching from the trees, could see the men-at-arms taking up positions on the newly fortified walls and palisades around the old castle tower. Soon they were joined by men from another wave of ships. Before long the defences were thronging with soldiers and there was barely space for anyone to join them on the makeshift walls.

Their bridgehead established, the disembarking of the bulk of the Scottish army began. Ship after ship sailed into the lough and disgorged men, horses, arms, armour and other materiel onto the beach. Within a short time the shore thronged with thousands of men and horses, so many that the defensive enclosures built around Corainne castle to protect their bridgehead could no longer contain them and they began spreading out to fill the open land around the shore. Tents were erected and the flags and banners of the Scottish Earls and Barons were raised to flutter in the wind as soldiers and men at arms began unpacking bundles and chests of arms and weapons.

Finally, a large ship flying a huge banner arrived. On the flag was displayed a silver lion, rampant on an azure background.

"The arms of Edward Bruce," MacHuylin commented. "Our new King has arrived."

The earlier rain returned in a steady, heavy downpour.

"Come on," MacHuylin said, standing up and pulling his hood up. "Let's go and see if we can find out what their plans are."

"Are you mad?" Savage said. "We can't just walk into their camp!"

"Why not?" The galloglaich said. "There's no more anonymous place than in the middle of an army. Especially at the start of a campaign. There's thousands of men down there from all over Scotland and they don't all know each other. Who's to say who we are?"

"There are not just Scotsmen there. You're the Captain of the Earl of Ulster's bodyguard," Savage objected. "If anyone recognises either of us we're both dead."

"Well let's pray it doesn't stop raining then." MacHuylin replied, pulling the front of his hood further forward to cast a shadow over his face. "Come on, before they start digging entrenchments. It'll be a lot harder to get in when they're finished."

Savage thought for a moment. It seemed madness but MacHuylin had a point. They just might be able to carry it off and any information they could glean about what way the Scots intended to march would help the Seneschal to draw up plans to repel them.

"Very well," he agreed, pulling up the hood of his own cloak. "If anyone challenges us, say we are scouts sent to check the headland for Irish troops."

As it turned out, no one stopped them as they strolled as nonchalantly as possible out of the woods and mingled with the Scottish army.

Along the edge of the army, spearmen were being barged around into ranks.

"See that? No entrenchments," MacHuylin said out of the corner of his mouth. "They're posting pickets instead. You know what that means?"

Savage nodded. "They don't intend staying around here too long."

They made their way to the heart of the camp that was at the beach just outside the wall of Corainne castle. All around them the army was unpacking weapons and equipment, lighting cooking fires and tending to horses that were more than a little disturbed by their passage across the sea. Suits of mail, suspended on poles passed through the arm holes were carried up from the beach suspended between two men like bizarre, rigid washing lines. Long rows of helmets, hung on similar poles by their chin straps were being disembarked too. Great sheaves of spear poles were carried up from the ships to armourers who were already untying them and nailing spear heads to their ends. Pots were hung over cooking fires and the aroma of stew began to drift through the damp air. Some men were at work digging trenches, not for defence but for soldiers to shit in. Everyone worked with an air of well-practised professionalism.

"Do you see whose banners are flying?" MacHuylin asked, pointing at the various flags that had been planted in the earth around the edge of the castle.

"How would I know?" Savage shrugged. "I've spent most of the last five years in a dungeon. Before that I was in Cypress with the Templars."

MacHuylin shot a bemused sideways glance at Savage. "A dungeon? You're full of surprises today. Well that," he gestured to a yellow banner with a blue and chequered stripe across it, "is the badge of Sir John Stewart, King Robert Bruce's right hand man. That," he gestured to another colourful banner, "is Sir Philip Mowbray's coat of arms, the turncoat who switched sides after Bannockburn. Sir John Ramsay of Auchterhouse is here too. Sir Fergus of Ardrosson and Sir Neil Flemming. The flower of Scottish Chivalry have come here. These are fearsome warriors. They're veterans of Bannockburn and Bruce's wars of independence from England. "

"And the first thing they do when they win their freedom is invade Ireland?" Savage grunted.

Several brightly dressed heralds came running towards them through the throng of the camp.

"Captains and Lieutenants!" They were shouting, "All Captains and Lieutenants are to report to the King for marching orders!"

Men began hurrying towards the beach where the flags of the nobles and Edward Bruce were flying.

"I think that includes us, don't you?" MacHuylin said.

Savage could not help but smile at the sheer audacity of what they were engaged in as they joined the others who congregated in a large semi-circle around the banners planted on the beach.

Several of the barons whose banners flew overhead were standing there, dressed in mail armour with surcoats over it emblazoned with the emblems that matched their flags.

The rain was getting lighter but Savage had no desire to take his hood down. Standing in the middle of a hostile army, not knowing who would suddenly appear beside him, his nerves were stretched taut in almost unbearable tension. At every moment he expected a hand to be laid on his shoulder as someone recognised him or MacHuylin and then it would be all over.

Remembering why they were there, Savage did a quick headcount of the captains gathered around the banners of the Scottish Earls. About a hundred men in total were there. Not every captain would have a lieutenant with him, but if even half of them did, and each captain led a company of roughly about a hundred men, that meant it was a fair bet that the Scottish Army was probably between five and seven thousand men strong.

Sitting on a travelling chest was a hardy looking young man who wore a yellow surcoat emblazoned with three silver lozenges within a red cross.

"That's Thomas Randolph, Earl of Moray." MacHuylin whispered. "He captured Edinburgh castle from the English a couple of years ago. He's Robert Bruce's nephew."

"And here's the man himself," Savage commented as the blond haired Edward Bruce, Earl of Carrick strode across the strand. His hair was combed straight, his beard trimmed and he too wore a bright yellow surcoat but his
was embroidered with a rampant lion. At the sight of him the soldiers all cheered. Bruce's eyes lit up with a fierce glare at the sound of their adulation. He held up two hands for quiet.

"Men," Bruce said, "eight hundred years ago our fore-fathers left this land and forged the kingdom we now call Scotland. Today, we have returned across the sea to take this land back from those who have stolen
it. Ireland and Scotland and now one once again. This land is now our land. I am its new King and you are my loyal subjects, and you are the men who will free this island from tyranny. With our help, the Irish will gain their freedom from the English yoke the way we Scots have won ours. We are here to help our Irish cousins."

"And if they don't want our help," Earl of Moray smiled "we'll slit their throats."

A rumble of laughter went around the gathered captains.

Bruce signalled for silence again. "To show that we mean to stay," he said, "I am sending the ships home again. They will leave before nightfall." A murmur of disquiet went through the troops. Bruce held up high a piece of parchment. "I have in my hand a letter, signed by thirteen Irish Kings, pledging their support for us in our fight."

"Sire," One of the captains near Savage and MacHuylin spoke up. "That's less than half of the Kings in this land. How will we know who is on our side and who is not?"

"Do not let that trouble you," Bruce replied. "Lord De Lacy is with us and has already done great service by luring the Earl of Ulster south. Everyone who is on our side in the north part of the Island east of the Bann River is with us today: Sir John Bysset, who led our ships safely into this haven, rules the coast north of here up to Rathlin Island."

Savage shrank further under his hood at the sight of Bysset, his eyes still black from the tournament, sauntering forward out of the crowd to acknowledge the cheers of support that came from the soldiers.

"Syr John, we are grateful for the aid you and your uncle have given us," Bruce said. "You will be handsomely rewarded."

Bysset looked sheepish. "Sire, there is one thing I wish for more than anything. I wish to see the Holy Grail."

Bruce nodded. "And you shall. The Grail is safe in the chapel of the Noquetran, guarded by Ulick Ceannaideach. Once we have secured our foothold here you can sail and meet him there and see the Grail"

Bysset nodded.

"Leave the Bysset lands alone," Bruce continued. "Everyone else must be taught a lesson. We will make an example of the Earldom of Ulster and show the rest of Ireland shall see how foolish it is to oppose us. The people here have chosen to stand against us, well so be it. Take what you want from them. Kill them. Rape their women, kill their children, burn their homes. Destroy everything. Plunder their churches; demolish their towns, their houses. Take all the gold you want and obliterate everything else. Leave nothing standing but blackened stones."

A raucous, bloodthirsty cheer erupted from the gathered soldiers.

"We march right away to take the capital," Bruce said. "We will form two battalions and march on Carrickfergus. Follow the standards of your liege Lords so you will know which battalion to fall into."

"What about forts?" Another captain asked. "How many are on the way?"

"There are hundreds of forts all over the country here," The Earl of Moray replied. "Most of them are too small to cause us problems so we will just march round them and deal with them later. There are a couple of strategic forts: Duncrue on the way to Carrickfergus and Donegore that guards the way to the north. Detachments of cavalry will ride fast and take both by surprise. Companies of spearmen will follow to re-enforce and garrison the forts once taken. Hugo Montmorency will lead the attack on Donegore. Syr Neil Flemming will take Duncrue."

"Now let us prepare to march." Bruce said. "God goes with us. He has shown his approval of our cause by delivering the Grail into our hands. We cannot fail. Victory will be ours!"

As the gathering of captains broke up to gather their men, MacHuylin grabbed Savage's sleeve and steered him aside.

"We've got to get to Donegore before the Scots," the galloglaich said. "If they take it the whole of the north as far as Coleraine on the north coast is wide open to them. It's a really strong fort: right on the top of the highest hill. If we can warn the garrison there they can shut the gates and the Scots will be forced to lay siege. It will slow their whole advance northwards."

"What about Carrickfergus?" Savage said, "Shouldn't we get back there and warn the Seneschal what is coming his way?"

MacHuylin shook his head. "Sir Thomas is gathering the army at Carrickfergus. By now they'll have enough men to meet this army in battle. If they take Donegore, then even if the Seneschal defeats them they can withdraw north and come back and hit Carrickfergus again. We need to get to Donegore and warn them."

Savage saw that he was right, but still he was uneasy, remembering his vow.

"Alys and Galiene are in Carrick castle. I promised to return," he said, his face reddening slightly.

"It's only a few miles from Donegore back to Carrickfergus," MacHuylin said. "Once we've warned the garrison at the fort you can ride back."

Savage nodded. Grimly, he followed the galloglaich as he lead the way through the decamping Scottish army, hoping fervently that Alys and Galiene would be safe, and that he managed to live long enough to get back to them.

Chapter 41

Savage and MacHuylin made their way back through the mustering Scottish army to the woods. As soon as they entered the trees they broke into a run, dashing back to where they had earlier tethered their horses.

"It's about sixteen miles to Donegore," MacHuylin said as he leapt into the saddle. "If we ride hard we'll get there before the sun gets much higher."

"As long as we beat Montmorency," Savage said as they dug in their spurs and took off at a gallop up the track through the woods.

Savage let MacHuylin lead the way as they headed inland. The rain stopped and after a short time they took a fork in the road as the ground began to gradually rise. After twenty five minutes of riding, the horses were breathing heavily and their flanks were covered in sweat.

The woods began to thin and soon they were riding up a very wide, gently sloping meadowland. Grass and heather coated the ground and here and there were large clumps of prickly, deep-green gorse bushes dotted with bright yellow flowers. A herd of the little, dwarf-like Irish cattle calmly chewed on the grass, barely raising their heads when the two men galloped past. The Irish still measured their wealth in the number of cows they owned. Unlike England, where the countryside was choked with flocks of sheep, the economy had not switched to large-scale wool production.

After riding some way further they came to a river. It was not wide and the horses easily forded it. They stopped on the far bank to let the horses drink and rest a while. About a mile down the river bank to the south was a small settlement. It was little more than a small fort on a mound around which several buildings and church were collected. Savage knew that this was what passed as a town in this part of the world.

"Belch Cláir," MacHuylin nodded in the direction of the settlement. "The river is called Abhainn na bhFiodh but you Normans call it the Six Mile Water because its six miles from Carrickfergus. This marks the western boundary of the Earldom of Ulster. On this side of the river we are now in the Kingdom of Ui Tuirtre which is run by the Ui Flainns. They're our allies. They maintain forts for us, let us garrison soldiers on their land and in return we protect them from their bullying neighbours, the Ui Neills in the west. God damn it they are coming already-" MacHuylin interrupted himself.

Behind them the ground sloped gradually back towards the coast, so they could see the several miles back to the woods. A group of horsemen were just emerging from the trees.

Savage squinted to try to discern their numbers. "It's hard to tell, but there's quite a few of them. Maybe forty."

"They'll outnumber the garrison at Donegore at least two to one," MacHuylin said. "With surprise on their side, they could take it before the garrison even get a chance to shut the gates."

"What about the garrison in that Motte?" Savage said, pointing at the fort in the hamlet down river.

MacHuylin shook his head. "There'll be four or five warriors there at the most. That's all it takes to defend that mound. The Scots will bypass them anyway and we don't have time to start riding down there to gather troops."

"Let's get going then," said Savage and they took off at a gallop once more.

Their progress became slower as the ground began to slope upwards more markedly and the journey began to tell on the horses legs. Savage regularly glanced over his shoulder as they rode, noticing with growing dread that every time he did so the riders behind them seemed to be a little closer.

After a couple more miles, they rode over a low rise and
to the north of them rose a very large hill. Its lower slopes
were wooded but the top half to the summit was cleared of
trees. On the top of the hill they could clearly make out a man-
made mound on which sat the wooden palisade of a fort.

"Donegore," MacHuylin shouted, changing course to ride
towards it. Savage took another glance over his shoulder and
judged the Scots cavalry were now less than a mile behind
them, then the track they rode on plunged into the woods at the
bottom of Donegore hill and he lost sight of their pursuers.

Their ride through the woods was short, but the horses
were now really labouring as the ground sloped upwards much
more dramatically. When they emerged from the trees once
again onto the open meadow of the hillside, they had slowed to
little more than a walk.

A trackway that led to the fort on the summit wrapped
around the contours of the hill, intersecting the track that
Savage and MacHuylin were on. To Savage's surprise, coming
from the trees to their left was a herd of cows. The animals
were accompanied by three armed warriors who were
whooping and shouting, driving the animals up the slope
towards the fort. They were wrapped in bright coloured cloaks
and prodded the flanks of the cattle with the butts of their
spears.

"The Ui Flainns," MacHuylin shouted over his shoulder.
"Their clan garrisons the fort."

The galloglaich made straight for them, waving his hand
to get their attention. Savage spurred his horse to follow.

The warriors saw them coming and one slowed down. The
other two kept driving the cattle on up the slope.

"Connor MacHuylin, what brings you here?" The warrior
asked. He was a man of about thirty, with long black hair and
wearing a huge gold band like a twisted rope around his neck,
a sign that he was the gaelic equivalent of a knight.

"Fergus," MacHuylin shouted, "the Scots are coming!"

"Sure we know that," the warrior replied, "messengers came this morning. That's why we're rounding up the cattle. We'll need some in the fort in case we're besieged and the Seneschal wants the rest driven to Carrick-"

"No: I mean they're coming now. Here." MacHuylin stopped him.

As if in answer, horsemen began emerging from the trees behind Savage and MacHuylin. A look of dismayed astonishment flashed across Fergus Ui Flainn's face.

"To the fort! Shut the gates!" Savage shouted, and they all dug their spurs in, mercilessly driving their horses up the hill amid squeals and whinnies of protest.

Over his shoulder Savage saw that there were forty to fifty Scottish horsemen, armed with spears and swords, riding side by side in a long line towards them. They were now about a hundred yards away, downhill.

The cows were in full stampede. Panicked by the galloping of the horses around them, they kept going in the same direction as the horsemen as they all desperately charged for the summit of the hill and the gate of the fort that gaped invitingly open.

Savage heard something buzz past his head. He looked back again and saw that several of the horsemen had crossbows and were losing them as they rode. They were shooting uphill and riding at the same time which made the shots wild but still dangerous.

There was a loud thwack from beside him and one of the cows let out a pained low before crashing to the ground, a crossbow quarrel embedded in its flank.

Donegore fort sat on top of an artificial mound on the summit of the hill. The sides of the mound were too steep to ride a horse up, however a track that curled around the contour of the mound allowed the gate to be approached on horseback. The gate was set back from the outer palisade wall, so the final approach to it was walled on both sides, allowing defenders to assault anyone approaching from both sides at once.

Accompanied by the cows, Savage, MacHuylin and the three Ui Flainns burst through the gates of the fort. To Savage's surprise, there were even more cows inside the fort. They squeezed into a crush of bodies that filled the centre of the ring fort, packed so tightly there was hardly room to move. The inside of the fort was literally jammed with cows, mooing and pushing each other.

Defenders-Irish warriors dressed like the Ui Flainns and armed with axes and spears-were up on the walls on platforms behind the palisades but Savage didn't have time to count them. One thing was sure was that there were not that many of them. A couple more were on the ground and they struggled to shut the gates behind Savage against the heaving bodies of still more cows that were trying to push their way in. The gates were almost closed when the foremost Scottish riders arrived. Two of them, dressed in chainmail and swinging swords, burst through into the fort before the heavy wooden gates slammed shut. The gate guards finally slammed the gate closed and threw the massive latch. They then began struggling to slot a heavy wooden bar across the back of the two gates to lock them shut.

The Scots turned on the men at the gate straight away, realising that once the bar was in place their compatriots outside would not be able to force the door back open. They wheeled their horses around and swung their swords down at the gate men who dropped the bar and ducked to avoid the deadly blow.

Savage tore his sword from its sheath. It was a beautiful German-made weapon De Thrapston had lent him from the castle armoury. Unlike the massive Cladh Mor he had wielded during the tournament, this was a side sword: lighter, well balanced and small enough to be welded in one hand.

He managed to get his horse turned, despite the crush of the cows inside the fort and rode to the gate, swinging a stroke at one of the Scots horsemen. The man somehow caught sight of the sword coming out of the corner of his eye and just turned in time to counter the blow with his own sword. Savage swung again, suddenly remembering that unlike his opponent he wore no armour. The Scot again countered his strike. Then his face suddenly creased in pain as behind him one of the gate guards drove a spear into his back, bursting his chainmail and gouging deep into his chest. Bright red blood bubbled up into his mouth and he fell off the horse.

His companion was also quickly dealt with, going down in a prickly forest of spear thrusts from the men above on the battlements.

As both Scotsmen lay dying on the ground, Fergus Ui Flainn dismounted and drew a large Danish axe from a saddlebag. On each man in turn, he planted his right foot on the man's chest and in one swing of the huge weapon clove the heads from their bodies. Ui Flainn then picked both severed heads up by the hair and tossed them out of the fort over the gate. He then turned to Savage and MacHuylin.

"You two make yourselves useful," He said, gesturing with his bloody axe towards a low wooden hut beside the wall on the other side of the fort. "Get yourself armed with long weapons then get up on that wall with the rest of us. This fight is only just starting."

Like most Irish "forts", Donegore was little more than a roughly circular palisade wall about twice the height of a man and made of sharp topped wooden stakes, built on a steep sided mound on the hilltop. A battlement walkway was on the back of the walls, near the top, for defenders to stand on and rain missiles and blows down on anyone outside. The middle of the fort was an open courtyard with a beaten earth floor that was now being churned up by the cows. Hammocks for the defenders to sleep in were slung on the walls, sheltered from the elements by the wooden battlements above and some cloth curtains that could be pulled over. There was also a small hut for storage and it was there that Savage and MacHuylin pushed their horses through the cattle throng to.

When they got there, they dismounted and pushed open the door.

Savage gave a low whistle. The hut was filled with every sort of weapon imaginable. Throwing and thrusting spears stood against the wall, along with swords, helmets, maces and axes. There was every sort of knife and barrels of what looked like small pebbles.

"There might not be many of them, but they have enough weapons here to hold off an army," Savage said.

"They might have to," MacHuylin said as he grabbed a long pole axe from a rack. He also picked up a léine croich, the long padded linen jerkin that served as armour in Ireland. "You'd better get that on you. It's not chainmail but at least it's something."

Savage took off his hooded cloak and pulled the léine on over his head. Then he grabbed a mace and thrust it into his belt. He lifted a long spear from the rack and then put his cloak back on. MacHuylin and he ran back outside and clambered up a nearby ladder to mount the battlement walkway.

Savage was impressed at how light the léine croich was. Unlike when he wore chainmail or plate, he felt he could move much faster and strike with greater dexterity. On the other hand, he did not fancy his chances much if someone hit him a direct blow with an axe.

On the walls were Fergus Ui Flainn and eleven other warriors. Outside the fort the rest of the Scottish riders were trying to get in. The narrowness of the entranceway funnelled ten of them into a close-packed mass that pressed against the fort gates. They were now in the killing pen, designed to concentrate attackers in one small area where they could be dealt with more easily than in a widespread assault.

One of the Scots stood up on his saddle and leapt upwards to grab hold of the top of the palisade wall. Hanging on with both hands, he began to pull himself up to the top of the wall.

MacHuylin spotted him as soon as he reached the battlements. Holding the pole axe near the head he delivered a short chop on the wall top and the Scotsman was falling backwards towards the ground, his severed fingers still grasping the top of the wall.

A couple more riders tried the same thing, but the defenders on the walls quickly repelled them, either stabbing them with their spears or pushing them back off the wall with the shafts. Because of the narrowness of the entranceway, the bulk of the Scots cavalry had to wait at the bottom of the mound, unable to get close enough to the walls to attack.

After several failed assaults the horsemen at the gate realised that they could not get the gates open, and if they stayed where they were they were at the mercy of the stabbing spears from above. They wheeled their horses and began to retreat but their close-packed ranks made it difficult. Frustrated at the speed of the retreat, one of the riders took his horse sideways off the trackway that ran up to the gate, hoping to attack again at a different point on the walls.

Savage spotted him and shouted a warning. A couple of the Ui Flainn warriors broke away from the gate and began tracking the horseman along the wall as he rode round the mound. He did not get far, however. Once off the track, the side of the mound proved too steep for his horse, it missed its footing, tried to turn, then stumbled, pitching the rider off before it tumbled down rest of the mound, rolling its bone crunching weight over the rider as it went.

The Scottish riders withdrew to the base of the mound, accompanied by the derisory jeers of the defenders in the fort.

Savage counted them and-after deducting the casualties-there were now forty three of them. Four times the number of defenders, but thanks to the design of the fort it had held out against the superior numbers, at least initially. The Scots attack had relied on speed and surprise. Thanks to MacHuylin and him they had lost the surprise and their gamble had failed.

The Scots began to regroup about twenty yards from the bottom of the mound. They all dismounted. The eight of them with crossbows began loading them.

"Get the stones," Fergus Ui Flainn ordered. Savage suddenly realised that the barrels of what he had thought were pebbles in fact were exactly that. A couple of warriors jumped down off the battlements, ran to the hut and returned, struggling with the barrels, back up onto the wall. The rest of the defenders grabbed handfuls of stones and took out long strips of leather. Slingshots. Savage knew that there was no one in the world deadlier with these weapons than the Irish.

The Scots crossbowmen loosed a volley of arrows at the fort. The defenders all ducked down behind the palisade as the arrows thudded a tattoo on the wood. Immediately they rose and returned a hail of pebbles from their sling shots. Some stones rattled off helmets but where they struck flesh on hands and faces there was a loud thwack followed by gasps of pain. One of the crossbowmen collapsed holding his face, blood streaming from a ruined eye socket.

"Isn't this how David beat Goliath?" winked Fergus Ui Flainn, the confidence of his grin inspiring confidence in his hopelessly outnumbered men.

Unlike the crossbows which took up to a minute to reload, another volley of stones was launched almost immediately, followed by another. Under the onslaught, the Scots hurriedly withdrew further from the fort until they were about one hundred yards from the base of the mound and out of the range of the deadly pebbles.

Consequently, they were also now out of crossbow range.

Savage peeked over the wall and observed the Scots as they regrouped. They had injured another couple of them and the odds had been reduced further, but now there was a stalemate. The Scots could not get in, but he and the rest of the defenders were trapped inside the fort.

One thing was sure: There would be more fighting.

Chapter 42

Realising that they could not take the fort easily, the Scots spread out and encircled the bottom of the mound so no one inside could slip out. They then lit fires and began cooking.

"They'll not attack again tonight." Fergus Ui Flainn surmised. "If they do they're mad. Once they've lost the advantage of surprise there's no way cavalry can take a fort."

"There is a contingent of spearmen coming to re-enforce them," Savage said. "When they arrive I think it's safe to expect another attack."

"Well let's hope our re-enforcements arrive before theirs do," Ui Flainn said.

No one arrived for either side that night. As darkness fell the defenders split the night up into watches. Each man would take a turn to watch what the Scots were up to while the rest found somewhere to sleep. This was not easy, given that the fort was filled with lowing, milling cattle.

"Can we not do something about these cows?" Savage asked. "Why are they in here anyway?"

"They're worth a fortune," Ui Flainn said. "I'm not letting them out for those Scots bastards to get their hands on. Anyway, if we're stuck in here much longer some of them will become our dinner."

"If we don't drown in cow shit first," MacHuylin grunted.

Savage spent an uncomfortable night perched on the battlements wrapped in his cloak. Thankfully the rain stayed away. At dawn he awoke and took a look over the battlements. The view from the fort was superb. He could see for miles in all directions. To the south the land stretched away into the far distance for many, many miles, eventually rising into the dark masses of the Mourne Mountains. To the west the waters of Lough Neagh shimmered an amazing pink-gold in the early morning light. On it far western shores rose the distant hazy mountains in the Ui Neil's kingdom of Tyr Eoghan. To the East was the coast. He could see the sea, and in the extreme distance the dark hazy lump of north England rose from the water on the other side of the sea.

Frustratingly, the land dipped towards the coast so Corainne, Vikingsford and Carrickfergus were out of sight. Ominous black plumes of smoke were rising from that direction.

"Beautiful, isn't it?"

Savage turned to see MacHuylin was standing beside him also admiring the view. "No wonder we all fight over this land. How could you not love that?" He swept his hand around the stunning vista.

"Is that why you're still here, Connor?" Savage said. "Because I can't figure it out. You're a mercenary: You could just get out of here. You could have gone South with the Earl but here you still are, still fighting. What for? Who for? An Earl who'd betrayed you for his own ends? His Overlord, the English King? For a nice view? What's it all about?"

MacHuylin laughed. "You just don't understand do you? Yes, I am a mercenary. I come from a long line of professional soldiers. My forefathers have fought for everyone from the Viking Jarls of Orkney to the King of England. If truth be known, sometimes the King of France too," he winked. "And we've made good money from it. But it's not really about the money. We fight because we're good at it. It's what we do. But it's also about the people you fight with. I respect the Seneschal. As my father did his father. And it's about where you fight. We came here shortly before you Normans arrived and our roots are entangled here now as much as yours are. They stretch down into the land. This is our home. And no one comes into our home and pushes us around. You were born here, but I don't think you feel the same way about this country."

Savage shook his head. "I suppose I have been away from her too long. I've seen other places. I've broken the spell she casts."

MacHuylin laughed again. "And now you come back to old Ireland and find you'd put some roots down here after all." His face became serious. "I hope you get to see your woman and daughter again. Nothing is more important than family. Blood."

"I wonder what's going on in Carrickfergus," Savage said.

"People are dying." MacHuylin grunted, pointing at the plumes of smoke rising in the distance. "That's not farmers burning gorse. Its houses, farms, churches being fired by the Scots. The war has started and we're stuck up here scratching our arses."

He spat in frustration.

The rest of the fort was stirring. As Savage looked around his face creased in puzzlement. There seemed to be ten defenders plus Ui Flainn. The day before he had counted eleven. He counted again and came up with ten again. He must have miscounted the day before.

"I see your friend is down there." MacHuylin said, pointing at the Scottish troops outside who were also rising. A figure wrapped in a black cloak was moving among them.

"Montmorency," Savage growled. "What I wouldn't give for a longbow right now."

MacHuylin laughed. "Sure a wee man like you couldn't even draw a longbow, never mind shoot somebody a hundred yards away. How do you know him anyway?"

"Before he was a Knight of Saint John, he was a brother Templar," Savage said. "Though not much of a brother. It was him who betrayed me and my brethren at the Templar Commandery of Garway."

Savage told MacHuylin the whole story of the two fugitive French brothers and their mysterious treasure and how Montmorency had betrayed them to the sheriff.

"Knowing what I do now," Savage said when he had finished his tale, "I'll wager those French Templars had the Holy Grail with them. It makes sense that they would have taken it to Scotland because Robert Bruce had been excommunicated for the murder of Red Comyn. The Pope had no authority there and they would be safe from the Inquisition. That's how the Scots must have got their hands on the Grail. Montmorency must have followed their trail to Scotland."

"The Scots have the Holy Grail?" MacHuylin looked confused.

Savage nodded. "The mad priest in the Church in Carrickfergus told me."

"And you believe a mad priest?"

"It makes sense: Think of the support the Scots are getting from lords and barons here. They are half English so why support the Scots? It makes no sense unless they have something very special. Likewise why would a religious fanatic like Montmorency follow an excommunicated King like Robert Bruce unless he possessed something that justified his cause in the eyes of God?"

"The Holy Grail...." MacHuylin breathed. "There's an ancient Prophecy, you know, that soon the crowns of Ireland and Scotland will be united. They say the wizard Merlin foresaw it and the army that will make it come true will bear a sacred treasure."

Savage nodded. "It is said that whatever army bears the Holy Grail is invincible."

"Invincible or not, we'll beat them." MacHuylin smiled. "Maybe not today, but we'll beat them."

The day dragged on. No re-enforcements arrived for either side and the Scots seemed content just to wait it out. As the day passed the biggest problem for the defenders of the fort began to be boredom.

Early in the afternoon strange sounds began to waft through the air. Carried on the wind they drifted in and out hearing. They seemed to consist of shouting and roars of men, great crashes and the whinnying of horses but they were very far away and it was hard to tell exactly what was going on. Fergus Ui Flainn joined MacHuylin and Savage on the battlements as they strained their ears to try to discern the source of the sounds. To the east, towards Carrickfergus, many thick columns of black smoke were rising into the air.

"There is a battle," MacHuylin said. "The Seneschal's army must be fighting the Scots."

They all stared in the direction of the smoke. Savage could almost taste the galloglaich's frustration at not being part of the fighting. All Savage could think of was Alys. He hoped more than anything that she and Galiene had got out of Carrickfergus and were well on their way to Dublin.

The afternoon wore on. Still no re-enforcements arrived for either the defenders or the Scots. The sounds of battle eventually began to fade. Ominously, the plumes of black smoke appeared to grow thicker and more numerous.

As evening began to fall, there was movement at the bottom of the hill and a contingent of about a hundred spearmen emerged from the trees. They were led by a horseman in a bright coloured surcoat. As he approached Savage could just make out the red cross and three silver lozenges emblazoned on it.

"Sir Thomas Randolph, Earl of Moray." MacHuylin said.

Savage looked at him. "The man who captured Edinburgh castle from the English?"

MacHuylin nodded. "I don't like the look of this."

The Scots outside the fort hailed the approaching spearmen with warm greetings. The spearmen joined the besiegers and for a time there was a lot of laughing and shouting. Eventually a horseman rode forward from the Scots camp, carrying a white flag tied to the shaft of his spear.

Fergus Ui Flainn gestured to his men to let the man approach. "He carries the flag of parley. Let's hear what he has to say."

The rider halted his horse outside the gate. "I'm here to offer you the chance to surrender." He announced.

Fergus Ui Flainn popped his head above the parapet. "Now why would I want to do that?" He asked. "Haven't we already beaten you once?"

"Because you are surrounded, you are outnumbered and you have no chance of re-enforcements," the Scots rider replied.

"I've sent a messenger calling for re-enforcements," Ui Flainn shouted back. "It will be you who will be surrounded soon, not us."

The Scotsman gave a rather unpleasant grin. "No one will be coming to rescue you. The army of Ulster met in battle today with our army. Your side was slaughtered. Just like at Bannockburn our spearmen destroyed your knights. Your soldiers were annihilated and we have taken Carrickfergus."

There were a few moments silence as he let the impact of his words sink in.

"The English power here is broken. Why continue to hold out?" the Scotsman continued. "Surrender the fort and join our crusade. You will be welcome as brothers in our fight against the English."

Ui Flainn made a gesture behind his back and one of his warriors stood up. Before the Scotsman had a chance to react the warrior had launched his spear down at him. At such short distance he stood no chance. The leaf-bladed spear point went in over the top of his chainmail jerkin, entering the base of his throat and ploughing downwards through his chest. A bright jet of blood shot upwards from the wound and splattered across the wall of the fort as the Scotsman collapsed off his horse.

"What?" Ui Flainn challenged Savage when he saw the disapproving look the knight shot in his direction. "He was annoying me."

"He was under a flag of truce," Savage said.

"This isn't the Round Table, friend." Ui Flainn said.

A brief skirmish ensued. The Scots, provoked by the murder of their messenger, surged forward and launched a few arrows and spears at the defenders in the fort. The defenders replied with stones and throwing spears but the half-hearted attack soon petered out, leaving no casualties, bar one Ui Flainn warrior who ducked to avoid an arrow, lost his footing and fell off the battlements.

From the angle his hand sat to his arm, his wrist was obviously broken.

"You won't be able to hold a weapon. You're of no more use to us," Ui Flainn said, examining the man's injury. "You can go home when it gets dark."

"Do you think the Scot was telling the truth?" Savage said. "The Seneschal was beaten? Carrickfergus has fallen?"

"Who knows?" MacHuylin shrugged. "They might just be bluffing to try to get us to give up without a fight."

Ui Flainn nodded. "I'd like a damn sight more proof than the word of a Scotsman before I open these gates. I have to admit though, I don't like the way our re-enforcements haven't arrived. I sent for them last night."

"I thought you were just bluffing about that," Savage said. "How on earth did you do that?"

"There has been a fort on this hilltop since the first man walked on this island," Ui Flainn said. "And like most ancient forts, there is a secret tunnel in and out. It's just about big enough for one man to crawl through and it goes underground from the inside of the fort to somewhere down there." He gestured in the direction of down the hill.

"You might have told me." Savage said. "I was sure that someone disappeared last night. I thought I was just going mad."

"Sure if we told everyone it wouldn't be a secret, now, would it?" Ui Flainn retorted, his voice heavy with impatience.

Instinct told Savage not to push it further. Now outside the Earldom, whether in an allied Kingdom or not, he could see that the civility he had grown used to between Irish and Norman could no longer be expected once the heavy military presence that ensured politeness was removed. The relationship between the Earldom of Ulster and Ui Tuirtre was one of military convenience that suited both sides. It did not mean either party necessarily liked the other.

As the day drew towards evening the Scots re-organised. Most of the cavalry, led by Montmorency, rode off in the direction of Carrickfergus leaving only a few horsemen behind with around eighty foot soldiers. Sentries were posted at various points around the fort and as evening began to fall Sir Thomas Randolph himself did a tour of the perimeter, keeping a respectful distance away from the walls and out of slingshot range.

Savage and MacHuylin watched him as he carefully examined each side of the fort.

"Do you think this place will be harder to take than Edinburgh castle?" Savage said.

"They've got the numbers to do it." MacHuylin assessed the situation with the clinical eye of a professional soldier. "If they make a determined effort they should do it."

Darkness fell. Savage again wrapped himself up in his cloak and settled down on the battlements. The smell of the cows was now overwhelming and they were starting to get agitated as there was nothing for them to eat. Sleep took a long time to arrive but eventually he drifted off.

He did not get to sleep long.

Chapter 43

Savage was awoken by raised voices and the sound of feet pounding along the wooden platform he was sleeping on.

His first thought was that another attack was underway but a quick look over the battlements showed no one was outside the walls. Most of the defenders had left the battlements though so he decided to join them.

He pushed his way through the cows towards a crowd that had gathered around the little hut in the fort courtyard. To his surprise he saw Guilleme le Poer and Aengus Solmandarson-MacHuylin's Hebridean cousin-standing in the doorway of the hut.

-At least I know where the entrance to the secret tunnel is now, Savage thought to himself.

Lit by torches, the two men were bedraggled figures. Their arms and knees were caked with mud. Both wore chainmail armour over leather jerkins but many links were broken and the leather beneath creased from sword cuts. Le Poer's hands were blistered and caked with dried blood and he had a deep cut on his left cheek. Their faces were dirty from sweat and helmet oil.

"You've been in the wars," MacHuylin commented.

Le Poer gave a sardonic laugh, "Aye," he said. "While you've all been lying around up here we've been fighting the Scots."

"What happened?" Savage said. "They told us the army was beaten."

Le Poer nodded. "It was a disaster. The Scots fight in these formations of pike men called shiltrons. It's impossible for horsemen to get in amongst them."

"That's how they beat the English at Bannockburn," MacHuylin said. "Horses simply won't charge into tightly-packed spearmen. The heavy cavalry of the English knights were useless. The only way to deal with them is to use archers: Stand back and rain arrows on them either till they're all dead or they break formation and run for cover."

"That was supposed to be the plan," le Poer spat. "Most of our troops are light cavalry. That's the way we have to fight in a land of bogs and woods. But the Seneschal had managed to gather up every available archer north of Dublin and we had a couple of hundred of them. The battle plan was that two companies of horsemen would make a feint towards the Scots battalions, then turn and run to see if they would follow, at least get them to advance into arrow range-"

"The old Hastings tactics," Savage nodded.

"Then the archers were supposed to launch an arrow storm," Le Poer continued.

"Sounds like it should have worked. What happened?" MacHuylin wondered.

"We reckoned without the treachery of Syr Hugh Bysset," le Poer spat again. "He and his men formed the battalion who were supposed to be our rear-guard and protect the archers but they switched sides. As soon as the rest of the army charged he turned on the archers and massacred them, then charged on our cavalry from behind. Our horsemen were caught between the Scots in front and Bysset's treacherous men behind them. We were cut to pieces."

"So his nephew John is not alone in his treachery," Savage said.

"What about the Seneschal?" MacHuylin asked. "Is he alright?"

"He got away, but only just." Le Poer said. "He was leading the charge at the Scots. I wasn't far behind him. We had to turn fight our way out. At least we took a lot of that bastard Bysset's Glens men out on our way. It was a rout though. Those who got away fell back to Carrickfergus but there was chaos. There weren't enough soldiers left to man the walls. The Scots pursued, there was a lot of fighting in the streets and in the end the remnants of the army fell back to the castle. Aengus and I did not go: I need to get to Dublin to report what happened to the Justiciar and Aengus here wants to get back to the Hebrides so we rode out of the town just before it fell to the Scots. The castle is now under siege."

"What about Dame Alys and her daughter?" Savage asked. "Were they still in the castle? I sent a message that they should head for Dublin."

Le Poer's eyes flicked away and Savage could tell there was something else to tell. "And?" he demanded.

Le Poer took a deep breath, "As the Scots were landing at Vikingsford, King Domnall Ui Neill's troops crossed into the South west of the Earldom and cut off Carrickfergus completely. The road to Dublin is cut off. If they were in the castle they are besieged there with everyone else."

Savage rolled his eyes and stared at the starry heavens. Suddenly they seemed to be so hostile to him. Well so be it. It was time to challenge fate.

There was a long silence as everyone in the fort considered what had been said.

"Why are you here now?" Ui Flainn finally asked.

"Your messenger got through yesterday, so the Seneschal knew you were besieged here." Le Poer explained. "He asked we bring you a message: everyone not trapped in Carrickfergus is to fall back to Coleraine on the north coast and re-muster there. The Justiciar will be marching north with another army from Dublin to take on the Scots so we need to hold out until they arrive. The strongholds at Carrickfergus and Coleraine must not fall."

"We have other news," Aengus Solmandarson said. "The outside entrance of the tunnel we used to get into this fort is close to where the main body of Scotsmen are camped. We had to sneak our way through them to get to the tunnel and we heard what they are planning. They are going to attack this fort at dawn."

"What do you want to do?" MacHuylin addressed Ui Flainn. "This is a disaster. The Earldom is shattered. It will take a miracle to reverse this defeat. The Seneschal will understand if you decide to surrender."

Fergus Ui Flainn sighed. "There's too many of them for the fifteen of us to defend this fort against. You're right: The power of the Earl is broken, but surrender? It's just not in me. Not in me or any of my blood. I don't fancy the chances of me or my people at the hands of the Ui Neills either."

"Are you going to fall back to Coleraine?" Le Poer asked.

"And end up besieged behind the walls up there too?" Ui Flainn shook his head. "No way. I'm sick of being cooped up here already. Hiding behind walls and forts is the Norman way of war. I've had enough of it. It's time we took to the old ways. We'll take to the woods and the mountains and hide out there. We'll hit the Scots and the Ui Neills every time they move, and then disappear back into the trees. That's the way we fight when we're outnumbered. It's the way we always have. It works."

"What about you, cousin?" Aengus laid a hand on MacHuylin's shoulder. "I came here with Le Poer to offer you passage with me to the Hebrides. This war extends beyond these shores. Robert Bruce has hit us hard and we can use a warrior like you. My ship waits off the coast just north of here. It's ready to set sail as soon as we arrive."

MacHuylin paused. For the first time since he had met him Savage detected genuine indecision in the galloglaich. Finally he shook his head. "No. I owe it to the Seneschal to stay and continue the fight."

The Hebridean nodded. "I can't say I'm not disappointed, but I understand."

All eyes turned to Savage. "What are you going to do?" Le Poer asked. "The Seneschal is trapped in Carrickfergus castle and the army is smashed. It will take a small army to break Dame Alys and Galiene out of there. Right now I can't think where you will get one of those."

Savage sighed, trying to think.

"You could try to ransom them," MacHuylin suggested. He looked Savage up and down then shook his head. "I doubt you would have much to offer in exchange for them though, and it would take something very special for them to allow the woman and the girl to go free. It would make Ui Neill look soft, or worse: greedy."

Savage suddenly smiled.

"I think you've got the answer, Connor. Something very special you say? Aengus: Would there be room for me on your ship?"

"Plenty," the Hebridean replied.

Le Poer looked disappointed. "You're going to run away? Abandon them to their fate?"

"No. I'm going to get the one thing we can bargain with that Edward Bruce will really want." Savage said. "I'm going to Scotland to steal the Holy Grail."

There was silence. All eyes were on Savage.

"Robert Bruce has the Holy Grail. While he bears it, more and more people will join his side," Savage reasoned. "MacHuylin said it yesterday: The legend says that an army that bears the Grail is invincible. Connor and I infiltrated the Scots army when they landed and we know where they are keeping it. Some place called 'the Noquetran'. I'm going to go there and steal it, bring it back to Ireland and we can use it to negotiate with Bruce. I'll try to bargain with him to let Alys and Galiene go and lift the siege on Carrickfergus castle."

MacHuylin smiled. "It just might work."

"Even if you only take away their talisman, it would stop more men joining them. One person might succeed where an army wouldn't. Its madness, but it's the only plan we have," le Poer laughed. "I wish you the best of luck with it."

"That leaves us with the small problem of how we all get out of here before the Scots attack." MacHuylin said.

"What about the tunnel?" Savage asked.

Everyone else shook their heads. "There's only room for one man at a time," Ui Flainn said. "It would take all night for us to get through there one at a time."

"It comes out nearly in the middle of the Scots camp," Le Poer said. "It was hard enough for the two of us to creep in to it in the dark, but fifteen of us suddenly popping up in the middle of them? They're bound to notice."

"We'll have to fight our way out." Ui Flainn stated the obvious conclusion they were all coming to.

"There's a lot more of them than us," MacHuylin said. "Not all of us will make it."

"We don't have any choice," shrugged Ui Flainn. "We'll just have to charge out the gate and then it will be every man for himself. If there was some way to even the odds up a bit I'd be happier but that's just the way it is."

Everyone was quiet for a second as each man calculated the possibilities of any of them making it away from the fort alive.

"Don't any of you know your history?" Savage said suddenly.

Questioning eyes looked at him.

"When the Normans first came to Ireland, Raymond le Gros found himself in the same situation as we do now down in Wexford," Savage said. "I think we should follow his example. Listen: I have an idea."

Chapter 44

As the cold, grey light of dawn began to touch the sky, Sir Thomas Randolph led his men towards Donegore hill fort. Fifteen hand-picked men followed him, they moved quickly and quietly towards the gate, carrying scaling ladders to throw up against the walls. Four of them hefted a middle-sized battering ram slung between them. The rest of the foot soldiers followed in a column that snaked up the path to the gate. Ten crossbowmen, their weapons primed, moved into positions around the fort within range of the walls.

As he approached the gate, Randolph recalled a similar dawn two years before. Then he had scaled the near sheer cliffs beneath Edinburgh Castle to take the defenders by surprise and win a famous victory. He did not anticipate today's assault would be anywhere near as difficult. From observation, he reckoned there to be a maximum of twenty defenders in the fort, so his men would outnumber those inside by four to one. Numbers alone would ensure their victory. Even if the first men fell the swift onrush of the men behind would simply overwhelm the defenders. It should all be over before breakfast.

When within easy sprinting distance of the gate, Randolph stopped and let his vanguard troop go ahead. When they were close enough to the gate he held up his hand to signal that everyone should pause. He looked around to check everyone's positions. Everything was set for the attack.

If he was honest with himself, he was surprised that they had made it that close without being spotted. He could see several men up on the battlements but they were huddled down into warmth their thick cloaks. They were probably asleep, he surmised. That would their fatal mistake.

From inside the fort sound finally came. An agitated mooing of cattle and the thumping of hooves against the walls and ground could be heard. Something was disturbing the cattle, probably the defenders getting up. As if in confirmation, a glow of light appeared from within the walls which must be them lighting fires for breakfast. They were up, but it was too late.

Randolph stood up so all his men could see him. He dropped his hand and the crossbowmen rose as one and loosed their arrows at the men on the battlements. At the same time the rest of the men, led by the four with the battering ram, charged the gate, screaming war cries that would have woken the dead.

Randolph suddenly realised something was wrong. The four men on the battlements were riddled with arrows, but each still stood in his position. One suddenly tipped sideways, revealing that it was little more than a scarecrow: A long Irish cloak propped up on three spear shafts to look like a man.

The noise of the cattle inside the fort had now reached a frantic squealing. The glow of fire inside was too intense to be a mere cooking fire.

"Stop!" Randolph yelled, but his shout was drowned by the roaring of his men's war cries and the moos of frantic cattle.

The men with the battering ram reached the gate and ploughed straight into it, the weight of the ram given further impetus by the speed of their charge.

Randolph began sprinting himself towards the gate. "Stop! Stop! It's a trap!" he shouted.

At the merest touch of the battering ram the gates of the fort burst open, much too easily for them to have been barred or bolted.

The gates swung inwards and a tide of panicking cattle stampeded out. A huge fire had been set in the middle of them and they desperately ran to escape the flames. The men in the lead with the battering ram went down beneath the cattle's charge, obliterated beneath the thundering hooves.

Behind the cows stormed the defenders of the fort, riding on horses, whooping, screaming and poking spear points into the rearmost cows' flanks to incite their terror further.

Sir Thomas Randolph had to throw himself off the track to avoid the stampede that gushed like a waterfall out of the fort, sweeping aside everything in its path. He tumbled down the side of the mound. Two of the cows missed their feet and tumbled off the path also, narrowly missing Randolph as they tumbled down the slope.

The rest of the Scottish spearmen had no choice but to turn and flee before the onrushing tide of cattle. Some jumped off the track and scrambled down the slope while others just ran as fast as they could back the way they had come. At the bottom of the mound they scattered in every direction down the hillside.

Reaching the bottom of the fort mound the cows continued to run blindly down the hillside in a herd but the riders following them turned sharply towards the woods and rode as hard as they could, savagely driving their horses as they went.

Sir Thomas Randolph scrambled up to his feet just in time to see the last of the fort's defenders escaping on horseback into the trees down the hill, pursued by nothing more than a couple of desultory crossbow shots that had no hope of hitting any of them.

"Shit." Randolph commented, wondering how Edward Bruce would take this news.

Behind them the fort of top of Donegore hill, its walls and ramparts carefully fuelled with pitch and oil, began to dissolve into a blaze of fire.

Chapter 45

Savage stood on the stern of the ship, near the steering board, watching the coast of Ireland recede behind him.

After the hectic ride from Donegore they had left the fort to burn and galloped hard west through woods. Finally they arrived at a fork in the path and the place of parting. MacHuylin, Le Poer and the Ui Flainns were going to Antrim, while Savage would go north-east with Aengus Solmandarson, back towards the coast.

"Good luck," Savage saluted Le Poer and MacHuylin.

"May the Big One look down on you," MacHuylin replied with the Irish version of the same sentiment.

As they rode back towards the coast, Savage could see the fire at Donegore fort blazing away on top of the hill, now to the south of them. By the time the sun was high in the sky they finally rode down a steep wooded valley that ended in a little natural harbour. Riding on the clear azure waters of the bay was the Hebridean galley of Aengus Solmandarson.

"There are ships patrolling the crossing. They stop and sink anyone they don't like," Aengus's forecastleman told him as they boarded. "We will need to be careful."

In no time they had cast off and were underway. Savage was pleased to find he experienced none of the terror of his former of sea journeys. The tang of salt water was in his nose, the wind tugged at his hair. Beneath his feet the ship moved, above his head the sun shone and ahead lay uncertainty, mystery, even danger. He looked back at the shore of Ireland behind, recalling the countless times he had spent on the same shore as a boy, throwing stones into the sea while watching the ships leaving and aching to be going with them, not caring where they were destined, just wanting to go. Now here he was, for the second time in his life sailing away again. This time however he knew the meaning of leaving home.

Aengus Solmandarson was dangling precariously over the side between two sets of oars. After a moment's hesitation he plunged his head into the icy sea, then wrenched his head from the water, sending showers of droplets everywhere and whooping with unbridled delight. Sweeping his sopping wet hair back from his face, he gave a satisfied sigh and commented "That's better! Gets rid of the cobwebs." He made his way through the arranged ranks of oarsmen to the back of the boat where Savage stood.

"It's a beautiful day, we have the tide with us and soon as we get out into the open sea we should have a good wind behind us." Aengus said. "We'll to be in Galloway by nightfall -at the latest."

Savage nodded. "What if we run into those patrol boats? You don't have many men here to fight anyone off."

Aengus grinned. "This is a very fast ship, Syr Savage. I have no intention of putting up a fight."

Savage surveyed the galley, noting just how sleek it was. Smaller and thinner than most ships, Aengus's boat was shaped like a leaf-bladed spearhead which scythed through the water with ease. At present it was propelled only by the oars which were arranged in rows on port and steering board sides, but a big square sail could be unfurled on the mast when the wind was right. The oars themselves were manned by a motley, dangerous looking band of islanders.

Once out into the open sea the youngest and nimblest member of the crew, Col, was sent up the mast to undo the lashings of the sail to catch the wind. With a creaking of wood the mast took the strain, the canvas filled with the stiff sea breeze and the galley surged forward. The crew pulled their oars aboard and almost to a man wrapped themselves in whatever they could find and curled up on the open deck to catch up on some sleep.

Aengus remained awake, standing on the platform at the stern with the handle to the great wooden steering oar grasped steadily in his hands. Col also had to stay awake to keep an eye on the sail.

Savage remained at the prow, watching the nose of ship slice through the emerald, opaque sea, churning the water to white froth. Behind him the land got further and further away as the ship sailed north east towards Scotland. To the south were the little islands called the Maidens and far to the south east were the scattered rocks of the islands owned by the Copeland family.

Turning away from the prow, Savage picked his way carefully through the sleeping crew to the stern where Aengus stood.

"Where can you land me in Galloway?" Savage asked.

"That will depend on the wind, the tide, and the whim of Aegir." The Hebridean said. "There are only a few natural harbours and my preferred landing would be at a sea lough called Lough Ryan. However, if the wind carries us further south, then we'll round the Mull of Galloway and land in Luce Bay. From there it'll be up to you on your own. We'll be sailing north to the Islands and."

"Do you know where this 'Noquetran' where the Grail is kept, is?" Savage asked.

Aengus shook his head. "Never heard of it. You could try by asking some locals but the name sounds French to me. They probably have a different name for it."

Savage nodded grimly. The prospect of having to fend for himself alone on foreign, hostile soil in an area famed throughout the world for the wildness of its natives was daunting.

"There's nothing much of interest to see after this, except sea." Aengus said. "If I were you I'd get some rest. I know I would if I didn't have to steer this boat."

Realising just how sound an idea this was, Savage made his way back to the prow and curled up on the deck, wrapping his cloak around himself and pulling his hood over his head to shut out the sun. As he lay awaiting sleep he tried to remember the story of a romance he had once heard about a knight's adventures in Galloway, but all he could recall from it for definite was the often repeated sentiment that Galloway was a wild, dangerous, inhospitable place peopled by barbaric savages, evil monsters, wicked knights and beautiful maidens. He finally slipped into unconsciousness smiling at the thought that the latter perhaps made up for all the other shortcomings of the place.

His, and the rest of the crew's, awakening was a rude one.

Either by accident or carelessness, the top fastenings of the sail came loose. The great canvas sheet collapsed forward to envelope those slumbering at the front end of the boat. After a lot of general swearing and grumbling, Col was blamed for the usual reasons: He was youngest and smallest. Up the mast he was sent again to retie the sail which was again hoisted by the rest of crew.

Looking around him, Savage saw that the coast of Ulster had disappeared over the horizon behind them. Up ahead the dark coast of Galloway was just starting to ascend into view. The bright sun had been masked by clouds and the sea was no longer green but slate grey.

"Make a better job of it this time!" Aengus warned Col.

"It wasn't my fault!" Col grumbled from the top of the mast as he finished tying the ropes. He was about to begin climbing down when he suddenly caught sight of something.

"Ship!" Col shouted down from aloft. "There's a ship following us."

"Where?" Aengus shouted up the mast.

"One vessel. Dark sail. About the same size as us." Col said, smiling down at them, pleased at his own cleverness and the keenness of his eyesight.

Aengus and Savage looked astern. Sure enough, there was something just on the horizon, as yet just a fuzzy blob in the distance.

"His eyes are the sharpest I've come across in my life." Aengus said aside to Savage. "If he says he can see a dark sailed ship I believe him."

"It could be a fishing boat." Savage suggested. "Anyway: It's not necessarily following us. People sail from Ulster to Scotland all the time."

"Not when there's a war on." Aengus replied through gritted teeth. "I'm not taking any chances. I don't like being followed by anyone."

"What are we going to do?" Asked Savage. Without his feet planted firmly on dry land and a sword in his hand he was starting to feel utterly helpless. Some of his old fear of sailing began to crawl in his gut.

"We run." Aengus replied. "Right you;" he shouted up to Col, "Make sure that sail is fixed properly this time or you're walking home. The rest of you," He addressed the crew, "it's back to the oars. Let's see if we can leave this bastard in our wake."

Chapter 46

The crew sprang into action. They grabbed their oars from the deck and slid them out through the rowlocks, cracking a few unfortunate heads during the process. The crew took their places on the rowing benches and to Savage's amazement, Aengus began singing in a loud, clear voice.

The reason for this quickly became clear as the crew joined in. On the third line of the verse they all pulled together a mighty stroke of the oars and the galley surged forward. The singing continued, and the oars beat in time to the music. Col finished his job and descended the mast as Aengus returned to the steering oar at the stern. The ship powered on through the waves, now propelled by both wind and oars.

"Look ahead." Col shouted over the rush of the water and wind.

Both Savage and Aengus did so. To Savage's surprise the coast of Galloway seemed to have disappeared. Strangely, the tops of the mountains were still visible, but they seemed unnaturally high in the air.

"Excellent!" Aengus's broad grin reinstalled itself on his face. "Sea mist. We'll disappear into it. That lot behind us will never find us. Aegir the ale brewer is looking after us today."

They raced on for a time towards the floating mountaintops and the thick mist, but all the while Savage could see that they were getting slower and slower. It was not that the rowers were tiring. They still pulled on their oars as resolutely as ever, but the canvas sail was getting looser and baggier by the minute. The wind was dying.

Aengus Solmundarson's face became deadly serious. Savage joined him at the stern again.

"This is bad." The Hebridean said.

"Surely not? They need the wind as much as we do." Savage said, presuming Aengus referred to the ship chasing them.

"I wasn't talking about them." Aengus replied dismissively. "It's not just that the wind has dropped. Haven't you noticed how flat the waves are?"

"Isn't that a good thing? Easier for rowing."

"It would be, if we were a good few miles closer to the coast." Aengus replied grimly. "Smell the air. Can't you tell? There's a storm coming. This is the calm before it."

Savage's jaw dropped a little. In a flimsy open boat miles from land a storm was the sea traveller's worst dread. His old fear of sailing surged once more through his guts.

"Will we make it ashore before it breaks?" He asked, his voice husky from the sudden tightness that gripped his throat.

"It depends on that mist," Aengus said. "Once we enter it whoever is following us won't be able to find us, but we won't be able to see where we're going. We'll have to slow down in case we run into an island or rocks. We might get lost. I had planned sailing north towards Lough Ryan but now I reckon we'll just go straight for the coast. Old Aegir isn't on our side after all: A mist and a storm he's decided to throw at us. He must be lonely today."

Fingers of the mist were already reaching out to curl around the mast.

"I want you and Col up at the prow." Aengus ordered. "One on each side. Keep a watch up ahead. I'll need you to look out for rocks, reefs, islands: - anything that could sink us. If you see ahead in the water then shout. Loud."

Savage and Col took up their posts as directed. The galley slipped into the white oblivion of the mist. Perception reduced drastically and the wide, open seascape dissolved into the mist's blankness. Vision was cut down to fifteen feet around the boat and even though they knew they were outdoors, the encroachment of a creepy feeling of claustrophobia was hard to shake off.

Aengus began singing a low, haunting song in words unintelligible to Savage. The oarsmen joined in and the tempo of their rowing changed accordingly. By now the sail hung limp and useless. The wind had died entirely.

"Who is this Aegir he keeps talking about?" Savage asked Col.

Col chuckled. "The old ale brewer? He's the God of the sea our ancestors worshipped. Sailors from our part of the world still have a healthy respect for him. They say when the waves are frothy-topped and stormy it's the froth from the ale Aegir is brewing ale for a feast. If you are caught out in the storm you'll be joining Aegir's feast in his hall."

"Where is his hall?" Savage asked.

Col did not reply, but simply pointed downwards, beneath the sea.

Savage was unsure of exactly how much time they spent, creeping along through the fog's strange closeness, but it was certainly a long time. All the while he and Col strained their eyes at the prow, gazing intently into the blankness in an effort to make out a sign or shadow of anything that could be of danger.

They saw nothing. Ever onwards the boat moved, for all they knew going round in circles.

All the time it grew ominously dark. Savage knew that it could only be afternoon so it must be the unseen gathering overhead of black storm clouds. The first stirring of a breeze began to tug at the sail but this time it was far from welcome. It was the herald of the approaching tempest.

Soon they felt the first kiss of raindrops and a stronger gust grasped the sail. All conversation aboard died except for muffled complaints about getting soaked. At first the rain was light; hardly warranting even pulling up their hoods but suddenly and without warning great gouts of water began to gush down from the heavens, soaking everyone to the skin within seconds.

All around raindrops hissed into the sea, adding themselves to what there was already so much of. A swell was gathering on the sea and soon the boat was rising and falling in gentle rhythm with the waves.

The wind grew stronger and stronger.

"At least this mist should be cleared by the wind. We will soon be able to see where we're going." Aengus said. "Eric, Ewen:" he addressed two of the oarsmen. "Start bailing, will you? It's bad enough being rained on without the herrings playing tig between our toes as well."

The two crewmen left their oars and picked up a couple of hide buckets and began using them to reduce the level of the rain water which was gathering in the boat.

Despite Aengus's hopes the mist remained thick as ever while the wind grew ever more ferocious and the waves got higher and higher.

"Get that sail down before the wind rips it to pieces or it pulls down the mast!" Aengus shouted over the rising tumult.

Four men left their oars to spring to the mast. Col left the prow and shinned up the mast to undo the sail tying. The great canvas sheet collapsed onto the deck, the sailors bundled it up and pushed it beneath the steering platform on which Aengus stood.

The men returned to their oars but as the elements took control their part was becoming increasingly redundant. Any attempt to power the boat or influence its course was futile. Savage could see with a cold dread that their fate was no longer in their own hands. They were no longer masters of their own destiny.

At the prow Savage crouched, soaked and miserable, trying to quell the waves of fear that surged like the sea around him. With his feet on solid ground and his sword in his hands he had faced countless foes and dangers without experiencing terror but now the sheer helplessness of their predicament overwhelmed him.

The ship pitched and rolled between waves which seemed to be growing to ever more impossible sizes. The high wind whipped the heavy rain so it lashed the sailor's skins till they stung.

A new affliction struck Savage. The lurching of the boat suddenly began to be echoed by his stomach and nausea seized his jaw muscles. The rest of the crew, all experienced mariners, did not suffer with him. Despite their situation, a few even managed to smile as Savage violently vomited over the side.

Savage could not remember ever feeling more wretched. He was sick, soaked to the skin, cold, lashed by the wind and racked by the terror that at any moment the ship would roll over or break up and pitch them all into the dreadful, opaque sea where an inescapable watery death awaited.

If there was a Hell, then surely this was what it was like. Not fire and torture but this helpless misery, tossed about like a straw entirely at the mercy of heedless powers which at any moment could smash the ship to pieces.

Despite Ewen and Eric's best efforts, the level of water in the galley kept rising. Sea water foamed over the sides to add to the rain bucketing from the sky. Aengus, his voice barely audible over the howling wind, shouted orders for everyone to abandon their oars and start bailing.

Finally the wind began to have an effect on the mist and it began to thin out. This proved to be small comfort. By now the waves were massive and when rising up on one the ship was tilted backwards so all the mariners could see was the wave behind. When they came down the other side into the trough all they could see was the wave behind and the one in front. All they could hear was the screaming wind and the roaring sea.

The ship was tossed about so violently that the bailing had to be abandoned. Everyone aboard simply clung to whatever they could for dear life, with the exception of Aengus who resolutely stayed at the steering oar.

It was impossible to tell how long they were washed to and fro by the sea and wind but it seemed to Savage an absolute age, every second prolonged by the terror of expectation that the next wave would plunge them all into the water. He desperately wondered if he could still swim. As a child he had loved swimming and indulged himself whenever he could until one day the parson had caught him and a friend swimming and that had been the end of it.

The priest had told their mothers, warning the worried parents that swimming was a skill inspired by the Devil. Floating in water was proof of the sin of Witchcraft so swimming for Savage became forbidden.

Now it might save his life if the ship sank. Then again, he agonised, God knows how far out to sea they were, and if pitched into the water how could he even hope to struggle against such unstoppable might as the waves possessed. Perhaps being able to swim would just prolong a very cold, very lonely, utterly hopeless death.

Around him the mariners were praying to be delivered from their peril. Some were obviously hedging their bets as the name of Aegir could be heard amidst cries to Jesus, Mary and Saint Christopher for help.

Suddenly Aengus's voice was heard above the rest, shouting "Listen! Shut up will you and listen."

The crew fell silent and strained their ears to find out what he was shouting about. Amongst the howling wind and rain and the roaring sea, there came a strange, rhythmic booming followed by a hissing sound.

"What is it?" Savage shouted to the nearest sailor to him.

"Waves!" The man yelled back. "Waves crashing onto the shore!"

Savage's heart surged. At last a source of hope. They had reached land and after beaching the ship safety would only be a short wade away.

There was no sign of hope yet on the sailors' faces. They knew that a ship could only be beached on a sandy shore. Anxiously they strained for a sight of the shoreline.

As the ship breasted another wave they could plainly see the mountains and glimpsed the dark outline of the shore. They were very close. Aengus did his best to steer the ship straight in that direction but in reality they could only hope to reach it if the waves carried them that way.

"Row! Row you lazy sods!" The Hebridean Captain shouted and the crew sprang to their oars again desperately trying to influence their fate in any small way they could.

The ship once again rose on the swell of a huge wave, then dropped suddenly down the other side.

Suddenly there was an awful thud and the crack of splintering wood. The ship stopped dead. The crew were sent sprawling in every direction. Before Savage's horrified eyes the black, wet ruggedness of a big rock exploded up through the deck between him and the rest of the sailors.

The wave had smashed the ship down onto a massive rock.

Chapter 47

Before anyone could react the next wave arrived. The ship, skewered on the rocks, was unable to move with the swell. Like a gigantic hammer the wave smashed down onto the boat. Battered by such awesome power, Aengus's galley splintered like matchwood. Within a second it had ceased to exist.

Savage tumbled headlong into the water. The wave carried him along spinning over and over, head over heels, upside done, unable to tell which way was up or down. He expected to strike the rocks himself and feel his bones smashing like the ship but all around him was only black, freezing water.

Suddenly his head broke the surface and he gulped air. An instant later he sank again. Frantically he kicked out and struggled but kept sinking. Desperately he wondered if he had indeed forgotten how to swim, then remembered that a fully clothed man in the water sinks as fast as a stone. In an instant he had unclasped his cloak and unbuttoned his belt and baldric, abandoning his sword, purse and daggers to the anonymous depths. He was still sinking. Lungs beginning to ache he struggled out of one of his boots and got his jerkin off.

Finally he started to rise. Kicking his legs and beating his arms he came back to the surface, lungs now burning from oxygen starvation. Once again his head burst into the sweet air and he gasped frantically.

Despite how hard his arms beat the water, the weight of his other boot dragged him under again. After another submarine struggle his remaining boot was consigned to the deep and he made it back to the surface. This time he stayed afloat.

He was able to breathe the welcome air, but the shock of the cold water seized his chest and his breath came only in short gasps. He allowed the swell to carry him backwards as he fought to control his frantic breathing, knowing it would play havoc with his heart which thudded wildly behind his ribs.

As his breathing calmed down he took stock of the situation. There was no sign of anyone else from the ship, but there were plenty of pieces of the galley floating amidst the troughs and crests of the awesome waves. There was no sign of the rock they had floundered on, or rather it was impossible to tell which way he had been carried by the waves. Another wave lifted him and he tried to look about himself as he reached its crest. Far to his left, behind another wave, he finally spotted the site of the wreck. He saw the pathetic remnant of the mast, still upright but at an impossible angle, before it was engulfed in an explosion of white spray as another wave broke over the rock.

He was still in deep water, so the ship must have struck an offshore rocky outcrop. Now with some bearings he waited for the next wave to lift him so he could try to see which way the shore was. As he waited in the trough, surrounded only by grey sea, above the wind and rain he heard the tantalizing booming of the waves breaking on the beach.

The next wave came and lifted him. He rose and looked about. No sign of a beach. As he sank down into the trough the horrifying thought came to him that the rock that had been the ship's downfall was an isolated cluster, far out at sea. There was no shore. The booming was just the waves striking little islets. He was alone and waiting to die, with no hope of rescue.

Angry at himself he put these thoughts aside as the next wave lifted him. He turned round as much as he could in the water. Suddenly he saw it. Only a momentary glance amidst the waves but they were there: The dark mountains and a black line that could only be the shoreline. It was ahead, in the direction the waves were travelling.

Treading water he contemplated that if the tide was going in he would have a better chance of making it than striving against an ebbing tide. Either way he was wasting energy staying where he was.

Now with something to aim for he struck out for the shore, counting his lucky stars it was not dark as well.

As he swam, each wave lifted him and he felt its power surge him forward. Encouraged, he kicked harder. Despite the iciness of the water, the wind on his wet face was painfully cold. He plunged it under the surface as he swam, lifting it up every few strokes to breathe. It was strange that the water should seem warmer than the air, then he realised that his skin had become numb where enveloped by the water.

On he swam, unable to tell how close he was to the shore. He just kept doggedly going, rising and falling with the sea. All around the storm raged with no signs of abating. The effort was exhausting. A strange sleepiness started to creep over him, starting in his fingers and toes and working in. His strokes became slower and slower until he felt content to rest a little, floating face down, relaxed, resigned to let the tide carry him on in. It would be all right to take a break for a bit. He would be able to redouble his efforts with renewed vigour later.

A spark seemed to ignite within Savage and he raised his head out of the water with a gasp. It was Death who had been whispering these things in his ear. He would not-could not-give in. To stop was to die and he had no intention of dying, not when so close to the shore and safety. He began to swim once more, denying the tiredness in his limbs.

A wave lifted him and he saw it. The black rocks jutting into the sea and running up to the land on both left and right. In between was a little crescent of sandy beach.

Savage redoubled his desperate efforts, his heavy arms and legs protesting with exhaustion.

Another wave took him and he surged forward, this time the wave started to break as it passed him. As he fell behind the wave he felt his right foot hit something soft. Land. Before he could react the next wave caught him, breaking as it did so.

He was careered forward uncontrollably with the surf, bouncing through the shallows propelled, spinning, by the violent power of the wave. It passed and he found himself on hands and knees in the water. The broken wave began to go out again. Savage felt its awesome sucking power pulling him back into the sea.

Wailing forlornly he tried to grasp purchase on the sand but it just melted away, running through his fingers with the wave. Back down the beach he was dragged.

The next wave hit him, knocking him almost senseless and propelling him back up the beach. Savage realised that this shuttling up and down the shallows could be the death of him. Exhausted, he would drown, his feet on land but lungs filled with water he could no longer fight to keep out.

When the wave passed him, with supreme effort he rose off his knees to his feet and half staggered, half lurched forwards through the water, feeling the strength of the undertow tugging his legs and the sand from under him.

Another wave came and knocked him off his feet, but also shoved him further up the beach as if the sea, realising that this morsel was not going to be easily swallowed, had decided to vomit him up instead. His mind was now virtually a blank, he knew only that he had to keep struggling forwards. Savage rose to his feet once again and waded further forward before the next wave hit him. Again he was pushed further up the beach, the wave's power being spent as it was expelled on hitting the land.

With only the energy to get to his knees left, Savage crawled onwards; the water around him now only inches deep. Utterly exhausted, he collapsed onto his back.

Only dimly aware of his surroundings, he thought he saw two human figures coming down the beach towards him. Weakly he croaked to them for help and waved a pathetic arm before he passed into unconscious oblivion.

Chapter 48

Savage knew time was passing, but the days to him were a confused blur of lucid moments and strange dreams and visions. Interchanging dark and light told him days had gone by, but how many he could not tell. He drifted between sleep, wakefulness and a strange state that was somewhere in-between.

In his more lucid moments he found himself to be in a richly decorated bedchamber lying in cool, clean linen sheets. A beautiful young woman soothed his hot brow with damp cloths and coaxed him to drink bitter tasting infusions which could only be herbal medicines. He was unsure, but he thought she had said her name was Repanse de Schoy.

His less coherent hours were filled by nightmares of drowned sailors and terrible sea creatures coming to drag him back into the waves. Through it all a vision of a shadowy woman and a little girl ran, for some reason frightened and calling for help.

Eventually he awoke from a mercifully deep, untroubled sleep to find himself feeling the closest to what he could describe as normal since Aengus Solmundarson's ship had sunk.

Taking stock of his surroundings, he saw the bed was surrounded by beautiful tapestries. Beside his bed sat the dark haired maiden who had called herself Repanse de Schoy.

When she saw he was awake, she put down her embroidery and regarded Savage with dark, sloe-like eyes.

"So you're back among the living." She smiled. Her accent was slightly odd. There was a broad hint of Scots in it, but also something else Savage could not quite trace.

"Where am I?" Savage asked.

"You are safe," the woman replied. "My uncle's servants saw your ship floundering in the storm and picked you up off the beach, half dead from exhaustion and cold."

"Did they find anyone else?"

She shook her head and laid a hand on his shoulder in a sympathetic gesture. "Were they close friends?" She asked gently.

"I'd only just met them, but ..." Savage trailed off, trying to come to terms with the news. The smiling face of Aengus surfaced in his memory. It was hard to think of him as being cold and dead, floating alone in the black depths.

"You've been very ill." The woman explained. "Because of the cold and the soaking you caught a dangerous fever. For a while we thought you weren't going to live. You've recovered admirably, though."

"How long is it since the shipwreck?" Savage wanted to know, memories of the urgency of his mission surfacing.

"Nearly a week." Repanse told him.

A week? Savage was dismayed. Anything could have happened in that time. Perhaps he was already too late. Seeing the agitation igniting in his eyes, the woman laid a calming hand on his brow.

"Rest yourself." She said. "You are not fully recovered - far from it. You are still weak and tired so no more questions for now. You will have time to ask all you wish later."

"I've had such strange dreams ..." Savage began.

"That was due to the fever and the poppy draughts we've been giving you," said the woman, getting up. "I'll leave you alone now. Take some rest. There are clothes for you if you wish to get dressed. Feel free to explore the castle if you want, but don't stray too far. You're still weak and we don't want you passing out. It is a beautiful day, though. Perhaps some sunshine would do you good." With that she left, closing the door behind her.

Savage was unable to remain in bed. His mind was a mess of agitation. The ship had been wrecked on the coast of Galloway, but where? Where was he now? Who were his saviours? They had saved his life, but he was still in the enemy country so he had to be very careful what he said. God knows what he had already let slip in feverish ravings. What was happening in Ireland? Were Alys and Galiene alright?

He got out of bed but had to steady himself momentarily as his head spun with the adjustment of standing up after so long being perpendicular. Once his dizziness subsided he examined the clothes which had been left for him. These were a brand new shirt of fine woollen cloth, off-white in colour and wonderfully soft and comfortable, green woollen breeches and a new pair of leather boots.

He dressed then set about exploring his surroundings. The woman, Repanse, had said he was in a castle, and the walls behind the gorgeous and impressive tapestries were indeed made of stout stone.

The room had an unusually wide window through which Savage studied the castle's environs. Repanse had been correct; it was a beautiful summer's day. The Sun blazed in a cloudless blue sky and in its rays danced a sea of green-a thick forest alive with the newness of fresh spring leaves. There was no sign of the real sea, but the castle seemed to be in a wide, steep sided valley so the water must lie beyond the valley, invisible to sight.

On trying the door he found it unlocked.

At least he was not a prisoner, Savage consoled himself. Opening the door he discovered a spiral staircase that went up and down. Savage descended, passing two doors on his way down, both of which were locked. Finally he arrived at ground level and a door which was unlocked. He opened this and went outside to have a look around, hoping to find someone he could talk to and perhaps discover some useful information.

On leaving the building he saw that he had been in a tower of a castle. It was one of two small towers which flanked a much larger keep. Savage's military eye surveyed the keep appreciatively and judged that in all his travels it was about as well built a stronghold as any he had seen this side of Beirut. Constructed of dark grey stone, the keep was square, as broad as it was tall and radiated the impression of solid, unshakeable strength.

In front of the keep was the hall. Most castle banqueting halls were long, rectangular buildings but unusually, this one was square like the keep. All the buildings were surrounded by a round curtain wall with galleries built into it. Savage could only marvel at how well designed the castle was, for both peace and war. He wondered that he had never heard stories of such a civilised place existing in the wilds of Galloway.

There was no sign of any living soul about the place. It was such a beautiful day that the denizens of the castle must be out in the forest hunting or at some other sport.

Savage decided to venture further and made for the castle gate. His legs felt weak after so long in bed, but he was enjoying the enlivening fresh air.

Above the gate was an anonymous tower with arrow-slit windows but no sign of access to or from it, save for the murder hole above the castle entrance used to pour boiling oil down on unwelcome visitors. Although no sound came from the tower Savage felt the distinct impression that eyes were watching him from it.

He called a loud "Hallo".

No one replied. With a shrug Savage continued on his way.

The gate itself was open and led to a drawbridge which had been let down to cross the moat that surrounded the castle. Beyond the moat was a forest into whose depths wound a little twisting path. Along this Savage sauntered, enjoying the healing coolness of the green shade dappled with golden sunlight amidst the ancient oaks, elders, ash and yews.

He had not gone far when the cheerful gurgling of running water reached his ears and he came across a river, running between moss-covered rocky banks. The path led alongside the river and for ten minutes Savage walked beside the crystal clear waters that ran deep and fast over the stones that made its bed. His worries were momentarily pushed aside by the peace and beauty around him. In the green canopy birds sang melodious ditties of their own understanding and the sun danced across the river in a million dazzling reflections.

As he came around a large rock, Savage saw a small boat, riding at anchor midstream. The boat was a hide and wicker coracle and in it sat two men. The man at the back of the boat was enjoying the sun while his companion fished with a line. Both were very finely dressed and it was plain to see that these were no humble peasants who relied on fishing to eat.

Savage called hallo and waved to them. "Excuse me, Sirs," he said, "can you tell me who owns that castle back there through the woods?"

"I can, brother." The fisherman looked up at him and smiled. Judging by the well groomed, long grey hair which hung down from his head, Savage took him to be rather old. He spoke with the same curiously mixed accent that the woman Repanse had possessed. "You're the young man the sea washed up, aren't you? Good to see you're better."

"You're from the castle?" Savage asked.

"It is my castle," the fisherman replied. "And I'm pleased to welcome you to it -now you're in a better state to comprehend that welcome."

"I've much to thank you for," Savage began but the fisherman held up a hand to quiet him.

"Pardon me if I seem rude, Sir," The fisherman said, watching the water with the eye of a hunter, "but fishing is the only kind of recreation I can enjoy these days and I like to indulge myself. We shall talk at length tonight at supper."

Realising he was being dismissed, Savage left the grey haired castellan to his fishing and began trekking back along the path towards the castle.

Repanse De Schoy's warning came back to him and he feared that perhaps he had ventured too far in his weakened state. Sweat was beading across his forehead and his breathing had become laboured. His legs felt as if someone had attached lead weights to them.

Pushing himself onwards he made it back to the castle drawbridge. When he reached the watchful gate tower, Savage was met by four serving lads who, seeing his fatigue and guessing his reluctance to climb all the stairs back to his bedroom, led him up to the galleries in the walls instead.

In the cool restfulness of the surrounding stone Savage found a couch upon which he laid down and without further ado fell asleep. He drifted off wondering where on earth he had ended up and just how friendly this mysterious fisherman who owned the castle would be if he knew the real purpose of his mission.

Chapter 49

Savage awoke. The cooler air and change in light told him it was evening. Two serving lads who were hovering nearby saw he was awake and showed him the washroom before leading him to the castle hall for dinner. The howling emptiness in his belly affirmed to him just what a good idea that was.

Entering the square hall, Savage saw that its interior was different from most castle halls. It was large enough to comfortably seat well over a hundred people. There was no raised dais at one end where normally the lord and his lady would sit. Neither was the fire situated along one wall. Instead, a great blaze roared right in the centre of the room. Around the fire, aligned with the corners of the hall itself, were four stone pillars. The strong, stout pillars supported a high, wide chimney made of bronze that efficiently extracted the fire's smoke from the room.

Savage was led into the middle of the room, near the fire. Close to the fire was a couch, on which an old man with long iron-grey hair reclined, leaning on one elbow. Savage realised that this was the lord of the castle who he had met earlier, fishing. Now closer, he saw that he was not, in fact, elderly: He was middle aged certainly but must have gone prematurely grey. The lord wore a sable hat the colour of blackberries, the crown of which was covered by purple cloth that matched the colour of his flowing robe.

Seeing Savage, the man smiled.

"My friend who the sea threw up," he said. "Forgive me for not getting up to welcome you properly. I'm not able to."

The lord struggled to raise himself a little higher on the couch. Savage saw that one of his legs was sticking out of the purple robe and noticed how withered and stick-like it was.

"Old battle wound." The lord said, patting his hips sadly. "I took a spear right through both thighs. They're useless now. Still, mustn't dwell on the past. At least I can still indulge one passion: Plenty of time for fishing."

As he spoke Savage tried to place his accent. He spoke Norman French which had a lilt of Scots to it, but only as much as someone who has spent time in a country rather than been born there would pick up. There was a hint of something else too, perhaps eastern.

The lord smiled. "We have much to talk about. Sit down brother."

Silently and unseen, servants had placed a plush, upholstered chair behind Savage so that all he had to do was sit down. The heat from the fire was uncomfortable but the invalid lord probably needed extra warmth.

"I suppose you're wondering where you are." The lord said.

"I admit I'm puzzled," Savage said. "I was under the impression that Galloway was a wild, savage place but this castle is the height of sophistication. It's as excellent as any I've ever seen- and I've travelled quite a bit."

The lord beamed but looked a little embarrassed at the praise. "Thank you, brother. Castle Corbenek is indeed a pleasant home, but, I'm sad to say, the tales you've heard about Galloway are true. You were very lucky it was my servants who found you on the beach. Some of the natives who haunt the mountains and forests of this land wouldn't have hesitated to cut your throat for what little possessions you had."

"They wouldn't have got much," Savage grunted. "The sea took everything I own. Even the shirt off my back."

"What were you doing sailing in such a storm?" The lord of Corbenek asked.

Savage took a deep breath and prepared to launch into the cover story he had concocted for himself.

"I am Richard de Clare," he said, announcing the pseudonym he had decided on. "My family were from Ireland but I have been in the East for a long time. I heard of King Robert Bruce's struggle for freedom and I was coming here to lend my sword to his struggle. Unfortunately my ship got caught in the storm."

The lord nodded thoughtfully. "Damned bad luck," he said. "So you are a knight? Bruce would indeed welcome you into his ranks. But you are now a knight with no horse, no armour and no sword. Not much use to anyone."

"I hear his brother has sailed for Ireland," Savage said.

"He has," the lord replied. Strangely, the man's grey eyes seemed filled with deep sadness.

"You seem sad. You wish you were going yourself?" Savage asked.

The man gave a little ironic laugh. "Quite the opposite. I wish he had not gone."

"You have cousins across the Irish sea?" Savage probed.

The paralysed castellan shook his head. "No. I just think it's sad that a country which has struggled so long to gain its own freedom should so soon seek to visit war and oppression on another."

"But Ireland supplies England with troops, weapons, provisions," said Savage. "It is hostile to Scotland's interests."

"Doubtless there are many sound, tactical reasons why so much will be expended, why so many lives will be sacrificed," the grey haired lord said, "but it cannot be denied either that what drives Edward Bruce is ambition. He wants to be a king like his brother. No, he wants it more than his brother. Robert Bruce will be happy if the expedition succeeds and England's supply route is cut off. Also, if the expedition fails and his over ambitious brother is killed in the attempt..." he shrugged. "A dangerous rival is removed."

Their conversation stopped for a moment as both spotted a young squire entering the hall with a jug of wine. Two goblets were filled and Savage took a long draft from one, buying some time as he considered the nobleman's words. Was his dismay at the Bruce expedition real or was he just testing Savage, trying to trap him? The last time Savage had been called "brother" was as a member of the Templar Order. Was this nobleman referring to him by that sobriquet simply out of Christian fellowship? He decided to try a gamble.

"I'm glad there was help here for this son of the widow," Savage said, using the Templar recognition phrase as nonchalantly as he could manage, while carefully watching the lord's face to see if there was any reaction.

The paralysed castellan simply chuckled.

"Tell me," he said, seemingly ignoring Savage's line. "What makes you want to fight for Robert Bruce?"

"King Robert Bruce bears the Holy Grail," Savage replied. "The cause of anyone who bears such a holy relic must be just."

"Indeed, he says that he does," the nobleman said. "And I have seen it."

"You have seen the Grail?" Savage leaned forward eagerly. His eyes were suddenly bright with excitement.

"Robert Bruce showed his Grail to many Scottish noblemen to try to gain our support. I saw a grail, whether or not it was the grail is another question."

"You don't believe Bruce has the true Grail?"

The nobleman shrugged. "Who can tell? Perhaps you would know that better than me. He got it from the Templars, your former Order."

Savage smiled. "So you did recognise the Templar code word: Where you in the Order too?"

"Dinner should be ready," the nobleman said. "I hope you are hungry."

Savage was starving and as if on cue, a door opened in one of the walls of the hall. Savage noticed that there were doors all around the hall, probably leading to kitchens or other private rooms. As his hungry eyes turned to the opened door a veritable procession emerged.

Two male servants entered, each bearing a pure gold candelabra inlaid with black enamel. Ten candles glowed on each candelabrum. Behind the candle bearers came a squire carrying a white painted lance. To Savage's surprise, the tip of the lance seemed to have fresh blood on it.

Deciding that it must be some strange local custom, he said nothing in case it might give him away.

Next through the door came the beautiful young woman who had nursed him, Repanse de Schoy. In her petite hands she bore a deep, wide dish made of refined gold, set with many kinds of precious stones. Behind her came another young woman carrying a silver carving dish. The procession halted as servants came forward to erect a table before the nobleman and Savage, over which a stunningly white tablecloth was laid. Warm water and towels were brought so that they could wash their hands, then the food began to arrive.

Repanse laid the silver carving dish on the table before the grey haired nobleman as the first course came: A haunch of venison in hot pepper sauce. A servant carved the meat on the silver dish, setting the slices on flat loaves of bread. Savage noted that slices of the rich, dark brown meat were also placed in Repanse's golden dish which she then carried through another door in the East wall of the hall.

"Your daughter won't be eating with us?" Savage asked.

The lord of the castle gave one of his customary chortles. "My daughter? Unfortunately no, she is my niece. She lives here with me and helps to look after me. I don't know what I would do without her. She is such a selfless girl. Even now she is taking that food to serve someone else who cannot join us."

Golden cups were set before them and clear, smooth wine poured out liberally.

"This is excellent," Savage said as he tasted the pepper sauce. "I prefer hot spicy dishes but it is so hard to get anything more exciting than stew in these Islands."

"I do as well," the nobleman said. "They so add to the flavour of the meat. It is a taste I acquired while living in the East."

"You were in Outremer?" Savage exclaimed. "I thought I detected an oriental sophistication in your castle. I take it you served there with the Order? It that where you were wounded?"

"Sir Richard: How long where you a Templar?"

"Just over two years. I served in Cyprus and England."

"Two years is not long enough to have risen very far through the ranks. You would not have learned many of your Order's secrets," the nobleman said as he chewed on a juicy lump of venison.

"True. That was something that really frustrated me."

"Well I will tell you one now. Your Order is gone now-ceased to be-so I can't see that it will do much harm."

Savage leaned forward expectantly.

Chapter 50

"Two hundred years ago, Hugh de Payens founded the Order of Poor Fellow-Soldiers of Christ and the Temple of Solomon: The Templars," the lord said. "King Baldwin of Jerusalem granted him and nine other companion crusaders quarters on the Temple Mount in the heart of the Holy City. For nine years they didn't do very much. There were still only nine of them and they spent the time digging beneath the Temple. Then things changed. Within twenty years they were the most powerful military force in the Holy Land. Within thirty years they were the richest organisation in the world. How do you think that all came about so quickly?"

Savage shrugged. "A combination of luck and good planning?"

"Good planning, yes. But not by them." The lord of Corbenek lowered his voice to barely above a whisper. "There is another Order, Syr Richard. A secret Order. It has existed since the very dawn of Christianity. Its members are few in number but great in influence. They possess secrets of incredible power, much greater than anything the Templars or any of their brother military Orders knew."

Savage was suddenly aware his mouth was hanging open and closed it quickly. "I've never heard of this Order."

"You wouldn't have," The lord continued. "It is highly secretive. Unseen, and working covertly, they have their own aims and goals, and they guide the history of the world through influence and money. Every now and again, however, this order needs to intervene in the affairs of the world in a more direct manner. In that case they make use of an existing organisation or, if one does not exist, they create one."

"Are you saying that the Templars were set up by this secret Order to fulfil some hidden purpose?"

The lord of Corbenek nodded.

"For what end?"

"To further the Order's strategy in the East."

"And what was that? I need to know. I sacrificed a lot to join the Templars."

"Tell me," the lord said. "Who is Alys de Logan?"

Savage was astonished, and his face betrayed him. Seeing this, the invalid nobleman smiled. "It was a name you often mentioned when delirious with the fever."

"She's a woman." Savage grunted.

"With a name like Alys I should hope so." The nobleman laughed.

"I was in love with her when I was young." Savage said, suddenly wondering what else he had betrayed about his mission while raving. "But I was torn between her and what I saw as a higher purpose. In the end I chose the higher purpose. I joined the Templars."

"An admirable sacrifice," the nobleman said. Savage thought he detected a hint of sarcasm in the man's voice. "I'm sure you profited by it."

"No, far from it. I lost everything." Savage looked away into the flames of the fire.

"Perhaps your reward will not be in this world." The lord suggested. "But I understand how you must be feeling. You sacrificed everything for what you thought a worthy cause only to find the cause was false: an empty chalice."

Savage did not reply. This paralysed rich fisherman knew more than he guessed.

The lord smiled in a kindly way and laid a friendly hand on Savage's forearm. "Let me tell you a piece of wisdom I learned in Jerusalem." He said. "Take it as friendly advice from an older man who has made mistakes in his life. It is this: 'Wine is strong. The King is stronger. Women are strongest, but Truth conquers all.' You have to work out what is really important in life, and when you do, you have to be true to that. Everything else is illusion and not worth fighting for."

Savage nodded. "I have a question for you," he said. "Why did the Templars give Bruce the Grail? He is excommunicated. And how did they get it in the first place?"

The lord turned his attention back to his meal. "Your Order, Syr Richard, were inveterate relic hunters. And were so from the very beginning. What do you think Hugh de Payens and his nine companions were doing ferreting away in the tunnels and passageways under the Temple Mount in Jerusalem? They were looking for holy relics. Whoever bears relics holds great power and influence, and the Templars knew that. That's were their money and power came from. They fought the Saracens, yes, but most of their energy went into hunting holy relics. Then once they had them, they exploited them. They hoarded them, made powerful people pay to get them and supplied them-at the right price-to ambitious Kings and Bishops. Genuine holy relics attract pilgrims to cathedrals and shrines. Do you know how much money pilgrims bring to a town? Do you think it is a co-incidence that the burghers of Santiago, Canterbury or Paris are some of the riches in the world? Relics are good for business, Syr Richard."

"And they found the Grail?"

"They certainly claimed to have found it. Like a said though: Is it the real Grail? Who can say? It's all a matter of faith really. The Templar treasury in Paris was stuffed full of holy relics: Enough thorns from the Crown of Thorns to make a hedge. Enough splinters of the True Cross to crucify Jesus five times over."

"The treasury in Paris, you say?" Savage said. "Before I was arrested, two French brethren came to the Templar base I was in. They were carrying a holy treasure from the Paris Temple treasury. A treacherous brother Templar-Sir Hugo Montmorency-betrayed us in an attempt to get his hands on it."

The lord raised his eyebrows. "You were arrested for being a Templar? Well my brother, you really did sacrifice much for your beliefs. Montmorency, I fear, is a fanatic."

"You know him?" Savage was surprised and suddenly defensive.

"I know of him," the lord continued. "He is someone who sees the Grail and nothing else. He does not realise that the Grail is a symbol of a higher purpose. It is the quest for it-and more importantly what you learn on that quest- that is what is really important. Montmorency thinks the physical object is what will get him into Heaven, and God knows, after the things he has done to get the Grail, he needs something to get him in there. I believe what happened was that your French brothers escaped to Scotland. As you say, Robert Bruce was excommunicated for the murder of Red Comyn, so the Pope's authority didn't stretch to Scotland and they knew they would be safe here. Montmorency tracked them down here but by the time he found them they had already offered their service to King Robert and given him the Grail as a sign of good faith. Montmorency had no choice but to enter into King Robert's service also. The Grail obsesses him and he wants it more than anything in the world."

Savage was silent for a few moments as he considered what had been said. Repanse re-entered the hall with the next dish, a blancmange of chicken in spiced almond milk. She served Savage and the castle lord then once more she placed a serving in the wide gold dish and she left again, going out through the eastern door. Savage wondered just who she was going to serve from the gold dish, but decided he had more important questions to ask.

It was time to take another risk.

"I didn't really come here to join Robert Bruce's army," Savage said.

"I had already guessed that. You're not a very good liar." The lord of the castle smiled.

"Alys de Logan and Galiene her-my-daughter are besieged in Carrickfergus castle by Edward Bruce's army," Savage continued. "I came here to steal the Grail and take it back to Ireland. I want to use it as a bargaining chip: To exchange it for Alys and Galiene."

There was silence for a few moments. Savage began to worry that he had miscalculated.

"Well, now." The lord of the castle finally spoke. "That's probably the best reason I've heard for seeking the Grail for a very long time."

Relief flooded over Savage. "Sir: You speak as though you know of this secret Order who founded the Templars. I believe you are a member of that Order. I believe you know many secrets and know much about the Grail. Can you help me? Do you know where I can find a place called the Noquetran?"

The lord looked puzzled. "The Noquetran?"

"I heard Edward Bruce say that is where he keeps the Grail," Savage said. "There is a chapel there called Merlin's Chapel."

The clouds of mystery cleared from the lord's face and he began to laugh heartily.

"What's so funny?" Savage asked.

"The Noquetran!" The lord chortled. "Edward Bruce called it that did he? The man who claims to be King of the Gaels cannot even speak their language properly! Cnoc Dreann, my friend-or 'Noquetran' as Edward Bruce's Norman French tongue would say it-is a mountain in these parts. Its name means the Hill of Sorrow. The pagans used to climb up it at their Easter rituals. There's an ancient burial cairn on the top of the mountain they call Merlin's chapel. There's a very old church up there too."

"Is it far from here?"

"A good half day's ride east," the lord said. "Follow the valley inland then ride along the edge of the great forest.

Finally you will come to another wide valley. Cnoc Dreann is at the far end of it. You cannot miss it."

"I must go there," Savage resolved, rising from his seat.

"I agree you should go there, and I wish you good luck," the lord said. "But my friend, it is late and you will not get far in the dark. Cnoc Dreann will still be there in the morning and Carrickfergus Castle will still be besieged. You have dangers to face so sit down and enjoy the rest of your dinner, then get a good night's sleep. Your quest begins in the morning."

Savage realised he was right. He sighed, rubbed his eyes and sat down again.

"Now," the lord smiled, "it is so rare to have company here, and much rarer to have a guest who has travelled to the East as you have. I miss Outremer: the warmth of the climate, the exotic food. Let us talk more of that."

From there the conversation flowed freely. Savage found his host to be pleasant, intelligent and very knowledgeable. As they talked, a succession of courses were brought to the table, each one delicious and cooked to perfection.

After the excellent meal the nobleman and Savage, now feeling quite stuffed, sat long into the night talking. As they chatted about their eastern travels and other shared topics, they nibbled dates, figs and nutmegs, cloves and pomegranates, all washed down with spiced wine. Finally, electuaries were brought: medicinal concoctions to aid digestion. After this they drank old mulberry wine sweetened with syrup.

At length the nobleman yawned and beckoned to some nearby servants who came over.

"My friend," he said, "it's time to retire for the evening. Goodnight." Then, to the servants, "take me to my apartments."

The four servants each grasped a corner of the spread which covered the couch and lifted the nobleman with it, then carried him in the makeshift bier out one of the doors of the hall.

Contented and well feasted, Savage made his own way to bed in his room in the tower, hoping that so much rich food eaten so late would not bring him nightmares. He needed all the rest he could get, for in the morning he would face who knew what trials on the summit of Cnoc Dreann.

Chapter 51

Savage awoke to the sound of birdsong. It was well past daybreak. He got up and found clean clothes had been left for him. The same fine woollen shirt and green woollen breeches as the day before were there, but they had been augmented by apparel suitable for travelling: A dark green, hooded long cloak, a leather jerkin and a pair of leather riding boots.

Once dressed, he left the room and descended the spiral staircase to the base of the tower.

Outside the tower door waited a well-groomed chestnut palfrey. It was bridled, saddled and obviously intended for him. Behind its saddle was tethered a leather shoulder bag containing enough provisions for a day's riding. A heavy sheepskin jerkin and thick woollen cloak were bundled alongside it.

Savage took the horse and led it around the castle, looking for the nobleman so as to say goodbye. Like the day before, the castle was deserted. Savage could find no one anywhere. The hall was empty, the fire out. The only sound in the dark stone fortress was the twittering of birds.

Savage decided that the lord of the castle was once more at his favourite sport of fishing. Mounting the palfrey, he rode out of the castle gate and down the forest path to the river. Following the river, Savage found no sign of the moored coracle or anyone fishing on the banks. Nevertheless he rode on for about a mile downstream, until he came to a little lake. Bobbing on the water of the lake was a little boat with someone sitting in it.

Savage hailed the boat and waved to attract their attention. The occupant turned and Savage saw that it was the young woman, Repanse de Schoy. As he watched, she pulled on the oars, rowing the boat over to the shore while Savage dismounted from his horse.

"Good morning," Savage greeted her as the boat reached the edge of the lake. "I was hoping to see your uncle. I wanted to say goodbye and thank him for his generous hospitality."

He grasped the end of the boat to steady it as Repanse rose from her seat. She gathered up a bundle wrapped in sack cloth from the bottom of the boat and carefully stepped out onto the shore.

"My uncle asked me that I give you this," she said, passing the long bundle to Savage.

Savage unwrapped the cloth. Inside was a sheathed sword. Suddenly captivated, he gazed at the terrible beauty of the weapon. He could only guess at its expense. The pommel was of the finest Arabian or Greek gold. The scabbard was intricately embroidered with the sort of gold thread work which was specialised in by the Venetians. He half drew it and studied its blade. The fine, burnished steel blazed with reflected sunlight and Savage saw that runes were engraved on the sword, though what they said he had no idea.

"He said that a knight is not much use without a sword," Repanse smiled.

Savage snapped the sword back into its sheath. "This is too generous. I cannot accept such an expensive-"

Repanse held up a hand to silence him. "My uncle insists. He has no use for it himself and simply prays that you will put it to good use."

Savage girded the sword onto himself; amazed and grateful.

"My Lady, I am overwhelmed with his generosity," He said. "Tell me: what is your Uncle's name?"

"He is called Bron." Repanse said. "But let us waste no more of your time. You must be on your way if you want to reach Cnoc Dreann before nightfall. The top of the mountain will be cold so there are heavy clothes bundled on your horse."

"I have many questions-" Savage began, but Repanse just held up her hand again for silence.

"You must go." She said simply. From her tone it was clear this was an order, not a suggestion. "Follow the valley east."

Savage realised that she would answer no more questions. He saluted her and mounted his horse. With one more look over his shoulder he spurred the palfrey and rode off around the bank of the lake and along the river that continued from its far shore.

He had travelled several miles when he came to another path which branched to his left. Savage judged by the position of the sun and by what side of the trees the thicker branches grew on, that this new path went west, while the one he was on went south, so he took the new path.

It was not long before later he began to regret the decision. The path became little more than an animal track which twisted and wound its way through dense thorns and undergrowth beneath the tree canopy. At least it was getting steeper, which meant he was climbing up the valley side. Eventually the angle of the ground and the tugging thorns made him dismount. On and on he climbed, sweating and panting, until quite suddenly he emerged from the treeline into grassland, a few hundred yards from the summit of the valley side. He slogged on to the top then stopped to take his bearings, rest and break out the provisions packed for him.

As he munched his way through bread and fruit he looked back over the valley. Castle Corbenek nestled amidst the green trees that filled the valley, which was more of a Glen, and a great glen at that. What he was sitting on was the summit of a ridge of high hills which made up one side of the glen. From up here it was possible to see for miles around. Turning to look ahead he saw that gentle slopes made their way down from the ridge. These were wooded too, but much more lightly than the denseness he had just clambered through. Eventually these thinned out into a wide, level plane which was bordered on both sides by hills.

Then he saw Cnoc Dreann.

At the far end of the plane was the vast bulk of a huge black mountain. It stood alone, its sloping sides towering up from the ground to disappear into the clouds. It looked like it was holding up the sky. It looked enormous.

Savage mounted his horse and rode towards the mountain. It took some time and and when he got to the foot of Cnoc Dreann the sun was already high in the sky. The mountain looked daunting and he briefly hesitated, wondering if he had really time to scale it before darkness fell. There was no choice though. He had lost enough time already and who knew what had happened back in Carrickfergus.

He rode as far as he could but when he reached the edge of the forest beyond which trees would not grow, he had to dismount. He found a suitable tree to tether the palfrey to, put the shoulder bag over one shoulder and strapped his sword to his back to avoid tripping over it on the climb. Over his other shoulder he slung the bundle of heavy clothing, then began the ascent of the steep mountainside.

As a choice of place to keep something special, it was inspired. No fortress was as secure. No army was large enough to surround the mountain, and it would take an attacker so long to climb anyone on the summit would have plenty of time to quietly slip away while they toiled their way up.

There did seem to be a path but it was little more than an animal track. The climb was hard and gruelling. Many times the steepness of the ground reduced him to clambering on all fours. His thighs and calf muscles burned from the effort. Sweat streamed from him, running into his eyes and stinging them. As he climbed higher and higher it became colder and the wind grew stronger. Several times he slipped and had to grasp bunches of rough gorse to stop falling. The ground at first got muddier and darker but higher up it became little more than a skim of black peat over hard granite rocks. The higher he got the colder it was and soon the sweat that stung his eyes and soaked his clothes was chilled to cold dampness almost immediately. Unbundling his heavy clothes, he pulled on the sheepskin jerkin and the heavy black woollen cloak.

It took a long time to ascend the mountain and the sun was lowering in the sky. Savage could see that he had one more climb and he would be on the summit and he stopped for a moment. The wind was strong now and the clouds that had obscured the summit cleared away. He was exhausted and did not know what waited on the summit, so he had to rest, however briefly. Any ounce of strength he could recover would help him if there was any fighting.

Savage sat down on a rock and admired the view. It was stunning. He could see for miles. Southwards he could see as far as England and the mountains of Cumbria, while to the east he could see right to the Irish sea and even as far as Ireland that hovered on the horizon like a dark shadow.

Far away at the base of the mountain, someone was starting to climb along the route he had taken. It looked like there were two of them: it would be ages before they got to the top, but he could not afford to sit around.

He waited a few more minutes until the ache in his legs had subsided a little, then got to his feet again and recommenced his journey to the summit where the Holy Grail awaited.

Chapter 52

Savage approached the summit with caution. There was no point charging up: he had no idea what or who awaited him at the top.

As he carefully picked his way through the rocks the clouds rolled back in. His range of vision closed down to twenty or so feet of strange misty grey. The wind howled over the rocks and buffeted Savage so at times he staggered.

He reached the edge of the summit and crouched behind a crop of rocks. The top of the mountain was a wide, flat barren plateau about a hundred yards across and strewn with boulders. Just off centre of it was a mound, an ancient cairn built of rock with a doorway into it made of three large rectangular stones: two upright on either side and one across the top as a lintel. At the far side of the plateau was a little stone building that looked like the sort of chapel built by the early Christian missionaries. It was very old, moss coated its walls and there were holes in the slate roof. Through the gaps in the roof he could see the flickering glow of a fire.

Savage decided to make a tour of the edge of the summit to judge his best route of approach. He only got two thirds of the way round though, as the far edge of the plateau plunged away in a sheer cliff that disappeared off into the mists.

He was about to creep forward onto the summit when he saw movement. Several figures emerged from the doorway of the ancient mound.

Savage froze in astonishment.

Two of them he did not recognise. They were warriors. Hooded, clad in chainmail and with swords drawn they prodded three others in the direction of the little chapel. The other three were obviously prisoners: A man and a woman stumbled forward over the rocky ground, their hands bound before them. A little girl was with them but her hands were not tied. She clearly was not deemed a threat and was propelled forwards with a slap round the head.

The man was Connor MacHuylin, the woman was Alys de Logan and the girl was Galiene.

As they entered the chapel and the door was closed, Savage sank back behind a rock. What the hell was going on? What were they doing here? This turn of events complicated things considerably.

His first thought was to draw his sword and charge into the chapel to rescue them. The blade was halfway out of its sheath when his second thought-that he had no idea how many others were in the chapel-stopped him. He would be no use to anyone if he just charged in and got himself killed. He needed to find out more.

Carefully, Savage crept forward. Crouched and moving quickly, he went from boulder to boulder, pausing behind each one to make sure no one could see him. He had got halfway to the little chapel when the door opened. Quickly Savage ducked down behind the nearest large boulder. He heard raised voices: He could tell someone was shouting but with the roaring of the wind he could not make out what they were saying.

Risking a look, Savage popped his head out at the side of the rock to see what was going on. He saw Galiene, arms wrapped around herself in an attempt to ward off the cold wind, had come out of the chapel. Behind her was a one of the Scottish warriors he had seen earlier. They seemed to be arguing about something.

As they got closer to where he was hiding, Savage made out Galiene shouting "I can't go with you watching me!"

She stopped and the warrior walked up to her. The threatening bulk of the big man towered over the little girl. Savage gripped the hilt of his sword again, cursing himself for not already having drawn it. He tensed his thighs to run forward.

The warrior prodded a finger on the girl's chest.

"Alright," he said. "Go behind that rock. But if you try anything, if you so much as look like running away, I'll catch you and I'll gut you like a fish. Understand?"

Galiene nodded. She was doing her best to look defiant but Savage could tell from the way she held her shoulders and the look in her eyes that she was terrified. His hand itched to rip his sword and to do his own bit of gutting.

"Now hurry up. Go and piss so we can get back inside and you can make our supper," the warrior ordered, giving her a shove.

Galiene turned and scurried behind a rock near where Savage was hidden. She was almost level with him but now both of them were out of sight of the warrior who waited for her return.

Galiene crouched down, pulled up her dress and began to piss.

"Pssst!" Savage attempted to get her attention. The howling wind snatched his words away and he realised he would have to quickly move to where she was. He took a deep breath and slunk to the next boulder. He paused briefly behind it, but the warrior had not seen him. One more to go. He rolled across the pebble strewn ground and arrived beside Galiene.

The girl looked at him with a mixture of shock and extreme embarrassment.

"How dare you!" She vehemently whispered. "I am pissing!"

"I can see that." Savage said, realising to his discomfort that he was now lying in the stream of hot urine that trickled away from the puddle Galiene was making and already it was seeping through his jerkin. He could not move though. If he rolled back out the guard would see him. "What are you doing here?"

Galiene quickly pulled her dress down and tried to regain what little modesty she could. "We came to find you.

MacHuylin's cousin Aengus survived the shipwreck and sent word about what had happened."

"How did you get out of Carrickfergus castle? I heard it was besieged."

"When the news of the defeat of the Ulster army came, the keeper of the castle ordered all the women and children to make for Dublin. We just got out before the Scots arrived. The castle garrison came out and there was terrible fighting in the streets, but it gave us time to get away."

Savage thought of Henry de Thrapston and the desperate struggle that must have taken place against much greater odds. He was a brave man and now he would be surrounded and besieged in the castle. He could only hope that De Thrapston's faith in the strength of his fortress would prove justified.

"Connor MacHuylin met up with us as we were going south." Galiene continued in a rushed whisper. "He told us the news of your shipwreck and how he planned to continue your mission to steal the Grail. Mother refused to believe you were dead and insisted we come with him to Scotland. We were on our way up this mountain when those guards ambushed us took us prisoner."

"They must have seen you coming up the mountainside," Savage reasoned, realising just how lucky he was not to have been spotted also. There had been three of them, though, which would have stood out more. "How many Scots are in the chapel?"

"Three. And one Irishman." Galiene replied. "There's one man they call Ulick who is evil. He looks at me in an awful way and he longs to kill us, but the Irishman says he has to wait until Montmorency and John Bysset get here in case they want something else done with us. He says they are on their way here now."

Four of them to one of him. It was odds that Savage did not like, but if he waited much longer it would be six to one when the Hospitaller and Bysset got here.

"Mother and MacHuylin are tied up. They treat me like a slave." Galiene hissed. "I have to cook for them, clean their weapons and tidy up. It's hateful."

"Galiene, have they-" Savage hesitated, unsure if a girl her age would understand what he meant, "-have they touched you in any way you did not like?"

"Not yet." Galiene replied, and Savage saw that she understood full well. "The one called Ulick promised he will though. When he does, I will make sure he regrets it."

Savage was taken aback at such ferocity in one so young, but heartened all the same. "You're your Mother's daughter," he smiled.

"Why would I not be? I've had no one else to bring me up," the girl spat back.

Savage ignored the jibe and peeked round the rock to see where the Scottish warrior was. "I'll make up for that I promise, but first I've got to work out a way to get rid of your guards."

"Hurry up, will you?" The Scottish warrior shouted. "Or I'll come and get you."

"I must go back," Galiene said. "Mother and I have a plan to deal with the guards. Wait until a little while after they have eaten their supper before you attack."

Savage was about to ask why but the girl just said "trust me", and then was gone. He peered round the side of the rock and saw the Scots warrior propelling her by the scruff of her neck back into the decrepit chapel.

Savage contemplated what to do. The clouds that cloaked the summit were thinning and he could see that the sun was getting lower in the sky. Every moment he waited Montmorency and Bysset would be getting closer. He recalled the figures he had seen starting the ascent of the mountain behind him. That must have been them. Galiene said she had a plan, but could he afford to wait?

Now that the mountaintop was empty again, one thing he could do was get closer to the chapel and try to see what was going on in there.

Savage got up and took a look to see if anyone was around. The mountaintop was deserted now, which was good because the middle of the summit was flat and devoid of boulders that could provide cover to hide behind.

He quickly covered the distance to the ancient chapel and crouched down beside the wall. There was one, narrow window midway down the side of the stone wall that had long ago lost its glass. Through the gap he could hear voices from inside.

Peeking in through the window, Savage had a good view of what was going on. The chapel was a small, one roomed building, narrow but high-roofed. At one end of the church a simple stone altar stood. From its design Savage judged it to be very old, probably eight or nine hundred years and it had clearly been abandoned for some time. The roof was slate, but the years of extreme weather on top of the mountain had ripped many holes in it. The stone flagged floor was carpeted with moss and in the relative shelter given by the walls, weeds sprouted through its cracks.

Near to the altar was a crumbling wooden pillar that helped support the roof. MacHuylin and Alys were sat on the floor, their hands bound behind them around the pillar. One end of the chapel was completely filled with stacked firewood and a fire had been built in the middle of the church. A large iron pot was suspended over it and Galiene was stirring the contents. A rich, herbal aroma rose from the pot, prompting the saliva to flow in Savage's mouth. After the long climb he was absolutely starving.

The only furniture in the building were a few stools and a decrepit table at which sat four warriors. One was the warrior Savage had seen earlier with Galiene. There was nothing special or expensive about his equipment and he looked like a sergeant. He was no knight. Neither was one of his companions, a black haired man with a large knife. The other two of the warriors were different, clearly knights or noblemen. Both were middle aged but looked battle hardened. One of them was tall, blond haired and with a wild bristling beard. He was wrapped in heavy, colourful Scottish apparel and his eyes were bright and to Savage, a little bit too wild looking. He carried a wicked, heavy iron hand axe. He looked down at Alys and as he did so he ran his tongue along the sharpened blade of his axe, seeming to relish the harsh metallic taste. Savage recognised the sort of man this was: a dangerous, unpredictable killer who slew people for the pleasure it gave him. Knowing that Alys and Galiene were in the custody of such a man sent a chill through his blood.

The last man was thin, tall, black haired but greying, with a close trimmed beard. Savage recognised the purple lion rampant emblazoned on his expensive cloak: The arms of the Irish De Lacy family.

As Savage watched, he saw Galiene take something out of a leather pouch she wore and surreptitiously cast it into the pot, just before the Scots nobleman strode over to see what she was cooking.

Suddenly he realised what she meant when she had told him to wait until after they had eaten: She must be trying to poison them.

"Stew," the Scots nobleman grunted, looking down with disgust at what was in the pot Galiene stirred. "More peasant food. I've had nothing but this rubbish since Bruce sent me here."

"Oh be quiet, Ceannaideach." De Lacy said peevishly. "It smells good. Its ages since I've had stew." He took a deep, appreciative sniff of the appetizing steam rising from the pot.

"It's all I could make with the muck you have up here," Galiene said.

"Shut your mouth, wench," Ceannaideach growled. "Soon we'll have no more need of a skivvy. Then I'll slit you pretty white throat."

He gave her a look that showed he looked forward to that time with relish.

"Calm yourself," de Lacy said. "You know John Bysset ordered these prisoners are not to be harmed."

"Aye. I still don't know why."

"He'll be here soon with Montmorency and you can ask him yourself. But I know he intends to marry the woman to get legitimate claim to her lands."

Alys looked up at this. "I wouldn't marry him if he was the last man alive," she spat.

De Lacy chuckled. "I doubt you will have much choice," he said. "But you won't have long to suffer: You'll be killed after the wedding. Ulick," he turned to Ceannaideach, "if you aren't keen on the stew then join me in guarding the Grail. We shouldn't be leaving it unguarded and I wish to say my prayers before it before I eat."

Ceannaideach grunted his assent and both men left the chapel. Savage crouched back down beside the wall and made his way to the corner of the building so he could watch where they went.

Leaning forward against the driving wind, their heavy cloaks billowing out behind them, Ceannaideach and De Lacy battled their way against the elements across the mountaintop until they reached the entrance of the ancient mound. De Lacy stopped momentarily and made the sign of the cross, then they both went inside, stooping slightly to enter the low doorway.

So that was it. The hiding place of the Holy Grail.

Chapter 53

Savage felt torn.

Barely yards away lay the ultimate treasure, the actual vessel of God's grace. The pursuit of the Grail was the ultimate quest. Achieving the Grail was physical proof in this mortal world that something existed beyond it.

An old fire within him he thought long extinguished was beginning to glow once more. The old yearning. An insatiable, overwhelming, all-compelling desire to know what lay behind the mysteries of life. All the convictions that had shorn up his personality for the past five years began dissolving like sandcastles in the tide. It was such an enormous prospect.

He closed his eyes. Once it would have sounded insane to him, but there was now something more important. He forced himself to go back to the window to see what was going on in the church.

Galiene had dished out two bowls of the stew and was carrying them over to the table where the two Scottish sergeants sat.

They grunted their appreciation, picked up their spoons and were about to begin when one said "wait."

Savage's heart froze. Did they know Galiene had put something in the stew?

The sergeant held out the spoonful of steaming stew to Galiene.

"You first," he said.

Perhaps they did not know, but they at least suspected.

"No!" Alys suddenly shouted.

The sergeant leered at the little girl. "You wouldn't be trying to poison us, now. Would you?" One hand dropped to the hilt of his dagger.

Savage knew he had to act now. At least the odds were down to two to one. He grasped his sword hilt and tensed his thighs for action.

Without hesitation, Galiene took the spoon into her mouth and swallowed the stew.

The sergeants relaxed and began to tuck hungrily into the food, wolfing it down in uncouth mouthfuls.

Savage was confused. He had seen Galiene slip something into the stew but if it was poison surely she would not have so readily taken the mouthful?

Alys dissolved into a flood of tears. Could it be that the brave little girl had once again risked her life to save her mother?

As if she could sense his doubt, Galiene looked up to the window and caught sight of him looking in. She frowned, clearly annoyed that he might ruin everything by being seen and she flicked her eyes to tell him to get out of sight.

Whatever was going on, she seemed to know what she was doing. All Savage could do was trust her. She had asked him to wait, and he would do that.

He moved to the end of the wall where he could keep an eye on the ancient cairn in case Ceannaideach and De Lacy returned. For what seemed like an age he crouched, freezing in the battering wind, despite the heavy clothes he wore. A pelting rain began to fall and Savage began to contemplate the very real threat that he would freeze to death. The sun moved lower in the sky and eventually he decided that he would have to make a move or it would be too late. Ceannaideach and De Lacy would return or Montmorency and Bysset would arrive on the mountain top.

Then the screaming began.

Savage's sword was drawn and he was on his feet in a second. At least the screams were coming from a man but still it was far from a good sign. He kicked open the decrepit door of the church, the wood splintering around his boot as it sprung open.

The sight before him was astonishing. Alys and MacHuylin were still tied up and sitting on the floor. Galiene was crouched on the floor, her knees to her chest, her arms locked around her shins.

One of the Scottish sergeants stood before the altar, it was he who was screaming. His face was a mask of terror, sweat gushed down his face and he was pointing at the far corner of the church. His sword was grasped in his other hand and he was chopping at the air with it.

Savage took full advantage of the situation. He crossed to the altar in a couple of strides. His sword flashed down and across, catching the Scotsman a slashing blow that dug deep into his chest, cutting downwards from the shoulder. His screaming stopped instantly as he collapsed onto the floor, blood pouring out onto the flag stones.

Only then did Savage turn to see what had so frightened the man. To his astonishment there was nothing in the far corner of the chapel but thin air.

He had no time to wonder what was going on: There was another sergeant to deal with.

The other man stood beside the wooden table underneath one of the holes in the roof. He seemed oblivious to the steady stream of rain which was coming through the hole to soak him as he stared up at the sky with a faraway look in his eyes.

Savage ran straight at him, sword gripped at waist height, one hand on the hilt and the other halfway down the blade. The sergeant didn't even flinch, move or try to avoid the blow and Savage's sword went deep into his guts and exited from his back. The weight of Savage's charge propelled the sergeant backwards until he thumped against the wall. Savage felt the point of his sword grating on the stones of the wall. The sergeant looked at him with confused expression on his face, then the light died from his eyes and he sagged onto the ground, sliding off Savage's blade on the way down.

Savage made straight for Galiene and knelt beside her.

"Are you alright?" Savage asked.

The girl's face was deathly pale and sheeted with sweat. She too stared ahead of her, her eyes focused on something invisible in mid-air. The pupils of her eyes were huge and black, like two sloe berries. She was absolutely terrified.

"It's not real," she said through gritted teeth. "I know that what I am seeing is not real."

"It's henbane!" Alys cried. "I gave her some to put in the stew. The plan was for the guards to eat it so we could escape."

"Henbane? The weed?"

"It's a poison," Alys wailed. "If you eat it, it causes terrifying visions to appear before your eyes, then you fall into a sleep, your breathing slows down, then it stops altogether."

"That's why the sergeants were acting so strange!" Savage deduced.

"They made Galiene eat some too." Alys was distraught, tears streaked down her face. "We must give her the antidote or she'll die."

"Have you got it?" Savage asked.

Alys had no chance to reply.

The battered door smashed open once more. Standing in the entranceway were Ulick Ceannaideach and Sir Walter de Lacy.

For a couple of seconds they stood still, surveying the scene in the chapel: Both sergeants dead and Savage bending down beside Galiene. It was enough to work out what was going on.

"It looks like our prisoners have a knight in shining armour come to save them," Ceannaideach said.

De Lacy drew his sword, Ceannaideach hefted his heavy axe into a position of readiness. They both advanced warily towards Savage.

Savage rose to his feet, holding his sword before him in both hands. He knew he could not counter Ceannaideach's heavy butchery instrument with his blade so would have to try to avoid his blows.

Carefully he backed away from Galiene towards the middle of the church, to give himself plenty of room to manoeuvre.

Suddenly the two attackers lunged forward, screaming and swinging their battle weapons. Savage countered De Lacy's blow then leapt sideways to escape the chop of Ceannaideach's axe.

Da Lacy took advantage and stabbed at Savage's neck. Savage saw the blade coming but all he could do was desperately throw himself backwards to avoid it. The sharp point of the sword missed him by a hair's breadth, scything through the air centimetres from his eyes. Off balance he staggered wildly sideways then lunged towards the altar.

With the strange sixth sense that comes to a warrior in battle, Savage was aware of Ceannaideach bearing down on him as he ran. Instinctively he leapt clean over the crumbling altar. Ceannaideach brought his axe down in a crushing blow meant for Savage's back. Savage's leap took him clear of the blade and it sheared down into the stone of the altar, unleashing a welter of sparks and a hideous grinding noise.

Savage jumped up onto the altar. He might be outnumbered but height would give him an advantage.

Ceannaideach lifted one of the fallen stools and hurled it at Savage to try and knock him back off. The stool struck Savage a glancing blow on his right shoulder then bounced off, smashing itself to shards on the wall.

Savage did not fall, but was unbalanced. Seeing him momentarily sway both De Lacy and Ceannaideach rushed forward.

De Lacy slashed at Savage with his sword. Savage managed to parry and metal struck metal sending up a shower of bright sparks. The blow knocked him further off balance and Savage knew he was about to fall.

Ceannaideach swung his axe in a scything arc, meaning to cut Savage's legs from under him. Off balance and tottering, instead of dodging all Savage could do was jump up into the air. The axe which was supposed to sever his knees cut through thin air and instead struck De Lacy. The wickedly sharp blade hit him just below the right shoulder and severed the arm cleanly. The limb, still grasping his sword, clattered to the floor and de Lacy collapsed in shock and pain, screaming hideously while his blood sprayed across the altar.

Savage landed badly on the altar top. One of his feet skidded wildly in De Lacy's blood and he finally lost his balance completely, toppling backwards onto the floor.

He landed heavily on his back, grunting as the wind was driven from his body.

Sensing victory, Ceannaideach ran towards him, axe raised.

Suddenly the Scottish Lord stumbled and sprawled headlong across the floor.

The was a short laugh and Savage saw that MacHuylin, still tied to the wooden pillar, had managed to sweep his leg round and take the feet from under the running Ceannaideach.

Enraged, Ceannaideach scrambled back to his feet and turned his attention on MacHuylin. His axe had a wicked looking spike on the top of it and Ceannaideach reversed the weapon, stabbing downwards at the bound galloglaich. MacHuylin twisted away from the blow as best he could. He was unable to get out of the way completely and the point of the axe gouged deep into his thigh, unleashing a cry of anguish from him.

By this time Savage was back on his feet also. He charged Ceannaideach while he was still bending over MacHuylin and drove the point of his sword into the back of the Scottish lord's chest. With the full weight of Savage's body behind it, the blade skewered its way right through his body to burst out above his heart, unleashing a torrent of blood that showered down over MacHuylin.

Ceannaideach made a brief gurgling sound as blood bubbled up from his punctured lungs and overflowed from his mouth. Then he fell dead upon the moss covered flagstones.

There were a few moments silence as Savage got his breath back and surveyed the grim carnage. De Lacy was dead too. Killed by shock and blood, his corpse still knelt, propped up against the altar in a parody of prayer.

Galiene looked like she had fallen asleep.

"Release me!" Alys shouted.

Savage snapped out of his battle trance and ran to her. He grasped her head and kissed her fiercely.

"Thanks. That's nice, but we've got more important things to do." Alys said.

Savage took Ceannaideach's dagger and sliced the ropes holding her. She quickly ran to Galiene and examined her, pressing fingers against her neck and opening her eyelids.

"She's in a very deep sleep because of the Henbane. Unconscious." Alys said, her beautiful face wrought with worry. "We have to get her that antidote."

"Have you got it?" Savage asked as he cut MacHuylin free.

Alys shook her head as she came over to MacHuylin to inspect his wound. "You're going to have to go down to the forest to get it."

"How will I know what to look for?"

"I'll show you. I've a book in my bag with drawings of the plants needed but I've got to stop this bleeding first," Alys said as she unbuckled MacHuylin's sword belt. She wound it around the galloglaich's wounded thigh and pulled hard, mercilessly tightening the belt through its own loop around the limb.

"Sweet Jesus: go easy!" MacHuylin gasped through clenched teeth.

"I have to stop the bleeding or you'll die." Alys said.

"What can I do?" Savage asked, feeling superfluous as he stood helplessly nearby.

"Get the Grail!" MacHuylin shouted as Alys tightened the belt further. A thick globule of blood gurgled up from his wound. "Then at least this whole trip hasn't been a waste of time!"

Savage looked at Alys.

"You may as well." She said. "We can't do anything until I get this leg bound and the bleeding staunched."

Savage nodded. He sheathed his sword and ran out of the chapel.

Alys worked feverishly, twisting the belt ever tighter, ignoring MacHuylin's cries of pain. Sweat dripped from her brow with the effort but soon the bleeding slowed and then finally stopped. She looked up but MacHuylin had passed out from the agony.

"At least he's quiet." She said to herself as she opened her leather shoulder bag. Inside were various herbs and bandages and in no time she had packed MacHuylin's wound with sage, waybread and honey, then bound it in a new linen bandage.

Alys sighed and stood up, turning her attention back to Galiene.

At that moment the door of the church opened again. She looked round, expecting to see Savage returning with the Grail.

Instead she saw John Bysset standing in the doorway, his kidney dagger drawn.

"Hallo, my dear." Bysset said, an evil grin creasing his face. "So nice to see you again."

Chapter 54

Savage ran across the mountaintop towards the low burial mound. The weather had cleared up and the clouds that had cloaked the summit had blown away. Had he had time, he could have admired the stunning view that opened up, revealing a vista that stretched right to the Irish Sea and beyond it to Ireland itself. The wind still roared across the mountain but the Scottish countryside below was bathed in the warm orange glow of late summer evening as the sun dipped low towards the horizon and shadows began to flow into the valleys below like black water.

What this meant to Savage was that he would have to get down the mountain to pick the antidote for Galiene and back up again in the dark.

As he approached the stone mantled entranceway, however, thoughts of Galiene, Alys and MacHuylin slipped momentarily from his mind. Could this ancient mound really be the resting place of the Holy Grail?

The sun was setting directly opposite the mound and its last rays bathed the approach to the mound in golden rays that reached right inside. Savage walked up the short corridor of stones that lead to the door. He ducked his head to get through the low doorway and entered the cool darkness of the mound.

Inside was a round chamber, completely built of stone. Sheltered from the roar of the wind, the quietness immediately enveloped him like a calming bath. There were entranceways to many little chambers around the walls and the late rays of the setting sun lit up a round stone right in the centre of the mound. It was covered in carvings: Intricate spirals that looped and curled their way around the faces of the stone in ever-spinning loops.

On top of the stone was set a cup. It was gold, a long stemmed goblet which was studded with red and green precious stones. The evening sunlight glittered across it and sparkled on the gems. This must be the Grail.

Savage reached out tentatively then stopped, suddenly nervous about even touching such an object. Could this really be the actual cup of Christ? The vessel that bore his blood at the last supper?

Savage went to reach out again but paused once more. Had he just heard something? He thought it was Alys's voice but he knew that was impossible. He was inside the mound and outside the wind would snatch away any words spoken.

He grabbed the cup and shoved it into the leather shoulder bag he had carried since Castle Corbenek.

He had things to do.

Chapter 55

Inside the crumbling chapel, Alys de Logan was backed up against the altar. John Bysset stalked towards her, the long, pyramid shaped blade of his kidney dagger held before him.

"There will be no trickery this time, my dear Alys," Bysset sneered. "No secret passageways and escape routes. This time you are mine."

Alys felt the cold stone of the altar behind her and realised she had nowhere to go. The only exit was the door and Bysset blocked that way out. She had no weapon, though several were discarded on the floor.

"You worthless shit," She spat. "You're not in this for the Grail, for Ireland or for Scotland. You're just in it for yourself."

Bysset chuckled. "How right you are. And after all the crusaders, zealots, patriots and believers are dead, killed by their convictions, I'll be the one who comes out of this alive and richer."

"What would your friend Montmorency say if he heard that?"

"Oh he is one of them all right: A true believer in the Grail." Bysset said as he edged ever closer. "He believes in the Grail. He's obsessed by it. But he's every bit as treacherous, two faced and untrustworthy as me. The difference is that he excuses himself by insisting the end justifies the means. I like to think I'm a lot more honest."

Alys knew her only chance was to go for the door. She ran forward, trying to duck past him but Bysset caught her easily and tossed her back against the altar. His left hand snaked around her throat and tightened, squeezing the airway so she could not breathe or shout.

"Why do you think we are here anyway?" he growled. "I don't know how you did it but killing Ceannaideach and De Lacy has saved Montmorency and I the trouble of having to do it ourselves. With both Edward and Robert Bruce out of the country this is the perfect opportunity to sneak back here and take the Grail. We shall wield its power and no one-no princes, kings or popes-will be able to stand against us."

"We?" Alys gasped, her face reddening.

"Ah you know me so well, my dear." Bysset said. "Such a pity our marriage will be such a short one. Yes indeed I will also have to get rid of my friend the Hospitaller at some stage, but that is a battle for the future."

"Marriage?" Alys's vision was starting to darken, she could feel panic rising in her chest.

"Montmorency will marry us- he is a monk after all, albeit a warrior monk. Then I will be legally entitled to your lands."

"Who would know?" Her words came as little more than a strangled whisper.

"I would." Bysset smiled. "I'm a simple man and I despite what you might think I still believe in certain things. It will also please me to see you so humiliated. Just before you die: You and your bastard child."

Savage pushed open the crumbling door of the chapel. For the second time the scene that met his eyes shocked him.

Alys's eyes flickered towards Savage standing in the doorway. Bysset spotted this straight away and looked over his shoulder. He smiled and let go of Alys's throat, then drove his dagger down into her shoulder. She shrieked in pain then he punched her hard on the face, sending her spinning backwards into the altar and onto the floor.

"I'll deal with you later," Bysset sneered, sheathing his dagger and drawing his sword, "after I've dealt with your lover boy. I thought you were dead, Savage. No matter: That will soon be the case."

Savage drew his own sword and advanced into the church.

Bysset moved towards him. "You are another follower of the Grail, I believe Savage. You may have beaten me in the tournament but there will be no rules here to protect you."

Suddenly Bysset stopped, a look of stunned shock on his face. His grip on his sword loosened and he dropped it, then sank to his knees. Behind him stood Alys de Logan. In her hand was a dagger, taken from the corpse of De Lacy that still lay beside the altar. Its blade dripped blood from where she had driven it into Bysset's back, puncturing his liver and one kidney, then quickly withdrawing it again.

"I would have thought by now John, you would have learned never to turn your back on me," Alys said with bitterness, then she grabbed the kneeling Bysset by the hair, wrenched his head back and drew the blade across his throat, unleashing a torrent of blood that gushed out over the floor of the chapel.

Alys let go of Bysset's hair and his corpse fell forward face first onto the floor. She gasped and clutched her left shoulder where her own blood welled up.

Savage rushed to her and grabbed her in his arms.

"Are you alright?" he pleaded.

"It's not serious, just a flesh wound. The worthless bastard couldn't even stab me right," Alys replied. "I can treat it myself but I'm not the one you should be worried about. Galiene needs those herbs from the forest."

Savage looked at the pale face of the unconscious Galiene and felt utterly helpless.

"What can I do?" he asked.

Alys drew a leather bound book from a pouch in her dress. She winced in pain as she leafed through several of the velum pages, which Savage could see bore coloured drawings of different herbs and plants. She stopped at one page and pointed to the drawing of a star shaped, white flower with a black heart.

"This is henbane," she said, then drew her finger to the drawings on the page opposite. It showed a bell shaped purple-green flower with deep black berries. "This is belladonna: Deadly nightshade. It will be growing in the woods at the foot of the mountain. I need you to get some."

"Isn't that poisonous?"

"Yes. One of the most deadly I know of," Alys replied. "And by one of those odd contradictions of Mother Nature, a preparation made from it is also the only known antidote for henbane poisoning. If prepared correctly it induces massive purging of the body."

"It will be dark soon," Savage said. "I doubt I will be able to see what I am picking."

"There will be a full moon tonight," Alys replied. "When it comes up it will be a clear as day."

"I can't leave you here alone," Savage insisted. "If Bysset was here, Montmorency must be around somewhere too-"

"If anyone but you walks through that door I'll put that axe through their skull," Alys smiled. "Richard, I must stay here to tend to Galiene. Please: Just go. Quickly."

Savage nodded. There was nothing else for it. He took Alys in his arms and kissed her, then turned and ran out of the church.

Outside the wind buffeted him again and he leaned forward as he ran past the cairn towards the edge of the mountain summit. His legs still ached from the ascent, and he was not looking forward to the gruelling task ahead of him.

Savage reached the edge of the mountaintop and stopped. He had made a mistake. In his haste to get help for Galiene and still distracted from the fighting, he had gone the wrong way and made for the side of the summit that fell away in a cliff.

Now the clouds had cleared he could see that the mountainside plummeted away for several hundred feet of sheer rock until it terminated in a little mountain lake, its cold, still waters a deep peat-soaked black. There was no way down in that direction. He would have to go back the way he had come.

Cursing his own stupidity and the waste of precious moments, Savage turned.

Standing behind him was a figure robed almost completely in black, save for the white, equal armed cross that emblazoned the shoulder of his sable cloak. His sword was drawn and glinted in the evening sunlight.

It was Hugo Montmorency.

Chapter 56

"Richard Savage: The sodomite English King's tame Templar," Montmorency said, looking at Savage through narrowed, suspicious eyes. "I am getting bored with you turning up where you are least wanted."

"Hugo Montmorency," Savage returned, drawing his own sword, "the excommunicated Scottish King's pet Hospitaller. Tell me Montmorency, how do you reconcile working with the anathematized Robert Bruce with your vows to the Holy Father?"

"I have climbed all the way up this mountain," Montmorency ignored Savage's question, "and I find that a certain valuable item is no longer in the place where I left it. I assume you have something to do with the Grail not being in Merlin's burial mound where it is supposed to be. Thankfully God has ensured I was here in time to catch you before you made off with it. As it says in the book of Exodus: You shall not steal. Breaking the commandments of the Lord must be punished. Be assured, Savage, I will now do that."

"You accuse me of stealing?" Savage laughed bitterly at the man's audacity. "Montmorency: You're here to steal the Grail yourself."

"Steal? How can I steal what rightfully belongs only to God?" Montmorency shouted.

Savage frowned. With his left hand he drew the golden cup from his leather shoulder bag. "Is this what you are looking for?"

Montmorency's eyes lit up. He stared at the goblet the way most men stare at the naked flesh of a woman.

"How many men have you killed for this, Montmorency?" Savage asked. "How many have you betrayed, stabbed in the back, lied to? Your Templar brethren in Garway for a start: Do you know how painfully some of them died in that dungeon after you betrayed us?"

A look of recognition dawned in Montmorency's eyes and his smile broadened. "Garway? I knew I'd seen you before somewhere but could not quite place it. Yes, I remember Garway and the old fool who was Commander there. What was his name again?"

"De Vere."

"Ah yes, Commander De Vere. If he had listened and given over the Grail to me when those French Templars arrived with it, there would have been no need for the unpleasant outcome. I was forced to pursue them north here to Scotland. Unfortunately by the time I tracked them down they had already offered their service-and the Grail- to King Robert Bruce."

"And you were forced to do the same?" Savage concluded. "So you could wait for the day you could steal the Grail yourself and betray Bruce too?"

"Very clever, and correct in a way," Montmorency said, "but you use such critical language. What I do is God's work. Everything is for Him, so how can I be blamed for anything?"

Savage saw a strange look in Montmorency's eyes and realised that what he saw there was not the light of inspiration, but the cold, fish-like deadness of certainty.

"You speak of betrayal," Montmorency smiled, "but did you not abandon a wife and a daughter in Ireland to go and seek the Grail? Are we really that different?"

Savage thought of Galiene lying dying in the chapel while he wasted more time talking. He knew that if he bought his own escape with the Grail and left Montmorency up on the mountain top the Hospitaller would kill Galiene, Alys and MacHuylin anyway. He had to fight him and he had to end this, one way or the other. He dropped the goblet back into his shoulder bag and grasped his sword hilt with both hands.

"Come and get your trinket," he challenged.

Montmorency's smile faded. "Very well. A l'outrance: To the death!"

Savage stepped away from the cliff edge to give himself some room to move. Neither he nor Montmorency had any armour nor carried a shield, so they would have to rely on speed, manoeuvrability and swordsmanship for defence. This would not be the usual hack-and-slash battering encounter of broadsword fighting.

It seemed counter-intuitive, but the most effective defence relied on keeping the point of the sword still, and parrying blows by moving the hilt right and left. Savage planted his feet slightly apart and lowered the point towards the Hospitaller.

Montmorency did the same. For several seconds neither moved.

Montmorency lunged forward. He drove the point of his sword towards Savage's chest. Savage kept the point of his sword level but swept the hilt to the right, sending the Hospitaller's blade skittering sideways and away from its target.

Montmorency struck again. This time a sweeping chop from above. Now Savage had to move the blade point and raise his blade above his head crossways to stop the blow. Metal clashed on metal and a shower of sparks ignited where the blades met.

The Hospitaller bore down with his blade, aiming to force it lower onto Savage's head. Savage strained to hold the sword off as it inched closer to his forehead.

Montmorency had the advantage: It was much easier to push down than resist upwards. The only thing Savage could do to relieve the pressure was to move.

Savage ducked with his thighs and spun away at the same time. His sword scraped up the Hospitaller's blade as he pirouetted backwards. As Savage moved, Montmorency's blade came down, missing him and striking the ground instead.

Turning, Savage's eyes widened as he saw how close he was to the edge of the cliff. Some pebbles and gravel, kicked by his feet, skittered over the edge of the precipice and tumbled down through the evening air to splash into the black pool far below.

Montmorency's eyes lit up as he saw his advantage. He took another step forward, sweeping his feet across the ground instead of lifting them, so as to never be off balance. He swept his sword back up off the ground towards Savage's gut.

Savage could do nothing but move again. He leapt backwards, this time along the edge of the cliff and away from the blade. Despite his care his right foot skidded over the edge and his stomach lurched as he felt air beneath his toes. Panic gripped Savage and he threw himself sideways away from the precipice, springing off his left thigh.

Montmorency followed and advanced again. He launched himself forward from his back foot. Savage, still trying to recover balance could not counter in time. This time Montmorency's blade struck home: Savage heard the point of the sword tear through his sheepskin jerkin and felt the metal pierce his flesh on the left side of his ribs. It stopped momentarily, grinding into his six and seventh rib bones. Before it could penetrate deeper Savage smashed his own weapon upwards, hitting the Hospitaller's blade and knocking it away before it did any more damage.

Savage winced as he felt the angry burning of the stab wound. Warm sticky blood was already seeping into his sheepskin. A quick deep breath however, told him that his lungs were intact and his injury was just a flesh wound.

Quickly he resumed his defensive stance, once more levelling the point of his sword in the direction of Montmorency. If he was not more careful he would lose this fight.

Again he thought of Alys and Galiene and realised he could not afford to lose.

Montmorency pressed his advantage. He lunged forward, this time stabbing at Savage's face. Savage swung the hilt of his sword to the right, deflecting the blow again. This time however he used an intercepting attack: he continued the movement by driving his own sword forward.

Savage's blade scraped its way up the Hospitaller's, the point heading straight for his face. Montmorency, taken completely by surprise, only just pulled himself back in time. The end of Savage's sword still caught him on the cheek, opening up a slice just below his left eye.

Savage struck again, this time swiping a chopping blow aimed low at Montmorency's legs. The Hospitaller jumped and Savage missed. Montmorency attacked but once more Savage met his blade with his own, halting the Hospitaller's blow and pushing his sword sideways.

Montmorency hit at Savage's head again and once more their blades locked. For a couple of seconds they stood, each trying to force his own blade into the other man, their faces barely inches from each other.

Savage raised his knee, kicking Montmorency hard in the groin. The Hospitaller gasped and staggered backwards, breaking their deadly embrace.

For several seconds, both men stood apart, facing each other on the cliff top. They were panting hard from exertion and took advantage of the brief respite to try to catch their breath.

"We both learned sword fighting in the Templars, Savage," Montmorency said. "We know the same attacks and defence. This could be a long fight. We are not that different, you and I. Why should we fight? Whoever bears the Grail wields enormous power. Why don't you join me? Together we two could rule all this."

The Hospitaller swept his left hand around the stunning vista that lay to Savage's right, beyond the edge of the precipice on which they stood. From the great height of the mountaintop, three Kingdoms were visible: The distant blue hills of Cumbria in England lay to the South, Scotland lay beneath them and the Scottish Highlands, still capped with snow, could be seen far to the north. Nestling in the blue sea to the South West was the Isle of Man and beyond it the black, misty shores of Ireland.

Savage dropped one hand from his sword hilt and once more pulled the golden cup from his leather shoulder bag. For a moment he looked at it as the light played and danced across its glittering precious stones and the gold of its long stem.

Montmorency smiled, sensing victory and the final fulfilment of his quest. His eyes were fixed on the goblet in an intense, longing stare.

"Here's your carpenter's cup," Savage said, tossing the Grail towards the Hospitaller.

He threw it high, aimed above Montmorency's head so it tumbled through the air and out over the edge of the cliff.

Montmorency gave a shout of surprised dismay. He dropped his sword and headless of the precipice jumped, trying to catch the Grail, both hands outstretched.

The goblet began to fall, tumbling end over end down the cliff towards the black lake below. Montmorency, still reaching, fell after it, his black cloak billowing behind him like the wings of a raven.

They had both fallen about twenty feet when the Hospitaller caught up with the cup. His fingers grasped it and he pulled it into his chest, cradling it like a baby as he hurtled downwards. His body turned and Savage could not be sure, but he thought he saw Montmorency smiling.

Eighty feet below the summit, the Hospitaller struck a rocky outcrop of the cliff with a sickening crunch. His body bounced off the stones, spiralling and cart wheeling like a bag of broken bones the final twenty feet to the bottom of the cliff.

With a tremendous splash, Montmorency and the cup both hit the black waters of the little mountain lake below. A fountain of dark, peaty water erupted and they disappeared beneath it.

As the splash receded and the waves from it subsided, Savage continued to watch, expecting Montmorency's corpse to float to the surface. Minutes passed, the waves became ripples and eventually the glassy black smoothness returned to the surface of the lake. There was still no sign of the body.

Savage realised that like most mountain lakes, the water was probably just a sheen over a bog: A morass so deep as to be bottomless and once in it, there was no way to escape its sucking grasp. Even if he had survived the fall, the Hospitaller would now be on an unstoppable descent to untold black depths. Montmorency and his Grail had gone forever.

Savage sheathed his sword and turned from the cliff edge. He had wasted enough time already.

Chapter 57

Dawn broke over Cnoc Dreann. The first rays of sunlight struck the summit of the mountain, re-illuminating the trackway into the mound of Merlin's Chapel and pouring light into the ancient chapel.

The corpses of the previous evening's battle had been taken outside the chapel. The spilled blood had been cleaned up and a large fire blazed in the centre of the room. The delicious aroma of warm bread filled the room from flat querns of wheaten bread that baked on a griddle over the fire.

An exhausted Richard Savage sat perched on the altar of the chapel. Galiene, awake now and huddled in a heavy blanket beside the fire, stared into the flames, her gaze still haunted by whatever visions had manifested themselves before them the night before.

Savage knew somehow that she would be alright. Her strength of character was amazing and though her experiences would stay with her for the rest of her life, they would never overcome her.

Connor MacHuylin sat near the fire also. His thigh was wrapped in bandages and he was pale from the blood he had lost. Savage knew that he too would be fine. It would take much more than a stab in the leg to kill of that particular galloglaich.

"You did what?" MacHuylin asked.

"I threw it off the cliff," Savage replied.

MacHuylin shook his head. "Brilliant. Absolutely brilliant. We come all this way, find the Holy Grail and you throw it off a mountaintop?"

Savage nodded. "Into a bog."

Alys came in through the door. She had been outside watching the sun come up. She too looked tired, her face grey and drawn. She had been up all night, tending to MacHuylin and Galiene and using all her skills to keep the both of them alive while she anxiously waited for Savage to return with the herbs from the forest at the foot of the mountain. When Savage had returned, she had the extra strain of trying to prepare the medicine from the herbs he brought using only the limited tools she carried with her and the cooking pots that were on the mountain top.

Thankfully, it had worked.

"What do we do now?" Alys wondered aloud.

"We need to get off this mountain," Savage said. "There is a castle near here called Corbenek. I think the lord who owns it will let us rest there until everyone is fit again."

"I need to get back to Ireland," MacHuylin said. "There is unfinished business there. Edward Bruce and his lackeys still need kicked out."

"That won't be easy," said Savage. "They've already taken half the north of the Island. Ui Neill rules the west. De Burgh is fighting the FitzGeralds in Connaught…" he trailed off. It was obvious that none of these arguments had any effect on MacHuylin.

"It's my island," MacHuylin stated. "I have to fight for it. Why don't you come with us? We will need good knights."

Savage shook his head. "I don't know if it's my island any more."

"What are you going to do?"

Savage sighed and shrugged his shoulders. "Right now I don't know. The Scots will kill us all if they get their hands on us. I'm still an outlaw in England. King Edward said he would pardon me but now the Scots have invaded Ireland I doubt he will want my services any more so I've no job either. I have no money and no home."

Alys de Logan gave a laugh. "You're not much of a catch, are you?" She smiled.

"No." Savage agreed. He held her gaze for a long moment. "But would you marry me anyway?"

Alys laughed again. She looked at Savage for a moment then walked over to him and took both his hands.

"Yes." She smiled. She pressed herself to him and they kissed each other. After a few moments their lips parted.

Behind them a heavy sigh came from Galiene. The look on her face showed her opinion of her mother's behaviour.

"It's not just me you are marrying." Alys said.

Savage nodded. "I realise that. Don't worry she'll come to like me some day. Maybe when I'm dead."

Alys laughed. Galiene actually smiled.

"Do you think it really was the Holy Grail?" Alys said.

"With all that gold and precious stones, it certainly was grand enough to be the cup of the King of Kings." Savage said.

"Maybe too grand to be the cup of a lowly carpenter." said Alys. "It was certainly a Grail, but was it the Grail?"

Savage shrugged. "There's no way to tell now. I do know one thing though," he looked at Alys and Galiene. "I've found my Grail."

END

Authour's Note

While the main characters in Lions of the Grail are fictional, the events against which they have their adventure were very real, and many situations whose memories still haunt Ireland were foreshadowed in this time. Some of the minor characters are also artistic representations of real people who lived at the time.

Edward Bruce's Irish invasion of 1315 led to a war that unbelievably continued despite coinciding with a disastrous famine that swept northern Europe, killing millions.

Henry de Thrapston and Thomas de Mandeville carried out a heroic and dogged defence of the besieged Carrickfergus castle. An indication of how desperate things became is that at one point the defenders resorted to cannibalism, eating nine of their Scottish prisoners.

Richard de Burgh returned to fight against the Scots but the suspicion that he was somehow in league with the Bruce's never went away, and in the aftermath of the invasion he was arrested. He eventually retired to a monastery near Cashel and died in 1326. His title of Earl of Ulster only survived a few generations after him. When his grand-daughter Elizabeth married the Duke of Clarence the title passed into the English Royal family. Elizabeth moved to London and her household accounts show she employed a young page boy who later went on to great things, one Geoffrey Chaucer. The name de Burgh survives in the Irish surname of Burke, born by many notable Irish men and women over the centuries, from the illustrious politician Edmund Burke to the infamous "resurrection man" and murderer William Burke.

Sir Edmund le Bottelier (Butler) distinguished himself in the war against the Scots and died in 1321 while on pilgrimage to Santiago de Compostela. His interest in poetry in this book is a nod towards one of his more famous modern descendants, William Butler Yeats.

Some of the other Anglo-Norman names that appear in the book may seem unfamiliar to modern ears, but perhaps their modern forms are not so foreign sounding. Le Poer became Powers, Blanquet became Plunkett, Roche became Roach while names like Fitzgerald and Fitzpatrick remain unchanged. Logan and Savage are names still found in Ulster.

The ill-fated expedition to Ireland by Edward Bruce continued for another three years after the events in this book, and the story of the war is an epic and bloody one that deserves telling. Perhaps, if he proves popular enough, Richard Savage will be back for another adventure.